EXECUTIVE PRIVILEGE

EXECUTIVE PRIVILEGE

Two Centuries of White House Scandals

JACK MITCHELL

HIPPOCRENE BOOKS
New York

For information, address:
HIPPOCRENE BOOKS, INC.
171 Madison Avenue
New York, NY 10016

ISBN 0-7818-0063-3

Library of Congress Cataloging-in-Publication Data
Mitchell, Jack, 1950-
Executive privilege : two centuries of White House scandals /
Jack Mitchell.
   p.   cm.
Includes bibliographical references and index.
ISBN 0-7818-0063-3
1. Presidents—United States—History. 2. Political
corruption—United States—History. 3. United States—Politics
and government. I. Title.
E176.1.M67   1992
973'.099—dc20   92-2865

Printed in the United States of America

This book is dedicated, with love, to five wonderful children who are important in my life:
Ryan Adam Mitchell
Matthew and Nicholas Warren
Julia Rose Smolonsky
Schuyler K. White

ACKNOWLEDGMENTS

First and foremost, I'd like to sincerely thank my editor at Hippocrene, Tanjam Jacobson, for many months of patient, highly professional supervision and advice. This modest work has been substantially refined and improved by her expert editorial guidance and skillful hand. I'm truly grateful for her meaningful contribution. Editors remain an important element of any book writing process; that fact is clearly evident here.

Also, I take this opportunity to express my heartfelt gratitude to Hippocrene's publisher, George Blagowidow, for personally providing me with the opportunity to complete *Executive Privilege*, and thus having the pleasure of seeing it published. His encouragement and good will over an extended period of time, and through reams of correspondence, are immensely appreciated.

Thirdly, I must acknowledge a large body of work by a distinguished variety of historians, political writers, presidential scholars and journalists, perhaps not adequately credited in these pages, whose discoveries and views contributed to and shaped my own personal interpretation of two centuries of presidential perfidies and peccadilloes.

Finally, many thanks to friends and colleagues who put up with my complaining and endless promises about a project which was on the drawing board for a longer time than was ever initially envisioned. I hope the final product is worthy of their kind forbearance.

CONTENTS

INTRODUCTION

Scandal involving the White House certainly didn't begin with the Iran/contra imbroglio which crippled the second term of the Reagan presidency, nor the ill-fated June 1972 Watergate break-in which toppled the Nixon White House. Illicit bedroom romps involving chief executives were commonplace almost two centuries before the carefully concealed sexual adventures of the libidinous John F. Kennedy. Allegations of presidential misconduct during the days of our Founding Fathers were so severe, in fact, that they frequently make the titillating gossip of today's tabloids look somewhat tame by comparison.

It may be difficult to imagine, but the staid, powder-wigged gentlemen staring out from the pages of our history books had skeletons in their closets which dwarfed some of the shenanigans of their more straight-laced successors at 1600 Pennsylvania Avenue. Before the dawn of instantaneous communication, many vicious rumors which had no basis in fact were believed and repeated as true, because wagging tongues moved faster than official denials.

Few presidential administrations were spared the lash of scurrilous, often unfounded allegations of political double-dealing, malfeasance, financial cheating, or sexual misconduct. In chronicling the private and public scandals of our early presidents, one tendency seems apparent: the greater or more revered the man, the crueler and more widely circulated the charges against him.

George Washington, for example, was constantly subjected to outrageous published broadsides. A New York journal in 1793 described Washington as having "aristocratical blood" flowing through his veins, and claimed, totally without sub-

7

stantiation, that "gambling, reveling, horseracing and horse whipping" had been among the building blocks of his education. To top it off, the invective-laden piece accused the first chief executive of being a cheapskate and alleged that he was a "most horrid swearer and blasphemer." The rabid attacks by the ink-stained wretches of eighteenth-century journalism was one of the reasons Washington chose to retire from public life in 1796, rather than seek a third term as president.

Another Founding Father, Thomas Jefferson, gained a rather justified reputation as a libertine. In a charge not likely to be repeated even in today's rough-and-tumble electoral politics, a university president predicted that there would be an increase in prostitution if Jefferson was reelected in 1804. Our third president's amorous adventures, in the view of many historians, included fathering children by a black slave named Sally Hemings.

Old Hickory, Andrew Jackson, arguably the most dominating political figure of his era, was accused of being a bigamist; he fought more than one duel of honor to defend the reputation of his beloved wife, Rachel. Another of our presidents was an alcoholic as a young man and continued tipping the bottle after assuming the highest office. It's unlikely that any presidential candidate of the 1990s could be accused of fathering a child out of wedlock and still be elected president (twice), a feat accomplished by Grover Cleveland near the end of the nineteenth century.

Warts and all, our presidents were (and are) fallible human beings who've often lied, cheated, slept around, and placed their trust in aides and appointees who disgraced themselves. As we'll see, many of them rose above their shortcomings, sins and misjudgments to become outstanding or near-great leaders in the most demanding office in the world. Others, like Richard Nixon, were overcome by their own character flaws and saw their presidencies undone by scandal.

This work is a modest attempt to chronicle two centuries of that fascinating story dominated by forty American men. The vivid recounting of the foibles of our chief executives is meant to remind us, not that our leaders have feet of clay, but rather that those at the pinnacle of power struggle with their human frailties just like the rest of us.

Chapter 1

COLONIAL CAPERS
George Washington—John Quincy Adams

March 1789—March 1829

Few public officials have been more maligned in their times than George Washington. The Father of His Country was even accused of mistreating his mother, with whom he never enjoyed a close or warm relationship. As author Hope Ridings Miller has noted, "No famous American has ever been so slandered in life—and so idolized after death" as Washington. He regarded his eight years in the White House as something of an ordeal, which he bore with the grim, stoic countenance he believed proper for a public figure.

The first president's stern, foreboding public manner (which characterized much of his personal life as well) precluded him from developing an image of a dashing, romantic politician who could become the center of idle gossip among the circle of socially prominent women who dominated Washington and Williamsburg of the 1780s.

But the young Washington's own private correspondence shows that he had a long-term, obsessive romantic infatuation with a slightly older, dark-featured woman named Sally Cary Fairfax, the young wife of his best friend, Colonel George William Fairfax. He first met Sally when he was just sixteen, and a frequent visitor to the Fairfax home. She became the willing teenager's social tutor and wardrobe adviser, just as the rest of the Fairfax household looked after the

9

somewhat awkward Washington in other ways. By the mid-1750s, when Washington was in his early twenties, he was writing to his mentor's wife often from military camp, and his letters recalling their gay dancing and card playing together at the Fairfax estate were apparently a source of pleasure during what was a generally depressing time for the young officer.

His devotion to the witty, untouchable Sally, however, didn't completely dim his interest in other eligible ladies of the day. He courted and proposed to a young Virginian named Betsy Fauntleroy, but was rejected, partly because his financial prospects at the time didn't impress her wealthy father. And a few years he later met Mary Eliza ("Polly") Phillipse in New York, who was the friend of a long-time female acquaintance. But she was in love with another military man and this romantic interlude also ended in rejection for the young soldier.

Finally, in 1758, the 26-year-old Washington developed an interest in a widow of his own age named Martha Custis, and after a whirlwind courtship of just a few weeks, the couple came to an understanding that they would marry when he returned from his latest military duties. But, as historian W.E. Woodward noted, the engagement didn't take his mind off Sally Fairfax, for in a carefully-couched letter of September 1758 he wrote:

> Tis true, I profess myself a votary of love...The world has no business to know the object of my love declared in this manner to you, when I want to conceal it...But adieu to happier times, if ever I shall see them. I dare believe they are as happy as you say, I wish I were happy also.

Rather strange sentiments for a man so recently engaged to be married! For her part, the charming Sally, who was reputed to be more than a bit of a flirt, never responded directly to her admirer's thinly veiled outpouring of affections. So the troubled Washington, finding himself the victim of a classic case of unrequited love, married the wealthy, friendly widow Custis the following January, after he had resigned from the military and been elected to the House of Burgesses.

Never forgetting his overpowering lovesickness, however, he continued to correspond periodically with Sally, and wrote his last letter to her when he was 66 (and Sally, 68), a year before he died and long after his older friend Fairfax had died. Even in the twilight of his life, his half-century preoccupation with Sally was evident as he concluded:

> None of which events, not all of them together, have been able to eradicate from my mind the recollection of those happy moments, the happiest of my life, which I have enjoyed in your company.

Martha Washington, secure in her husband's faithful love for her, considered Sally a friend and there is no record of any marital jealousy because of the warm, fifty-year bond between the friends. His fortunate marriage to Martha, however, didn't take the Washington name off the lips of Virginia's more sanctimonious scandal-mongers. In the Puritan-influenced colonial times, nothing (with the possible exception of adultery) stirred up the back-fence gossips like the hint of illegitimacy. Rumors of Washington's having fathered bastard children swirled around his family for decades, though no shred of proof ever surfaced to substantiate the whispers which followed him right into the White House.

The first recorded instance of such talk centered around a Captain Thomas Posey, a ne'er do-well who owned a farm near Washington's own Mount Vernon and who frequently visited Washington to drink wine and unload his considerable personal troubles. The irresponsible Posey was always in debt, and several times Washington signed loans and unsecured notes to bail his dissolute neighbor out of trouble. He also took on the role of generous "uncle" to Posey's children, even allowing one of Posey's daughters to move into Mount Vernon for a time. Although Washington was known to often lend money to those in need, his continuing patronage towards an obvious deadbeat led some to believe that he had an ulterior motive.

When it was noticed that Posey's son Lawrence had a strong resemblance to his family's benefactor, stories circulated that the young man was Washington's bastard son, fathered years before, when Washington was in the Barbados Islands, and that Posey had agreed to raise the boy as his own in return for monetary support. The idle gossip was completely without foundation, but Washington continued to be the center of such tales right through his White House years, when some erroneously believed the first chief executive to be the true father of his gifted and controversial Treasury secretary, Alexander Hamilton.

Legend and American folklore have always portrayed Washington as a supremely strong and gifted military commander, and that he was, but he certainly wasn't without his critics before and during the Revolutionary War. Torrents of abuse and invective were heaped on a general burdened with the toughest military assignment seen to that time on this side of the Atlantic. Conditions could hardly have been worse as the rebellion came towards a head in 1776; supplies were short, communications ineffective, and the ranks of the ragtag American army had to be continually replenished with a largely unsuitable pool of men who had been bribed, threatened or cajoled into service.

Pro-British sympathizers, sensing that a contribution to General Washington's moral disgrace would add a crushing blow to the rebels' cause, spread every sort of false propaganda in an effort to further demoralize the sagging rebel troops and their increasingly disconsolate supporters. Loyalist publications suggested that Martha Washington was one of their own and that her constant separation from her husband was deliberate. Those whispers continued until Mrs. Washington joined George at his New Jersey military headquarters some months later. Bolder propagandists, meanwhile, published the alleged account of a trial linking a woman named Mary Gibbons to the general, and falsely claimed that, in the course of their intimacy, she stole secret documents and passed them to the British through intermediaries. Sadly, the lies and half-truths caused a worried stirring among many of the American commander's restive soldiers.

As if that wasn't enough, many of Washington's own senior officers plotted to have him replaced behind his back. One such effort was led by General Thomas Conway; he and his fellow conspirators were known as "Conway's Cabal." The plotters sought to convince Congress through anonymous letters that Washington's military background was inadequate and that he should be demoted in favor of General Horatio Gates, the victorious strategist of the battle of Saratoga.

But Washington learned of the back-biting and had his fellow officers demoted. Later, another jealous officer, General Charles Lee, denigrated Washington's abilities and compared them unfavorably to his own. Only a few members of Congress seemed to take Lee seriously, and even after he was wounded by a defender of General Washington in a duel of honor, Lee continued his campaign of vicious criticism. Washington finally had the persistent Lee court-martialed.

Pilloried incessantly by a legion of detractors, including an army of the most merciless "yellow" journalists of the day, Washington's war years probably at times seemed an endless torrent of unfair abuse. But if the reviews of his military performance were mixed, the monetary rewards, apparently, were not. His personal ledgers showed that, financially, the Revolution was quite profitable for the commander in chief.

George Washington, as his biographer Marvin Kitman discovered, was not only the first among equals as a Founding Father, but he was probably the originator of expense account living in America. As the fledgling republic's finances were in serious doubt during the war years (for any money loaned or contributed to the revolutionary cause would have been lost if the British had prevailed), Washington was forced to dig deep into his own pockets even while he served as chief military officer.

But he recouped his investments—handsomely. Much credit has been heaped on Washington for his repeated refusal to accept a salary, insisting only that his expenses be reimbursed. That decision showed extremely sharp business acumen on the part of the new nation's number one military figure, for Washington turned in total expenses of $449,261 for the revolutionary war years. Even taking a unrealistically conservative inflation figure of ten to one for the Continental dollar, the general claimed virtually millions in expenses from the taxpayers.

While it's true that he would have forfeited everything if the Revolutionary cause had been lost, it's also fair to note that the First Father, by any standard, lived in regal style with the help of his expense ledgers, according to Kitman's richly detailed account. And the largesse wasn't just for himself; he picked up the dining and lodging tab of a sizable entourage, including a secretary and aide-de-camp, and charged much of the expense of keeping his slaves to the government as well. In addition to his other firsts, Washington may also have been one of the original junketeers, whose travel was completely underwritten by taxpayers. Besides his own considerable personal expenses, which over several years included barrels of wine, the best food, and visits to the barber, Washington also charged the Revolutionary bookkeepers for trips made by his wife, Martha, their stepson and even neighbors, when they came from Virginia to visit the general's military outposts. Mrs. Washington's travel bill alone exceeded $27,000, which would probably represent the equivalent of several hundred thousand dollars today.

True to his well-deserved, penurious reputation, Washington even charged 6 percent interest on the personal funds for which he was later reimbursed during his military service. The $449,000 compares to the $48,000 the high-living officer would have received on the payroll with the other generals for the time he was busy recording every handkerchief he had laundered during the revolutionary turmoil. The reader, of course, is free to judge whether Washington's clever record-keeping was merely fair compensation for his enormous personal risks and service to the fledgling nation, or whether he was practicing a sophisticated version of expense account padding.

The final hurdle of gossip Washington had to overcome prior to entering the White House was a series of vague but persistent charges that he had been dishonest in business dealings. This turned out to be a rare occasion when Washington answered his critics directly and put an end to the loose talk, which centered around tracts of land in the Shenandoah Valley which he had acquired before the war. While he was off fighting the British, squatters took possession of some of the land. When Washington reclaimed title after returning to Virginia, there was a heated dispute over the farmers' rights to part of the holdings. Such a tempest ensued that he was finally forced to take out space in a newspaper to explain how he had acquired the tracts, challenging anyone to prove that he didn't legitimately own the rights. That stopped the whispers, as no one came forward publicly to dispute the aggrieved general.

But if the gossip, slanders and jealousies of his enemies hadn't been enough of a torment, the personal trial that the weary Washington faced after the war hurt more deeply even than accusations that he had cheated in business. For the source of the new embarrassment, which was to become public, was his mother, Mary Ball Washington.

Despite efforts by some biographers to paint their relationship as sentimental, a controversy over his mother's financial support during the 1780s highlighted a fact that Washington wanted kept undisclosed; he wasn't emotionally close to his mother and apparently was far from being the apple of her eye. Again, according to the revelations of an outstanding scholar of Washington's life, W. E. Woodward, after the Revolution, when George and Martha's Mount Vernon estate became an attraction for notable visitors, the elderly Mrs. Washington wrote to say she'd like to spend time there. In reply, however, Washington wrote that he didn't want her to come; that she would be miserable in the society he was keeping and that her discomfort would make him unhappy.

Mrs. Washington and her famous son saw each other only infrequently. Occasionally he gave her money, but he also often reminded her of the various financial demands made on him (in fact, Washington, though the owner of considerable real estate, was cash-poor throughout much of his later life and actually had to borrow funds to attend his own inauguration). His explanations didn't deter his mother's increasingly strident pleas for more money. Once, in a 1787 letter to another son, John Augustine, she complained, "I never lived soe poore in my life." Were it not for friends and neighbors, "I should be almost starved," she lamented, perhaps with more than a touch of exaggeration. Nevertheless, she did accept various gifts from her neighbors during this period, and her incessant complaints finally caused a movement for a pension to be initiated on her behalf by the Virginia Assembly, noted writers Sid Frank and Arden Davis Melnick.

Naturally, when news of this development reached the president-to-be, Washington was shocked and dismayed. He wrote to a friend in the legislature to explain the situation, saying that "has not a child that would not divide his last sixpence to relieve her from real distress. This she has repeatedly been assured of by me; and all of us, I am certain, would feel much hurt at having our mother a pensioner, while we had the means of supporting her; but in fact, she has an ample income of her own."

In a self-pitying tone, he remonstrated with his mother saying, "I am viewed as a delinquent, and am considered perhaps by the world as an unjust and undutiful son." Mrs. Washington's protests, which were symbolic of a deep, long-term rift with her son George, continued until her death. The gulf between them was never really bridged. Mary Washington lived to see her son elected first president of the United States, but she didn't attend his inauguration, and died several months after her son reached the pinnacle of his military and political career.

Of all the myriad far-reaching decisions made by the nation's first chief executive, perhaps the most important was a choice which was never really made, but left to develop through the course of events. To a great extent, it determined the young nation's future fiscal direction, informally allied Washington with the country's first budget chief, and led to repeated rumors that the First Father had sired a bastard son.

At the epicenter of the overriding power struggle of the first Washington administration was the brilliant, ambitious, financially astute Alexander Hamilton, the bastard son of a Scottish planter and a French mother. His precocious intelligence had landed him a position as an aide-de-camp to General Washington, and he later married a society belle. A meteoric rise to the inner circle of the first federal cabinet encouraged Hamilton's grandiose schemes for a national bank, and in short order created a schism between him and other key Washington advisers, notably Secretary of State Thomas Jefferson and James Madison. The split was almost catastrophic for the uncertain financial health of the struggling new nation in the early 1790s.

Economists troubled by the huge debt burden of the modern federal government have the elegantly dressed, stylish Hamilton to thank for originally proposing that the new central government refund the considerable national debt of the revolutionary era, *and* assume the debt burden of the individual states. Indeed, the young (35) Treasury secretary's tireless insistence that repaying the debt was "the price of liberty" led to the greatest wave of speculation in the colonial era and the first national financial panic, in 1792.

What the persuasive Hamilton was twisting legislators' arms for was revolutionary in itself. He wanted to provide payment for a combined domestic, foreign and states' debt of as much as $80 million, a staggering sum in 1790. If today's conservative economic advisers would have applauded Hamilton's determination to establish a reliable, hard currency and a firm credit standing for the fledgling federal government, thousands of soldiers and farmers who had been paid in Continental scrip were not so sanguine. They were desperate for cash, and sold their uncertain paper money to eager speculators, who were ready to make huge profits on Hamilton's plan to refund the debt and toughen the government's financial backbone.

News of Hamilton's scheme to certify the paper scrip with government revenues led to a field day for a horde of unscrupulous speculators armed with insider information. As chronicled by Nathan Miller in *The Founding Finaglers*, the Treasury secretary was not accused of personally profiting from the massive redistribution of public wealth, but Hamilton's relatives, friends and former business associates realized a windfall bonanza. Philip Schuyler, his father-in-law, and John Barker Church, the secretary's brother-in-law, raked in large profits on the burgeoning securities. Church wasn't in the country at the time of the hectic horse-trading, and Hamilton audaciously acted as his relative's agent in the purchase of the golden paper hoard so he wouldn't miss out. Representative James Wadsworth of Connecticut, a former business partner of Hamilton, bought all the scrip he could find.

Worse yet, one of the biggest opportunists in the entire sorry episode was Hamilton's own vice secretary of the Treasury, William Duer. Conflict of interest apparently was unknown to Duer, who was dubbed "the Prince of the Speculators." Hamilton brought Duer into the Washington administration as his chief assistant despite Duer's rather unsavory business reputation, which included allegations of bilking and intimidating various government contractors. He used the public treasury to start financial pyramiding schemes which would make today's dark villain of stock cheating, fugitive financier Robert Vesco, blush with envy. Duer's conduct was so outrageous that Hamilton was finally forced to make the devious speculator resign his government post. Duer finally died in a debtors' prison, but only after his greed had helped precipitate a widespread financial panic.

Hamilton, meanwhile, wasn't without his opponents, who included a determined Thomas Jefferson, who thought the nattily dressed Treasury secretary an unreconstructed monarchist, and the tiny but energetic, articulate James Madison, who was appalled by the unbridled greed being unleashed by Hamilton's manipulations. A debate over the measures raged in Congress for months, but Madison's objections were so strongly presented that Hamilton's proposals were narrowly defeated, much to his shock and dismay.

Hamilton immediately set out to reverse the decision, using as his trump card a promise to rally political support for a capital located in the South, in return for votes in favor of his plan for the federal government to assume the states' debts. Up to that time, much of the official business of the government had been done in New York, which was regarded as only a temporary home; dozens of new locations had been proposed along the eastern seaboard. Hamilton, born in the British West Indies, had no sectional interest and was willing to use his influence to make a deal on the capital's ultimate locale. But there could be no compromise without Jefferson or Madison.

It was, therefore, the feuding triangle of Hamilton, Madison and Jefferson who came to a quiet arrangement on both the debt assumption vote and the future of the capital. Afraid he would be defeated and ready to resign if he were, Hamilton made a last-ditch effort to persuade his articulate opponent Madison to swing the vote his way. According to Jefferson's account, the powerful triumvirate met over dinner and Madison finally agreed to bring Southern votes over to Hamilton's side (although he did not promise to vote for the measure himself). Sensing victory, Hamilton then offered to swing Northern votes in favor of a Southern capital, to be established at a low-lying, rather swampy location not far from Washington's beloved Mount Vernon.

A reflective Jefferson later regretted his part in the meal-time bargain, and subsequently even attempted, unconvincingly, to claim ignorance of what Hamilton plotted. He had helped seal the future monetary fate of the young nation, and though his rival had the backing of the man he idolized, George Washington, Jefferson felt Hamilton was the head of a "corrupt squadron" of greedy businessmen and cheap speculators who could bleed the country dry. (Indeed, he and Hamilton spent a good part of the administration flailing at each other in the newspapers and encouraging favored editorial writers to launch vicious, thinly disguised attacks on the other.)

But neither he nor the determined Hamilton were ever to know the true, awesome results of the forces they had jointly set into motion. In this vitally important drama, Washington was the least active player; but however hesitatingly, he had cast his lot with Hamilton's grand design, a federal financing system which was to be the foundation for the nation's future growth, but also the apparatus of many corrupt schemes.

Even if Washington had a quiet pride in his young protege Hamilton, the weakness of the flesh of the Treasury secretary would soon cause the major sexual scandal of the Washington presidency, an episode which shattered a number of careers and was the direct cause of a famous duel to be fought years later. Hamilton's disgrace came to be known as "the Reynolds Affair," and was triggered by the a revenge-minded, cuckolded husband.

The sordid tale, as related by author William P. Cresson, began in 1791, when a woman named Maria Reynolds presented herself to Hamilton and beseeched him for financial assistance. Although married and a father, Hamilton was strongly attracted to Maria, and when he later visited her rooming house with the money, he was pleasantly surprised that, as he later confessed, "it was quickly apparent that other than pecuniary consolation would be acceptable." Unfortunately for Hamilton, Maria's husband, a con man named James, learned of their prolonged affair, and blackmail ensued. The Treasury secretary would have lost only money and

pride if the profligate Reynolds hadn't been arrested the following year, with a partner in a complex swindle aimed at
wartime veterans.

The licentious Reynolds told his cellmate not to panic, for
he had "friends" in high places, namely the eminently re-
spectable Hamilton, over whose head Reynolds now hung a
sexual liaison which threatened to ruin one of the president's
most trusted aides. But if Hamilton might be willing to pay
blackmail, he wouldn't accede to political intimidation. Undaunted, Reynolds leaked word from prison that he had information which would "hang the Secretary of the Treasury."
Reynolds' revelations, which hinted at financial improprieties as well as adultery, came to the attention of several congressmen, including James Monroe. Not afraid of admitting
his extra-marital romp in the hay to the legislators, and certain of his ability to refute Reynolds' other charges, Hamilton
invited the congressmen, Republican opponents of the administration, to meet with him personally, promising to prove
his innocence.

True to his word, he managed to convince his political
antagonists that he had done nothing to compromise his office, and they in turn pledged to keep his bedroom confession
a secret. (Monroe, however, broke his part of the bargain and
caused a confrontation which will be discussed later.) Then,
in an extrordinary *mea culpa*, Hamilton published a pamphlet
giving his side of the Reynolds imbroglio, admitting that he
had fallen prey to the wiles of a seductress, but claiming that
he was guilty of no sin worse than gullibility. "There is nothing worse in the affair than an irregular and indelicate amour.
For this, I bow to the just censure which it merits. I have paid
pretty severely for the folly, and can never recollect it without
disgust." And recollect it he would, many unhappy times in
the years to come.

But if the favored Hamilton's frank indiscretions provided
fodder for the genteel gossip mills of privileged society, a
more serious breach of ethics by another cabinet official sent
a shocked Washington into paroxysms of rage. The offender
was Edmund Randolph, a former governor who had replaced
Thomas Jefferson at the helm of state during Washington's
second term. Randolph's disgrace came at a most inoppor-

tune moment for the president, who was agonizing over the implications of signing the pro-British Jay Treaty, which was adamantly opposed by a large portion of the post-revolutionary population of the thirteen colonies.

Purely by accident, in the midst of the 1795 controversy over the future direction of the United States' relations with Britain and France, a cache of letters was discovered. They contained secret dispatches from French official Joseph Fauchet to his superiors in France. In guarded, diplomatic jargon, they suggested that Randolph had solicited French bribes to assist in the crushing of the Whiskey Rebellion of 1794. This had been a tax revolt by moonshiners from the western territories against the authority of the new central government. Washington had personally led an army of 15,000 men to quell the short-lived disturbance. Fauchet's eyes-only report intimated that Randolph blamed the British for the rebellion and was secretly and unofficially asking for French intervention.

Washington was livid at the apparent breach of national security and at what he saw as an attempt by Randolph and pro-French republicans to enrich themselves at the expense of sound foreign policy. He read the dispatches aloud at a hastily-convened cabinet meeting, and when the surprised Randolph couldn't provide a satisfactory explanation, the president forced his resignation on the spot. The humiliated ex-secretary published a pamphlet in his own defense, but it was more an attack on Washington's policies than an attempt to shed light on the mystery of the secret French letters.

Even eight years in the presidency he never wanted wasn't enough of a service to completely curb Washington's critics, who hounded him with a catalog of charges right through retirement to his beloved Mount Vernon. One of the most persistent attackers was Benjamin Franklin Bache, the grandson of Old Ben and the editor of the anti-Washington, anti-federalist *Aurora* newspaper. According to historian Nathan Miller and others, Bache had a personal grudge against Washington, who he believed had once blocked the appointment of his father to the office of postmaster general. The writer discharged his spleen by accusing him of being "debauched" and deceitful. The virulent slanders, which Washington's defenders accused Thomas Jefferson of promoting, continued almost to the time of John Adams' inauguration. The retiring president seemed to most resent the publication of phony letters alleging that he'd had a liaison with a black mistress, a rumor he sought to refute through friends and former aides.

There was to be, however, no respite from controversy for Washington during his lifetime. Charges of his having fathered a variety of bastard children followed him to his grave in 1799, despite firm evidence to the contrary. And long after Bache's low blows had been disproved, critics peddled the canard that Washington had committed miscegenation with his black slaves at Mount Vernon because of a series of mysterious marks in his personal ledgers, scribbles that most historians have decided were his own short-hand code for the slaves' work records. So the First Father, while perhaps the best loved man of his time, was also one of the most hated, and certainly was no stranger to the type of scandal which was to haunt his successors in the office first occupied by himself.

*   *   *

The larger-than-life Washington would have been a tough act for any man to follow as president, but the somewhat pretentious John Adams was perhaps an unfortunate choice to be the second man to hold the highest office in the land. One of the most learned but irascible men of his day, Adams had assumed the vice presidency when he finished second in the balloting, as the prevailing electoral system dictated. His vice presidential tenure, distinguished by a number of critical policy decisions, is memorable for his incessant demands that Washington assume various royal-sounding titles as chief executive. Such grandiose suggestions made him a laughing-stock of many in the legislature, some of whose members began addressing him behind his back as "His Rotundity," and "His Superfluous Excellency." Washington more often turned to Adams for advice and companionship during his second term, after losing the services of Jefferson, Hamilton and Randolph. For his part, however, the scheming Hamilton did everything he could to block Adams' road to the White House, including supporting one of his opponents, Thomas

Pickney, in the 1796 election. A disappointed Jefferson, meanwhile, finished just three votes behind his bitter political rival
and took the number two spot in the new administration.

In fairness to Adams, he was aware of his own shortcomings, including his personal vanity, and the United States he
was elected to govern in 1796 was headed for a period considerably more troubled than the eight years of Washington's
tenure. Even the defeated Jefferson was forced to concede that
Washington "is fortunate to get off just as the bubble is burst-
ing, leaving others to hold the bag." Economic times were
hard as the prosperity of the 1780s dissipated. Much of
Europe was at war, the western territories of the new nation
were wild and unsettled, and partisan political differences
were reaching a fever pitch. Adams made foreign policy decisions with the threat of war hanging over every wrong move.

Worse yet, the second chief executive didn't get much assistance from a cabinet largely inherited from Washington,
which quickly showed itself to be disloyal. Several key officials, including Secretary of State Timothy Pickering, Secretary of War James McHenry and Secretary of the Treasury
Oliver Wolcott had either worked for or idolized Hamilton.
During Adams' long absences from the capital, these three
cabinet officials regularly sent Hamilton's suggestions for
policy and official appointments to Adams at his home in
Quincy, Mass., under-cutting their leader. The conniving
Hamilton, in effect, became a surrogate president from his
New York offices, dispensing advice on patronage, fiscal policy and government contracts to his eager cabinet worshipers.
Meanwhile, Adams was unaware that many of his administration's policies were being dictated by one of his most
hated political rivals.

It was small wonder, then, that Adams was a man truly
alone at the top when the biggest foreign policy scandal in the
brief history of the republic broke in the spring of 1798. The
"XYZ Affair" so outraged American public opinion that war
with offending France was averted only by a narrow margin.
It was a fantastic tale, the details of which have been related
by Jack Shepherd and other colonial-era writers. Franco-
American relations, which had been so cordial during the
years after the American Revolution, began to sour in 1793,

when France declared war on Great Britain and waited impatiently for the United States to jump into the hostilities on the side of Paris.

When it became increasingly clear, from the pro-British Jay Treaty and several embarrassing diplomatic incidents between the two countries, that the U.S. preferred a "hands off" policy towards the European power play, French pro-American sentiments cooled considerably. Blundering by James Monroe, the U.S. representative in Paris, didn't help. The unabashedly pro-French Monroe took it upon himself to blast the British government and insist that the United States stand behind its long-time French allies. His controversial statements made such a splash in London that he had to be recalled. In retaliation, angry leaders of the revolutionary French government's Directory refused to accept the diplomatic papers of his replacement, Charles C. Pinckney, and ordered U.S. cargo ships seized.

This was the ugly situation Adams inherited, and he soon took the advice of Hamilton and other bipartisan advisers to send a special group of envoys to France to forestall the threat of war between the quarreling allies. After weeks of consideration and a blunt refusal by Jefferson to serve in the diplomatic mission (a rejection which alienated Adams from his vice president once and for all), three men were chosen and approved: the previously rejected Pinckney, future Supreme Court Chief Justice John Marshall, and Elbridge Gerry (oddly reshaped voting districts designed during his later governorship of Massachusetts were named "gerrymanders" after him).

Months passed with no word from the delegation, but when secret dispatches arrived from the envoys for Adams on March 4, 1798, they shook the president to the bone. The real story, in fact, was so scandalous Adams didn't dare release it all, even to Congress. He informed the legislature that the mission had failed and that the French had passed an edict that all neutral ships carrying goods bound for England would be seized. Backed by his Federalist party, the president suggested strong measures of defense, including a larger army and weapons for merchant ships on the high seas.

Republicans reluctant to discard pro-French sympathies weren't so quickly convinced and concluded that Adams was rushing the nation into a premature war. Jefferson, among others, felt that Adams was exaggerating the diplomats' confidential warnings in order to whip the country into a frenzy against France. A rancorous, closed-door session of Congress ensued, and the Republicans demanded that the White House release the full text of the diplomatic cables from Paris.

Jefferson's supporters won that argument but may have wished they hadn't, for the sordid details subsequently disclosed made even the most pro-French Americans shudder. Treachery and bribery had become the new tools of French diplomacy under the slippery foreign minister Talleyrand. After refusing to receive the extraordinary American delegation personally, he sent three lackeys of his own to quietly visit the confused Americans. Talleyrand's messenger boys were named Hottenguer, Bellamy and Hauteval, but their identities were concealed in the dispatches with the letters X, Y, and Z.

Their terms for peace were quickly apparent—they wanted money, and lots of it. Talleyrand would be willing to settle American grievances for a princely bribe of fifty thousand pounds sterling (or about a quarter of a million dollars at the period's exchange rate), plus a loan to the French government of several million dollars. Nor was that the end of the incredible demands. The agents wanted the American diplomats to agree in writing to disavow all the attacks made on France by Adams and his Federalist supporters. "You must pay money," taunted the mysterious Mr. Y. in the *Adams Chronicles*. "You must pay a great deal of money."

Pinckney, twice rejected by the French, gave the midnight messengers a blunt answer which was to make him more famous than all his patient, fruitless diplomacy. Our response, said Pinckney, "is no, no...not a sixpence!" Talleyrand's conduct, which Madison cited for its "unparalleled stupidity," gave Adams and the Federalists the war whoop they wanted; Jefferson and the pro-French Republicans fell into deep despair. "Millions for defense but not one cent for tribute" was the rallying toast which greeted Marshall on his return from France.

Hysteria gripped Congress; vengeful Federalists even threatened to impeach Vice President Jefferson to curb Republican opposition to the rapid arms build-up and tough anti-civil rights legislation aimed at French residents and foreign nationals such as the Irish, who were then mostly Republicans. The Sedition Act imposed fines and prison sentences on those who wrote, published or even uttered remarks critical of the president or Congress. Adams, a supposed defender of civil liberties, shamefully stood by and allowed the more frenzied of his political allies, the arch-Federalists, to control the day.

While war loomed over the nation, more behind-the-scenes skulduggery underminded Adams' intentions; and again, his political antennae seemed not to sense it. Hamilton was receiving secret information restricted to top government advisers from the president's duplicitious cabinet officials. In his chronicle of the Adams presidency, Ralph Adams Brown documented that Secretary of State Pickering, one of the Hamilton's ardent admirers, sent him confidential details of John Marshall's report on the XYZ incident, leaks which Adams probably knew nothing about. Anxious to form an alliance with Britain, Hamilton used his White House connection and the top secret reports to foment a "palace revolt" against Adams. His cause was given a boost when Adams was forced to ask Hamilton's aging mentor, Washington, to come out of retirement to head the armed forces during the threat of war with France. Hamilton's supporters then lobbied the ex-president aggressively and Hamilton, after a lengthy period of bickering, was named second-in-command of the armed forces.

The conflict between commander-in-chief and frequently unscrupulous subordinate didn't stop there, however. Hamilton pushed for a build-up of the army, while Adams remained firmly convinced that the U.S. could avert a war only with a stronger navy. More ominously, Hamilton and the arch-Federalists pushed for war with France at the same time that Adams, determined to avoid armed conflict, pursued peace negotiations. The patient Adams finally prevailed, but at a terrible political price to himself and his party. His stubborn insistence on peace hurt him politically when the presidential ballots were cast in 1800.

As with the man who preceded him in the highest office,

not all Adams' presidential problems were political; he experienced family crises which would have tested the patience of Job. Indeed, the cruelest disappointment Adams received while in the White House wasn't from his arch-rivals Jefferson or Hamilton, nor from the double-dealing cabinet officials. Rather, the most painful and personal scandal linked to Adams involved the debaucheries of his son Charles, who spent his father's White House years in a constant state of alcoholic stupor, and died of his devotion to booze little more than a month after the elder Adams was defeated for re-election.

No one could have foreseen the miserable end of the president's second son, who as a youth had always been the most gregarious and outgoing of the Adams children. He'd been a brilliant law student, had a promising legal practice, and a lovely wife and family. But while his father was striving to save the nation from war, and his older brother, John Quincy, was beginning an outstanding career as a diplomat, Charles was sinking in a sea of drink, debt and despair from which his alarmed family ultimately couldn't save him.

His son's decline was a crushing blow for Adams, who wrote to his youngest son Thomas, "Oh! that I had died for him if that would have relieved him from his faults as well as his disease."

Adams' quiet agony didn't stop the vicious accusations of nepotism from journalistic critics. Adams was taken to task by Benjamin Bache, Washington's old nemesis, for bringing his son John Quincy into government service and thereby collecting two government salaries for the Adams family. The president ignored the exaggerated fusillade, although it enraged him.

He may not have been so innocent, however, in the case of Colonel William S. Smith, his son-in-law, whose name he submitted to the Senate in 1798 for the rank of commander of a regiment of provisionals. No sooner had Adams forwarded Smith's name than his back-biting secretary of war, Pickering, was urging Federalist senators to vote against Smith, claiming he was a crooked businessman and had been nominated only because he was related by marriage to the president.

Adams was livid. He had patiently accepted Pickering's

other disloyalties, which had been legion, but this challenge he regarded as the height of hypocrisy. Pickering himself was a nepotist extraordinaire. He had installed his eldest son and one nephew in the diplomatic service, another son and nephew in the navy, a cousin as a postmaster and his brother as an insurance agent for the navy. Nevertheless, object Pickering did, and the intense lobbying from the war secretary hurt. When the votes were counted, Smith had only three Senate tallies in his favor, a humilation for the president. Adams was beside himself when the news came, but somehow managed to control his explosive temper.

Pickering actually expected to be fired from his post for his irksome meddling, but Adams didn't ask for his resignation. Calmly, he had Smith's name re-submitted for a lesser office and the colonel was confirmed by Federalist senators who were not anxious to cross their president twice. In this particular instance, however, Pickering's opposition wasn't entirely personal or petty; other politicians seemed to agree with his low opinion of the presidential son-in-law. One Republican leader in Congress, Albert Gallatin, later wrote to Jefferson that "Colonel Smith is a bad officer; he does not attend to the duties of his office; he has presented fallacious statement of his emoluments [compensation], with intention of keeping a portion which by law ought to be paid in the Treasury."

Four years of vituperative insults and double-dealing came to an ugly head during the summer and fall of 1800, when Adams' army of political enemies launched an all-out effort to deny him a second term. In spite of his family troubles, the coarse disloyalty of key advisers, and the embarrassing XYZ scandal, Adams decided to seek re-election, after initially indicating that he was considering retirement. For months, the brickbats flew in a presidential campaign beside which modern mudslingers would pale by comparison. Slurs were circulated which would result in immediate libel and slander suits today. Adams' frequently impetuous and hot-headed personal manner brought charges that he was senile and lacked full possession of his senses. Although his origins were lower-middle class, he was branded an aristocrat and a monarchist. Unbelievable stories were conjured up about Adams' planning to marry one of his sons to a daughter of King George III and produce a dynasty linking Britain and the United States.

Worst of all, the man who had become his political arch enemy, Hamilton, "the bastard brat of a Scotch pedlar," as Adams referred to him, continued his plotting against the president. Hamilton published a pamphlet, later widely circulated by Adams' political opponents, accusing him of "vanity, extreme egotism," and bizarre behavior in the dismissal of cabinet officers Pickering and McHenry. In turn, the president's supporters were far from guiltless; Federalist campaigners attacked Jefferson as an infidel and an atheist.

The barrage didn't stop at the bedroom door; one well-traveled rumor said the president had sent his vice presidential candidate, Charles Pinckney, to England to "procure four pretty girls as mistresses, a pair for each of the elderly gentlemen." But this tavern story amused more than outraged Adams, who wrote to a friend that "I do declare upon my honor, if this be true General Pinckney has kept them all for himself and cheated me out of my two."

The lies, innuendo and fencepost gossip produced a hairsplitting three-way race for the presidency; Jefferson and Aaron Burr tied with 73 electoral votes each, and Adams ran a close if disappointing third with 65; under the election rules of the day, the final selection was left up to the House of Representatives. After much behind-the-scenes politicking by all sides, the legislature chose the man from Monticello as the third chief executive. Selection for the presidency only seemed to step up the personal attacks on Jefferson, who soon was being painted as some sort of diplomatic and executive Casanova. He found himself accused of seducing at least two matrons while serving as minister to France.

Much of the licentious gossip was nothing more than that, but Jefferson was far from blameless; he had enjoyed the pleasures of much female company as a young bachelor, and again after his beloved wife, Martha, died at the age of 33 in 1782. One episode, which he later admitted in his own correspondence, didn't come to light until he was in the White House and caused him and his party considerable chagrin. It also almost embroiled the president in a duel of honor with a man who had once been one of his closest personal friends.

The "Walker Incident," which Jefferson probably thought had long since been forgotten by 1805, apparently began as a mild flirtation more than thirty years before, in 1768. Young Jefferson was strongly attracted to Mrs. Betsey Walker, the comely wife of his friend John Walker, who was often away on business. Although she rejected his advances, Jefferson showed the same tenacity towards the object of his affections as he had in politics, and kept trying to seduce Betsey for the next three years. Her husband learned of his friend's indiscretions, but never made anything of them until a newspaper published a list of grievances against the president in January 1805, which included insinuations that he had cuckolded Walker.

Jefferson's political antagonists, seeing a savory tidbit to turn against him, persuaded Walker that the only way to save his honor was to humiliate Jefferson and detail the whole sordid affair of a generation before. Not satisfied with embarrassing the president, they goaded Walker into demanding "satisfaction," a duel of honor, an impossibility for the 62-year-old president, particularly after the public revulsion that followed the infamous duel the year before, in which Vice President Aaron Burr had shot and killed Alexander Hamilton.

Even if he was willing to tolerate the savage attacks on his own reputation, Jefferson realized that he would have to defend Mrs. Walker in some way. Manfully, he confessed his guilt in a private letter to Attorney General Levi Lincoln, which is quoted by Hope Ridings Miller: "You will perceive that while I plead guilty to one of the charges, that while young and single I offered love to a handsome lady, I knowledge its incorrectness. It is the only one in truth of all those allegations against me." The official communique was circulated to other members of the Jefferson administration, and soon the general public also knew that their president had freely confessed his decades-old romantic indiscretion. Mrs. Walker was never specifically named, but by that time everyone in the capital knew the players involved. The confession brought an end to the controversy, and years later Jefferson made amends to the Walkers with gifts of Monticello fruit.

The biggest and most titillating sexual puzzle of Jefferson's life has never been solved, however. The mystery centered around Sally Hemings, a handsome, black slave woman on the Monticello plantation, nicknamed "Dusky Sally" because of her light-skinned, mulatto heritage. In some historical circles, it has come to be regarded as fact that Jefferson took Sally as his concubine, fathering several racially mixed children by her. Since the relationship was reputed to have lasted for thirty years, it would have been the longest sexual liaison of Jefferson's life.

The debate over who occupied Sally's bed at Monticello has gone on for 175 years. In modern times, the historian most responsible for popularizing the alleged long-term affair between the black slave and the president has been Fawn Brodie, author of *Thomas Jefferson: An Intimate History.* It was "serious passion that brought Jefferson and the slave woman much private happiness over a period lasting thirty-eight years. It also brought suffering, shame and even political paralysis in regard to Jefferson's agitation for emancipation," she wrote.

But Professor Brodie's conclusions, shared by a number of other Jefferson experts, have been disputed in recent years, most notably by Virginius Dabney, author of *The Jefferson Scandals.* Dabney maintains that the villain of the Hemings tale was a dissolute pamphleteer and journalist named James T. Callender, a muckraking hachetman who bore a grudge against Jefferson because of the late refund of a government fine which the president had ordered remitted to Callender. Examples of his earlier work include broadsides against Washington as a "scandalous hypocrite" who had "authorized the robbery and ruin of his own army" in the Revolution. Callender also had castigated John Adams as a "British spy" and "one of the most egregious fools upon the continent."

The real sires of the dark-skinned children at Monticello, according to Dabney, who is backed by John Miller in *The Wolf by the Ears*, were Jefferson's nephews, Peter and Samuel Carr. A question mark remains today, nevertheless, about Jefferson's real relationship to Sally and his possible fathering of as many as five illegitimate children.

After the wild antics of his first vice president, Jefferson probably deserved a more loyal number-two man to succeed Burr: but what he got was a tired, cranky old man, George Clinton, who, according to one account, "whiled away much of his time at his boarding house." To put it bluntly, Clinton, the seven-time governor of New York, was senile and could barely count the votes his party rolled up in the Senate, where he presided with remarkable ineffectuality.

Besides Clinton's cantankerous behavior, Jefferson had to contend with his former vice president, Burr, who'd been sent into exile after killing Hamilton, then traipsed around the country and attempted to organize a western revolt. The president got himself and his party into hot water in late 1805 with the passage of a piece of legislation called the Two Million Act. Jefferson and his secretary of state, James Madison, wanted Congress to approve the appropriation of two million dollars, then a very healthy sum, to buy Florida border lands under the control of the Spanish. Unfortunately for them, they chose to exercise "executive privilege," and declined to tell Congress exactly how much money they wanted or why.

When legislative leaders learned of the president's plans, they angrily opposed the appropriation, as key Federalists feared the money would be used to bribe the French into pressuring the Spanish to relinquish the properties. The administration got what it wanted, but only after Jefferson used his considerable political muscle to have the powerful chairman of the House Ways and Means Committee, John Randolph, replaced with one of his party "yes men," giving rise to (justified) charges of presidential meddling in the affairs of Congress. This was one time Jefferson forgot about the separation of powers that he so cherished, and in the process squandered a measure of the respect and loyalty he enjoyed from the capital's legislators.

The Jefferson era didn't end happily, for the weary chief executive was plagued by headaches caused by a long, losing confrontation with Congress in the months before his retirement to Monticello. His condition became so severe, in fact, that Madison and Treasury Secretary Gallatin assumed most of Jefferson's presidential duties in the waning days of his second term, to keep the government from grinding to a

complete halt. Having left office, he found peace at his beloved Monticello estate, troubled in his last years only by a
lack of money, squabbling relatives, and two idiot nephews
who, while drunk, chased down a runaway slave in Kentucky
and cruelly dismembered him, much to the shame and outrage of their uncle.

In the year of his death, Jefferson was so strapped for funds
that a public lottery was planned in his behalf. Fortunately,
however, friends were able to raise thousands of dollars instead, rescuing the former president from bankruptcy and the
humilation of having his estate sold out from under him. He
died, still the master of Monticello, on July 4, 1826, the same
day, ironically, as his long-time political rival, John Adams.

*　　*　　*

James Madison's woes started right on inauguration day,
March 4, 1809. The fourth president had a seventy-year-old
problem whose name was George Clinton. The old curmudgeon's rantings and ineptness had already embarrassed Jefferson who, after eight years of Burr and Clinton, grew used to
ignoring the bizarre habits of his vice presidents. It would be
more difficult for Madison. Clinton detested Jefferson's successor, and he didn't mind letting anyone within earshot
know it, at least those who were still listening to him. Disgusted at the choice of Madison for president, Clinton
snubbed his political colleagues by refusing to attend the
inauguration, and reportedly never even spoke to engaging
First Lady Dolley Madison, long a favorite at the Jefferson
mansion. After the swearing-in, Clinton seemed to spend
even more time than before at his boarding house, denouncing practically everything Madison said or did. That farce
went on for three full years until Clinton died in the spring of
1812, no doubt much to the private relief of his party's leaders, who were facing an election year. Frail, tiny and seemingly helpless, Madison was certainly a change from the robust, hulking Washington, the short, stout but imposing
Adams, and the healthy, ruddy-cheeked Jefferson. "Little
Jemmy," in fact, was even sicklier than he looked. Fearful
always of discovery, Madison concealed an epileptic condi-

tion which he knew might ruin his rising political career, for in 1809 epilepsy was widely considered a disease of madness.

Jefferson cared for Madison one day when he was seized with an attack, and the older man's discretion in keeping his successor's medical secret earned him the tiny politician's undying loyalty, a relationship which was to benefit Jefferson many times over during the trials of his own presidency. Jefferson pressed his advantage during Madison's administration by trying to manipulate a number of cabinet appointments and major policy decisions, moves which the crafty Jemmy successfully parried.

Madison hardly seemed a Don Juan, but the undersized legislator and author, dubbed the "Father of the Constitution" for his key role in drafting that historic document, made a highly successful career out of allowing people to underestimate him. His physical infirmities masked a formidable intelligence, which caused women as well as his fellow politicians to seek him out for counsel.

Although some would have guessed him an unlikely seducer, Madison had a few romantic secrets which he wished concealed from the public eye. At the age of thirty-three, for example, Madison became infatuated with and engaged to a lovely young woman named Kitty Floyd. Alas, the object of his affections fell head over heels for a medical student and married him after brushing the heartsick Madison off with a "Dear John" letter sealed with rye bread dough. Thereafter the rejected suitor made every effort to hide the evidence of this romantic debacle.

Luckily for the "great little Madison," as he was called by Aaron Burr, he later attracted the affections of Dolley Todd, a buxom widow who became his amiable consort for life and considerably brightened Madison's middle and later years. Dolley, who was several inches taller and about thirty pounds heavier than her devoted husband, enjoyed his undying trust, but she became the target of sexual innuendo around the capital, rumors intended to damage her husband. Her full figure, accented by plunging necklines and complimented by a gay, witty personality, made Dolley an easy mark for society tattlers anxious to spread discord.

The furor over Dolley's behavior started during the Jefferson administration. Mrs. Madison's gracious parties then caused many to wonder if the sage of Monticello, who'd gone after other men's wives, might not have wandering eyes for her. Others tried to undermine Dolley by spreading the slur that she was nothing more than a common tavernkeeper's daughter. Madison's political enemies, including John Randolph, started whispers that both Dolley and her sister, Ann Cutts, the wife of a Massachusetts congressmen, were engaged in numerous affairs with prominent men around town. The biggest cad in all the gossip was Burr, who confided to friends in England that he had slept with Dolley, a tidbit which quickly made its way across the Atlantic. None of these stories bothered Madison, who was confident of his wife's love, and the presidential couple had a harmonious marriage despite the idle sexual chatter.

The only thorn in the Madison family's life was Dolley's surviving son from her previous marriage, a determined wastrel named Payne Todd, whose dissolute ways constantly embarrassed his mother and tolerant stepfather. A compulsive gambler, young Todd wallowed in debt and forced Madison to pay $40,000 worth of gaming losses. His betting sickness was so out of control that it finally cost his mother her family home.

The first lady, who greatly enjoyed the executive life style, got her more penurious husband into a few minor scrapes over expenditures with the federal legislature. Once, Dolley bought an imported mirror for $40, whose origin, rather than cost, infuriated a protectionist-minded Senate. Upset that she had furnished the White House with something purchased from abroad, senators launched an investigation which cost several thousand dollars. There was also some controversy over Dolley's handling of the presidential Furniture Fund, granted by Congress so that the first family could furnish the executive mansion to their own taste. Actually, most of the backstage furor was over the fact that the president had allowed his wife to take over the handling of monies usually accounted for by the chief executive himself, or a male bookkeeper. Madison's unshakable faith in the first lady's extraordinary domestic and social abilities allowed him to ignore the complaints.

Madison's reliance on his wife in such matters was probably a prudent course of action, for the president had already shown himself to have limited acumen in business affairs. He and his successor-to-be in the White House, James Monroe, once entered into a land speculation venture in the Mohawk Valley, contracting to buy about a thousand acres of land. Initially, Madison had no money and Monroe was forced to come up with the down payment; later, Monroe lacked funds to continue the payments and his partner had to bail him out and then sell the land himself to avoid further debt.

Politically, Madison's first term was dominated by the prelude to the War of 1812 and its horrendous consequences for the capital. Feelings against the president ran so high that the conflict became known as "Madison's War." If the conflict itself wasn't the president's fault, his critics merely had to point to his lackluster cabinet officials to make their case. As secretary of war, Dr. William Eustis was a good physician. Writer Alfred Steinberg quotes one observer as relating that the burly doctor from Massachusetts "consumes his time in reading advertisements of petty merchants to find where he may purchase one hundred shoes or two hundred hats...instead of forming general and comprehensive arrangements for the organization of his troops."

For the key post of secretary of the navy in that maritime-dominated age, Madison had unwisely chosen Paul Hamilton, the former governor of South Carolina. The pathetic Hamilton knew nothing of the sea and was a confirmed alcoholic, "drunk by noon" every day. Such were the chiefs of the team that Madison assembled to rival the armies and armadas of the British Empire.

The coming war and its conduct dominated both of Madison's terms, for he was re-elected in 1812 despite charges that he was a warmonger and an inept commander-in-chief. His cause wasn't harmed by some timely, sensational American naval victories just prior to the election. But the situation had deteriorated by August 1814 to the point that the British invaded the capital and burned it, including the executive mansion which Dolley had so carefully refurbished. Despite almost being captured by the advancing British troops, Madison was greeted with calls of "serpent" and "coward," because at the last moment he had fled to the nearby Chain Bridge to evade capture. The capital escaped total destruction only because of a hurricane which extinguished most of the British fires, and a false report that American reinforcements were advancing on Washington.

Following the British army's withdrawal, Madison returned to the capital, but was unable to move back into the charred remains of the "Palace," as the president's residence was called then. Instead, the president relocated at the small F Street house he had once occupied, and later finished his term at a complex known as the House of the Seven Buildings on Pennsylvania Avenue.

Not surprisingly, the razing of the capital precipitated a major cabinet shakeup, which led to a sleazy incident involving threats from Gideon Granger, Jefferson's postmaster general and political bagman. The ailing Granger, who had enjoyed unchallenged control of a giant patronage machine for thirteen years, suddenly found himself dismissed for insubordination with a Madison footnote that "bodily infirmity with its effects on his mental stability" had contributed to the sacking. A seasoned political in-fighter like Granger wasn't leaving without a show, however. The patronage chief already was angry with the president for failing to appoint him to the Supreme Court, and for opposing him on the appointment of a postmaster general for Philadelphia. So when Madison announced that he intended to nominate Return J. Meigs, former chief justice of the Ohio Supreme Court, as the next postmaster general, Granger was ready.

He had a blackmail scheme planned, which he thought would force the president to back down from firing him. If Madison removed him, Granger warned privately, he would be forced to reveal publicly that he had defended Dolley and her sister Ann Cutts against charges of promiscuity by offering to duel the slanderer. Moreover, he would tell the voters how he had blocked the publication of details of the attempted seduction of Mrs. Walker by Madison's bosom friend Jefferson. To Granger's astonishment, however, Madison refused to waffle, and the patronage boss was thrown out on his ear after failing to initiate a Senate investigation of his firing.

The peace treaty ending the War of 1812 and the establishment of a chartered Second Bank of the United States with an attendant upsurge in the economy ended Madison's eight-year reign on a generally positive note. Even former political opponents praised the president's leadership, a refreshing experience for Little Jemmy, who had been branded a coward and warmonger only a few years before.

*   *   *

If a Hollywood movie were to be made of James Monroe's political career, it might be titled "How to Succeed in Politics Without Really Trying." The tall, elegant Monroe was the consummate "climber" of his day; he always managed to be in the right place at the right time. "He was not the equal of Washington in prudence, Marshall in wisdom, of Hamilton for constructive power, of Jefferson for genius in politics, of Madison in persistent ability to think out an idea and persuade others of its importance," acknowledged one perceptive Monroe critic. But Madison's successor had been a political cat throughout his career; he had always managed to land on his feet. Since the days when young Monroe had the good fortune to have as his law tutor the governor of Virginia, one Thomas Jefferson, the ball had bounced his way. He had the connections and wasn't shy about using them. That Monroe was a rank opportunist there can be little doubt; though an early admirer of Washington, he later decided that Jefferson was the man of the future and attacked Washington's Federalist policies and Hamilton's banking schemes. Apparently unperturbed by the criticism, Washington sent Monroe to France as diplomatic minister in 1794. By most accounts, Monroe proved himself an abject failure as a diplomat. He was too outspoken and allowed his post to become a forum for anti-British diatribes which embarrassed his chief executive, who was trying to get the pro-British Jay Treaty passed in Congress.

Despite getting himself into several more scrapes involving Hamilton and others when he returned to the U.S., Monroe continued his steady political ascent and was elected the fifth president of the United States in 1816. Following his 1817 move into the repaired executive mansion in Washington, now called the White House for the first time, Monroe was greeted by yet another favorable turn of fortune; economic prosperity combined with the relative calm of the post-war years to produce what has been referred to as the "Era of Good Feelings." A triumphant, three-month presidential tour of New England got the fifth chief executive off on the right political foot. The general public euphoria, however, didn't prevent several particularly nettlesome scandals from rearing their ugly heads.

One such embarrassment involved Vice President Daniel Tompkins, a former governor of New York, and at forty-two one of the youngest presidential running mates to win the second office up to that time. As related by author Sol Barzman, the progressive Tompkins became one of the hardest-hit victims of the political fallout over the War of 1812. He had been chosen for the unenviable task of defending the New York frontier. The militia cost a pretty penny to keep fed, clothed and armed, even with copious loans from his friends at the New York state treasury. When the unpopular conflict ended in victory, Tompkins confidently submitted an expense account of $660,000 to the government auditors, who almost went into shock.

Not surprisingly, the federal bookkeepers made it clear they that wanted a full, itemized listing of the unoffical defense minister's expenses. While no one thought Tompkins had cheated the government, the new vice president had insufficient records on how he had spent the money, and an inquiry was launched which resulted in his pay being withheld for a time. The controversy was never fully cleared up, partially due to Tompkins' own stubbornness (at one point he was offered a special arrangement to satisfy the full measure of his debt, but held out for more money, and then infuriated his political enemies by trying unsuccessfully to regain the governorship of New York.) His financial woes made him a disinterested and frequently absent vice president.

More ominously, the economic high which greeted Monroe's entrance into the Oval Office soon dissipated in the Panic of 1819, one of the earliest and most severe depressions suffered by the young nation's fragile economy. The financial calamity's most illustrious victim was Thomas Jefferson, who got caught short on a promissory note and had to be supported with cash gifts from friends during the last years of his life.

Much of the misery could be blamed on changing international economic conditions which buffeted the United States' sea trade and foreign commerce. At least a portion of these woes, though, were directly attributable to Monroe's support of a new Second Bank backed by federal funds, a venture which largely degenerated into an exercise in futility and corruption. The first president of the bank, former Navy Secretary William Jones, should have stuck with plotting maritime strategy, for his tenure was marked by lamentable ineptitude. At least one congressmen, Sam Smith of Maryland, along with other prominent citizens, was caught looting the Baltimore branch of the beleaguered bank, whose stringent credit policies ruined hundreds of small businesses and raised an outcry against Monroe's tight-fisted fiscal policies. The president felt that the only cure for the depression was to ride it out, and he did just that.

Whiffs of political scandal weren't confined to his bank and vice president, although Monroe himself was never personally accused of anything worse than poor judgment. His secretary of war, John Calhoun, himself a presidential aspirant and once described as looking as though he were made of cast iron, made several government contracting decisions which caused Monroe considerable consternation. In 1818, Calhoun was so eager to promote westward trade that he over-extended exploration efforts by almost a quarter-million dollars, partly at Monroe's insistence. The administration's critics in Congress lost no time in charging mismanagement, waste and extravagence in the "Yellowstone" contracts, named after the river area to be explored. For more than a year, Monroe's and Calhoun's enemies used the pretext of congressional investigations to force a reduction in the war secretary's ambitious defense spending plans.

Calhoun was also guilty of allowing his subordinates in the War Department to abuse their positions and enter into government contracts at favorable terms with businesses in which they had an interest. In fairness to the forceful South Carolinian, however, he fully cooperated with subsequent congressional probes of the malfeasance which had taken place under his nose.

In late 1823, the "A.B. Plot" severely damaged Monroe's political reputation. "A.B." was the signature of an anonymous author who published serious allegations of financial impropriety against Treasury Secretary William Crawford, who was a bitter rival of Monroe despite serving in his cabinet. Crawford's ghostly accuser charged that he had mismanaged public funds and had favored certain banks by depositing federal funds in local institutions without notifying Congress, and had then tried to cover up his nefarious actions.

Partly because the gregarious Crawford was popular in Congress, a sympathetic committee cleared him of wrongdoing in three separate investigations, noted historian C. Vann Woodward. Others remained unconvinced of the treasury secretary's innocence, however. Being ultimately responsible for the financial folderol, Monroe fulfilled his humiliating political penance by obtaining the resignation of his ambassador to Mexico, former Senator Ninian Edwards, who was widely suspected of being the mysterious A.B.

Meanwhile, the president himself got into hot water over his official furniture fund, which had caused his predecessor, James Madison, more than one headache. Once the White House had been restored after its burning in 1814, Congress appropriated $20,000, then a small fortune, to refurbish the presidential residence in style. Since the new furnishings would take time to select and bring to Washington, Monroe offered to sell his private collection of French furniture to the executive mansion for a price to be determined by an outside expert.

So far, so good. The rub came when Monroe twice borrowed against the value of the fund to finance presidential trips. In effect, since his journeys had political overtones, Monroe was accused of using these public funds for his private benefit. Since Monroe intended to repay the money, there would never have been any objection to this, had the overseer of the presidential Furniture Fund, William Lee, not died with $20,000 unaccounted for. That discrepancy launched two congressional probes, in 1822 and 1823. The hearings caused a serious executive-legislative branch confrontation, for Monroe refused to appear, claiming that the money was part of a discretionary presidential fund over which he had complete control. He won that round when auditors failed to find any evidence of fraudulent behavior.

Actually, Monroe's family and social embarrassments probably caused him more private agony than the political scandals laid at his door. First Lady Elizabeth Monroe, bluntly, was a snob, and made no effort to hide her feelings for those she considered her social inferiors. She ordered a complete about-face from the gay, open-door days of the exuberant Dolley Madison. Formality and tightly restricted guest lists came back when Elizabeth Monroe took over the newly decorated White House. Her older daughter, Eliza Monroe Hay, was a bit of a society bitch who seemed to get her kicks by ignoring her father's prominent guests and telling others just what she thought of them. The two female hellions apparently had the hapless Monroe tied to their apron-strings, for they were so obstinate about protocol and proper etiquette that Monroe had a reluctant Secretary of State John Quincy Adams prepare a volume on the subject for the edification of his cabinet. Finally, official Washington decided that enough was enough and instituted a social boycott of the Monroe women, which left the presidential family with a pretty dull guest list for state dinners.

Suffering as a social pariah wasn't all that Monroe had to endure from his oddball family. Monroe's brother, Joseph, evidently was a nineteenth century precursor of future ne'er-do-well presidential brothers, such as Jimmy Carter's sinning sibling, Billy Carter, and Lyndon Johnson's headache, Sam Houston Johnson. Joseph Monroe had been married three times, was constantly in debt and forever pestering his successful brother to help him become financially solvent. Monroe hired Joseph as his secretary, largely to keep an eye on his untrustworthy brother. He also had to find a place for another wastrel and gambling man, Samuel Gouverneur, his shrewish wife's nephew.

The president later regretted that move because his youngest daughter Maria fell in love with Gouverneur, despite the fact that the young suitor's only real interests seemed to be horse racing, liquor and the gaming tables. Probably just to keep domestic peace, Monroe allowed the young lovers to be married at the White House. That proved to be a disastrous decision, however, for daughter Eliza hated her brother-in-law, and his marriage to Maria turned the White House into a family battleground.

A tired sixty-seven when he left office in March of 1825, Monroe was near bankruptcy because of his family's grand style of living and the declining value of his Virginia properties. Like the man to whom he had attached his political star more than forty years before, Thomas Jefferson, he died virtually broke, six years after leaving the White House.

*   *   *

No president who enters office under the charge that he gained it through a "corrupt bargain" is going to have an easy time. But that was how it started for John Quincy Adams, the well-educated but politically limited son of the second president. Political blood must have run thick in the Adams family, for in that respect John Q. was exactly like his father, intellectually suited for high office, but somewhat inept when it came to the political subtleties which separate good leaders from great ones.

That notable lack turned what should have been an understandable political deal into a major election scandal in 1824. The presidential sweepstakes that year had started out like a free-for-all; for a time it seemed as though every prominent politician in the nation thought he had a chance to succeed the aging Monroe. His cabinet provided much of the competition, including Secretary of State Adams, Secretary of War Calhoun and Treasury Secretary Crawford. Other names popped up, such as perennial Federalist favorite Rufus King, and South Carolina's William Lowndes, whose state legislature made him the earliest formal candidate. Not to be left out, the fiercely ambitious Speaker of the House, Henry Clay, thought he could translate his popularity in Congress into a serious bid for the nation's top job. And last, but certainly not least, the immensely popular war hero, General Andrew Jackson, wasn't to be forgotten.

Ill health and dirty politics had key roles to play in the mounting electoral drama. In September 1823, fully a year before the balloting, the insiders' favorite, Crawford, came down with what appeared to be a paralysis; it rendered him an almost helpless invalid for many months. Then an Adams family friend published portions of correspondence between John Adams and son John Quincy, in which the elder Adams blasted Jefferson and his followers, causing some nasty political fallout.

As with the Jefferson-Burr deadlock of 1800, the voting in the fall of 1824 produced a four-way split which had to be decided by the House. The three true contenders left were General Jackson, who had garnered the most popular and electoral votes, Adams, and the recovering Crawford, whose illness had since been diagnosed as a violent allergic reaction to a drug. Clay, who had finished fourth, was left to become either a swingman or a spoiler; he chose the former. During the months between the popular vote and the climactic House vote in February 1829, Clay and Adams, former antagonists, met several times, and while the substance of their conversations was not recorded, gossip circulated that the two had made a deal to assure Adams' rise to the presidency over Jackson, a man whom Clay despised.

When Adams was victorious on the first ballot in the House vote, Jackson and his supporters cried foul, claiming that a "corrupt bargain" had been made for the highest office, and that the war hero had been cheated out of the victory that he had won at the polls. (The general was, however, polite in Adams' presence, and when they met, most observers judged that the loser had shown the more cordial behavior of the two.) Clay was offered Adams' former post as secretary of state, and although he feared that the whispers of his alleged intrigues might damage his future aspirations, he accepted the position. This left Adams to begin his term with a lot of Monroe holdovers in his cabinet, and the excess baggage of voter suspicion that a quiet backroom deal had frustrated their will.

If he started out on shaky ground as president, however, it must be said that the stiff-necked John Quincy ran a tight shop when it came to political corruption. Hardly any notable shenanigans occurred during his four-year term. The only real disgrace befell to presidential friend Dr. Tobias Watkins, who was caught embezzling $7,000 after being appointed as an auditor at the Treasury Department. Adams was never implicated in his friend's thievery, and the incident didn't even come to light until after Adams had left the White House in 1829.

John Quincy's wife, Louisa, and their three skirt-chasing sons provided most of the gossipmongers' entertainment during their White House years. The first lady, for example, had some rather strange habits—she gorged herself on chocolates until her teeth fell out. In fairness to Mrs. Adams, it wasn't just a sweet tooth raging completely out of control. She had developed severe psychological problems, partly due to the boredom and loneliness of her life at the White House.

Her husband considered her a hypochondriac given to "fits," and indeed there was a mystery to her behavior; once a strong, self-reliant woman, she turned into a self-pitying mess when her spouse became chief executive. In *Cannibals of the Heart*, Jack Shepherd theorizes that Louisa Adams' problems were caused by the excessive sentimentality popular among women of the age. Illness, grieving and death became favorite preoccupations for mothers, wives and young females; many escaped their troubled, repressed lives by "ailing" and retreating to health spas and sanitariums.

Louisa's outlet was the bizarre chocolate binge, in which her family indulged her like a child. She became a "chocoholic," and even losing her teeth didn't stop her obsession; in fact, she found chocolate easier to consume with false teeth, which she carried around in a bottle. Her letters to John Quincy and their sons when they were out of town always included entreaties for chocolate, which the men mailed or carried home with them.

Like his father before him, John Q. served only one difficult term; and also like Old John, his term ended with a no-holds-barred, disappointing election. Neither the cries of "bargain and corruption" nor the long shadow cast by Jackson ever really left Adams' door. The Jacksonians had inflicted the worst political blow of Adams' administration when their supporters took over the House as well as the Senate in the 1826 congressional elections; the "Old Hero" was determined to avenge what he regarded as the stolen election of four years earlier. Jackson's backers had also displaced the president's man, House Speaker John Taylor, by successfully smearing him with sexual allegations. The supposedly lascivious Taylor, claimed the Jackson forces, brought his girlfriend over from Baltimore, set her up in a hotel, and slept with her every night. Taylor denied the stories vociferously, and although Adams didn't quite believe his political ally, he backed him for re-election, only to see him lose in a close vote which forever destroyed his presidential influence in the House.

Given the bitterness between the Adams and Jackson forces and the four years it had to fester, it is no surprise that the campaign of 1828 was a classic mudslinger. Jackson's minions went for a familiar soft spot, the presidential Furniture Fund, which had caused embarrassment for three past chief executives. The president's purchase of a billiards table and a chess set was proof he had used the taxpayers' largesse for "gambling furniture," charged his critics.

Adams was also castigated for supposedly swimming nude in the Potomac (Adams was a daily swimmer and reputedly occasionally a skinny-dipper), and was reviled as a monarchist, a spendthrift and, like Jefferson, a gourmandizer who plied his guests with rich meals paid for from the public dole. Many of the president's own political appointees, meanwhile, particularly those in the Customs office, were actively and disloyally lobbying for Jackson's candidacy. Yet, mired down with family problems and perhaps sensing his own political end, Adams seemed reluctant to get down in the dirt and scuffle with his enemies. His supporters, however, detested Jackson and fought fire with fire; they revived old charges that Jackson's beloved wife Rachel wasn't divorced when they married. Technically true (her ex-husband had falsely told her he'd obtained a legal divorce), this smear led the hot-tempered general into more than one armed duel of honor.

In the end, Jackson finished first in the popular vote, as he had done in 1824, only this time he also gained the electoral ballots necessary to propel him into the presidency. John Quincy, for a last time following in his father's footsteps, left office without attending his successor's inauguration.

Chapter 2

AN OLD HERO FOR A TROUBLED AGE

Andrew Jackson—James K. Polk

March 1829—March 1844

Of all the men who have attained the highest office in the land, the unhappiest on his inauguration day was the "Old Hero," Andrew Jackson. The sixty-one-year-old general had reached the zenith of a long and legendary military career, crowned by a belated yet triumphant entrance into the fractious world of American politics in the 1820s. Nevertheless, his swearing-in in March 1829 occurred in the midst of one of the most miserable periods of the cantankerous Old Hickory's life.

The chief cause of his depression was the unexpected death, just three months before, of his beloved wife, Rachel, for whose honor the hot-tempered Jackson had shot more than one man. Less than a month after Jackson had wrested the presidency from his longtime rival, John Quincy Adams, Rachel suffered a fatal illness. The simple, kind spouse of the president-elect had been a reluctant future first lady to begin with, saying that she would "rather be a doorkeeper in the house of God than live in that palace in Washington." She yearned only to be back at their Hermitage estate in Tennessee.

A stranger to the hidden corners of the capital's gossips, Mrs. Jackson unwittingly became the target of cruel campaign attacks from her husband's enemies, who were determined to keep a man they regarded as an unschooled frontier ignoramus from moving into the White House. Slander alone wouldn't do, for General Jackson seemed utterly impervious to even the most disgusting epithets. The tall, spike-haired military commander did have an Achilles heel, however; his devoted wife of 37 years had once been a bigamist.

The bizarre tale had begun more than a generation before in 1785, when the future Mrs. Jackson, then Rachel Donelson, had wed a Captain Lewis Robards, an unstable and insanely jealous Kentuckian. His lovely teenaged wife attracted courteous male attention with no encouragement, but the masochistic Robards seemingly needed to satisfy a sick urge by accusing her of infidelity. His wild tirades produced more than one marital separation, until finally even the saintly patience of Rachel ran out, and she left her husband's home for the safety of relatives. She was accompanied by Jackson, then a fledgling prosecuting attorney and a boarder at her mother's house.

Looking for a confrontation, Robards accused Jackson of alienating his wife's affections and suggested a fistfight, but backed off when Jackson offered to escalate the disagreement into a duel of honor and later threatened to cut Robards' ears off. The ugly estrangement went on for months; finally the unbalanced Robards played his trump card. Although rejected by Virginia courts in his bid for a divorce petition, he maliciously wrote back to Tennessee in 1790 that the marriage had been legally annulled. Rachel and her loyal protector Jackson traveled to Natchez and married the following August.

Two years later, when his friend John Overton told Jackson that Robards hadn't successfully filed for divorce until late 1793, and then only on the grounds that his wife was living adulterously with another man, Jackson was enraged. Quickly, he and Rachel repeated their marriage vows, but the gossip had already spread like a virus. For years afterward, armed with his dueling pistols and famous hickory cane, Jackson defended his wife's honor against innumerable slurs. In one duel, a slanderer named Dickinson put a bullet into Jackson which was to remain in his body for the rest of his life, but the severe wound didn't prevent the war veteran from killing his opponent on the next shot.

The Jacksons' innocent mistake and the general's violent

reaction to it became the most formidable weapon in the campaign arsenal of his detractors. Although sheltered by friends from the worst of the calumnies, Rachel Jackson was well aware that the tragedies of her earlier marriage were being thrown in her husband's face twenty years after he had been nearly killed defending her. "The enemys of the Gels have dipped their arrows in wormwood and gall and sped them at me," she wrote to a friend after Jackson defeated Adams, who had outmaneuvered him for the presidency in 1824.

How much her depression over the burden of gossip and the unwelcome prospect of living in the White House contributed to her premature passing will always remain a mystery. But there was never any doubt in the Old Hero's mind. At her graveside, just before Christmas 1828, the president-elect exclaimed bitterly: "In the presence of this dear saint I can and do forgive all my enemies. But those vile wretches who have slandered her must look to God for mercy."

A crushing combination of depression and ill health left the new president with little taste for his inaugural festivities, which degenerated into a riotous affair featuring window and crystal smashing, drunken fistfights, faintings, and wholesale destruction of furniture. The saturnalia didn't do much for the image of Jackson and his followers, who were already widely regarded as barbarian frontiersmen by much of Washington society. Jackson's personal illnesses, which he bore with unflagging stoicism, paled beside the sickness which was soon to infect the body politic and rock the very course of his presidency. The disease was called "Eaton's Malaria," and it swept self-righteous Washington tastemakers like a social bubonic plague.

As author Noel Bertram Gerson related a detailed account defending her actions, the incipient virus was let loose by a dark-haired beauty named Peggy Eaton. Because of her charm and ambition, a dark-horse candidate became president of the United States, a vice president was cast aside, an entire cabinet was forced to resign, a major political party split in disarray and a social war began, with echoing reverberations felt in faroff European capitals.

It may be hard to believe in light of today's more permissive sexual climate, but the question of Margaret O'Neale Timberlake Eaton's chastity and marital fidelity was the most hotly debated social issue of Jackson's entire two-term presidency, and dozens of political careers rose and fell, depending on whether the subject was an accuser or defender of the much-maligned lady. The center of the years-long controversy was an unlikely shaper of destiny. The daughter of a Washington hotel keeper, the flirtatious Peggy O'Neale was considered one of the prettiest young women in the capital, and her father's hostelry assured that she came into contact with some of the leading political lights of her day. In 1817, at about eighteen (her exact birthdate is uncertain, but she claimed to have been be born in December, 1799), Peggy fell in love with and married a rugged, handsome navy purser named John Bowie Timberlake. Like many newlyweds just getting started, the couple took up residence with her parents in the O'Neales' fashionable Franklin House Inn. That would have been the end of the story had the indolent, hard-drinking Timberlake not become friendly with a wealthy Tennessee landowner and newly elected senator named John Eaton. Scion of a distinguished family, the twenty-eight-year-old Eaton was already considered one of General Jackson's closest unofficial advisers, despite his tender years.

Eaton had served under Old Hickory in the Indian wars, and had acquired family ties to the general by marrying a ward of Andy and Rachel Jackson, Myra Lewis, who had died a few years later. A Jackson biographer, Eaton took the Old Hero's every word to heart and believed that the general's every wish was his command. The younger hero-worshiper knew Jackson would be president someday, and he wanted to be at his commander's right hand when the time came. In the meantime, the freshmen senator Eaton promised his new friend Timberlake that he would do all he could to obtain a profitable government-sponsored voyage for the unemployed purser.

The senator's repeated efforts were ultimately successful, and in 1821 Timberlake set out for long sea duty, his first steady work since he married. Eaton's apparently innocent campaign to assist his friend and boardinghouse companion may have been the greatest mistake of his life, however.

Peggy Timberlake had become disgusted with her husband's constant drinking and had gone back to working in her father's tavern, both to help support her new baby and to ward off boredom.

When Timberlake embarked on a job which would keep him at sea for many months, Peggy's appearances at the tavern and her frequent social outings with her husband's friend Eaton soon had tongues wagging. The social ostracism which would plague Peggy throughout her controversial life began almost seven years before the Old Hero occupied the White House.

First Lady Elizabeth Monroe fired the first snobbish salvo during her husband's administration. The priggish wife of President Monroe wouldn't have as a White House guest any married woman who would be seen in public with another man while her husband was at sea. She sent the startled Peggy a note telling her as much. Mrs. Monroe's brush-off was a portent of much worse to come for the strong-willed tavern-keeper's daughter. The first lady's rebuff soon made Peggy a social pariah among Washington's prominent hostesses.

Defiantly, she continued to see Eaton, and through him became friends with General Jackson, whose political star was rapidly rising. Peggy, who preferred the company of men over women, couldn't have had a more loyal pair of friends than the aging, blunt-spoken military hero and his devoted acolyte Eaton. The shunning of Mrs. Timberlake by the clucking hens of Washington society reminded Jackson of the vicious whispering campaign that his beloved wife had been subjected to, and Peggy's proud, forthright attitude further endeared her to the spike-haired warrior, who never suffered hypocrites gladly.

No one but Senator Eaton knew his true intentions towards his friend Timberlake's wife, but he continued to use his growing influence to help the purser get assigned to voyages which paid handsomely, even stepping in when naval officials cancelled one job because of Timberlake's sloppy bookkeeping. Despite the rumors flying around Washington drawing rooms, the Timberlakes' marriage seemed on the firmest ground for years, thanks to the purser's renewed sense of financial responsibility to his family. As the whispers about

Peggy's behavior might have abated, though, her husband died aboard ship in April 1826, just when she was preparing to join him in Spain, and the woman who had long been a favorite of town gossips went into seclusion for months.

Thus the stage was set for the political brouhaha which was to taint the entire Jackson presidency. Eaton, now a senator, had been spending most of his time organizing Jackson's triumphant rematch against John Adams in 1828, but he hadn't lost interest in the welfare of his late friend's wife. Timberlake's unexpected death drastically complicated the situation, for now it was rumored that Timberlake had killed himself on the high seas after learning of an affair between his wife and Eaton. That ugly lie ignored the fact that Timberlake had left his watch and navy ring, two prized personal possessions, to his "best friend," Eaton.

The senator began to fret, with good reason, that the backroom whispers might hurt his president-elect, Jackson. Now mourning the loss of his own wife, Jackson rallied even more determinedly to the side of the young woman who reminded him of his beloved late spouse, Rachel. If Eaton was in love with the widow Timberlake, snorted Jackson, "go marry her and shut their mouths." As always, Eaton took his mentor's advice and did just that; the wedding took place on New Year's Day 1829 in the office of the chaplain of the Senate. The timing of the ceremony left many Washington matrons shaking their heads in dismay and warning of the dire social consequences to be visited on the heads of the Tennessee country bumpkins who would soon be running the country.

"The Ladies' War," unprecedented in the capital's exclusive drawing room circles, was quickly enjoined, much to the chagrin of virtually every high-ranking male member of the Jackson cabinet. The wives of Vice President John Calhoun and almost every other politician who hoped to gain a post in the Jackson administration snubbed Peggy Eaton in every imaginable way, to the point where several of the president's advisers begged him not to give Eaton a cabinet position, for fear of the continued embarrassment it would cause. As always obstinate to a fault, however, Jackson refused to budge an inch. Eaton had been his most effective campaign organizer, a loyal supporter; standing by one's friends was an unshakable commandment in Jackson's moral universe. Besides, he knew that Peggy Eaton had to be a decent, God-fearing woman, or his adored wife Rachel would not have liked her so much. The bereaved general also wasn't about to forget that Peggy Eaton had helped him through his darkest hour of misery following Rachel's death. The Old Hero was well aware of the Eatons' critics. But they could burn in hell; he was president and would do as he pleased. Eaton could have any government post he wanted, except secretary of state, which would go to New York's "Little Magician," Martin Van Buren. Senator Eaton became secretary of war.

If Jackson was quick to throw down the presidential gauntlet at the feet of his friends' critics, they were just as swift in picking it up and throwing it back in his face. "The Petticoat War," as the newspapers called the ladies' social battle, became the sole topic of conversation in the capital, to the exclusion of almost everything else. Mrs. Calhoun and most of the cabinet wives soon made it clear that Mrs. Eaton wasn't a welcome guest in their homes, and the ladies of Washington's social register followed their lead.

A humiliated Eaton considered resigning or taking an ambassadorship to limit the political damage to his friend and benefactor, the president. The stubborn Peggy had other ideas; she'd lived in Washington all her life and wasn't about to let a clique of old biddies drive her out of town now that she finally had the social standing she thought she'd always deserved. Her hard-line attitude won the backing of her most powerful admirer, Old Hickory, whose instinct was always to give a blow for every one received. In any event, Jackson was convinced that his enemies, such as Henry Clay, were using Peggy as a cowardly means to strike at him.

Within months, the president realized that the conspiracy against Peggy was even more widespread than he had imagined. Undaunted, he decided he would set the record straight once and for all, and charged one of his closest aides, William B. Lewis, a former brother-in-law of Eaton, to gather evidence establishing Peggy's feminine virtue. Thorough as usual, Lewis didn't let his commander-in-chief down; he gathered a hundred and fifty pages of testimony from almost ninety people, including congressmen and high-ranking Washington officials, all in Peggy's favor.

Still, despite the president's best efforts, the capital continued to choose up sides for "The Ladies' War," and Jackson was soon outraged to learn that Peggy was under attack by no less a personage than the Reverend John Campbell, minister of the church that the president attended. The good reverend made the fatal mistake of circulating an unconfirmed story that Peggy had suffered a miscarriage a year after her husband had sailed on his last voyage. That slander sent Jackson into paroxysms of rage, and he and Eaton hounded the frightened, contrite Campbell until he resigned his pastorate and fled to New York.

The bitter feuds over the wife of the war secretary, meanwhile, caused more important tensions at a higher level. Old Hickory had never been close to his vice president, but although Calhoun had steered clear of any personal involvement in the social sniping, the fact that his wife was one of Peggy's severest critics didn't do much to improve his stock with Jackson.

Secretary of State Martin Van Buren, on the other hand, being one of the most astute (some said conniving) politicians of his day, decided early on to champion Peggy's cause, and his unswerving loyalty to the Eatons caused Jackson to grow much closer to the tiny, ambitious New Yorker. Van Buren threw a dinner party, inviting the Eatons, and his standing made it difficult for other cabinet members and their wives to refuse.

The cagey secretary of state also played the conciliator in another incident in which Madame Huygens, the wife of the Dutch foreign minister, was rumored to be having a grand ball for all the cabinet ladies except Peggy. Jackson was furious when he heard of the plans, and he called in the House majority leader, Congressmen Richard Johnson of Kentucky, for a private chat. If the Eatons weren't invited to the ball, the president told Johnson, the other cabinet officers had better not show their faces, either. Three of the cabinet members reacted indignantly, and said that their social obligations were none of the chief executive's business. That rebuttal precipitated a real crisis, but Van Buren saved the day by making a personal call on Chevalier Huygens and apparently persuading him that such party plans might not be diplomatically advisable. The party was not held.

Never known for his patience, Jackson finally had enough of the drawing room fencing and called his cabinet together to give them the word—they had better get their wives in line, for any further affront to Secretary or Mrs. Eaton would thereafter be considered an insult to the president. General Jackson's famous fiery temper no doubt intimidated several of the meeker souls present, but nothing really changed; for it was the women of Washington, not the men, who were in control of this genteel war of nerves. The old general was sadly mistaken if he thought that the influential men before him at the meeting could turn the vindictive tide. As Jackson's political foe John Quincy Adams wrote, "the influence of that Eaton woman is still all-pervasive."

The Eaton affair finally indirectly destroyed John Calhoun's chances to ascend to the highest office in the land. Eaton and Lewis heard at a dinner for former President Monroe that it had been Calhoun, secretary of war under Monroe, who had recommended a court martial for Jackson after he had invaded the Spanish Floridas years before. The news shocked the Old Hero, who had always believed his antagonist, former Secretary of the Treasury William Crawford, to have been the one after his hide.

When additional proof of his guilt surfaced, Calhoun was forced to confess to an angry Jackson, who considered the action an unforgivable backstabbing. A friend was a friend to Old Hickory; any explanation about different political context was balderdash. He had been betrayed by a man who was now his second-in-command. As far as Jackson was concerned, Calhoun became a non-person from that moment on. If there had been any doubt that Van Buren was the general's favorite to succeed him, it was quickly dispelled.

But the wily Van Buren, not called "The Red Fox" for nothing, had saved his master stroke. If the "Eaton Malaria" afflicting Washington was allowed to rage unchecked any longer, his own bright future as Jackson's political heir might be ruined. A bold solution was required, and Van Buren had an unorthodox solution up his sleeve. If he should resign, he confided to a surprised Jackson, it would give the president a perfect opportunity to clean house and be rid of the wounding whispers against Peggy Eaton and her husband once and for all.

Initially, Jackson was aghast and feared that Van Buren, too, had betrayed him. But he agreed to think about it and seek the counsel of his most trusted cabinet members, Eaton and Postmaster William Barry, one of the few who had stood up for Peggy throughout the long ordeal. Fortunately, Eaton played right into Van Buren's hands. If the secretary of state was resigning, he must also resign, Eaton told Jackson.

The political advantages were obvious; the controversy surrounding Peggy would be ended and those who had stubbornly resisted Jackson's counsel to accept her could be purged. But the general wasn't about to lose his two closest confidants, so it was agreed that Van Buren would become minister to Great Britain and Eaton would remain in Washington and re-enter the Senate as soon as the president could prevail on one of Tennesee's ranking officeholders to resign.

Several of the key cabinet members in the anti-Eaton faction soon showed themselves to be politically dense as well as rude. They refused to take the hint and join Van Buren and Eaton in self-imposed exile. So, within twenty-four hours, on April 24, 1831, Jackson demanded the immediate resignations of Attorney General John Berrien, Secretary of the Treasury Samuel Ingham and Secretary of the Navy John Branch, against whom Eaton was particularly bitter.

To save face for Jackson, Van Buren tried to claim that he had resigned because he might be considered a presidential candidate in the upcoming elections and didn't want to put the administration in an awkward position. Many in Washington knew the real reason for the sudden, wholesale defections from the Jackson camp, though, and that was Eaton's sharp-tongued brunette wife.

With no libel laws in existence, the press had a field day at Peggy's expense, accusing her of using her influence to obtain government jobs for friends and hinting at a wide variety of romantic liaisons. The discharged cabinet members didn't distinguish their exits with good grace when they gave whining interviews to the press, blasting Jackson for firing them without cause. The public exchanges became so ugly that an enraged Eaton finally tailed a frightened Samuel Ingham all over town, trying to challenge him face-to-face to a duel of honor. The cowed ex-Treasury boss left town without even packing, much to Jackson's amusement.

Peggy's enemies had won a Pyrrhic victory, but John Eaton had the last word. Following his retirement from the cabinet in 1831, he wrote *A Candid Appeal to the American Public*, a book which turned the tables of popular opinion against his wife's enemies. "Detraction has struck everything around me," he wrote of his ostracism. "And, although it has been uniformly pretended that the persecutions against me originated in great regard and delicacy for public feeling and morals, yet where are the proofs to authorize the rumors about which Mr. Ingham and Mr. Berrien would not trouble themselves to inquire, but which, notwithstanding, they could slyly and secretly whisper into circulation? They have produced none!"

Public opinion, always flighty, tilted toward the Eatons in short order, and they returned home to Tennessee in triumph, ending four acrimonious years in Washington's close-knit social circuit. The adventures of the spirited innkeeper's daughter were far from over, for she would return to Washington and be the center of attention yet again at soirees in Florida and Spain, stopoffs on her husband's extended political career.

After John Eaton's death in 1856, she would make a dramatic reappearance in the capital's social headlines by marrying a twenty-year-old Neapolitan dancing instructor, Antonio Buchignani, who later humiliated her by running off with her teenaged granddaughter and a large chunk of the family fortune. Peggy O'Neale Timberlake Eaton Buchignani carried on in grand style until just before her eightieth birthday, when the ravages of time finally caught up with one of the most fascinating women of her era. But it was Martin Van Buren's gutsy roll of the political dice which may have saved Jackson's presidency from dissolving into chaos over what began as a parlor room feud.

Between bouts with ill health and warding off the Eaton's Malaria, it was a wonder the cranky, besieged Jackson accom-

plished anything at all. One act which he was bound and
determined to complete was the overhaul of the federal government's patronage system. Jackson introduced the "rotation in office" concept to the bureaucracy, believing that a
frequent changeover of officeholders was the only way to
prevent families and small, powerful cliques from controlling
the burgeoning federal payroll, and the thousands of jobs
(and votes) which went with it.

Supposedly, this was the birth of the notorious "spoils system," an electoral grabbag which permitted the winner of an
election to replace competent government employees with
whichever political hacks and cronies he chose. In fairness to
Jackson, however, he was far from the wild-eyed radical he
has been portrayed on this issue. His henchmen replaced only
about 20 percent of the holdovers from the Adams bureaucracy.

And there was certainly good reason to replace some of the
deadwood that he had inherited. A number of Treasury clerks
had taken the bankruptcy oath a dozen times, and eighty-
seven were found to have prison records. Petty theft was
widespread and unchecked. Much of the bureaucracy had a
life of its own and was totally impervious to the change of
occupancy at the White House.

The axe fell swiftly for a time. Spies were turned loose in
targeted departments, gathering gossip and tattling on those
critical of the shakeup. When John McLean, the postmaster
general, refused to participate in the political housecleaning,
Jackson had him kicked upstairs to the Supreme Court, where
he couldn't interfere with the important task of doling out
patronage. His successor, William Barry, performed so admi-
rably in passing out contracts that he created a giant postal
scandal for his boss. Barry was charged with favoritism, inept
management, and all-around incompetence, and although the
charges were undoubtedly true, he had been an unswerving
supporter of Peggy Eaton, which earned for him the undying
loyalty of President Jackson.

If Jackson's minions were able to locate and gleefully discharge a number of small-time chiselers and grafters from the
bowels of the bureaucracy, the thieves who replaced them had
much more ambitious plans in mind. One of them, named

Samuel Swartout, became the first man to steal a million dollars from Uncle Sam. To his credit, or perhaps for the sake of his own political future, secretary of state and patronage boss Van Buren, who knew the slippery Swartout from their New York days, tried to dissuade the president from appointing the flim-flam man, with no success. Luckily for Jackson, he would be long gone from the White House when the same Swartout was apprehended diverting federal customs duties to a pyramiding scheme of land and railroad investments. Several years later, when he went on the lam to Europe, a check of his books produced the startling evidence that he had stolen $1.225 million, according to an account in *The Founding Finaglers*.

Even Swartout's notable larcenies, however, were small potatoes compared to the briberies and favors handed out in an attempt to recharter the Second Bank of the United States. Old Hickory, an implacable foe of all banks, held a special hatred for the federal bank, whose twenty-year charter was coming up for renewal during his second term. The easy credit and cheap money produced by the Second Bank's policies, fumed Jackson, made it a "hydra of corruption—dangerous to our liberties by its corrupting influence everywhere." That antagonistic attitude put him in direct conflict with the bank's boyish, brilliant president, Nicholas Biddle. If there ever was a child prodigy in finance, Biddle was he. Graduated from the University of Pennsylvania at thirteen and from Princeton (as valedictorian) at fifteen, he helped handle the complex financial details of the Louisiana Purchase as secretary to the minister of France while still a teenager. Biddle had become the bank's third president in 1823 at the age of thirty-seven, after the first two financial chiefs had seriously damaged both the bank and the national economy. The young financial whiz turned the fortunes of the bank around and thus gave American currency a healthy boost.

Biddle realized that he would need friends in high places to neutralize Jackson's dogmatic opposition, and he wasn't shy about using the bank's formidable resources to get them. Postmaster General William Barry got a long-overdue note extended and the chief clerk of the Treasury, Asbury Dickens, was permitted to pay off a loan for 50 percent of what he owed. Several influential newspaper editors, who were so deep in hock to the bank that they would have been ruined if their loans had been called in, were also given extensions.

Nevertheless, the shrewd Biddle wasn't inclined to take on the combative president in a head-to-head confrontation unless absolutely necessary. The bank's charter wasn't up for congressional renewal until 1836, and Biddle wanted to wait four years, in the hope that he'd then be dealing with a different chief executive. But Henry Clay still thought he belonged in the White House, and he was determined to make the bank and Jackson's obstinate opposition to it the main campaign issue of 1832.

To their dismay, both Clay and Biddle had underestimated the president's tenacity. "The Bank is trying to kill me, but I will kill it," he vowed to Van Buren. The bank's backers hoped to make Jackson's political position untenable by forcing his hand on the charter renewal, but when the bill was passed Jackson vetoed it with relish. This was one battle that the Old Hero had been spoiling for, and he would not only defeat, but humiliate his enemies with a devastating counterattack.

His veto message to Congress was a masterpiece of propaganda, and the business interests behind the bank now found their lobbying efforts described as a "concentration of power in the hands of a few men irresponsible to the people." Later, Biddle made a terrible blunder by distributing thousands of copies of Jackson's veto message as campaign literature for Clay. The ploy backfired, for he'd badly misjudged popular sentiment against the bank, and his *faux pas* put another nail in Clay's electoral coffin. He was outpolled more than four to one by Jackson in the electoral college.

Flushed with triumph, Jackson was determined to crush the pro-bank forces once and for all; and Biddle, Clay and their big business army were spoiling for another confrontation soon after the elections. This time the aging general was sure he had a scheme which would utterly destroy the bank. He was sick of hearing about Biddle using taxpayer money to influence congressmen. When Biddle asked for a postponement on a Treasury Department request for several million dollars worth of government funds, Jackson sensed that the Second Bank was in trouble. He decided to strike, announcing plans to withdraw all federal funds from the bank and placing them instead in state banks around the country, a suggestion offered by his slovenly but brilliant attorney general, Roger Taney.

Neither the House nor the Treasury secretary, Louis McLane, received the proposal favorably, and while Jackson couldn't force his withdrawal scheme on Congress, he could replace the recalcitrant McLane. Bumping the uncooperative cabinet officer over to the State Department, Jackson tried to stack the deck in his favor by appointing as McLane's replacement William Duane, a Philadelphia lawyer and outspoken Second Bank critic. To his sponsor's astonishment, Duane switched his position soon after his confirmation, and steadfastly refused to withdraw the bank's federal funds as the president ordered. Given Jackson's legendary outbursts of temper, Duane must have been either an exceptionally brave or a foolish man. For once, though, Jackson withheld the famed hickory stick, and after prolonged efforts to change the stubborn Duane's mind, he fired him. Attorney General Taney, who had put the final touches on the administration's plans to empty the bank of federal funds, was asked to move over from the Justice Department and finally get the dirty job done right.

The disheveled Taney, who would later reign as chief justice of the Supreme Court for twenty-eight years, was hardly a disinterested bystander in the bank's affairs. He was a stockholder in a state bank in Baltimore, one of the "pets" (as Biddle's people called them) to which he himself directed the bank's federal funds. Biddle wasn't going to give up without another fight, though. He almost single-handedly created a recession by calling in many loans from the south and west, hoping the resulting hardship would put political pressure on Jackson to ease his determined opposition. Unfortunately, Biddle was apparently as poor a judge of character as he was brilliant in financial affairs. He never understood the depth of Jackson's stubbornness or gritty determination to have things his way at any cost.

When special interest groups came to the president, begging him to end the money squeeze which was ruining businesses and farmers across the nation, Jackson thundered, "Go to the Monster!" (his favorite term for the bank). He wouldn't be swayed by pleas; only Biddle could end the suffering by fully submitting to his will. The do-or-die attitude won Jackson a stinging censure in the Senate and an unprecedented rejection of several of his nominations, including Taney for formal confirmation as Treasury secretary.

Despite the rebuke, Jackson was the eventual winner, but his victory came at a dire cost to the nation's economy. His bullheaded attitude about the bank may have made him an even greater hero to ordinary citizens who saw him as the gallant curmudgeon willing to stand up to Big Business. His refusal to compromise, in the long run, helped cause a financial panic whose full fury was visited on the head of his unlucky successor.

More than a year later, just months from the end of Jackson's presidency, his protege Sam Houston's revenge against the perpetrator of the Alamo massacre extricated the chief executive from yet another potentially embarrassing gaffe. Sometime before, eager to acquire the Texas territories for the Union, Jackson had appointed a greedy land speculator named Anthony Butler as minister to Mexico. The selection had appalled Houston, who referred to Butler as a "swindler and gambler." The commander wasn't so far off the mark, for when Butler failed to convince the Mexicans to sell the Texas lands, he bluntly informed the president that the territory could be had for several hundred thousand in bribes to the right bureaucrats. Jackson consented to the payoff, but was later outraged when Butler botched the deal and advised Jackson to seize the area outright. He was recalled to resounding presidential curses. Houston's later, successful military foray made further bribe attempts unnecessary.

Bone-weary and half-sick, as he had been through much of his two tumultuous terms in the White House, Jackson left Washington in March 1837, after overseeing one of the most eventful administrations the country had yet seen. He "swept over the government, in the last eight years, like a tropical tornado," concluded his long-time foe, Henry Clay.

*   *   *

Few men were better prepared for the presidency when

they entered the White House than "The Little Magician," the dapper Van Buren. Widely regarded as the most capable (and scheming) politician of his day, the pint-sized New Yorker had worked his way up through the ranks in state and national politics. From humble beginnings, with almost no education, he'd risen as a young protege of Aaron Burr to the New York State senate, then to the attorney generalship, and finally had became a much-feared Tammany Hall-connected political boss and kingmaker.

But the bowing and scraping in Albany wasn't enough to satisfy his grandiose ambitions. Van Buren's powerful political base had assured him of a position in the Jackson administration, and as secretary of state, minister to England, vice president and the president's closest unofficial adviser, he became the most influential man in the capital next to the Old Hero himself. After Jackson's bitter estrangement from John Calhoun, his first vice president, Van Buren's ascension as Old Hickory's hand-picked successor was assured.

Sadly for the "Red Fox of Kinderhook," as the red-whiskered New Yorker was sometimes called, his election day victory, followed by an inaugural triumph with the admiring Jackson at his side, was probably the highlight of his four years in office. He had come a long way for a man whose schooling had ended at 14, and whose grammar and spelling were often so bad that his friends and fellow legislators couldn't read his letters and memos. The tubby little man whom others had laughed at behind his back was at the pinnacle of power, and he intended to remain there for two full terms.

But as Van Buren had reaped the benefits of Jackson's political charisma, so he would now pay for the Old Hero's stubborn mistakes, follies of judgment which threw the nation into a devastating financial panic just as the Van Buren presidency was beginning. Jackson might have beaten the Monster, as he called the Second Bank, but his successor would have to take the consequences. Just a few weeks after his inauguration, Van Buren was confronted with warnings of a coming depression.

Speculation was rife, with hundreds of banks extending vastly inflated paper credit, much of which was used for wildcat land purchases. Jackson had thrown fat on the fire when he signed the Surplus Distribution Act, which legislated the disbursement of extra federal revenues to the states. Overinflated paper currency became worth even less as the states used the money to create another destructive tidalwave of borrowing and spending.

A moribund economy wasn't the only politically thorny problem Van Buren inherited from Jackson, who had retired to his beloved Hermitage estate. Samuel Swartout's epic thievery surfaced in the midst of Van Buren's other headaches, and the scandal was laid at his White House door. In 1838, the nation was outraged to learn that a public employee had absconded with more than a million of the taxpayers' dollars. Insult was added to injury in a separate incident when a New York district attorney named William Price followed the sleazy Swartout into exile abroad with a bundle of stolen lucre.

Van Buren's choice to replace the notorious customs man was one of the worst that he made in his long political life. He gave the job to a New York crony named Jesse Hoyt and told him to give the scandal-tainted customs house a thorough cleaning. Jesse must have misunderstood his patron's meaning, for he cleaned out the taxpayers, not the patronage workers. The grafters, cheaters and bribers in control of the customs house apparently got the best of old Jesse, for at the end of Van Buren's troubled term Hoyt was found by Congress to have stolen government deposits for his own speculation, and committed just about every possible breach of the public trust. The Swartout-Hoyt fiasco, and the resulting long congressional investigations, didn't do much for Van Buren's sagging reputation.

By this time, the man who had once been respectfully addressed as "the American Talleyrand" was becoming an easy target for his growing legion of detractors. Van Buren's colorful and fastidious mode of dress, a lifelong habit, became the object of derision and scorn from critics who denounced him as a preening peacock and a free-spending wastrel. His congressional opponents accused him of turning the White House into a palace furnished with the "costly fripperies of Europe." Visitors were said to dine with gold and silver cutlery, when in truth Van Buren had spent far less on refurbishing than Jackson or his other predecessors. Four years of unprecedented economic woes had recast Martin "Van Ruin" from worldly statesman to a pompous aristocrat. His young son was branded by the opposition press as Prince John and much was made of a foreign trip that he had taken.

Van Buren's dream of a second term was now shattered. A leader increasingly looked upon as an upper-class snob, his re-election prospects against the frontier military hero General William Henry Harrison were slim in 1840. The Little Magician was about to retire, but not to the statesman-like seclusion he had envisioned.

*   *   *

The Whigs seized the presidency from the Jackson Democrats with two weapons: a crushing depression which they could blame on the hapless Van Buren, and "Tippecanoe and Tyler, too," one of the most catchy campaign slogans in the annals of American electoral politics. General Harrison, medical student-turned-soldier and the victor of the Indian battle of Tippecanoe, became the Whigs' presidential standard-bearer almost by accident. Most knowledgeable observers expected the ticket to be headed by either perennial congressional power Henry Clay, or the oratorical favorite of the special interest groups, Senator Daniel Webster. But the stage had been set for the dark horse Harrison four years before, in 1836, when the Whigs devised the unsuccessful strategy of sending four regional candidates up against the then-formidable Van Buren. Harrison surprised even his supporters by garnering more votes for a losing cause than his three Whig allies put together.

Perhaps it shouldn't have been such a shock to the political bosses, for Old Tippecanoe was no stranger to elective politics. He had run for office no less than ten times before the Whigs plucked him out of obscurity in Ohio, dusted him off and sent him into his second battle against Van Buren. A loser seven times out of his ten tries for office, the general nevertheless seemed to have a habit of winning the important ones; his victories had elected him to the Ohio senate, the House of Representatives, and the United States Senate.

The father of ten children, Harrison seemed to relish being on the public payroll. When he wasn't running for office, he was lobbying for a political sinecure. His party connections, military record and relentless self-promotion won him several choice posts, including secretary of the Northwest Territory, territorial governor of Indiana, and minister to Colombia. He certainly left an impression on President John Quincy Adams, a frequent target of Harrison's pleas for appointment, who noted in his diary that "this person's thirst for lucrative office is positively rabid."

If that was true, Harrison must have been frothing at the mouth at the Whig party's Harrisburg, Pennsylvania, convention in December of 1839, when New York political boss Thurlow Weed craftily out-maneuvered Henry Clay's backers to put Harrison at the top of the ticket. For the vice presidential nomination, Weed, called the "Lucifer of the Lobbyists," settled on former senator John Tyler of Virginia, whose hard-line states' rights views seemed to be chiseled in stone.

The Whig election strategy was straightforward; keep Harrison quiet, out of sight, and let Van Buren's dismal economic record do the job for them. "General Mum" was the nickname he earned from the critical Democratic press. The real gem of this election, however, was a series of rallies at which Harrison was piously presented as a simple frontier man, whose humble log cabin and cider jug origins contrasted sharply with the "lily-fingered aristocrat" Van Buren had supposedly become.

Distorted as it was, for Harrison was neither poor nor humble, the image worked like a charm, and the cry of "Tippecanoe and Tyler, too" gave the Whig candidates a crushing victory in the electoral college over a disappointed Van Buren, who declared that he had been a victim of election fraud and corruption.

In the months before his inauguration, Harrison learned what it was like to be a dispenser rather than a seeker of patronage, as he was hounded day and night by voracious job-seekers until he fled the capital and embarked on a pre-inauguration trip with Tyler to the vice president-elect's home state of Virginia.

Ironically, the most fateful day of Harrison's brief presidency was the first. His inauguration took place in bone-chilling, blustery weather, and for some inexplicable reason the general declined to wear a coat or hat, either on the ride to the swearing-in ceremony or when he later rose to speak. Loving to hear himself declaim and fond of sprinkling his oratory with classical allusions, Harrison for once had a captive audience of thousands. Despite the freezing weather and the crowd shivering around him in overcoats and furs, the new chief executive droned on in the icy cold for well over an hour.

It was a fatal mistake. So thoroughly chilled that his lips had turned blue, Harrison still refused a coat and insisted on riding his white charger at the head of a parade to the executive mansion, where he presided over a gala party. No one should have been surprised that the sixty-eight-year-old president began his term with a heavy chest cold.

His subsequent rapid decline caused the only real scandal of his thirty-day administration: the abysmally poor quality of medical care that he received. Judged even by the guesswork medical practices of the day, the treatments that Harrison was subjected to probably hastened, rather than postponed, his death. The description of his care in the weeks following his inauguration sounds more like procedures at a medieval torture chamber than the expert ministerings of presidential physicians.

One favorite was the "cupping" procedure; it involved heating a cup over a candle and then placing it on the wrinkled, parched skin of the agonized president. The cooling cup drew the skin under it into a lump; apparently the hope was to draw out infections and poisons lurking beneath the treated area. That painful process was just the beginning. Blood was drawn from Harrison's withering body, and his skin was blistered repeatedly with stinging ointments.

Harsh purgatives such as castor oil and calomel (which contained traces of mercury—similar treatments had probably poisoned Andrew Jackson's tougher system) were poured down the throat of a chief executive then too weak to resist. Understandably, Harrison sank into a delirium, as much from the attempted cures as the fever and cumulative effects of his age and ill health. When conscious, he begged the physicians to stop the seemingly endless round of external and internal "medicines."

Finally, on April 4, one month to the day after he had condemned himself to a consumptive death from his own inaugural reviewing stand, old Tippecanoe succumbed. His only claim to fame would be that he had been the first president to die in office. It would have pleased the man who had spent his entire adult life running for elective office that the crowds surrounding his funeral procession near the capital were as large as those at his arctic inaugural.

Vice President Tyler, suspected by his own Whig party bosses of being a renegade Democrat and bored because the Senate he presided over was out of session, had retreated to his home in Williamsburg soon after Harrison's fateful inaugural. Young Fletcher Webster, Daniel's son and the chief clerk of the State Department, was dispatched to Virginia along with another messenger to bring Tyler back to the capital after the president's untimely demise. Members of Harrison's cabinet, many of whom detested Tyler (the feeling was mutual), decided that although the 51-year-old Virginian would be carrying out the duties of the late chief executive, he should officially hold the unwieldy title "Vice President Acting President."

The controversy over Tyler's executive role went unresolved for weeks. Even Tyler's most determined detractors, and there were plenty, admitted he *looked* like a president— tall, lean, with an angular face, an aquiline nose and the imperious bearing of one born to power. True to his outward appearance, Tyler never had any doubt that he was president in fact as well as name, and his every action during the fateful spring of 1841 was a calculated step towards fulfilling his destiny.

A resolution was proposed which called for Congress to treat Tyler as a vice president carrying out the duties of president; when it was finally defeated, the last official shred of doubt about the legitimacy of the fledgling Tyler administration was removed. The end of that crisis signaled the start of a brutal political tug-of-war which would last through His Accidency's entire term.

It wasn't long before the Whigs, now in control of both

houses of Congress, realized what a colossal blunder they had made by choosing the uncooperative, arrogant Virginian as Tippecanoe's running mate. The one-mile gap between the executive mansion and Capitol Hill seemed to widen with each passing day. The White House was flooded with letters threatening Tyler's assassination. In a planned move in September 1842, his entire cabinet resigned, hoping to politically cripple the unpopular president. His Accidency remained unperturbed. Expecting to be abandoned, he was ready with a list of acceptable replacements for the deserters, and he was satisfied to see them all go, asking only Secretary of State Daniel Webster to remain in the cabinet.

When the mass resignations failed to unhinge Tyler, the frustrated Whigs decided to go for broke. Calling a caucus, they drummed the President of the United States out of his own party. Any "alliance" between the Whigs and the political renegade in the White House was over, declared the party bosses. Let the obstinate pretender see what he could do without a party or any political allies. He would get no help from responsible Whigs.

"Executive Ass" and "the Second Benedict Arnold" were now added to the list of Tyler's slanderous nicknames as public criticism of his leadership rose to almost unprecedented heights. A former friend in Congress, John Botts, had also been stunned by Tyler's behavior and became one of the president's most implacable adversaries. At one stormy congressional session, he alleged that Tyler had offered him a bribe to help win four more years in the White House after his inherited term was up. Botts introduced a move in the House to impeach the president who had betrayed his own party. The motion was defeated, but 83 of the 210 votes cast had been against the besieged chief executive.

Their frustration wasn't groundless. Once content to pontificate his states' rights theories from the floor of the Senate, Tyler now suffered from a virulent case of "Potomac fever," or the virus of self-importance, brought on by the rush of circumstances which had propelled him into the presidency. He liked being the chief executive, despite the flaying he was taking from his enemies and the press, and he wanted to stay in the White House. To do so meant carrying out an age-old political duty, namely patronage, which his predecessor Harrison had once fled the city to avoid.

Tyler didn't mind playing the patronage game, though, and saw in the dispensing of political favors a chance to eliminate his future rivals. When Supreme Court Justice Smith Thompson died, for example, Tyler offered the post to Martin Van Buren, who harbored hopes of returning in triumph to the executive mansion in 1844. The Red Fox rejected the attempted bribe, but that didn't deter His Accidency, who then offered the job to Senator Silas Wright, the Democratic leader in the upper house. He also tried to derail the rapidly rising career of former House Speaker James ("Young Hickory") Polk by offering to appoint him as navy secretary. Tyler was again rebuffed.

Jackson had introduced the concept of rotation in office to prevent the burgeoning bureaucracy from being controlled by a political clique, but Tyler's idea was to get rid of any jobholders who weren't prepared to boost his reelection hopes. As detailed by Alfred Steinberg, dozens of influential bosses in key collectorships and agencies were fired in favor of Tyler loyalists. Competence wasn't a deciding factor for the key federal posts, only political connections and fealty to the president without a party counted.

Leaving little to chance, Tyler's minions also attempted to buy control of various newspapers and made their peace with notoriously corrupt political organizations such as Tammany Hall. Honest John was the nickname that Tyler hoped to acquire in time for the 1844 elections, but "Old Veto" was added to his unflattering sobriquets after particularly divisive fights with Congress over the Second Bank and tariff legislation.

Tyler seemed to delight in concocting little secrets to keep from Congress, projects which prompted howls of protest when they were discovered. Several of Tyler's *sub rosa* deals, in fact, weren't uncovered until after he'd left office and the opposition had a chance to survey the damage.

Perhaps the most serious of these misadventures involved Tyler's "secret service fund," a discretionary presidential cache which he frequently dipped into for special projects. During Tyler's tenure, the United States and England came perilously close to war over the exact location of the bound-ary between Maine and Canada. Negotiations were delicate, and Maine officials adamantly refused to cooperate. Believing quick action was necessary, Tyler dispatched his silver-tongued Secretary of State, Daniel Webster, to get things moving with the British emissaries.

That action was routine enough, but Tyler also secretly authorized Webster, an old hand at influence-peddling, to use money from the presidential contingency fund to bribe Maine editors and state legislators to support the upcoming talks. Bluntly, the president was using taxpayer money to buy officials to accept his foreign policy decisions. His unique brand of "dollar diplomacy" wasn't investigated by Congress until 1846, during the Polk administration, but the inquiry then let Webster's enemies give the former secretary of state a public "hot foot," and demonstrated that Tyler had been utterly contemptuous of the threats made by Congress against his authority.

Tyler's presidential stewardship left a record of resentment which made his reelection almost impossible. The hatred was so pervasive in the capital that, even after his defeat, false rumors were circulated that he had attempted to avoid going to the inaugural ceremony of his successor, Polk.

The headstrong Virginian would once more be embroiled in controversy and be called a traitor for his election to the Confederate House of Representatives fifteen years later, in defense of his holy cause of states' rights. As always, he would go his own way. The inscription which he composed for the grave of his horse, General, provides a clue that one of the most combative chief executives of all knew his own weaknesses—"Here lies the body of my good horse, 'The General.' For twenty years he bore me around the circuit of my practice, and in all that time he never made a blunder. Would that his master could say the same."

*   *   *

"Who the hell is James K. Polk?" That query, credited to Henry Clay, quickly became the rallying cry for the Whigs in the 1844 presidential election. The living legend of the Old Hero, Andrew Jackson, still dominated the American political scene, even seven years after his retirement. But when the aging Van Buren failed to win enough votes to lock up the nomination at the 1844 Democratic national convention in Baltimore, the kingmakers began to look around for another, fresher candidate to run against the formidable Clay.

Van Buren's supporters in the party were now called the Barnburners, because they were quite willing to see the party go down to defeat if their man didn't head the ticket. However, the Barnburners couldn't convince enough of the conventioneers that the old Red Fox could carry the party's Jacksonian Democratic tradition back to victory. With the seventy-seven-year-old Old Hickory near death, they needed a Young Hickory, who could be counted upon to carry the banner.

James Knox Polk, an experienced Tennessee politician with sixteen years worth of close ties to Jackson, filled the bill perfectly. In fact, Jackson had even once saved the young Polk from Tennessee's ignominious gossips. It seems that Polk, then a lawyer in his early twenties, was acquiring a reputation as a woman chaser, despite a rather dour personality. Jackson, already a legend in his home state, took the aspiring politician aside and told him to find a proper young bride. The chastised Polk took the advice to heart and lost no time wedding twenty-year-old Sarah Childress, a strict Calvinist. That was the end of the tavern whispers, and Polk's career prospered.

As was now the practice in this brawling, expansionist age, the campaign was a slanderers' delight. The popular vote was exceedingly close, with Polk winning by less than 40 thousand votes out of over 2.6 million cast. The man who had been a virtual unknown outside of his native state just months before, carried the electoral college with a boost from the New York ballots; if Clay had won that state, he would have realized his career-long dream of becoming president.

Alas, Polk's administration turned out to be as tiresomely dull and honest as he was. Like his mentor Jackson, he wanted to expand the United States' borders as far as possible. He took the country into a war with Mexico which ended with the Mexicans surrendering a huge tract of land at a bargain basement price. While his foreign policy was perhaps overly aggressive, and he frequently clashed with Congress like most other chief executives, Polk enjoyed the reputation of a scrupulously moral man, even among his political opponents. There were partisan attacks, as always; and Polk's secretive, restrained manner helped to prevent him from becoming an exceptional leader, but no meaningful instance of malfeasance was traced to him personally.

When Congress accused Secretary of State James Buchanan of leaking sensitive information, Polk demanded an investigation, rather than stonewall as his predecessor Tyler would have done. Buchanan was cleared and Polk's stock rose even higher.

On the other hand, like Tyler before him, Polk may have known of efforts to buy a newspaper for use as a publicity organ. Polk officials used public money to fund the purchase of the *Washington Globe* by an editor friendly to the administration. While in the twentieth century such attempts to buy influence would ruin careers, this was considered accepted practice in the Jacksonian era, and in any event, Polk's knowledge of the transaction remains uncertain.

"The Presidency is no bed of roses," Polk once wrote in his diary, and those words proved prophetic. The workaholic president didn't seek reelection, and thus may have prevented another Harrison-Tyler fiasco for the nation, for he died just three months after he had retired to Tennessee. Only fifty-three, he may have been the first victim of the stresses and strains of the highest office in the land.

"He was the most laborious man I have ever known; and in a brief period of four years had assumed the appearance of an old man," concluded his secretary of state, Buchanan.

Chapter 3

THE SPOILS OF A DIVIDING NATION

Zachary Taylor—Andrew Johnson

March 1844—March 1869

As the quadrennial presidential sweepstakes rolled around in 1848, there was more than a whiff of regional factionalism in the air. The relentless expansionism of the Jacksonian era had collided headlong with slavery, already the burning moral topic of the day. The question of whether the newly emerging territories would permit or prohibit slavery dominated national politics at mid-century. The rumblings of sectionalism could be felt from Washington to the edge of the frontier. A crisis of leadership was quickly taking shape. But sadly, the men who would occupy the White House for the next twenty-eight years, with one heroic exception, would be second-rate chief executives chosen by circumstance rather than ability. Almost imperceptibly at first, the nation was dividing, and only in its bitterest hour was a president able to rise above the flood of corruption and ineptitude which dominated the politics of the age.

"An old oilcloth cap, a dusty green coat, a frightful pair of trousers, and on horseback looks like a toad." A vagrant? Or perhaps a farmer returning from a long trip to the market? No, these unflattering phrases were attributed to a soldier trying to describe the sight of "Old Rough and Ready," General Zachary Taylor, a vivid description uncovered by writer Irving Wallace.

One of the sloppiest (and most unpretentious) soldiers of his time, the rumpled Taylor professed no interest in politics even after his name was mentioned as a potential candidate in 1846, as biographer Brainard Dyer revealed. Old Zack had never even bothered to vote in a presidential election, although he confessed he would have cast his ballot for Henry Clay in 1844, if he *had* visited the polling booth.

Nevertheless, for the third time in the century, a hero-soldier was sworn in as president. Taylor's recently married daughter, Betty Bliss, presided at the inaugural ball, an overcrowded, riotous affair featuring bacchanalian drinking, feasting and fainting reminiscent of Andrew Jackson's orgiastic first party at the executive mansion.

Taylor's tenure proceded quietly enough until the revelation of the "Galphin Affair," which rocked his administration with conflict-of-interest charges at the highest level. Since Taylor had not established himself as a strong leader and instead became largely dependent on a mediocre cabinet for advice, political fallout which might otherwise have passed over the White House was laid right at the president's doorstep.

The main culprit was Taylor's secretary of war, George Crawford. For sixteen years he had represented, as legal counsel and agent, a trader named George Galphin, who was trying to settle a forty-year-old claim. During the pre-Revolutionary War period, Galphin and other colonial merchants had accepted, as payment for bills owed by the Indians, huge tracts of land in Georgia. The revolutionary turmoil prevented Galphin from collecting on his claim, and although London paid some of these debts after the war, Galphin was denied because he had supported the colonies.

Over the years, the Georgia legislature had acknowledged his claim as valid, but didn't have the money to reimburse him. The victims of a bureaucratic nightmare, Galphin and his heirs were bounced around from agency to agency, with no one accepting responsibility for the sizable debt. Finally, legislation was introduced authorizing payment of the principal, or value of the land deeded to Galphin, a sum of over $43,000. Unsatisifed, one Galphin family lawyer, Joseph Bryan, filed an elaborate claim the following year for payment of interest, which amounted to five times the original principal. That delicate decision was dumped in the lap of the secretary of the treasury, a former Pennsylvania lawyer named William Meredith. Passing the buck as quickly as he could, Meredith tossed it into the hands of the dour-faced attorney general, Reveredy Johnson, who took his own sweet time making up his mind.

When Johnson did give his legal opinion, it was a bonanza for the long-suffering Galphins, who learned they were eligible for the interest accrued over more than seventy years, or the entire disputed period of the claim. Upon receiving the respected Johnson's judgment, Meredith dutifully paid out more than $190,000 in interest to the Galphin litigants, making their total haul from the government more than $235,000.

The payment of a sum that size would have made news in any event, but soon it was learned that Crawford's services had been offered on a contingency basis. The war secretary had pocketed half of the original $43,000 payment as his fee, and now he was going to get half of the huge interest settlement on which his fellow cabinet member had passed judgment.

What a field day for the administration's opponents! The treasury secretary, on the advice of the attorney general, was handing over almost $100,000 to the secretary of war, who had already profited handsomely from the deal. Cries for Crawford's firing arose almost immediately, but after conferring with his war secretary, the president decided that nothing improper had taken place and declined action. Stung by the barrage of Democratic attacks, Crawford personally demanded, and received, a congressional investigation, a probe which failed to turn up any evidence that he had misused his official position for personal gain. But the administration's detractors weren't about to let the squirming cabinet members off the hook so easily. A congressional debate over whether the Galphin claims were legitimate dragged on for weeks, and Whigs joined Democrats in censuring the behavior of the three Galphin-tainted cabinet officials.

There were ugly side effects as well. Congress was now in an investigating mood, and public criticism of other cabinet members, notably Secretary of the Interior Thomas Ewing and Postmaster General Jacob Collamer, rose to a fever pitch in the wake of the Galphin fiasco. Ewing had been under fire for his controversial handling of patronage appointments, and in another slap at Taylor from Capitol Hill, a congressional resolution was passed authorizing an inquiry into Ewing's fiefdom.

Tired and disillusioned after only sixteen months in office, Taylor was beginning to realize, during the hot summer months of 1850, that changes would have to be made if his administration was to continue to function. He was in the process of choosing new key advisers when a unexpected and rather bizarre illness struck. The president wasn't feeling particularly well, close observers noted, as the scorching month of July began. On Independence Day, Taylor spent hours under a burning sun near the Washington Monument, walking a great distance in the stifling heat after listening to interminable Fourth of July orations from long-winded legislators. Later, back home, he indulged a voracious appetite. Legend has it that Taylor consumed copious amounts of cherries, washing them down with cold milk, but accounts differ as to exactly what the chief executive bolted down to relieve his growling stomach. One thing is certain—he suddenly fell quite ill.

Presidential physicians termed the sickness "cholera morbus," but it was more likely acute gastroenteritis, or a serious inflammation of the stomach and intestines. At first, Old Zack didn't appear to be in mortal danger, and rallied enough to attend to minor duties such as document signing. However, the gravity of his condition became quickly apparent to his doctors, who were unable to ease a growing fever. News of his deterioration spread to Capitol Hill, and a death watch began. Gamely, Taylor hung on until Tuesday, July 9th. That night, realizing that he was about to die, the husk of the man they had called Rough and Ready summoned the White House doctors closer to his feverish face.

"I have endeavored to discharge all my duties faithfully—I regret nothing, but am sorry that I am about to leave my friends." Those were his last audible words, and with them the twelfth President of the United States prematurely ended his term, dying on his sickbed, as the aging military hero

Harrison had done just nine years before. So for the second time in less than a decade, America's twenty-four million citizens began taking a closer look at an unfamiliar vice president, who was now assuming the reins of power.

The man they saw was the dignified, strikingly handsome Millard Fillmore, who as president would never incite the passionate hatred spurred by the self-righteous John Tyler, the last president-by-default. Like Tyler, however, Fillmore was stepping into a delicate political situation. Old Zack had expired before he could clean up some untidy problems with his administration's officials, and now the younger Fillmore would have to answer critics who were demanding that political heads roll. There was no time for second-guessing; he would have to make decisions in a hurry to keep the anti-administration wolves at bay.

Since almost all Taylor's major cabinet officers had become the subjects of public scorn or congressional investigation, they feared dismissal and beat the new chief executive to the punch by resigning *en masse*. The harried Fillmore turned to the aging Whig warhorse Daniel Webster as his secretary of state and chief cabinet adviser. With Webster's guidance, he made only one particularly ill-advised appointment, and the innocent folly of that choice wouldn't become apparent until he left office.

For postmaster general, Fillmore had turned to Ohio's most revered Whig, Thomas Corwin, who didn't want the job, but agreed to join the fledgling administration as secretary of the treasury. He replaced one of those ruined by the Galphin exposé, William Meredith. Corwin, while no crook, was nevertheless responsible for the only serious incidence of corruption uncovered during Fillmore's tenure.

While trying to reduce the public debt, the well-connected Corwin decided to use private Whig bankers, rather than Treasury officials, to back the government's bonds. Although it was a clear violation of the Independent Treasury Act, which Corwin was undoubtedly aware of, his politically inspired manipulations weren't disclosed until 1853, when the Democrat James Guthrie took over his Treasury post.

Fillmore made a more visible gaffe when he appointed the zealous Mormon leader Brigham Young to the post of territorial governor of Utah. It was an innocent misjudgment on Fillmore's part, for he thought that the Mormons, who disliked outsiders telling them what to do, might be more governable if one of their own was in a position of influence. This reasonable presidential intention backfired, however, when Young began ruling like a virtual dictator and caused friction which led to the resignations of a number of federal officials in the territory.

Fillmore's last presidential duty, on a snowy, blowing March afternoon in 1853, was to attend the inauguration of his successor, Democrat Franklin Pierce. It was a duty which led to a tragedy mirroring the premature end of the Harrison presidency. This time it was a presidential wife, rather than the chief executive himself, who took sick after sitting out in a freezing slush to witness the swearing-in. Abigail Fillmore contracted pneumonia as a result of her husband's last presidential appearance and died three weeks later, after a constant bedside vigil by her devoted spouse. A presidency which had concluded on a relatively high note suddenly gave way to emptiness for the retiring Millard Fillmore, who later tried unsuccessfully to regain the presidency on a third party ticket.

*   *   *

"The hero of many a well-fought bottle," was how one snide (but perceptive) critic described Franklin Pierce. He was yet another dark horse in an electoral age full of them, having gained the Democratic nomination when a deadlock developed between supporters of James Buchanan and Michigan Senator Lewis Cass, who had already gone down to defeat once as his party's standard-bearer.

The choice of Pierce shouldn't have been a major shock, as the forty-eight-year-old politician possessed an enviable track record; he was from a politically active family (his father had been the governor of New Hampshire) and he had never lost an election. In fact, he was a bit of a political boy wonder, having been elected to the House at the tender age of twenty-eight and the Senate at thirty-two, making him the junior member of that august body.

At the nagging insistence of his wife, Jane, a puritanical

woman who hated Washington's gaudy social circuit, he gave up his office in 1842 and returned to New Hampshire, where he continued to dabble in state politics. The only damaging whispers against him arose in 1847, when he accepted a colonel's commission in the army fighting the Mexican War. Ironically, he was serving with his future presidential opponent, General Winfield Scott, when he was injured as his horse fell in the battle of Contreras. Understandably, Pierce fainted from heat prostration and the agonizing pain of a wounded knee, but upon re-entering political life he found himself accused of cowardice by gossipers a thousand miles from the field of battle.

When he defeated his former military ally Scott in the close 1852 presidential balloting, Pierce had reason to be one of the happiest men in the country. From the obscurity of the New Hampshire woods, he'd led his party to victory. However, the combination of his wife's reluctance to serve as first lady, and a freak tragedy caused Pierce to begin his presidency in a depressive state.

On January 6, 1853, eight weeks before his swearing-in, the Pierces and their sole surviving child, Benjamin, were riding on a train between Boston and Concord. Suddenly, the train derailed. The president-elect and his wife were only slightly injured, but eleven-year-old Benny was killed instantly by a severe head injury which almost decapitated him, the sole fatality of the mishap. According to a letter written later by a relative, Jane Pierce "saw that dreadful sight for one moment, but Mr. Pierce threw a shawl over the precious little form and drew her away." The future first lady became the second victim of the accident, traumatized for life. Withdrawing into herself, she soon became a pathetic figure, writing love notes to her dead son. She refused to attend her husband's inaugural and later became known as "the shadow in the White House."

Worse yet, she transferred a lot of her grief and guilt to her spouse. His return to national politics and public life had caused little Benny's death, she fervently believed. God was punishing them for not staying in New Hampshire. Pierce's woes mercilessly piled up one on top of another during his first few months in office. His last child and heir had just been killed, and his wife was rapidly becoming almost catatonic. Abigail Fillmore, to whom he had become close during the presidential transition period, had recently died after contracting a fatal chill at his inaugural.

Just weeks later, his vice president, Rufus King, died of tuberculosis, following an unsuccessful recuperation in Cuba. His early foreign policy moves had been failures and his unwise support of "involuntary servitude" had placed him squarely in the middle of an increasingly raucous debate over slavery which pitted state against state. The nation was being led by a severely depressed man struggling unsuccessfully against his inner demons.

Pierce had been a functioning alcoholic for a good part of his adult life. He couldn't hold his liquor well, but that fact hadn't stopped from from bending the elbow long and hard since his college days. A bachelor during the first few years of his early congressional career, he'd spent much of this free time carousing with his political colleagues, a hard-drinking crew who frequently made fools of themselves in public.

His friends believed that only his marriage to Jane Appleton at the age of thirty saved him from eventual suicide by the bottle. His wife's strict habits, and their return to his native state curtailed his abusive bouts of drinking, but neither completely cured his fondness for the sauce. In times of stress, he often would drink himself into a stupor.

Now, he worried friends and aides by drinking heavily, despite chronic bronchitis and failing health caused by a lifetime of alcohol abuse and general neglect. The president's doctors told him that his problems were caused by unknown allergies; but the whispers around Washington said Pierce's only "allergy" was the bottle. The presidential couple must have been a sad sight during the first several months of 1853; a chief executive fighting a losing battle against a twenty-year drinking curse, and a first lady, who like Dickens' Mrs. Haversham, stayed alone in her room brooding about the past and talking to people who weren't there.

Luckily for the president, most of the sinners in his administration weren't ferreted out until long after he had left the White House. Issac Fowler was one such malefactor. Pierce appointed him postmaster of New York and was blissfully (or perhaps boozily) unaware that for years Fowler had been quietly stealing postal revenues and handing them over to Democratic office-seekers. The slippery postmaster must have covered his tracks well, for he was reappointed by Pierce's successor. Not until 1860, when his accounts were found to be a trifle short, about $160,000, did Fowler flee the country to avoid arrest. His disappearing act no doubt was met with a silent sigh of relief by many Democratic office-holders, who would have been embarrassed by testimony concerning payoffs by the sticky-fingered postal official.

Pierce had the good fortune to have several major scandals overlap into the next administration, with most of the blame coming down on the head of his unfortunate successor, James Buchanan. Naval contracts, for example, were often awarded on the basis of political contributions, an outrageous practice which wasn't exposed until just before the Civil War.

President Pierce did make one blundering appointment, noted his biographer, Roy Nicols, which came back to haunt him fairly quickly. Again the focus of the controversy was slavery, the *cause celebre* of the day. Kansas was opened up as a U.S. territory along with Nebraska in 1854. The two big questions concerning the newly mandated areas were: would slavery be permitted, and who was going to get all that fertile, invaluable land? Pierce tried to keep armed hostilities from breaking out by compromise appointments: a Southerner to administer the Nebraska territory and a Yankee to govern the wheat fields of Kansas.

Given the sectional greeds and passions of the time, that made sense. His choice for a Kansas governor, Andrew Reeder of Pennsylvania, did not. In the first place, Reeder was a notorious real estate speculator and as such had an immediate conflict of interest concerning the land-grubbing going on in Kansas. Indian tribes had land stolen from them by the square mile, and armed men from both North and South were coming in to establish or prohibit slavery, or just to seize what they could. In short, the situation was disastrous.

In the middle of the skirmishing, Reeder was being denounced as the thief he was by other government officials. He was up to his neck in the fraudulent purchase of Indian lands, and at last Pierce realized that the governor would have to go.

That decision was easier made than carried out. Reeder was
fifteen hundred miles away from the capital, and strongly
resisted firing when he learned that the president was about
to bounce him out of a cushy sinecure which was making him
rich. He even had a scheme to locate the Kansas capital in an
area where he had holdings. Governor Landgrab came back
East to lobby on his own behalf and must have done a good
job, for several of Pierce's closest advisers prevailed on the
president to let Reeder have another chance. True to form,
Reeder got himself into deeper trouble when he went back to
Kansas, and the chagrined Pierce finally pulled the plug on
him.

By the time of the Democratic convention of 1856, the party
leaders had seen enough and surprised Pierce by denying
him renomination. Delegates from key states short-changed
the incumbent president by a sufficient number of votes to
throw the convention to Pennsylvanian James Buchanan, who
managed to defeat both Republican John ("The Pathfinder")
Frèmont, and former chief executive Fillmore, who ran on the
anti-immigrant, anti-Catholic "Know Nothing" ticket.

*　　*　　*

Although sixty-five years of age when he won the White
House, bachelor Buchanan instantly became the most desirable catch in Washington. Emotionally traumatized as a
young man by the rejection of a socially prominent fiancee's
family, and her subsequent death, Buchanan had never married. His comparatively monastic lifestyle seemed to generate
more excited rumor and gossip than his routine pronouncements about the economy or foreign policy.

The president began to wish that his thorniest problem was
fawning elderly widows tugging at his sleeve at social func-
tions. His administration, in the phrase of one expert, represented the "nadir of ante-bellum ethics." Scandals involving
the post office, customs houses (always a patronage grabbag),
naval contracts, public printing, and massive military procurement frauds tarred Buchanan's term of office.

Buchanan's admirers (and there still are some) have insisted that the honest Keystone State native was merely in the
wrong place at the wrong time, and that all the oily wrongdo-

ing of the past decade gushed to the surface during his administration, like a well of corruption which couldn't be capped any longer. The record shows, however, that, while not guilty of personal malfeasance, Buchanan created most of his own woes. In the Illinois post office, for example, he replaced the eminent, learned Stephen Douglas, a fellow Democrat but political antagonist, with Issac ("Ike") Cook, a "known thief" who had held the job before he resigned in disgrace as a defaulter to the government. The notorious Cook still hadn't made good on his debt to the taxpayers at the time of his presidential appointment.

Boldly, he offered as payment a tract of land to which his ownership was highly questionable. Such a problem is quickly resolvable if you have a friend in the White House. Attorney General Jeremiah Black obligingly ruled Cook's title to the land as valid, and Treasury Secretary Howell Cobb was forced to accept it as full restitution. With that small detail out of the way, Cook and his cronies proceeded to siphon off postal revenues at will, pilfering even registered mail. Buchanan and his aides turned a deaf ear to the resulting cries of outrage, for the larcenous Cook was too valuable a political ally to force from office over a minor matter like stealing from the U.S. mail.

President Buchanan further laid the groundwork for his own political disgrace by hiring one of the most utterly incompetent, nitwitted cabinet officials in the history of the republic. For sheer bumbling idiocy, Secretary of War John Floyd rated four stars. He was a patsy even among his weak-kneed colleagues. While no evidence emerged that he profited directly from his blunders, administration hangers-on played the accommodating Floyd like a slot machine which was paid off at every drop of the coin.

Not wishing to upset his grasping friends, Floyd engineered transactions to sell government land at hugely inflated prices and made instant tycoons of scheming insiders, who had been tipped off to the details. The constant fixes became so brazen that finally, disgusted military officers refused to deal with Floyd's business buddies, and Congress had to step in to prevent the war secretary from taking revenge against honest government workers who refused to participate in the chicanery. Even after he became a hopeless laughingstock to members of his own party on Capitol Hill, Buchanan retained him.

Floyd's worst was yet to come, as detailed in *Responses of the Presidents to Charges of Misconduct*. Always ready to do a favor for a friend, Floyd signed payments for bills presented to his department before Congress had authorized the disbursements. When wide-eyed contractors realized that Floyd would sign anything they put before him, they inflated their bills and got his scrawl on five million dollars worth of contracts for non-existent supplies. The delighted vendors also secured sizable bank loans with the illicit vouchers, and one particularly greedy contractor traded on the secretary's signature for $870,000 worth of government bonds held in trust by the war department.

Understandably, there was a bit of a furor when the bonds were put on sale in the open market. Journalists rightly accused the sellers of stealing from the Treasury. One newspaper reported that the president's banker had purchased six of the controversial bonds for his personal portfolio, but Buchanan apparently knew nothing of the contractors' sleazy maneuverings.

Nevertheless, even after the momumental ripoff hit the front pages, Buchanan was reluctant to discharge his friend Floyd, a move which by then would have elicted silent prayers of thanks from every corner of official Washington. Vacillating and too squeamish to do the job himself, he dispatched Vice President John C. Breckinridge to fire Floyd, who indignantly refused to resign. The dunce stayed on the job until he could save face by quitting over what he claimed was a broken promise concerning the harbor of Charleston, South Carolina.

Pierce's earlier sacking of Andrew ("Governor Landgrab") Reeder didn't cool the conflict over slavery in the Kansas territory, and Buchanan managed to strike a match to that political powderkeg by authorizing the handout of contracts and commissions as bribes to those who voted with the administration on the LeCompton Compromise regarding slavery. Incredibly, cabinet officials dangled cold cash in front of wavering congressmen; the payoffs did little besides hasten the time when the factional strife would escalate into civil war.

Perhaps the single biggest money-making bonanza for Buchanan's light-fingered Democratic allies was their control of public printing. Until 1860, when a federal government printing office was established, most of Washington's printing needs were serviced by private contractors. Naturally, the system was a patronage boss's dream, for the usually inflated bids were disbursed only to loyal friends and supporters of the administration. There had been much abuse of this system before Buchanan came to the White House, but his henchmen and appointees fine-tuned the favoritism into an art form.

Graft and gross overpayments flowed as freely as ink in the printing rackets of the 1850s. One prominent Buchanan supporter, Cornelius Wendell, made millions of dollars in profits, raking them right off the top of the fixed printing contracts. During an attempt to reform these licentious practices in 1858, investigators discovered that the federal superintendent of printing, who had been named to his post by Pierce and retained by Buchanan, was demanding and receiving kickbacks from government contractors, and the grasping Wendell was getting a piece of that action, too.

When the superintendent was indicted and convicted, Buchanan appointed an honest overseer named George Bowman to crack down on the printing perfidy. When the new regime turned off the spigot on the steady flow of illicit profits to Wendell, he ungratefully announced that he could no longer support the *Union*, a pro-administration newspaper. Alarmed at the possible loss of a friendly press organ, Buchanan ordered Attorney General Black to cook up a sweetheart deal whereby Bowman would take over the ailing *Union*, and Wendell would regain control of the Senate's lucrative printing contracts. While the president wisely excluded himself from the actual negotiations, Wendell later testified at a congressional hearing that Buchanan had full knowledge of the bogus bargain.

The acquisitive Wendell, in fact, became the star witness for the Covode Committee, which was convened by a Republican-dominated Congress in early 1860 to pour salt into Buchanan's largely self-inflicted wounds. Throughout the spring,

Buchanan's fellow Keystone State native Congressman, John Covode, dragged witnesses into secret sessions, gathering a mountain of incriminating information against the president. One of the president's home state fixers, John Forney of Pennsylvania, testified that he was offered $80,000 worth of post office printing contracts in return for his support of the Le-Compton Compromise.

While the Republicans delightedly leaked the juiciest tidbits from the closed door sessions to the press as quickly as they were uttered, Buchanan stonewalled the investigators and launched a counterattack. The committee, charged the president, had no authority to investigate him unless it had been convened as an "impeaching body." As for the allegations, they were just a fishing expedition by his enemies, who were labeled as "parasites and informers." Wrapping himself in the flag, Buchanan self-righteously asserted that he was defending the sanctity of the constitutional separation of powers by refusing to hand over documents sought by the committee.

By the fall of the year, the Democrats had once more had enough of their incumbent and decided to go elsewhere for a nominee for the second election in a row. They chose as Buchanan's replacement the spell-binding speaker Stephen Douglas, who finally got the last word over his antagonist after earlier having been abruptly removed from his political appointment in the Illinois post office.

*   *   *

Many modern public opinion and historians' polls, including a 1982 *Chicago Tribune* survey, have rated Abraham Lincoln, who prevailed over Douglas and other candidates in the 1860 presidential election, as the greatest of all chief executives to have held the office to date. One wouldn't have known that, however, by the torrent of invective and abuse which was rained down on the gangling, mournful-looking Illinois lawyer when he prepared to assume residence in the White House in the spring of 1861. "Ape...gorilla...monster...mulatto...a rawboned, shambled-gated, bow-legged, knock-kneed, pigeon-toed, slob-sided, a shapeless skeleton in a very tough, very dirty, unwholesome skin," was just a sampling of the reaction which greeted both his candidacy and election.

It wouldn't have been unfair to suggest that the new president's prospects for a successful administration looked fairly dim. The country was being torn asunder by a civil conflict which had already kept his name off the ballot in a number of Southern states. The gray-suited armies of the Confederacy would be only his most visible adversaries. Greedy and careless administrators, scheming cabinet officials, inept generals, constant assassination threats, a crushing mental depression and a wife slowly going insane would be the staple of Lincoln's daily White House diet.

For starters, allegations that First Lady Mary Lincoln was less than an all-out Unionist caused more than just troubling whispers against her husband. Almost all of his wife's close relatives supported the South's rebellion; three of her half-brothers were serving in the Confederate army. Although she had never met them, no less than eleven of her second cousins were soldiers of the southern Carolina Light Dragoons.

When the secretary of state, William Seward (whom Lincoln had defeated for the Republican presidential nomination) unleashed a spying force of U.S. marshalls and detectives which arrested thousands of suspected Confederate sympathizers, the suggestion that the president's wife might be in secret league with traitors was no less than a national scandal. Even after Mary went out of her way to criticize the rebellion and its generals, she found herself accused of passing information to the Confederacy through her half-sister, Mary Todd White, despite the fact that the two were never personally close.

Ultimately, the finger-pointing and rumor-mongering became so vicious that a joint session of Congress took up the issue behind closed doors. To the legislators' astonishment, the tall, angular figure of the president was soon in the room with them, unexpected and uninvited. Silence reigned for several stunned and embarrassing moments, until the chief executive said quietly and firmly: "I, Abraham Lincoln, President of the United States, appear of my own volition before this committee of the Senate to say that I, of my own knowledge, know that it is untrue that any of my family holds treasonable communication with the enemy." As quietly as he had come in, the president turned on his heels and left his startled audience, which promptly adjourned for the day. While some disgruntled anti-Lincoln whispers were still heard, this impromptu speech put an end to any official inquiry aimed at Mrs. Lincoln.

Coming to his wife's rescue didn't stop her irrational fits of jealousy, which often exploded in embarrassing public incidents. Mrs. Edward Ord, the attractive spouse of the commander of the Union Army of the Potomac, made the mistake of innocently riding by Lincoln's side as he reviewed her husband's troops. When Mary arrived on the scene, she shrieked at the younger woman like a banshee. Ignoring the frightened woman's apologies, she stomped off and sulked for days. On another occasion, Mrs. Lincoln railed at General Grant's wife, Julia, after she had tried to intercede on behalf of Commander Ord's wife. The tirade upset Mrs. Grant so much that she refused to go out socially with the first couple thereafter.

While the president bore his wife's outbursts with characteristic patience, he was less understanding about her champagne tastes in clothing and furniture, noted writer Hope Ridings Miller. Several of her White House parties were so lavishly catered that they caused a political backlash when the president had to explain to Congress why his beleaguered Union troops hadn't enough guns or food to best the ragtag, poorly supplied Southern rebels.

It wasn't an unfair question, as Mary had overspent by one-third the $20,000 congressional appropriation earmarked to refurbish the presidential residence. Worried about the wrath of her husband when he found out, she beseeched the federal commissioner of public buildings, Benjamin French, to intercede for her. "It can never have my approval," Lincoln declared angrily, refusing to sign the cost overrun. "I'll pay it out of my pocket first—it would stink in the nostrils of the American people to have it said that the President of the United States had approved a bill of twenty thousand dollars for flub-dubs, for this damned old house, when the soldiers cannot have blankets." Sympathetic congressmen bailed out the president by including an amendment for the extra amount in a later bill. Ironically, the near disaster didn't cure Mary's extravagance, and only an assassin's bullet saved her from another day of reckoning over a $27,000 bill she ran up for clothing in late 1864.

His wife wasn't the only person close to him who caused grief for President Lincoln. Simon Cameron, his secretary of war, was a walking conflict-of-interest who turned the key department into a feeding trough for his big business friends and cronies. Complaints about Cameron's incompetence and favoritism were rife as early as 1861. A special investigation by a House committee produced a report of over 1,100 pages, featuring an encyclopedic list of abuses. The Union army was fighting with broken guns, eating tainted pork and sleeping under rotted blankets, thanks to the war department's inefficiency and corruption. "Colossal graft" was the phrase the congressional probers used to describe Cameron's management style.

Another Cabinet official, Treasury Secretary Salmon Chase, who thought himself better qualified for the presidency than Lincoln, presided over a highly lucrative but illegal system of trade with the South during the war. The enormous profits to be made from southern cotton were too tempting for many of Chase's subordinates; speculators ran wild, bribing agents to set up illicit cotton deals. Chase wasn't accused of being personally involved, but the under-the-table profiteering on his watch was a black eye for the Lincoln White House.

Navy Secretary Gideon Welles couldn't claim ignorance of the payoffs in his department, however. His brother-in-law, George Morgan, made a fortune as Welles' purchasing agent on navy contracts. When congressional critics of the administration learned that Morgan had kept a percentage of the contracts as payment, they loudly demanded Welles' resignation. He didn't deny the charges, but boldly insisted that the familial arrangments were standard practice at a time when his department needed materials in a hurry. Lincoln, already under fire for Cameron's criminal behavior, decided to back Welles and won when a vote to censure him was defeated.

Meanwhile, Seward was turning the capital into a police state. Seeing treason behind every corner, he organized a network of informants, Pinkerton detectives, and policemen to ferret out suspected sympathizers in the post office, customs houses and other nooks of the bureaucracy. The spying, coupled with Seward's extraordinary censorship of the mails and telegraph lines, caused Lincoln to be denounced as an enemy of civil liberties.

In the midst of the paranoia and corruption, the 1864 elections were held. More than three years of wearisome war plunged the presidential campaign to a new low. The Democratic standard-bearer, Union General George ("The Young Napoleon") McClellan, was called a "cowardly traitor" by the Republican press for his endorsement of the Democrats' plan to seek peace with the South as soon as any of the southern states sought reunification. Not to be outdone, Lincoln-haters in the North openly discussed his assassination, discovered biographer Stephen B. Oates. One Democratic newspaper in Wisconsin editorialized, "If he is elected to misgovern for another four years, we trust some bold hand will pierce his heart with dagger point for the public good."

Sudden, dramatic Union battlefield victories, and the soldiers' almost total rejection of the peace planks adopted by the Democrats at their Chicago convention kept Lincoln in the White House. It might have been a Pyrrhic victory of sorts: his domestic life was in shambles. The Lincolns' son, Willie, died in the White House, and Mary's unquenchable grief, together with her friendship with the dedicated Massachusetts abolitionist Senator Charles Sumner, caused more gossip about the possible dissolution of the first couple's strained marriage.

Only the end of the war and the final cessation of slavery brightened the president's weary outlook. But a bullet from the gun of actor John Wilkes Booth in Ford's Theater on the night of April 14, 1865, shattered the slowly growing optimism in the capital, and pitched the nation into a different but equally dangerous mood of political crisis.

*   *   *

"I have reached the summit of my ambition," said Andrew Johnson when he was elected to the United States Senate to represent Tennessee in 1857. The former tailor had reason to remember that remark in the years to come, for rising higher on the political totempole cost him dearly, and it was only upon returning to the Senate that he found renewed peace of mind and public acceptance.

At first, the coarse, rather uneducated Johnson might have thought himself a lucky man upon being selected to run with President Lincoln in 1864; but his good fortune had a sour aftertaste, as one chronicler of his poitical career, Gene Smith, learned. To calm a headache and queasy stomach on the day of the inaugural, Johnson had quaffed three tumblerfuls of whiskey and looked like he had just come off a three-day bender by the time he reached the VIP podium. His first intelligible words to the assembled listeners were, "Your president is a plebian—I am a plebian—glory in it." The fifteen minute diatribe which followed caused even the tolerant Lincoln to bow his head in embarrassed silence.

"An exhibition of drunken impertinence," wrote one disbelieving journalist of the boozy display. "One frail life stands between this insolent, clownish creature and the Presidency," sniffed the *New York World* in a scathing editorial lambasting the new vice president. Several senators privately suggested to Lincoln that Johnson resign immediately. "I've known Andy for years, and he ain't no drunkard," replied the president, who earlier had appointed his friend as military governor of Tennessee. Keeping his perspective as always, the reelected chief executive wasn't about to disgrace the administration and his party over one morning's headlined debacle.

The incident would undoubtedly soon have been forgotten, if not for the fateful night at Ford's Theater just six weeks later. While Secretary of War Edwin Stanton's security forces combed the countryside for the assassination's conspirators, Johnson was sworn in as the seventeeth president on the morning of Lincoln's unexpected death.

It has been the practice of more modern candidates to choose running mates who generally agree with their views; however, such was certainly not always the case in the nineteenth century. Two men could hardly have been less alike than Lincoln and Johnson. The Tennessean was poorly educated and had been taught to write by his wife; Lincoln tirelessly educated himself until he became a respected lawyer and writer. Johnson was crude and tactless in manner, whereas his predecessor had been restrained and courtly.

Lincoln had hoped to bury the mutual hatreds engendered by four years of war during his second term; his vice president had a reputation as an avenger. Punish the rebellious traitors, he'd repeatedly insisted. A dirt-poor boy from North Carolina, he'd come to hate the aristocratic planters of the Confederacy. The Radical Republicans, who wished to push the South's collective face into the mud, initially were delighted that Johnson had ascended to the highest office. "Johnson, we have faith in you," cried the Radicals' leader in Congress, Ohio's Benjamin Wade. "By the gods, we'll have no trouble running the government now." The ebullient Wade would soon come to rue that declaration.

Actually, although his stubborn, unyielding attitude toward Congress made him the first chief executive to come within a hairsbreadth of being removed from office, Johnson was a pretty honest and upstanding politician by the notoriously weak standards of the day. Editorial and congressional critics would call him every vile name imaginable during his term of office, but none would successfully accuse him of stealing, or knowingly placing grafters in positions of public trust.

His only truly reprehensible habit, apart from his marked lack of social grace, was a love for the bottle. Once, on a presidential trip, he was accused of failing to pay for half the liquor, as required, along various stops on the route. Most of the time his train, and everything else which went with Johnson, was a traveling barroom. His imbibing wasn't as habitual as Pierce's, but after the inaugural fiasco, gossipers kept close tabs on Johnson's elbow-bending, and the finger-waggers were rarely disappointed.

The worst scandal of the adminstration occurred after Johnson changed his mind about rubbing the South's nose in the dirt. While he continued to be rude to the former Confederate soldiers who came to the White House for pardons so they could own land and vote once again, the unelected president slowly became disaffected with the Radical Republicans' plan to permit immigrant Northerners to loot and land-grab in the southern states. No intellectual, Johnson nevertheless realized that the Radicals' gameplan would split the nation again, as surely as the first shots fired at Fort Sumter. He vetoed their package, which involved excluding Southerners from Congress.

His surprised opponents, thinking he was one of them, now comprehended that they were dealing with a fire-breather. The Radicals and their allies in Congress responded with the Tenure Act, which forbade the president from removing any federal official appointed by Congress, and thus block Johnson's ability to fire any of the northern carpetbaggers who already had gone south. Johnson refused to accept the measure, and showed his disdain by sacking Edwin Stanton, Lincoln's Radical war secretary, who'd been a burr in Johnson's saddle since he'd taken office. Having appointed General U. S. Grant in his place, Johnson was stunned when Grant refused to get caught up in the fray and turned the office back to Stanton. Irate, the president fired Stanton again, and this time replaced him with Major General Lorenzo Thomas.

The ambitious, aging Stanton, who had little else besides his work, knew that his political career would be over if he caved in, so he refused to leave. A constitutional crisis was quickly taking shape. Something had to give, and within several days House members voted to impeach Johnson, an extreme measure which earlier had been rejected.

His legion of enemies stopped at nothing during the dramatic, unprecedented two-month trial which followed. Johnson-baiters claimed that he had been involved in a Confederate plot to murder Lincoln, a bizarre suggestion considering the president's antipathy toward the South and his friendly relationship with the deceased leader. Then Johnson's name was linked with every moral turpitude from adultery to murder. Witnesses testified that while military governor of Tennessee, Johnson had sold pardons to ex-rebels. One prominent newspaper called the president "The Great Criminal." Unfazed, Johnson hired five lawyers to defend him at his own expense.

When he steadfastly refused to wilt under the incredible pressures applied, and the final outcome of the presidency was still in doubt, bribes, threats and blackmail were brought to bear on legislators who had the "swing," or deciding, votes. Illinois senators were warned they'd be hanged if they came home after casting a vote for Johnson's acquittal. The Radicals warned a young woman friend of Kansas Senator Robert Ream that if she had any influence with him, she'd better use it to get him to vote to convict. Other senators had past shady dealings held over their heads by desperate anti-administration forces.

The final deliberation was a moment of high political tension, and although 35 of 54 senators cast their ballots against him, Johnson survived by one vote, as a two-thirds majority was required to remove him from the White House. By then, of course, all hope of reelection was lost. Still determined to prove he'd been right, he returned to Tennessee and ran for Congress in 1869. He lost then, and again in 1872, but was vindicated by an election to the Senate in 1874, where a warm welcome greeted the aging senator from several of the colleagues who had voted to impeach him just six years before.

Chapter 4

GRANT'S GRABBAG, RUTHERFRAUD, AND BIG STEVE'S BABY

U.S. Grant—William McKinley

March 1869—September 1901

The youngest president ever elected up to that time and near the height of his personal popularity when he took office in early 1869, Ulysses S. Grant, a failed shopkeeper turned military hero by the Civil War, had no reason to believe that his administration would deteriorate into one of the most scandal-tainted in history. The pain of reconstruction and the burden of a weak post-war economy made Grant's leadership task a difficult one, to be sure, but in eight years he did what few thought possible; he made the shortcomings of Pierce, Buchanan and Johnson look good by comparison. If corruption could have been coined during Grant's stay in the White House, Washington would have been the wealthiest city in the world.

No doubt the limitless greed and cruelty of carpetbagging northerners would have spawned graft and plunder no matter who occupied the executive mansion. As a judge of men and talent, however, Grant lived up to his earlier, cruel nickname of "Useless." He chose many political and business figures whose ethics were, at best, highly dubious. When they were caught with their hands in the till, he stood by them, regardless of the cost to his presidency or the nation.

The Grant administration, in brief, represented one of the lowest points since the birth of the federal government ninety

97

years before. It was a storybook of scandal, a veritable tome
of venality, a catalog of corruption. An army of voracious
dealmakers moved in for a financial killing, and few were
disappointed. Among Grant's trusted advisers, it's easier to
list those not on the take than to inventory all the scoundrels.
His early cabinet choices were mostly losers. Grant had insisted that he wanted to stay away from the party hacks in his
appointments, so instead he turned to a variety of campaign
contributors and outsiders, whose nominations evoked cries
of consternation on Capitol Hill. One newspaper flatly stated
that Grant regarded the patronage selections as "a candy
cornucopia from which he is to extract a sugar plum for the
good little boys who have given him some of their plum
cake."

His initial choice for Treasury secretary, for example, was
one A. T. Stewart, whose qualifications for office included
owning the largest department store in New York and con-
tributing generously to Republican campaign coffers. Administration opponents were delighted to learn from Massachusetts Senator Charles Sumner that the business tycoon's
nomination was apparently illegal; an eighty-year-old federal
law prohibited anyone "concerned...in trade or commerce"
from holding the Treasury post. Grant was reluctantly forced
to withdraw Stewart's name.

He also blundered in his choice for secretary of state, first
asking Representative James Wilson of Iowa, who demurred,
claiming he couldn't afford the expense of serving in the
office. Stunned, Grant then turned to the aging Hamilton
Fish, who, though highly respected, had been out of politics
for twenty years. Only when the president's personal secretary, Orville Babcock, hurried to New York to beg Fish not to
humiliate the administration by rejecting the nomination did
the dutiful politician yield and agree to take the unwanted
position.

If a bumbler in his cabinet choices, Grant was a master at
doling out patronage to friends and family. *Nepotism* wasn't in
his vocabulary. Once the black sheep of the family, he was
now in a position to confer highly desirable jobs upon formerly disapproving relatives, who were eager for favors from
the man they once had mocked. The family of his wife, Julia

Dent, acted as though Grant's aides were running an employment office; a host of Dents found a new home on the public
payroll. Brother-in-law James F. Casey got the enviable post
of Collector of Customs. The president's sons, Fred and
"Buck" (Ulysses, Jr.), had military and banking careers which
administration critics alleged prospered only because of their
blood relationship. General James Longstreet, best man at
Grant's wedding and an army crony, was made customs sur-
veyor for New Orleans.

Another relative, brother-in-law Abel Cobwin, a former
lobbyist who had married Grant's sister Virginia, had a key
role in triggering the first major scam of the president's tenure. A long-time speculator always on the lookout for a quick
buck, Corbin fell in with two youthful but accomplished finaglers, Jay Gould and Jim Fisk. With the willing Corbin's inside
help, the conniving duo precipitated "Black Friday," one of
the most catastrophic financial panics in American history.
Grant's presidency wasn't three months old before Gould and
Fisk were utilizing their White House connection through
Corbin to try and corner the gold market. It was an audacious
scheme—there wasn't anyone on Wall Street in the summer of
1869 who hadn't heard of the outrageous business antics of
Gould and Fisk. Even in a free-wheeling, post-war era, they
were an odd couple. Only thirty-one, the flamboyant Fisk was
already legendary for his gaudy clothing, expensive jewelry,
mistress, and racetrack tout's manner. A relentless self-pro-
moter, Fisk believed anything could be sold with enough
hype. The only thing he had in common with his fellow
manipulator, besides a consuming greed, was youth. Gould,
who had just turned thirty, already had the stiff, calculating
mien of a robber baron twice his age.

Despite their relatively tender years, the pair were already
the veterans of the "Erie War," one of the most bold-faced
double-dealings ever. Working in tandem, Gould and Fisk
had astounded their big business elders by outfoxing no less
an opponent than Commodore Cornelius Vanderbilt, a
scheme detailed by Nathan Miller. The prize was control of
the Erie railroad. Gould now began to get even bigger ideas,
and the preening Fisk was only too willing to play front man.

Gould wanted gold—not just enough to make a man fabulously wealthy, but enough to control industries. With the considerable holdings of the Erie railroad, the value of which he and Fisk had pumped up with phony stock certificates, Gould cooked up a scheme to corner and then control the price of U.S. gold. There was a possible hitch in his plot, however; he had to ensure that suspicious Treasury Department officials didn't spot any abnormalities in the market and start selling vast reserves of gold once the price started to escalate.

Gould needed a pigeon with friends in high places, and Corbin, a business acquaintance, fitted the bill perfectly with his White House connections. Corbin was only too happy to convince his influential relative that selling off the government's gold to depress the price of the precious metal was against the national interest. In fact, he did better than that: he arranged for the two youthful tycoons to meet personally with the president. Throughout the summer, the underground campaign continued, with Gould pushing his cause on Grant and his aides, while surreptitiously buying and hoarding as much gold as he could.

Meanwhile, Fisk quietly began spreading the rumor that the fix was in on gold sales, and that government overseers, including members of Grant's own family, were in on the grab. He and Gould pumped up the market artificially with their own purchases, setting off waves of speculation which began to drive the price of gold even higher. As usual, Grant was slow to recognize deceit from his friends. In September 1869, he'd gone on vacation to Pennsylvania, traveling in a special railroad car furnished at no cost by his young admirer Gould. When the financier continued to press the chief executive about possible sale of gold reserves, however, Grant smelled a rat. Newspaper reports had hinted at Corbin's involvement in a gold price pyramiding scheme, and the president must have finally seen the light. He wrote a letter to Virginia, addressed to "Sis," ordering her husband to back out of the speculations.

Then the bottom fell out. Gould learned of Grant's warning to Corbin and realized that the Treasury secretary might soon be ordered to start selling federal gold to temper the rapid price hikes. Coolly, he dumped millions of dollars worth of his own purchases through his brokers, double-crossing his partner, Fisk, who knew nothing of the change in plans. September 24, 1869, was Black Friday: the golden house of cards came crashing down and over-extended speculators, including some of the biggest names on Wall Street, were ruined.

Incredibly, Gould, who almost single-handedly had caused a national financial panic, came out unscathed. He had made millions of dollars by unloading his gold before the bubble burst and shared the bonanza with Fisk, who publicly proclaimed that Grant and his family had been involved in the market manipulations. A congressional inquiry, headed by Representative (and future president) James Garfield, was convened, but the resulting probe was essentially a whitewash, which never touched on the key allegations surrounding the role of the first family and its hangers-on.

Because Congress at that time contained so many fortune-seekers and free-booters, it should have come as no great shock when a list of the most influential politicians in the capital was implicated in the next disaster of the Grant administration, the Credit Mobilier scandal. A gigantic bribery network arranged to ensure the continued profits and dominance of the railroad magnates, Credit Mobilier ruined the political careers of several of the most powerful legislators of the day. Grant's henchmen didn't start the influence-peddling ring, but his first vice president, Schulyer "Smiler" Colfax, was ruined by its exposure, along with a number of administration sympathizers and party stalwarts.

During the 1860s, the building of the Union Pacific railroad joined East and West for the first time. The companies laying the thousands of miles of rail, the Union Pacific and Central Pacific, were reaping windfall profits from subsidies and rights-of-way granted to them by Congress. The sheer magnitude of such a construction undertaking made the railroad a tempting honeypot for a wide variety of wheeler-dealers. A new firm, with the fancy-sounding title Credit Mobilier of America, was formed to handle the financing of the milestone project.

"The Great Train Robbery" was set into motion. Contracts were inflated to astronomical levels, resulting in millions of dollars worth of unearned profits for Credit Mobilier insid-

ers. When reports of the swindling became so widespread
that a congressional investigation was feared, the moneymen
hit upon a simple solution; cut as many legislators in on the
gold mine as it would take to keep the legislature from termi-
nating the sweetheart scheme.

Far from resisting the payola, a host of Washington officials
hungrily scrambled after the bribes. The paymaster of Credit
Mobilier on the Hill, Massachusetts congressman Oakes
Ames, actually suggested that a large block of the corporation's stock be distributed to his colleagues, so they would be
encouraged to look favorably upon the transnational railroad's needs. Among the recipients of the generous largesse
were Vice President (and Speaker of the House) Colfax, and
prominent House members Garfield and James Blaine, both
future presidential candidates.

Much of the sensational exposure of the Credit Mobilier
mess was portrayed as a politically inspired effort to discredit
the administration; besides, the main thrust of the probe
didn't begin until after 1872, and it took years to unravel the
full details. It had no discernible effect upon Grant's re-election; he crushed his Democratic opponent, the crusading editor Horace Greeley, in the 1872 presidential election, despite
the scandal and the other corruption which had been uncovered during the preceding four years. Colfax was denied a
second term, however, and faded into political oblivion after
unaccounted funds were found in his bank account, matching
the amounts in Ames' private Credit Mobilier payoff ledgers.

Grant had taken no money, and in fact had been chasing
Confederate armies when most of the secret railroad plotting
had initially occurred; but he was blamed, not unfairly, for
allowing such wide-scale thievery to go unchecked. He didn't
take that lesson into his second term, which was distinguished by forty-eight months of even more egregious violations of the public trust. Grant's cabinet officers couldn't have
been more inept and duplicitous; scandals popped up like
weeds in the White House garden. As soon as one was
plucked up, another rose to take its place.

Secretary of the Treasury William Richardson made his
contribution with the "Sanborn contract" imbroglio. Before
1872, informers who reported tax cheaters received a percent-

age of the uncollected tax as a bounty. Congress abolished this practice during the first year of Grant's second term of office, but Senator Benjamin Butler attached a little-noticed amendment to the repeal allowing for the collection of bounties on *specific* delinquent taxes. One of Butler's protegés, John D. Sanborn, signed a contract with Richardson, who at the time was assistant Treasury secretary, to keep *fifty* percent of whatever he could collect.

The wily Sanborn then went out and raked in taxes which Treasury agents would have received in the normal course of affairs, and by doing so, garnered $213,000 on $427,000 worth of "uncollected" taxes. By the time this was discovered in 1874, Richardson had been promoted to the cabinet. When his role in the skim-off was revealed, a congressional committee voted to "condemn" him, but he resigned before the axe could fall. Characteristically, Grant stuck by his erring friend and appointed him to the court of claims, outraging investigators.

Unfortunately, Grant's appointees caused him embarrassment even while abroad. Ambassador to Great Britain Robert Schenck allowed his name to be used to promote the British-owned Emma silver mine in Utah. Under congressional pressure, Schenck later backed out of the promotional deal, but he dragged his feet long enough that his business buddies could sell out their interests and avoid losses over the adverse publicity. Under the threat of legal action in England, the obliging Schenck resigned his post in 1876.

Back home, Grant's grasping cabinet officials were up to their usual tricks. Interior Secretary Columbus Delano and his son John had been charged by various western state officials with bribery, fraud and coersion. Land contracts were illicitly issued by the department after payoffs to the secretary's son. The elder Delano had kept busy blackmailing his own department's surveyors, and there were hundreds of illegal and fraudulent entries in Interior's land grant program. Weak-willed as always when it came to disciplining his cronies, Grant didn't pursue Delano's resignation until administration officials threatened to quit unless he was removed. Even then, Grant accepted the blackmailer's walking papers secretly and didn't appoint a successor for two months.

War Secretary William Belknap's Achilles' heel was being married to a woman with expensive tastes that he couldn't afford to satisfy. Due to this lamentable shortcoming, he allowed himself to be suckered into a deal cooked up by his scheming wife and a friend of hers, New York contractor Caleb Marsh. Using domestic pressure on her spouse, the money-hungry Mrs. Belknap pursuaded the hen-pecked secretary to see that Marsh got a share of the business at a federally controlled Indian trading post, with the Belknaps quietly getting a fifty percent kickback on the profits. When a congressional committee later investigated the cozy arrangement, Marsh turned state's evidence and testified that he had paid off the secretary in person on several occasions. Belknap tried unsuccessfully to wriggle out of a Senate trial by resigning, but the disgusted senators went after him anyway. Ultimately, Belknap was acquitted, but several of the senators who had voted for him stated that they had done so only because they felt it improper to judge an official who had already quit his post.

Not to be outdone, Navy Secretary George Robeson increased his net worth from a modest $20,000 to at least $320,000 during his seven years in office. The extra $300,000 wasn't a bonus for outstanding public service. Robeson arranged for a grain and feeding company called A. G. Catell & Co. to have a series of lucrative navy contracts funneled to it. There was also circumstantial evidence that the Catell company, in turn, made purchases for their benefactor, gifts which were difficult to trace: but, as the Grant administration was mercifully coming to a conclusion by the time Congress learned of Robeson's favoritism, the matter was left quietly hanging, and he wasn't even asked to resign.

Perhaps the most damaging of all the myriad, damning disclosures during Grant's second term were the "Whiskey Ring" frauds, in which the president's personal secretary and confidant, Orville Babcock, and several of Grant's friends, were directly implicated. Whiskey distillers had been trying to evade government taxes for a decade, often with the connivance of federal inspectors. The man who replaced the disgraced Richardson at the Treasury, the politically ambitious

Benjamin Bristow, went after the tax cheaters with a religious fervor.

In one widespread crackdown, 350 industry liquor manufacturers and pliant government agents were arrested in May 1875. One of those caught was General John MacDonald, a Republican party loyalist and social acquaintance of Grant. The president had appointed MacDonald, at Babcock's insistence, as revenue chief of Missouri. Bristow told Grant that MacDonald was a key figure in the gigantic fraud ring. "Let no guilty man escape if it can be avoided," Grant told his reformist prosecutors. The president may have regretted that order when he was informed that Babcock, one of his closest associates, had been implicated. Constant to his friends if nothing else, Grant believed Babcock's denials in the face of strong circumstantial evidence against him.

As the probe dragged on for months, accusations pointed closer and closer to the president himself. First his son Fred, and then his brother Orvil were alleged to have been involved in the massive tax ripoff. It was no wonder that by early 1876, almost a year after the Treasury raids, Grant felt besieged. Loyally, he wanted to travel to the trial site of St. Louis to personally testify for his secretary, but was convinced instead to send a statement to the court. This written testimony doubtless influenced the jury, which acquitted Babcock. Nevertheless, he was replaced as Grant's chief aide by the president's son Buck. Lucky to get off despite Bristow's damaging evidence against him, Babcock ended his career as a lighthouse inspector.

By this time, the president could have expected to have been one of the most reviled and disliked men in the nation. Yet his personal popularity had remained largely untouched by the corruption circus of the preceding eight years. His party wanted to nominate him for a third term, but retirement from politics proved to be generally sweeter to Grant than the seemingly endless tribulations of the presidency. Leaving the White House in early 1877, Grant and his wife Julia embarked upon a three-year tour of Europe and Asia, a public relations triumph which prompted the Republicans to again try and nominate him for the presidency in 1880.

Financially, however, matters took a turn for the worse

when he was swindled out of much of his life savings by a bank embezzler involved with one of his sons. He might have left his wife destitute, if it hadn't been for his old friend, author Mark Twain, who helped Grant complete a profitable serial of his memoirs, just prior to his death in 1885.

Near the end of his life, perhaps because he himself had once been written off as a hopeless ne'er-do-well, Grant made a revealing comment which explained why his friends, rather than his enemies, had been the source of most of his woes: "I have made it a rule of my life to trust a man long after other people gave him up."

*   *   *

The worst scandal of the presidency of Rutherford Birchard Hayes was how he got to the White House. The presidential election of 1876 was almost surely stolen. The vote theft, intimidation and backroom deals which were made in order to get the Republican Hayes into the White House tainted his presidency and almost caused an armed insurrection by supporters of his unhappy Democratic opponent, New York Governor Samuel Tilden. Initially, jubilant Democrats believed that they had won, for their man seemed to have slightly more popular votes in an exceedingly close election; Democratic newspapers, in fact, prematurely and wrongly declared Tilden the winner.

Republican strategists, aghast at the thought of losing the White House that they had controlled for almost a generation, were panicked until they realized that their candidate, the principled Ohio Governor Hayes, could still pull out a victory in the electoral college, but *only* if he won all the disputed votes in several southern states, where the final tally remained in doubt. With the presidency at stake, political honor was thrown to the wind, and GOP goon squads were sent out to Florida, Louisiana and elsewhere to buy, steal or beat votes out of local officials, according to writer Paul Leland Haworth.

When the celebrating Democrats saw defeat being snatched from the jaws of victory, they pulled out a few dirty tricks of their own, such as sending armed men to threaten black voters not to join Republican organizations. As weeks of fractious dispute over who would take the oath of office turned to violence the ominous cry "Tilden or Blood" was heard from Midwestern Democratic diehards convinced that their man was about to be cheated out of a legitimate victory at the ballot box. There was even discussion that Grant might have to remain in office while the electoral controversy was sorted out by Congress. After months of the most intense political negotiations and secret deal-making, however, a man with less than half of the popular vote was sworn into office.

In a way, the ugly election controversy was doubly unfortunate, for the intellectual, principled Hayes stood head and shoulders above many of the men who had occupied the executive mansion during the previous thirty years. Despite being a Civil War hero, Hayes' sterling military record was about all he shared in common with his predecessor, Grant, except for the physical similarities that both were bearded, often personally unkempt, and of approximately the same height.

In character, Hayes was as different from General Grant as Andrew Johnson had been from Lincoln. Unlike Grant's early history of failures, the hardworking Hayes had been an outstanding student who earned a law degree from Harvard and had become a successful lawyer at an age when Grant was swilling bourbon whiskey in his captain's tent. While the loyal Grant could easily lose his moral rudder when a compromising situation involved friends, Hayes was a paragon of personal virtue, a teetotaler and practitioner of Christian charity to whom personal dishonor was unthinkable.

The new president's term began rather inauspiciously. With Congress still squabbling over the election results, he had come to Washington only days before the inaugural, not knowing if he would be sworn in as chief executive. Friends had urged him to slip into the capital quietly, fearing an assassination attempt after months of election contretemps which had produced whispers of armed revolution in radical political circles. Grant swore in the new president early, to avoid any possible scene at the inaugural.

Those who paused to look beyond the months of post-election turmoil soon realized what a breath of fresh air Hayes was. At least three of the past five chief executives had been problem drinkers, but the even-tempered, sedate Hayes had a vivacious, plump wife whose aversion to allowing liquor inside the White House earned her the sobriquet "Lemonade Lucy." Unlike the more spirited presidential children of the past, who embarrassed their prominent parents by openly debauching or keeping mistresses, the Hayes boys were strictly forbidden to drink, smoke tobacco, play cards or shoot billiards. Moreover, the new president was one of the wealthiest men to assume high office in the century; a fortuitous combination of inheritance and wise investments made the prudent Hayes financially independent, and thus unlikely to be tempted by conflicts of interest.

Religious, well-read, with a number of scholarly pursuits and unflinchingly honest, Hayes seemed too good to be true; he was almost the perfect leader for a coming age of industrial growth, capital investment and social enlightenment. The nickname of "Rutherfraud," given to him by disgruntled Democrats, seemed an unjust misnomer.

Hayes' cabinet appointments, unlike Grant's, didn't cause him any subsequent humiliation. Departing from Grant's patronage practices, he totally rejected nepotism and instead filled top posts with regard to ability and political acumen. "He serves his party who serves his country best," became the Hayes motto.

He wasn't without his problems, however. Facing a Democratic congressional majority which felt it had been cheated out of legitimate control of the White House, Hayes was thwarted at every turn in his attempts to reform governmental misdeeds by spiteful opponents and jealous backbiters from his own party. Boldly, he made reform of the bloated, corrupt civil service a major administration goal, but he soon learned that he was taking on formidable enemies to whom patronage, graft and bribery were second nature.

Hayes chose as his chief target one of the few men in Washington whose company he could not abide, the striking, blond-maned New York Senator Roscoe Conkling, lord of his state's political machine and dispenser of thousands of party jobs. The castle of Conkling's patronage kingdom, the New York Customs House, was a morass of greed, inefficiency and indolence. Government workers there labored for the good of their party, not the public; and Conkling, not the president, was their liege and protector. Wading in against decades of entrenchment, Hayes knew the battle would be politically bloody.

A Treasury Department-authorized commission, headed by John Jay of New York (who disliked Conkling as much as the president) investigated the patronage plunder; two hundred jobs were found to have no function other than to reward loyal party errand boys. Jay's probe also judged Conkling's cronies, customs collector Chester Arthur (a future president) and naval officer Alonzo Cornell (a future New York governor), to have been derelict in their duties. Arthur was accused specifically (and accurately) of using politics rather than ability as the basis of choice for public service appointments. Not as stubborn or confrontational as the combative Andy Johnson, Hayes wished to avoid a direct showdown with the influential Conkling, who already viewed the commission's inquiry as a direct challenge to his considerable power. Diplomatically, Hayes sought Arthur's and Cornell's resignations on the grounds that his new appointees would have a better understanding of the revised system he wished to install.

The velvet touch failed—Conkling went on the offensive and flexed his political muscle in the Senate to block Hayes' chosen replacements. It took over a year, but the reformers finally prevailed, and Arthur and Cornell were ousted after additional charges which included Cornell's direct defiance of a Hayes edict forbidding government employees from participating in partisan political matters. Edwin Merritt and Silas Burt, the president's nominees, won confirmation only after a tendentious Senate debate.

The victory wasn't the end of the scandals during Hayes' one term. As another reformist measure, he had discontinued the collection of "contributions" from government officeholders for political uses. His direct and specific order disallowing "assessments for political purposes on officers or subordinates" didn't prevent GOP congressional campaign secretary George Gorman from putting the arm on patronage workers for $93,000 in 1878. Outraged Democrats screamed that the Republican solicitor had violated Hayes' own edict; but curiously, the president ignored the outcry, one of the few questionable actions of his tenure.

Perhaps the blackest mark on the Hayes blotter was the unearthing of the "Star Route" frauds, a major post office scam. A generation of expansion into Western territories had caused a need for improved mail service, and holdovers from the Grant administration saw an opportunity to cash in. Selected mail routes to the West were marked with asterisks, hence the name "star" routes. Recognizing the rapidly changing situation, Congress gave the U.S. Post Office flexible authority to alter its manner of handling Western contracts. If the service improved, more money would be doled out to the delivery companies.

Such decisions were in the hands of the second postmaster general, Thomas Brady, a Grant appointee. Unbeknownst to Hayes, Brady had organized a ring which was milking this system for a bundle. Brady's cabal was putting in requests for payment to the post office for non-existent delivery upgradings. The chief beneficiary was one Stephen Dorsey, later to head James Garfield's successful 1880 presidential campaign. The biggest mystery in the ripoff was why Hayes never displayed any curiosity about the obviously inept handling of the mail services. The Brady-Dorsey partnership was no secret, and it was common knowledge during President Hayes' tenure that the post office was in dire need of reform. Once the situation became a public embarrassment, Hayes sought to dissociate himself from controversy by claiming, "I am not party to covering up anything; Brady and his stalwarts were always my enemies."

The only other blight on the Hayes record was a minor flap involving Secretary of the Navy Richard Thompson. French planners who wished to construct a canal in Panama had sought influence with the Grant administration, which had rejected their overtures. The would-be architects found Thompson more accommodating, especially after offering him a public relations job with a hefty salary attached. Despite his boss's reformist zeal, Thompson thought he could get away with keeping his sinecure *and* remaining navy secretary at the same time. He received a rude surprise when he was told that his resignation, which the cabinet official hadn't submitted, would be accepted.

Given the multitude of sins which had surfaced during the previous era, Hayes had a largely enviable record when he retired from public life in 1880 following a precedent-setting tour of the West Coast in the fall of the election year. Narrowly escaping serious injury in a train accident near Baltimore after attending the March 1881 inaugural of James Garfield, Hayes returned to his beloved Ohio estate of Speigel Grove and lived twelve more prosperous years as an elder statesman of the party which he had helped to rejuvenate.

* * *

The Republicans' choice to replace the respected Hayes, James Garfield, showed his mettle in the means by which he captured the 1880 nomination. Garfield came through the back door when the GOP hierarchy couldn't decide between the "Plumed Knight," Maine's James Blaine, and the scandal-tainted but still hugely popular U. S. Grant, who had returned from his three-year global tour. Shrewdly, the conniving Garfield allowed his rivals to neutralize each other's strengths and then presented himself as a compromise choice.

This cunning political ploy was vintage Garfield, as scheming as the man himself. Philandering and self-indulgent wouldn't be unfair descriptions, either. The intelligent, moody Garfield was an ambitious, unpredictable politician quite unlike his fellow Ohioan, Hayes. The product of an unbridled childhood, Garfield lacked emotional maturity. As a bachelor and later as a married man, he'd had a variety of love affairs, occasionally even two at a time, despite being devoutly religious. His amorous, rebellious streak didn't prevent him from being something of a prodigy, however. At twenty-six, he became president of Hiram College (then known as Hiram Eclectic Institute), and four years later became the youngest general in the Union Army. These accomplishments and his outstanding skills as an orator got him elected to seventeen years in Congress, beginning in 1862, while he was still serving on active military duty.

Hayes was delighted with Garfield's nomination, regarding the selection of his friend as a vindication of his own administration. Democrats weren't too down in the mouth about the outcome, either; Garfield had been implicated in the Credit Mobilier bribery ring by the alleged payment of $329 credited to his account by ringleader Oakes Ames. Garfield swore that he hadn't accepted the money, but the campaign slogan "329" was scrawled on many a wall and street corner. Democrats also circulated an earlier charge against Garfield; that while in Congress he had taken $5,000 in legal fees to represent a construction company which had spent almost $100,000 to influence a paving contract in the capital. The Democratic dirty tricks squad also publicized a phony letter in which Garfield was supposed to have declared his support for cheap Asian labor in America's burgeoning factories. Meanwhile, Garfield's Republican backers were busily setting up a slush fund to buy votes while extracting "campaign contributions" from party officeholders, a favorite GOP election tactic.

Garfield survived these shenanigans, as well as being saddled with Roscoe Conkling's waterboy as his vice president, the obedient Chester Arthur, who'd been dismissed from his job as collector of customs by Hayes. He overcame the propaganda war waged against him to defeat the Democrat's General Winfield Hancock. Garfield would have only 199 days in the White House to savor the fruits of his long rise to power, however.

It proved to be a tough six months. His cabinet had barely begun to function when it broke into warring camps because of Garfield's protracted feud with the powerbroker Conkling, a blood war Hayes had started. Conkling's former spear carrier, Vice President Arthur, kept himself busy by trying to thwart Garfield at every opportunity. Just three weeks into the administration, three cabinet officers threatened to resign over Garfield's controversial patronage decisions. Hayes' four years were already beginning to look like a vacation by comparison. "The last Administration was sort of a dove; this is more like a porcupine," remarked one senator, observing the hurly-burly.

Then insult was added to the president's considerable political injury when the continuing revelations of the Star Route postal frauds caught in their web Stephen Dorsey, who had been Garfield's *de facto* campaign manager and political godfather. Garfield was trapped between his duty and his personal loyalties, and the postal fraud's ringleader, Brady, didn't help matters any when he unsuccessfully attempted to implicate Garfield in the four million dollar scam.

Nevertheless, the president was in good spirits, sensing that he had prevailed in several key political battles, when he entered the Baltimore and Potomac railroad station on the morning of July 2, 1881, to travel to his college reunion. There, for the second time in sixteen years, cruel fate struck again. A deranged office seeker, Charles Guiteau, was convinced that Garfield was personally responsible for his repeated failure to win a government post. Believing the Conkling-Arthur machine could reverse his dismal fortune, the unstable Guiteau tracked the president like a rabid bloodhound for weeks, waiting for an opportunity to take his misdirected revenge.

He struck at the rail station in the presence of Blaine and War Secretary Robert Lincoln, who was forced to relive the nightmare of his father's assassination. Guiteau squeezed off two close-range shots at the startled Garfield, who was struck in the back by one of them. Sensing doom, the wounded, prostrate president listened to his physician's diagnosis that he wasn't fatally injured and replied, "Thank you, doctor, but I am a dead man."

The president's morbid prediction eventually came true, but not before an agonizing, almost bizarre ten-week struggle for life which left the nation hanging on the edge of its seat, rooting for a chief executive who hadn't been overwhelmingly popular before being gunned down. Garfield showed his best side in the shadow of death, bravely enduring an endless series of tests and treatments designed to locate the imbedded bullet, which had mysteriously disappeared inside his fevered body.

Like "Old Tippecanoe," William Henry Harrison, the dying Garfield was subjected to medical ineptness which at the very least hastened, and perhaps even contributed, to his death. Various presidential surgeons repeatedly stuck their unsterilized fingers directly into the gaping wound, no doubt aggravating the festering infection. Hundreds of sure-fire remedies were sent to the White House by well-wishers, including one failed experiment by the telephone's inventor, Alexander Graham Bell. All were to no avail, and Garfield rallied time after time only to suffer new infections.

His long-suffering wife, Lucretia, or "Crete," had just recovered from a prolonged bout with malaria and depression. A jungle-like heat in Washington added to the tense political atmosphere; Garfield couldn't perform any official duties, but Republican leaders prayed for his continued survival, dreading the increasing probability that Arthur might soon take the oath of office. Actually, although a lifelong political hack and errand boy, Arthur rose to the tragic occasion, steadfastly refusing to become "acting president" while any chance remained of Garfield's recovery. His self-effacing actions temporarily placated his critics and averted an ugly constitutional crisis over what to do with a living but incapacitated leader.

By September, after sixty days of pain, brutal heat and insufficient rest, Garfield had lost a life-threatening amount of weight from a once-impressive 200-pound frame. Ironically, the dying president was now almost a folk hero for his grim determination to hang on, and in the words of one pundit would "rise from his bed the most popular man in America", if he had been able to stave off the recurrent infections. No miracle occurred, though, and finally the former boy dynamo who had politicked his way into the White House succumbed on September 19, 1881, after being moved to a seaside cottage in New Jersey for his final days.

*   *   *

"Good God! Chet Arthur President of the United States!" was a reaction heard loud and often about the second man to take the oath of office in 1881. The presidency was one prize "The Gentleman Boss" had never publicly coveted; on the contrary, one Arthur intimate recorded that the vice president broke down "sobbing like a child" at the news of Garfield's expected passing. He was crying as much for himself as for the end of his running mate's immense suffering. Every man who took up residence at the executive mansion has had his detractors, but of Chester Arthur it could fairly be said that never was so little expected of an incoming president. "A mere tool and whipper-in for Conkling" was how one major newspaper disrespectfully described the new chief executive.

The much-maligned "Dude President," whose greatest claim to fame at one point were the hundred pairs of slacks that he owned, fooled them all. While not without his foibles, the underrated Arthur managed to chart a relatively scandal-free course during his three and a half year tenure. So successful was he, in fact, that disaffected party stalwarts, feeling betrayed by his inattention to their incessant demands, worked long and hard to deny him the nomination in 1884.

Few presidents had ever started so far back at the gate. Already dismissed as a nattily dressed, socially obsessed lightweight by most of the public, the press and his fellow politicians, Arthur had the displeasure of hearing rumors that he had been behind a treasonous plot to hire the lunatic Guiteau to murder Garfield, with whom Arthur had never been overly friendly. Almost no one took the whispers seriously, but their very existence demonstrated the general lack of respect for the "accidental" president.

Initially, it appeared as though the muttonchopped former patronage chief would give his critics plenty of ammunition. A procrastinator, he came to work late, left early and seemed happiest when throwing elaborate (as many as twenty-one-course) dinners for friends, entertaining in a grand style which would have made Mary Todd Lincoln blush with envy. "All his ambition seems to center on the social aspect of the situation," wrote Mrs. Harriet Blaine, wife of one of Arthur's main political rivals and a frequent White House guest. "Nothing like it ever before in the Executive Mansion—liquor, snobbery, and worse," carped former President Hayes after reading of the White House finery.

Arthur's reputation for high living didn't dim when he had twenty-four cartloads of furniture and bric-a-brac hauled out of the White House to be sold at auction. The more fashionable replacements were chosen by society designer Louis Tiffany. The "Dude President" further satisfied his penchant for going first class by ordering suits by the dozen and becoming the capital's best-known fashion-plate. Always immaculately groomed, with sideburns fastidiously coiffered, he presented quite a contrast to the earlier, comparatively untidy appearances of Hayes and Grant. His taste for luxury extended to his transportation; he was squired about in a gorgeous, lace-festooned carriage custom built in New York.

The White House partying became so habitual that the late hours favored by the widowed Arthur finally provoked rumors that he was keeping secret guest lists and had a paramour closeted away in the White House. "This is worse than assassination!" blustered Arthur on hearing of the rumormongering. At the same time, the president's wish to remain at the head of all the "A" social lists in Washington led to at least one embarrassing incident. Accustomed to being regarded as an arbiter of taste, Arthur was shocked to find himself accused of moral turpitude for attending the garish wedding of Colorado Senator Horace A. W. Tabor, a mining millionaire who gained office only briefly, by serving out an unexpired term.

After acquiring a fortune almost overnight, Tabor indulged his fantasies by dumping his middle-aged wife and taking up with a beautiful divorcee nicknamed "Baby Doe," whom he later married secretly. Proud as a peacock of his female acquisition, Tabor wanted to show off his sweet young bride and threw a wedding party with a star-studded political guest list which included Arthur, his interior secretary and a number of members of Congress. Washington matrons and religious leaders clucked their disapproval of the Byzantine affair, which featured a $7,000 gown for the bride and a ton of flowers. But Arthur remained non-plussed over the indignant whispers and tut-tutting in the press. Luckily for the president, the free-wheeling Tabor wasn't elected to a full term and left Washington shortly after his headlining nuptials.

It may have come as a shock to Arthur's legion of critics, but there was to be more to his administration than one long state dinner. The dandified chief executive shocked friend and foe alike by actively pursuing civil service reform and turning his back on his former mentor, Conkling, and his army of sycophants. As Conkling's subservient lieutenant, Arthur had become a powerful man; but as president, he knew he had to break the tie or forfeit any chance of running a credible administration. His sudden burst of independence created enemies, who regarded the president as an ingrate and would snipe at him at every opportunity thereafter.

As with Hayes and Garfield before him, the stickiest political problem of the day was the continued unraveling of the Star Route frauds, which had caused Hayes considerable chagrin and was very much on the mind of Garfield when he was fatally wounded. Whether or not Arthur would aggressively investigate the far-reaching post office scam and prosecute the malefactors would be the true litmus test of his presidential intentions. By most accounts, the party-giving president did his duty.

Although under intense pressure from former cronies to ease up on the probe, Arthur ignored the lobbying and ordered fired a number of federal employees who had been implicated in the scandal. When perpetrator Stephen Dorsey asked for a personal interview with Arthur, he was refused, despite his close ties with the administration and the recently deceased Garfield. Indictments were returned, and government attorneys assiduously pursued the prosecutions, even after one trial was aborted by of an attempted bribe to the jury foreman. The second trial lasted six months and produced almost six thousand pages of record, attesting to the thoroughness of the investigation.

It wasn't a complete victory, however, for Brady and Dorsey, the two main culprits, got off scot free despite a mountain of evidence against them, and Arthur was blamed for the failure to put them behind bars. Critical press accounts suggested Arthur was still an ineffectual political hack after all, and one Arthur biographer later hinted that the attorney general resigned because the president hesitated to move against his friends.

The only other notable flap to beset Arthur in the closing days of his term involved Commissioner of Pensions William W. Dudley, who took a leave of absence from his post during the campaign of 1884 to lobby for Republican candidates. The overzealous Dudley had the temerity to suggest that pensioners' claims could be expedited if they voted for James Blaine, the GOP standard-bearer. Dudley's outrageous conduct brought a torrent of criticism down on the administration, but Arthur did nothing to stop the pensions chief's abuse of his office. Planning to quit his post anyway, Dudley went on to become Republican National Committee treasurer, a job he had certainly "earned" with his illicit politicking. Arthur's defenders claimed that he didn't want to hurt the party by firing Dudley, but that was a lame excuse for permitting the questionable electioneering to continue.

On balance, however, the Dudley episode was an exception to what turned out to be a surprisingly clean administration. For once, an "accidental" president surpassed expectations. When Arthur retired from public life in the spring of 1885, as acerbic a critic as Mark Twain wrote admiringly, "It would be hard to better President Arthur's administration."

*   *   *

Yellow journalists had a field day during the presidential campaign of 1884. There was enough dirty linen to keep both sides happy, and little effort was made to tone down even the most scurrilous charges. It was the most vicious campaign since the beginning of the century. The candidates provided an interesting contrast for eager purveyors of gossip. The GOP's James Blaine had a spotless reputation as a devoted family man; it was Blaine's questionable financial dealings and fondness for cash-dispensing lobbyists which made the Democrats lick their chops with glee. While Speaker of the House, Blaine had made a ruling in favor of a secret railroad deal in which he had a large personal investment. Not only was Blaine believed to have made a huge profit, but letters were later discovered which implicated him in the fix. Worse yet, the words "burn this letter" were found scribbled in his handwriting on a document offering $10,000 for the return of the incriminating evidence. Blaine boldly proclaimed his innocence, but even some of his more gullible supporters remained unconvinced.

That was tame stuff, however, compared to the sexual innuendo trotted out to discredit the Democratic candidate, Stephen Grover Cleveland. The Republicans came across a truly juicy tidbit in Big Steve's background; he had apparently fathered an illegitimate child by one Maria Halpin, a woman companion from his days as a sheriff in Erie County, New York. Even more shockingly, the rotund Cleveland didn't deny the allegation. "Tell the truth!" was his reply to supporters who asked him how to handle the potentially devastating bombshell. Not only did Big Steve admit his relationship with Maria and his probable parentage of the child, whom he had supported financially for years at an orphanage, but he was outraged to learn that well-meaning but busybody Democratic backers were attempting to whitewash the admission and pin the fathering of the child on another man. As forthright as he was huge, Cleveland ordered such efforts stopped, knowing full well that it could mean the end of his lengthy political career.

Victorian morality came down on him like a thunderbolt, and the cruel singsong ditty "Ma, Ma, where's my Pa? Gone to the White House, ha, ha, ha!" became the Republicans' unofficial campaign slogan. Ironically, Cleveland's political and financial reputation was as spotless as Blaine's family life. The Democrats soon tried to make use of that dichotomy, seeking revenge by spreading rumors that Blaine's wife was three months pregnant when they married. To his credit, Cleveland wanted nothing to do with the sexually oriented attack on his opponent. "The other side can have the monopoly on all the dirt in this campaign," he told his astonished partisans. Cleveland's honest confession must have elicited some sympathetic votes, for despite the vituperations he eked out a narrow electoral victory against Blaine by carrying his home state of New York, and became the first Democrat to move into the White House for a generation.

The win wasn't the end of whispers concerning his private life. A bachelor for carefree decades during his terms as sheriff (when he was known as "The Hangman" for pulling the noose on two condemned prisoners), the 260-pound president finally took a wife at age 49. Not just any wife, either. On June 2, 1886, President Cleveland married, not a middle-aged spinster or widower, but the lovely, twenty-one-year-old Frances Folsom, the daughter of a friend and former law partner. He had known Frances since her infancy and she had called him Uncle Cleve most of her life. Naturally, the same fishwives who denounced the president's extra-marital relationship with Maria Halpin were the first to voice their displeasure over the president's romance with a woman young enough to be his daughter. But frustrating the nay-sayers again, Cleveland and his young bride led a joyful life together, producing five children and a happy home in the White House.

If this president had a somewhat checkered personal background, his enemies soon learned that his sterling reputation for honesty had been earned the hard way. Like Rutherford Hayes, the portly Cleveland was personally incorruptible, and not without political insight; thus he was spared major scandal during his first term. A few of his cabinet officials didn't measure up to his integrity and humiliated the chief executive, but the misdeeds weren't of the magnitude of those which had haunted several previous administrations.

Attorney General Augustus Garland, a former Arkansas senator, showed some outstandingly bad judgment by refusing to divest himself of stock in the Pan-Electric Company when he assumed office. Pan-Electric's Rogers telephone patent rivaled the Bell firm's landmark invention, and a challenge to invalidate the Bell version fell into the Justice Department's lap. When action was taken by the solicitor general, critics pointed out that Garland's Pan-Electric stock would be worth a fortune if the Bell patent was thrown out. Alarmed at the news, Cleveland personally ordered a halt to the suit, and a congressional inquiry was convened. Garland escaped censure because he was found innocent of "dishonorable" conduct and he retained office, thereafter considered blind to conflict of interest rather than corrupt.

Interior Secretary William Vilas wasn't so lucky with his stock misadventures. A close personal friend of Cleveland, he became embroiled in a flap over his ownership of stock in the Superior Lumber Company, which had received Interior Department rulings facilitating logging on Indian reservations. A bipartisan congressional probe cleared Vilas of personally profiting from his subordinates' actions, but Senate Republicans condemned the Interior boss for actions unbecoming to his office.

With so few public embarrassments during his first term, Cleveland might well have expected an easy reelection, but many of his political crusades, while based firmly on principle, were widely unpopular. Determined to effect tariff reform, Cleveland led an executive campaign in that cause which made him a host of enemies, as did his unflagging opposition to the burgeoning free silver movement, which he viewed as potentially inflationary.

These weren't insurmountable obstacles until inept campaign managers made a mess of his 1888 reelection organization; instances of wholesale bribery by the Democrats in Indiana and New York tipped the balance against the incumbent. Nevertheless, Cleveland won the popular vote by a narrow margin; but Benjamin Harrison, a lackluster campaigner and grandson of the thirty-day president, William Henry Harrison, pulled victory from the raw statistics by outpolling Cleveland where it counted—in the electoral college. Widespread fraud and voting chicanery cost the Democrats dearly in the big states. One of the main culprits was W. W. Dudley, the Republican National Committee treasurer. The unscrupulous and opportunistic Dudley was accused, probably correctly, of being the driving force behind a particularly brazen vote-purchasing scheme in the key state of Indiana. Democrats hollered foul when evidence was uncovered that huge blocks of votes had been bought outright, but Harrison waffled and refused to pass judgment on the slippery Dudley. As President-elect, he allowed him to remain at his party post, although reportedly he never spoke to him again.

The defeated Cleveland was actually relieved to return to private life, but his sprightly wife had other ideas. Prophetically, she told her servant Jerry Smith, "Now, Jerry, I want you to take good care of all the furniture and ornaments in the house, for I want to find everything just as it is now when we come back again...we are coming back four years from today."

*   *   *

The man who displaced the Clevelands was the short, stout scion of a political family famous since colonial days. Little Ben Harrison, former senator from Indiana, son of former congressman John Harrison and grandson of the hero of the Indian battle of Tippecanoe, was also the great grandson of a signer of the Declaration of Independence. Like every successful Republican presidential candidate between the Civil War and 1900, he had been born in Ohio and had served in the

Union Army. Although his personal integrity was unquestioned, he had a dour, humorless personality which made leadership a difficult burden. Even supporters in his own party felt he would be an easy mark for manipulation by the charismatic Blaine, who had backed Harrison's nomination and was subsequently appointed secretary of state.

Expansion was the by-word of the Harrison years in the White House and, strangely enough, several of Young Tippecanoe's problems revolved around the booming economy and the surplus it poured into the federal treasury. A brigadier general, Harrison, like Andy Jackson, had a soft spot for retired soldiers. That attitude led him to appoint a former army corporal named James Tanner to the scandal-tainted post of commissioner of pensions. Tanner, who had lost both legs in the Civil War battle of Bull Run, opened not only his heart but the public coffers to every military veteran he could find.

Harrison proclaimed that the nation should not use "an apothecary's scale to weigh the rewards of the men who saved the country," and Tanner said "amen" to that. Before he was finished, the crippled pensions chief declared he would "drive a six mule team through the Treasury." The president said, "Be liberal with the boys," and Tanner took that as a blank check to throw as much of the federal surplus at the pensioners as he could. Former soldiers who hadn't even asked for a pension unexpectedly received a healthy dose of Tanner's largesse.

Not everyone was thrilled, of course. Treasury Secretary John Noble wasn't overly enthused about a relatively minor official siphoning off the Treasury's revenues at will. He tried to clamp down on Tanner's free-wheeling giveaways, but the pensions boss ignored him and shoveled the money out the door even faster, much to the delight of thousands of veterans. An embarrassing and highly publicized scrap between Tanner and Noble ensued, with most editorialists taking the Treasury secretary's side. "If Tanner does not go soon," warned the *New York World*, "the surplus will—and the Republican party with it." At the same time, Harrison's supporters in his Midwest homebase told the president that Tanner had risen to the status of folk hero, and firing him would ruin the party's prospects in the next election. Finally, after months of barbed exchanges with Noble, Tanner acknowledged the predicament into which he had trapped Harrison, and resigned.

Unfortunately for the relieved president, the pensions scandal was only half over. The antics of Dudley and Tanner had branded the pensions post as an appointment to be avoided at all costs, and Harrison had a tough time finding anyone capable to take over. He finally settled on an Illinois veteran with the unusual name of Green Raum, who had Noble's backing. Unlike Tanner, Raum's problem wasn't an insatiable desire to help his fellow veterans; he wanted to benefit himself. It wasn't long before he was accused of pocketing fees from pensions lawyers to expedite their clients' cases through the bureaucracy. The findings of a couple of congressional investigations were inconclusive, though the Democrats accused him of "prostituting" his office. Not too surprisingly, Harrison sided with the milder Republican interpretation of Raum's behavior and allowed him to serve out the remainder of his term.

The president's wife, Caroline, who had married Little Ben when he was only nineteen, innocently precipitated one of the lowest moments of Harrison's term because of her fondness for a particular seaside cottage. The furor started when Harrison pandered to a traditional Republican officeholders' fascination with wealthy businessmen by appointing Phildelphia merchant John Wanamaker as postmaster general. The influential Wanamaker and the president had become fast friends shortly after their initial meeting in January 1889, just before Harrison's inauguration.

To display his gratitude, Wanamaker and several Philadelphia cronies raised enough private money to purchase a breezy, twenty-room cottage at Cape May Point for the Harrisons. The president was still unsure about accepting the gift when his wife visited the palatial seaside manor during the sultry summer of 1890, while the White House was undergoing extensive repairs. The first lady was so taken with the beach retreat that her husband sent Wanamaker a check for $10,000 along with a note of thanks to the generous benefactors who had overseen the construction and furnishings.

What started out as a quiet business transaction between friends quickly blew up into a major controversy. Leading newspapers attacked the first couple for accepting such a sizable gift. "The President who takes a bribe is a lost President," intoned the *New York Sun* gravely. "Gift Grabber" was just one of the epithets heaped on Harrison. Once the news was out, real estate speculators began trumpeting the virtues of owning land near a presidential retreat. The president's personal check to the postmaster general, while representing a fair market value at the time, didn't stave off the criticism, for published reports noted that the cottage was being built as an outright gift before the chief executive had reimbursed Wanamaker. The storm finally passed, though, and the Harrisons continued to occupy the cottage for years to come. Later, after leaving office, the former president would resell the controversial cottage to another friend of Wanamaker's for the same purchase price. The flap didn't disturb the close relationship between the president and the department store magnate.

The early 1890s, rife with restless expansion and reform, were exciting years; a new America of immigrants, teeming cities, and big business was emerging. The election of 1892 didn't mirror the electric atmosphere of the times, however. The rematch of Harrison and Grover Cleveland was dull in comparison with the past three or four mudslinging elections. The big difference this time was that Cleveland wanted to regain the White House and didn't intend to stand idly by while blundering party leaders ruined his chances. His rekindled enthusiasm, and his campaign handlers' willingness to bend to the tax and tariff-related demands of industrial titans, paid off when he crushed a surprised Harrison by a large margin at the polls and became the first president to regain the White House.

*   *   *

Mrs. Cleveland, who had been so eager to return to the White House, soon had cause to wish that he had stayed in private life. While Cleveland's first term had been relatively serene and free of major upheavals, the mood and the economy of the country were quite different when Cleveland reassumed the reins of power in the spring of 1893. The tariff and free silver issues which had bedeviled him during his first term had by now combined with social unrest and a sagging economy to create a political powderkeg ready to explode at any time. Moreover, labor relations were strained to a breaking point by the pressures of an industrial revolution which left slum-residing urban dwellers and downtrodden farmers in despair. Railroads and Wall Street businesses were going bankrupt at record rates, and cities overflowed with the unemployed.

The portly president had mixed success dealing with a currency crisis and violent labor strikes which threatened to seriously damage the nation's previous growth. But little did the American public of 1893 realize that the seemingly robust, healthy chief executive was secretly battling a malignant cancer inside his mouth, a small growth which might have set off a greater panic than even the most pessimistic industrialist could have imagined.

Cleveland's second term was barely into its tenth week when he made the disturbing discovery of a rough spot on the roof of his mouth while brushing his teeth. His worst fears were confirmed when pathologists concluded that the suspicious tissue was cancerous and that the growth may have spread to one side of the president's jaw. The biopsy quickly became a top secret, national security matter. "We cannot risk any leak that could touch off a panic," Cleveland warned his aides. "If the rumor gets around that I'm 'dying', then the country is dead, too."

For that overriding reason, Cleveland did something which went against the whole grain of his being; he engineered and carried out a big lie—one of the boldest in the history of the presidency. If an operation must take place, as his physicians insisted, it would be conducted in absolute secrecy. Only a handful of people were to know the details of the president's dread illness. It would prove to be a formidable task. Removing the president from the public eye for any length of time would arouse comment, especially among the horde of curious reporters assigned to dog Cleveland's every step outside the White House. Checking into a hospital was out of the question; too many people would then learn what was really wrong with the chief executive, and speculative reports might be even more inflammatory than the awful truth.

Various options were considered and rejected, until Cleveland himself hit upon a possible solution. During his first term, he had frequently taken pleasure cruises with his friend Commodore Elias Benedict. He made arrangements to have full use of the commodore's huge boat, *Oneida*, and the medical team progressed so well aboard ship that even a second, briefer operation to cut out some suspicious-looking tissue went off without incident. Tired and a bit thinner, Cleveland managed to recover enough within a month to return to Washington and resume his duties. Nothing but a few whispers leaked out in the capital; the affair was so clouded in mystery that presidential aides were easily able to quash as a falsehood a fairly accurate report about the president's death-defying operation, which was published several weeks after his reappearance. Almost unbelievably, it wasn't until 24 years later that the full details of Cleveland's bout with cancer were revealed, in an article by one of the doctors who participated in the surgery.

The travails of the presidency undoubtedly seemed lighter to Cleveland following the three-month ordeal. He had survived intact, and his personal integrity remained unquestioned, even if the same couldn't be said for a couple members of his cabinet. Both Treasury secretary John Carlisle and secretary of war Lamont were accused of cashing in on insider scams involving the sugar industry, outgrowths of Cleveland's eagerness to accept big business money and favors during the 1892 campaign.

*   *   *

A two-man tag team ran for the presidency on the Republican ticket in 1896, but only one went to the White House. The man who set up housekeeping in the executive mansion was the affable, moralistic, posing William McKinley, an undistinguished former congressman and governor who hailed from what was by now considered the birthplace of presidents, Ohio. He defeated the very young (36) "Boy Orator of the Platte," William Jennings Bryan, who wowed audiences throughout the country with his impassioned pleas for the freer coinage of silver and a cheaper, more plentiful currency. McKinley, who conducted a homebound, "front porch" campaign from his house in Canton, Ohio, didn't beat back the Bryan challenge by himself, however.

There was a power behind the throne, and his name was Mark Hanna, a rich and unscrupulous tycoon who saw in McKinley a willing vessel to make all his political fantasies come true. The shrewd, calculating Hanna was the most feared kingmaker of his time. If any presidential election was ever "bought," 1896 was the year. Hanna scared big business by painting Bryan as the bogey man of inflation and ruin. The ploy worked and the campaign turned into a free-spending frenzy. He raised the unheard-of amount of three million dollars to put his man over the top. Standard Oil matched almost the entire Democratic war chest with a contribution of $250,000 to McKinley and the GOP; financier J. P. Morgan kicked in the same amount: peanuts, even allowing for inflation, in the mediagenic elections of today, but an unbelievable sum to spend on electioneering at the turn of the century.

McKinley's adroit handler also made him the first "media candidate." The movie camera had just been perfected, and carefully-orchestrated pictures of the Republican nominee were distributed as part of the campaign propaganda. Then and later, McKinley became the first politician to make wide use of the telephone and telegraph as instruments of popular appeal. The new president wasn't ungrateful; aware of his friend's own political ambitions, McKinley chose the septuagenarian Ohio senator John Sherman as his secretary of state after his first choice turned down the job. To the vacant Senate position, he appointed none other than his political alter ego, Hanna, who warmed his seat to cries of political fix.

Like the several presidents immediately preceding him, McKinley was widely considered a basically honest broker of the public trust. Hanna and other cronies might wink when faced with moral turpitude, but McKinley enjoyed a largely unblemished reputation. After all, how could one bear malice toward a man who bore with such love and saintly patience the infirmities of an invalid wife?

Ida McKinley, in her youth the beautiful daughter of a banker, was the one and only true love of McKinley's life.

Their early married life was mutual bliss, but the tragic death of their two daughters, the second after a particularly painful birth, left Ida a physical and mental wreck. While still in her child-bearing years, she began a slow, tortuous decline, punctuated with attacks of incipient epilepsy. To his credit, McKinley proved a model husband. During his years in Congress, he turned over every spare moment to the care of his deteriorating wife. His political enemies sought to capitalize on his unflagging devotion by spreading slanderous rumors that McKinley was running around behind the helpless woman's back, and that he beat Ida behind closed doors.

McKinley's other problems revolved around foreign policy and the disturbingly aggressive mood of the electorate. "Jingoism" was the shorthand term coined to describe the blustering bellicosity given shape in the enormously influential New York-based publications of William Randolph Hearst and Joseph Pulitzer, the two journalistic giants of the day. Their papers' rantings stirred the public into a frenzy, and when the Spanish rattled their sabers at Cuba, McKinley unsuccessfully tried to keep his finger in the dike to plug up the mounting sentiment for armed hostilities. The War Department's sorry performance, under the inept and underqualified leadership of Russell Alger, gave the McKinley administration its blackest eye.

It wasn't the fighting readiness of the American troops which was called into question, for in the Spanish and later Phillipine military campaigns, U.S. troops won crushing victories with startlingly few battle losses. Rather it was the War Department's bureaucrats, who sent soldiers into Cuba's tropical heat with wool shirts and spoiled canned meat to eat, prompting a congressional probe by the Dodge Commission. "Algerism" became a synonym for incompetence. Few men died in the jungle fighting, but hundreds perished unprepared for tropical diseases, bacteria-tainted water and scorching heat. Newspapers which had goaded McKinley into the rash adventurism now blasted him for its deadly results, touting ghastly and often exaggerated accounts of American boys being gruesomely butchered by uncivilized Filipinio guerrillas.

Domestically, things went a bit easier for the nursemaid

president, despite continuing controversies over tariffs and "cheaper money." The president found himself caught in an embarrassing jam when he turned loose an investigator named Joseph Bristow to ferret out the frauds in the Cuban post office, which by 1900 was part of the United States postal service. One of the major targets of the probe was Estes Rathbone, director general of the Havana office. Rathbone happened to have close ties to Mark Hanna, who warned the presumptuous bureaucrat Bristow to back off. By then, however, although still close to Hanna, McKinley knew who was president and told Bristow to forge ahead. He tied up the threads of a long-standing post office scandal which went back to Cleveland's terms of office.

On September 5, 1901, at the Pan-American Exposition in Buffalo, anarchist Leon Czolgosz fired a .32 caliber handgun wrapped in a handerchief at McKinley and what followed was by then an old story: inadequate medical care for a wounded chief executive. To remove the bullet an operation was performed, too quickly and in less than ideal conditions. The wounded president hung on for nine days, but his most memorable comment before expiring was made just after he had been shot, when he muttered to his faithful personal secretary, George Courtelyou, "Be careful how you tell my wife, oh, be careful!"

Chapter 5

THE ERA OF THE MUCKRAKERS
Theodore Roosevelt and William Howard Taft

September 1901—March 1913

"Now that damned cowboy is President," lamented powerful kingmaker Mark Hanna, shortly after McKinley's death. The disgusted senator, his dreams of continued power and glory dead along with his presidential protegé, was referring to Teddy Roosevelt, who at 43 had just been sworn in as the youngest chief executive in history. As when Chester Arthur ascended to the highest office following Garfield's assassination twenty years before, audible gasps of consternation greeted the boisterous T.R.'s incoming administration. Wall Street collectively shuddered, for although a Republican, the former New York governor was known to be an impetuous, implacable foe of unbridled corporate influence.

For the nervous tycoons, McKinley's death couldn't have come at a worse time. Roosevelt had not yet dubbed them with the sobriquet "muckrakers," but a new breed of crusading journalists had already taken the offensive against what one foreign writer called "a country overrun by a house of robber barons, and very inadequately policed by the central government and certain vigilance societies." When the hero of San Juan Hill took the oath of office in September 1901, the America of the twentieth century was becoming an oligarchy, controlled by a feudalistic ruling clique rivaling the worst of Latin America's tightly ruled aristocracies.

During the first year of Roosevelt's presidency, estimated Frank Parsons in the progressive *Arena* magazine, one-eighth of the populace owned seven-eighths of the nation's growing wealth; one percent of the rich industrialists controlled fifty-four percent of the United States' resources. An incredible 94 percent of the all-important railroads were dominated by no more than 14 individuals, who thus had among them effective control of land transportation. Super-rich tycoons such as J.P. Morgan and J.D. Rockefeller were titans of political as well business life, for at the turn of the century there was no politics without business, and woe be to the candidate who forgot that incontrovertible fact of life.

The race and slavery issues which had split the nation less than forty years before had taken a back seat to commerce, both in government and the courts. More than half the crucial decisions rendered by the Supreme Court between the Harrison and Roosevelt administrations were related to business and corporations—only a handful applied to racial controversies. The miserable labor conditions which had ignited violent strikes during Cleveland's second term were, if anything, worse a decade later. Exploitation was the rule rather than the exception in America's grimy factories.

The oppressive social stagnation brought forth vigorous new voices of dissent and protest; the determined reformers of the century's first decade were armed with typewriters and a sense of outrage over the inequities of the age. The horrors of the nation's urban slums were laid bare by Lincoln Steffens in *The Shame of the Cities*. In graphic terms, the impatient Upton Sinclair exposed in *The Jungle* the filth and poisonous wastes intermingled with commercially-sold beef in the meat packing houses. Ida Tarbell traced the grasping tentacles of the giant oil companies and their domineering hold on the American economy.

It was truly an "era of the muckrakers," and the politically austute Roosevelt did everything he could to put himself on the side of the angels. He was widely perceived as the boy-wonder president, defying the greedy chieftans of commerce on behalf of the downtrodden citizens who felt that they no longer had a voice in their government. He carefully cultivated that white hat, underdog-boosting image, while at the same time genuinely believing in the need for a strong federal government led by a decisive chief executive.

The rapid consolidation of the industrial goliaths, their concerted attempt to seize control of the nation's resources and the government's role in curbing their insatiable appetites were the central conflicts of T.R.'s seven and a half years in the White House. His constant battles with the "Brobdingnagians" of business led to several of his worst embarrassments.

Wall Street magnates may have despised the presidential "trust-buster," but he was after all, a Republican, and the tycoons might have been stuck with the indefatigable Roosevelt for as long as eleven years if he won two elected terms. So when the GOP's moneymen extended open palms during the 1904 campaign, the big boys decided to cover their bets. Although the facts didn't become fully known until eight years later during a Senate investigation (there being no campaign contribution laws then), the Republican National Committee's reelection coffers contained a virtual "Who's Who" of what are now called the Fortune 500 corporations. The crusty financier J.P. Morgan personally donated $150,000 in cash; a friendly banker close to Morgan dished out another $165,000; industrialist H.C. Frick anted in $50,000; the New York Life Insurance company $48,000; and railroad financier E.H. Harriman personally collected $200,000 after kicking in $50,000 of his own. In fact, it was later discovered that almost three-quarters (72.5 percent, to be exact) of the Republicans' contributions came from corporations. Not bad for a president who was rattling the saber against big business!

For his part, Teddy claimed to have no knowledge of the plate-passing, or of a rumored $100,000 contribution from Standard Oil. He insisted that he'd ordered Republican National Treasurer Cornelius Bliss to return Standard's donation if it had been given. However, in later testimony to the investigating Clapp committee, a Standard Oil employee named John Archbold swore that GOP boss Bliss had solicited a $125,000 cash donation from his company, with President Roosevelt's full knowledge. Luckily for Teddy, he was able to prove that Bliss had high-handedly ignored his orders regarding campaign contributions, apparently thinking that the less the president knew, the better.

In fairness, some reform did come out of the Clapp committee's sordid findings. Bliss's deceptions and the extortionary fundraising tactics of "Cortelyouism" (named after T.R.'s Commerce and Labor Secretary, George Cortelyou, who strong-armed contributions from the corporations he regulated) led to the first major reform of the laissez faire campaign practices. Besides, the "payoffs" to the Republicans did little to keep the boisterous Roosevelt out of the industrialists' hair. "We bought the son of a bitch and then he didn't stay bought," complained Henry Frick, one of the disappointed contributors.

Of course, not all T.R.'s headaches revolved around the Morgans and Fricks of the world. The energetic president, who despite a wide-ranging intellect loved action above reflection, always had plenty of balls in the air, and frequently wasn't able to keep them all aloft at the same time. Longstanding feuds in the post office undercut his crusading image. The ever-vigilant Joseph Bristow had continued the housecleaning he had begun under McKinley, and by 1903 over forty Republican officials and federal employees had been indicted, including Perry Heath, Secretary of the Republican National Committee. Against his better judgment, Roosevelt was forced to appoint a special prosecutor to oversee the wide-ranging investigation.

Embarrassingly, scandals popped up in other agencies. The bounty of the West's cornucopia of natural resources was too much for the bureaucrats in the General Land Office and the Indian Service, who succumbed to the temptations of bribes. The commissioner of the land office was forced to resign after suppressing a report exposing an extensive fraud ring operating inside his department. It wasn't clearly evident at the time, but such flaps were the precursors of a developing struggle for control of the nation's vast, unclaimed wilderness resources, which would later become the focus of the most heinous crimes of the Taft and Harding administrations.

Roosevelt had nicknamed the muckrakers who chronicled the age, and he was personally close to several, including Steffens and Sinclair. Nevertheless, he caused the young century's first and most serious challenge to a free press. The president's temper flared over press coverage of his key policy initiative, his covert backing of the 1903 Panamanian revolution and the subsequent building of the Panama Canal. T.R.'s inveterate jingoism and his obsession with a waterway across the isthmus of Central America, which had been under discussion for twenty years, led him to insert himself into Panama's ongoing struggle for independence from Colombia.

The rough-riding president did a lot more than merely root on the sidelines for the Panamanian rebels; he did everything but lead American troops into battle on behalf of the would-be revolutionaries. Briefed secretly by U.S. military experts who scouted the situation in hopes of becoming mercenary soldiers of fortune, Roosevelt covertly did all he could to encourage a Panamanian uprising. Delighted when the revolutionaries finally succeeded in November 1903, he dispatched American warships to prevent any Colombian reprisals against the new provisional government. "I took Panama without consulting the Cabinet," he boasted indiscreetly in his memoirs.

There was an overriding political goal to Roosevelt's scheming. With Panama independent of Colombia, the United States wouldn't be in danger of losing a forty million dollar investment in the planned canal zone area. That princely sum had already been paid to the French government, which owned title to the canal land, an invaluable tract now that an alternate location in Nicaragua had been discarded. The Colombians had been cheated out of both the territory and a fair payment for their canal holdings, grievances which they would spend the next fifteen years trying to redress (finally accepting a $25 million "apology" from the U.S. government in 1921 after Roosevelt's death).

The episode further enlarged T.R.'s reputation as a man who, as he loved to say, could "speak softly and carry a big stick." However, a backlash developed when editorialists began to wonder aloud whatever happened to the forty million supposedly paid to the French government. "Forty Millions for Forty Thieves," stormed one unsympathetic writer, giving credence to whispers that insiders had profited handsomely from the murky canal transactions. Other editorialists com-

-pared the disappearance of the forty million with the Credit Mobilier scandal. "A more palpable confidence game, a greater robbery, was never perpetrated upon a people's treasure house," wrote the respected Henry Watterson, of the *Louisville Courier-Journal*.

The president didn't help his cause by being unable to specify who pocketed the gigantic payment. "There were speculators who bought and sold in the stock market with a view to the varying conditions in the course of the negotiations, and with a view to the probable outcome." That rather vague assertion was about all the public would learn, as two congressional investigations failed to disclose a complete list of the stockholders in the French-owned companies.

T.R. was taking a public beating and he didn't like it. At one point in the years-long controversy, he took the extraordinary step of suing for libel two newspapers, the *New York World* and the *Indianapolis News*. Each offending paper had published reports suggesting that a court action would charge Douglas Robinson, T.R.'s brother-in-law, and Charles Taft, brother of Roosevelt's vice president, William Howard Taft, with participation in a syndicate which had taken over the French rights to the canal companies and reaped a huge profit. Since the charges were been circulated during the presidential campaign of 1908, and stoked the fires of a smoldering story which had plagued Roosevelt for years, he struck back with the lawsuits.

Bitter exchanges followed, with the *World* counter-attacking the president and accusing him of "flagrant untruths" concerning his explanations about the mysterious disbursement of the forty million in taxpayer dollars. Despite a lack of precedent, Roosevelt bull-headedly went forward with his libel charges, forcing government lawyers to fish around for legal arguments to advance his cause. The allegations by the newspapers had possibly been circulated on government property in Washington and New York and thus libeled the government itself, contended Roosevelt's lawyers lamely, hoping to further the president's cause with that rather over-stretched assertion. Fortunately for the First Amendment, the presiding judge threw out that claptrap argument in an opinion upheld unanimously by the Supreme Court. Questions

about the curious payments would continue for years to
come, but few believed T.R. had profited personally from the
convoluted series of events. To Roosevelt, it was all slanderous nit-picking. The canal had been built—what else could
anyone have asked?

His greatest heartache at the White House, however, was in
leaving it. Many of his predecessors had regarded their stay
at the executive mansion as an oppressive burden, but T.R.
revelled in every moment of it. Until Ronald Reagan was
sworn in 73 years later, he was perhaps the happiest president, regardless of the tribulations of office, and he and his
family had taken constant delight in the "perks" of the presidency. The tragedy of Roosevelt's political career was too
much, too soon; he was but fifty when he faced retirement
from the most exciting job in the Western world, and although
overweight, he was still more vital than many men half his
age. A third term wasn't to be, however. A financial panic and
resulting slump hurt the economy in 1907 and carried over to
the election year of 1908.

Also lessening his chances for a further extended stay in the
White House was the fact that Roosevelt had greatly antago-
nized Congress, including a number of influential members
of his own party, to the point where in the final weeks of his
administration he received a stinging rebuke unheard of since
the reign of Andy Jackson. During the last eighteen months of
his second term, rumors circulated around the cloakrooms of
Congress that T.R. was illicitly using the Secret Service to spy
on legislators and gather incriminating evidence, ostensibly
for political blackmail purposes.

The president's bodyguards were supposedly slinking
around disreputable brothels and taverns with an eye out for
debauched or drunken congressmen; their confidential reports to Roosevelt could then be used to twist arms in favor
of the president's unpopular legislative package. No concrete
proof of the spying scheme was uncovered, and the president
denied the illegal abuse of his intelligence agents. But his
rude reply to an official congressional request for further
information in January 1909 outraged even loyal Republicans, who determined to teach the combative chief executive
a lesson in manners. Three days after receiving Roosevelt's

insulting letter, the House rejected his message, and in effect censured the president by an overwhelming vote of 212-35. The rebuff killed the president's program as well, but it had undoubtedly been doomed before the Secret Service flap.

Months earlier, when Roosevelt realized that the tradition against a third term included him, he threw his considerable incumbent weight behind his 330-pound Secretary of War, William Howard Taft, who had been in federal service for 27 years and who T.R. trusted (mistakenly, as it turned out) to carry out his progressive programs.

The Falstaffian Taft, often called "Uncle Jumbo," was a fish (or in his case, a whale) out of water in the White House. The Republicans had continued their forty-year domination of the executive mansion (broken only by Grover Cleveland) when the slow-moving, procrastinating Taft was able to make a three-time electoral loser of the tireless Democratic populist, William Jennings Bryan. But he was far from overjoyed by the outcome. "When they say 'Mr. President,' I always look around and expect to see Roosevelt," remarked the new chief executive, only half-joking. Actually, the passive Taft was doing just what the women in his family wanted, as usual. His mother, recognizing his legal talents, wanted her son to gain a seat on the Supreme Court, but it was his wife Helen who had pushed his career toward the presidency. Uncle Jumbo would have been happier with what Mommie wanted, and both eventually got their mutual wish when Taft was appointed Chief Justice of the Court in 1921, eight years after he left the White House.

Roosevelt had leaned heavily on Taft during the later stages of his presidency, appreciating the considerable intellectual skills of the affable, overweight former judge, while being worlds apart from him in temperament, character and outlook. For his part, while a year older than his political mentor, Taft looked upon the vital, decisive Roosevelt with unstinting admiration, regarding him almost as a father figure. Their later, bitter falling-out was probably the most painful emotional experience of Taft's life.

It's difficult to understand why the hard-charging Roosevelt ever considered the ponderous, deliberate Taft as a fitting heir to his political mantle. Action was T.R.'s middle name, while his successor was known to fall asleep after meals and in the midst of social gatherings. Roosevelt was king of the outdoorsmen, braving an African safari well into his middle age; Taft was a sedentary figure, who loved, in his own words, "personal ease," and whose idea of rigorous exercise was a leisurely game of golf. When things weren't moving fast enough to suit him, T.R. was infamous for taking the law into his own impatient hands and governing by executive fiat; to the judicially minded Taft, the law of the land was sacrosanct and no man or cause was above it. Roosevelt was the most recognizable, larger-than-life character in a sprawling age of social upheaval; Taft was the quintessential "stand-patter," a living embodiment of traditional, conservative Republican values.

Such marked differences, and Roosevelt's inability to retire from the hero worship heaped on him, dogged and ultimately spoiled Taft's term of office. The self-indulgent Taft cast a giant physical shadow, but he was the one forced to live under the cloud of his predecessor's stifling political dominance. The ugly and increasingly personal clash between Taft's limited, legalistic concept of the presidency and Roosevelt's growingly strident, activist progressivism colored every major event of Taft's presidency and eventually doomed him to a single term.

Taft's unquestionable personal probity, which later helped elevate him to his life's ambition on the highest court, precluded any headline-grabbing scandals from being dumped on his White House doorstep. His indecisiveness repeatedly embarrassed him, though, and his preference for compromise over bare-knuckles confrontation made him, by his own description, "a man of straw." Those executive short-comings created the biggest brouhaha of his administration, a nasty public airing of dirty linen known as the Ballinger-Pinochet controversy. Teddy Roosevelt was partly behind the feud, and characteristically, Taft wavered just long enough to cause maximum potential damage.

This domestic policy fight, as were most of the coming twenty years, was over natural resources. As part of his national conservation drive, Roosevelt reversed a long-standing policy of automatically opening up settled federal lands to private developers. Instead, he transferred large tracts to the public domain for regulation, and he brought to Washington a brace of bright young men who shared his vision of a more carefully planned future. Naturally, T.R.'s well-intentioned but dictatorial move outraged real estate speculators, timber barons, ranchers and farmers alike, and set off what became a decades-long struggle between conservationists and developers. It didn't take long for the policy disagreement to become an all-out war, with each side believing it had a monopoly on the public intererst.

In 1907, this dispute became personal when a disagreement erupted between Richard Ballinger, who had replaced the disgraced Binger Hermann as commissioner of the General Land Office, and a 24-year-old bureaucrat named Louis Glavis. A man named Clarence Cunningham had filed for an exemption from Roosevelt's set-aside program for five thousand acres of Alaskan coal lands he owned. Glavis investigated Cunningham's request and found his claims to be illegal, but he was overruled by Ballinger. Interior Secretary James Garfield (son of the assassinated president) complicated the dispute by ignoring Ballinger's approval and continuing the Cunningham probe. Soon afterward, Ballinger quit the government in frustration to return to his law practice in Seattle.

The fur began to fly again the following year when Taft asked Ballinger, who had campaigned for the president, to become his Secretary of the Interior. Old wounds were opened up, and it quickly became clear that no fence-sitters would be tolerated in the holy war of conservation. In addition, Taft's decision to discontinue the National Conservation Commission established by Roosevelt caused one of the first major cracks in their close friendship. While it might have been true that fifteen businesses held half the timber in the country by 1910, Taft didn't intend to change the near-monopoly by resorting to what he perceived as T.R.'s overly enthusiastic, extra-legal tactics. Roosevelt had taken the executive too far down the road without consulting the legislative branch, in Taft's view, and that wasn't his style.

That a blow-up would occur was now a certainty, the only question was when. The final catalyst for the coming explosion was added in the person of Gifford Pinochet, the federal forestry director. He'd become famous during Teddy's conservation campaign and was later dubbed "Sir Galahad of the woodlands." Pinochet, like Robert La Follette and several other determined progressives of the time, was a rather humorless fanatic. He unabashedly worshiped the crusading Roosevelt, and looked upon the easy-going Taft as a tool of the vested interests and a traitor to generations of unborn Americans. His cause needed a martyr, and the zealous Pinochet could hardly wait to volunteer.

Working from his forestry office at the Department of Agriculture, which administered over 190,000 acres of federally owned woodland, Pinochet jumped headfirst into the Ballinger-Glavis fray. As a powerful Washington official in his own right, he gave the inexperienced Glavis a letter of introduction to Taft and instructed the young whistleblower to take his protests right to the top. When Ballinger learned of this, he authored his own, thousand-page version of events for his friend in the White House. Taft read the materials, turned them over to Attorney General George Wickersham and asked for full explanations from his subordinates.

Not shockingly, Taft decided that his appointee Ballinger had done nothing wrong, but that the presumptuous Glavis had acted in total disregard for proper relations between the Interior and Agriculture Departments and should therefore be fired. The president communicated this to Pinochet in a message the forestry director dismissed as "the whitewash letter."

The anti-Ballinger forces were far from surrender. With the help of Pinochet's aides, Glavis went public with his charges against the Interior Secretary, writing a lengthy article for the muckraking magazine *Collier's Weekly*. Among the serious allegations he had published were charges that Ballinger had represented Cunningham's interests as a private lawyer between the time he resigned as General Land Office Commissioner and returned to government service as Interior Secretary. Disastrously, Taft tried to placate the Pinochet forces instead of cleaning house following the insubordination. For months, Pinochet stabbed Ballinger in the back every chance he got, publicly denouncing him as "actively hostile" to conservation interests. Now Taft was in a real fix; if he should fire the well-known Pinochet at this juncture, it would be viewed as a frontal assault on Roosevelt's policies and a clumsy at-tempt to silence a critic within his own administration.

The determined Pinochet would have it no other way, and Taft was finally forced, albeit reluctantly, to discharge the Machiavellian bureaucrat, an action which incited a congres-sional investigation and gave Taft's enemies a golden oppor-tunity to humiliate him.

The results were mixed. Both Ballinger and Taft were exon-erated of any wrongdoing, but the Interior Secretary was roundly criticized for having little real enthusiasm for conser-vation and for being a tool of western development interests. Worse yet, Glavis' counsel, the future Supreme Court justice Louis Brandeis (hired by *Collier's Weekly*), proved that Taft had inadvertently used a predated report from the Justice Department as evidence to dismiss the young whistleblower, a fact which the president initially denied because he was unaware of the fact. When Brandeis documented that Attor-ney General Wickersham could not possibly have produced the government's official report on Glavis in the few days which had elapsed, Taft was publicly, if unfairly, portrayed as a liar.

The whole unfortunate affair made Taft look like a wimper-ing failure in Roosevelt's eyes, and hastened the coming split between them, an estrangement which caused the increas-ingly radical Roosevelt to form a third, Progressive party after being denied the Republican nomination by Taft's effective control of the party machinery. Taft's record had been far from the worst, for his trust-busters had been more active than Teddy's, filing a record number of antitrust suits. But T.R.'s so-called "Bull Moose" candidacy caused Taft to suffer the most humiliating defeat ever for an incumbent president. He finished a woeful third behind the Democrats' Woodrow Wil-son and Roosevelt. Much of the blame for Taft's end must be placed squarely on the shoulders of the egocentric former president, whose obsession with denying his former cabinet official a second term put Wilson in the White House, a man whom Roosevelt openly despised and complained about until his death.

T.R.'s enmity hurt Taft far more than losing the election. "Roosevelt was my best friend," he repeated over and over, unable to truly comprehend the single-minded disdain of a man he had once admired more than any other. But he regained a measure of popular acclaim by leaving the White House good-naturedly, saying, "the nearer I get to the inauguration of my successor, the greater relief I feel." Taft also managed to comfort himself by carting off a haul of valuable silverware given to him and his wife in honor of their twenty-fifth (silver) wedding anniversary, a list of items which covered no less than twenty-one typewritten pages!

Chapter 6

PRESIDENTIAL AMORISTS AND A TEAPOT TEMPEST

Woodrow Wilson—Herbert Hoover

March 1913—March 1933

Bespectacled, graying, looking the middle-aged college administrator he once had been, Woodrow Wilson hardly seemed a presidential playboy when he took the oath of office at the age of fifty-seven in early 1913. Happily married for twenty-seven years, the intellectual Wilson was as devoted to his gentle spouse, Ellen, as the loyal McKinley had been to his ailing Ida. Mrs. Wilson, the one person the president "loved utterly and trusted utterly," would not share for long the burdens of the highest office with her husband. A victim of chronic kidney disease, she died on August 14, 1914, leaving her presidential widower in a deep depression in the midst of a growing crisis over war in Europe. "God has stricken me almost beyond what I can bear," the crushed Wilson wrote to a friend. He was inconsolable for months, and aides began to worry about his fragile health.

Always closer to women than men, the sensitive Wilson depended emotionally on the admiring affections of females, and seemed lost without the intimate relationship that his wife's understanding love had provided. Fate, aided by the matchmaking intentions of Wilson confidantes, intervened the following spring, when the still-mourning chief executive was introduced to Edith Bolling Galt, a rather plump, attractive 42-year-old Washington widow. In a matter of weeks, the

145

president had fallen head-over-heels in love with Mrs. Galt, and began writing passionate love letters to her daily, missives which seemed penned by an infatuated adolescent rather than the former, respected head of Princeton University: "God has indeed been good to me to bring such a creature as you into my life. Every glimpse I am permitted to get of the secret depths of you, I find them deeper and purer and more beautiful than I knew or dreamed of..."

Almost overnight, public sympathy for the grieving chief executive was transformed into suspicious curiosity over his boyish courtship and the obvious fervor with which he pursued the object of his intense affections. Rumors mushroomed that Wilson had been a philanderer even while married, and false stories were circulated that the president and Mrs. Galt had been involved much earlier, and that it was the discovery of the adulterous liaison that drove the first lady to her deathbed. "That Galt woman" became the subject of scorn and ridicule to many in the anti-Wilson camp.

To his dismay, Wilson the retiring college don became Wilson the lascivious skirt-chaser in the eyes of some indignant Americans. Much was made of an innocent friendship he'd established with a divorcee, Mrs. Mary Hulbert, whom he had visited in Bermuda years before (when she went by her married name of Peck). Although there was no evidence that their relationship had been anything more than a warm friendship encouraged by Mrs. Wilson, Mrs. Hulbert was hounded by reporters and sensation-seekers for more than a year. Less-principled Republicans allegedly offered Mrs. Hulbert substantial sums of money to turn over her personal correspondence with the president, but she refused.

The vicious gossip didn't deter the love-struck chief executive from wooing the widow Galt. Longtime chief White House usher Irwin ("Ike") Hoover was ordered to keep researchers at the Library of Congress busy finding romantic poems for the enamored president to include in his messages of endearment. In May 1915, he asked her to become the second Mrs. Wilson, although he'd known her only for a short time, and his beloved Ellen had been dead just nine months. Recognizing the political backlash that such a whirlwind courtship was causing in official Washington, the president's paramour tried to put him off, if only temporarily.

Wilson's inner circle feared election disaster when the president announced his engagement so soon after his first wife's passing. At a secret Cabinet session, he was warned that he courted voter rejection as well as a second wife, and that overblown tales about his relationship with Mrs. Peck would be used against him. Somewhat surprisingly, however, news of the betrothal was well received amid less joyful tidings from Europe's theater of war. The happy couple was wed in the White House on December 18, 1915.

Wilson faced tough reelection victory the following November, barely defeating Republican Charles Evans Hughes at the electoral college on the basis of late West Coast returns. Thereafter the president's remarriage became a political issue of another sort. High blood pressure, combined with cerebral and arterial disease, struck him down on September 25, 1919, when he sustained a stroke which left him partially paralyzed. Alarmed at his own drawn, wasted appearance, Wilson grew a beard and moustache to cover his sagging, gaunt face, but he was unable to receive visitors for weeks.

The new first lady and the president's chief physician, Dr. Carey Grayson, kept the worst details of Wilson's illness from him and the public, and refused to permit Vice President Thomas Marshall to assume the presidential duties. Cabinet officials were not allowed to see Wilson, and their orders were transmitted via scrawled, often unintelligeible messages carried by Edith Wilson. Virtually incapacitated, Wilson never fully recovered, and his physical disintegration became so grave that the Senate dispatched a special delegation to the White House to determine if the ailing president was fit to continue leading the nation from his sickbed. The sinking chief executive rallied long enough to convince his skeptical visitors that he was still in command of his dry sense of humor. When New Mexico Senator Albert Fall, a Republican opponent of the administration, told Wilson, "We've been praying for you, Mr. President," the chief executive shot back, "Which way, Senator?"

Edith Galt Wilson claimed she never usurped power from her husband during his lengthy medical crisis; nevertheless, critics charged that she became the first female president, in fact if not in title, and that her determined sheltering of Wilson altered the course of major events during the final thirty months of his administration. Despite her protests to the contrary, it was evident to all but a few observers that Wilson was increasingly short-tempered, lethargic, petulant and unable to control his emotions after the fateful stroke.

At the same time, the explosion of military contracting during the war effort produced predictable waste and procurement abuses, resulting in an inquiry into allegations that the government's wartime aircraft industry was rife with corruption and ineptitude. A 1918 congressional investigation blasted Wilson appointees for incompetence and lack of preparation, but found no wholesale thievery. Chief target of the administration's wartime mobilization critics were the "dollar-a-year" men, private industry executives who served as unofficial advisers for the military build-up.

Some of the worst shortcomings weren't discovered until after the physically spent Wilson left office. The Alien Property Office, under the direction of A. Palmer Mitchell, was found to have skimmed off the proceeds from the sale of German-owned property. Mitchell's director of sales, Joseph Guffey, was accused of siphoning off money from the sales and using the profits to speculate on the stock market; Mitchell himself later came under attack for allegedly diverting property sales to cronies.

Interior Secretary Franklin Lane managed to reopen the long-festering Ballinger-Pinochet rift of the Taft years by allocating government lands to private developers and oil companies at a pace which outraged a new breed of conservationists. The climax of the ongoing controversy occurred in the "Kearful Affair" of February 1918, when Attorney General Francis Kearful made the startling charge before Congress that he believed Lane would permit government land leases "where charges of fraud had been made and without [further] investigation." That inter-agency squabble would soon blossom into the biggest and most notorious land scandal in U.S. history. Fraud was about to become a way of life around the White House.

*   *   *

At least Warren Harding looked like a president. A once-handsome man, whose middle age had provided him with a graying, distinguished appearance, the former Ohio newspaper editor-turned-politician was nearing the end of his first term in the U.S. Senate when his party convened in Chicago to select a presidential candidate in 1920. Harding wasn't the GOP's first choice by any means; in fact, he may have been nominated in part because he was almost everyone's *second* choice among a rather lackluster crowd of hopefuls. When a divisive stalemate developed inside the oppressively hot convention hall, Harding's mentor, Harry Daugherty, was ready to suggest his affable friend as the compromise choice.

"We drew to a pair of aces and filled," was the nominee's characteristically jaunty response to his rather surprising selection. Copying his fellow Ohioian McKinley's "front porch" campaign (right down to having McKinley's flagpole shipped to his own front yard for good luck), Harding trounced James Cox and his running mate, Franklin D. Roosevelt, in a comparatively dull contest. Journalistic curmudgeon H.L. Mencken didn't need much time to assess the new president: "No such complete and dreadful nitwit is to be found in the pages of American history."

While Harding's cabinet included such luminaries as Secretary of State and future Supreme Court Justice Charles Evans Hughes, and Secretary of Commerce Herbert Hoover, a highly regarded engineer and administrator, the president's "Ohio Gang" of thieving, boozing cronies were the men who would put their stamp on his administration. Setting up shop just blocks from the White House in "the little green house on K Street," the chief executive's poker-playing buddies quickly established a nest of bootlegging and influence-peddling. This group of political misfits, through newly appointed Attorney General Daughtery, unofficially controlled a great deal of administration policy.

The boys' clubhouse was no hole in the wall, either. The cozy palace of perfidy featured a cook and a butler, and cost tens of thousands of dollars a year to maintain. Almost as many VIPs dropped by each day as visited the White House: congressmen, oil tycoons, business magnates, and bootleggers who brought in illicit liquor by the barrelful, even while

Prohibition was the law of the land. Everything was up for sale: pardons, appointments, judgeships, political favors—anything that would bring in a buck for Daugherty, his ubiquitous sidekick Jess Smith, a Justice Department flunkie, and the host of shadowy characters who skimmed off what they could from the orgy of corruption. Harding rarely came by the green house, preferring instead to have his "poker cabinet" come to him at the White House for frequent parties which lasted well into the wee hours of the morning.

One of the regulars, a con man and womanizer named Charlie Forbes, gained the dubious distinction of becoming possibly the most prolific thief of government funds since Sam Swartout became the first man to steal a million dollars from Uncle Sam ninety years before. An energetic backslapper whom Harding had met on a trip to Hawaii, Forbes found himself entrusted with the leadership of the newly formed Veterans Bureau, created to assist thousands of disabled, unemployed, and displaced World War I survivors. Forbes' departmental budget of $500 million dwarfed most other cabinet expenditures, and taking care of the soldiers was something that Harding, a compassionate man, wanted done right. The breezy, irresponsible Forbes turned out to be one in a long line of men to disappoint his political patron. Hospital contractors, seeing a gold mine, bribed the willing official with thousands of dollars worth of kickbacks, treating him to the finest in hotels, restaurants and occasionally even their wives, for the convivial veterans' chief seemed irresistible to women.

While not pocketing bribes or enjoying all-expenses-paid junkets around the country, Forbes emptied the contents of his agency's medical warehouses as quickly and cheaply as he could. Buildings full of crucial hospital supplies were unloaded as unnecessary war surplus and sold to his new-found friends for a tiny fraction of their value. Seventy thousand brand-new sheets were practically given away; over a million towels worth fifty-four cents each were sold for three cents apiece; almost a hundred thousand pairs of pajamas donated by the Red Cross were dumped for thirty cents a pair. To balance the scales, the generous veterans' boss over-purchased other items from his business cronies: thirty-two thousand gallons of floor wax, worth about two cents a gallon (enough to last a hundred years) was bought for the ridiculously inflated price of eighty-seven cents a gallon. Trainloads of material, worth between five and seven million dollars, were hauled away from what amounted to a government-authorized fire sale; the bureau received a paltry six hundred thousand dollars, or ten cents on the dollar, in return for the merchandise.

This stupendous graft was too much for the usually tolerant Harding. When he belatedly recognized the scale of mismanagement and outright stealing that his slippery friend had perpetrated, he got Forbes alone in the Oval Office, and according to witnesses outside, screamed, "You yellow rat! You double-crossing bastard!" The shaken Forbes was then unceremoniously shipped off to Europe to keep him out of the hands of congressional investigators. Not all the bureau's chiselers fled the country, however; Forbes' compliant counsel, Charles Cramer, who joined him in the ransacking of the agency, saw the handwriting on the wall with his partner's sudden departure abroad. Locking himself in the bathroom of his house, he put a bullet into his head.

Daugherty, meanwhile, was up to his neck in the continuing mess at the Alien Property Bureau. His errand boy Smith was busily expediting and rigging claims made by speculators and lawyers on property formerly owned by the defeated Germans. For their kind assistance, he and the cooperative director of the bureau, Colonel Thomas Miller, were rewarded with payoffs of Liberty Bonds and expensive cigarette cases by the grateful recipients. Simultaneously, Smith was also raking in a bigger fortune by selling illegal liquor permits, along with immunity from federal prosecution for those bootleggers unfortunate enough to get caught by the honest enforcers of Prohibition.

Their president, who'd been indulging in extra-marital affairs for twenty years, was reaping some nasty fallout over his repeated infidelities. One of Harding's previous mistresses, Carrie Phillips, had been bought off for twenty thousand dollars when his Republican handlers feared their affair might come to light, according to the account of Harding biographer Charles Mee. After Carrie departed the scene,

Harding had become infatuated with a young woman named Nan Britton, who was smitten with her older admirer. Shortly after she'd written to him asking for an employment reference, they began a torrid romance which continued through part of his White House years.

While a senator, Harding had found it easy to get away for New York hotel trysts with the adoring Nan. In the White House, President Harding had loyal Secret Service agents guard the Oval Office during his young lover's visits, lest his stern wife Florence, "The Duchess," catch them in the act. Nan had a baby in October 1919 which she claimed was Harding's; out of fear for his politial career and his wife, he agreed to support the child, who it was said bore a striking resemblance to him.

The first lady, who had helped push her philandering husband into the political limelight, wasn't unaware of his wandering eye. She called in Gaston Means, a gunshoe for the Bureau of Investigation (later to become the FBI), to dig up dirt on Nan. Means wasn't exactly the starched-shirt kind of agent later demanded by J. Edgar Hoover; unkempt and disheveled, he was more sleazy than straight arrow.

To Mrs. Harding's dismay, Means claimed that Nan had no other lover besides the president; to prove his point, he is reported to have handed over piles of short-story-length love letters written by her husband to his younger lady love. Means' report prompted an ugly confrontation between the first couple, in which an angry Harding berated his wife and then threatened to fire Means immediately. (Years after Harding's death, an older Nan Britton scandalized the nation with the publication of *The President's Daughter*, which revealed intimate details of their adultery. Neither she nor her child ever received a settlement from the Harding estate, and they faded into obscurity.)

By the final year of his life, a tired and discouraged Harding, who had at least tried to be a good president, was becoming fully aware of the depth of betrayal by trusted friends and associates. In fairness, Harding had taken office during a deep and prolonged post-war recession, and he'd taken stern measures to turn the economy around. Also, his administration's major disarmament treaty, in 1922, was a foreign policy triumph.

But it was Harding's misplaced trust in third-rate men, and his own personal weaknesses of the flesh which forever scarred his reputation. The thieving Forbes was under federal indictment and about to return from his exile in Europe. The pathetic Jess Smith was under investigation and would soon kill himself with a gun in Daugherty's apartment, under rather mysterious circumstances. The self-inflicted wound added fuel to heated whispers that there was a homosexual relationship between Smith and Daugherty, who had lived together for years. Before the fatal shot was fired, Smith had burned many of the Ohio Gang's ledgers, which recorded payoffs taken by the president's closest friends.

By this time, Harding's personal life was in a shambles and blood-thirsty Democrats were hot on the trail of a half-dozen of the president's top aides. Hoping to reverse his badly sagging political fortunes, he embarked in June 1923 on a cross-country "voyage of understanding" to reach voters less disgusted than those in Washington, who had seen the disaster from close range. Thinner and looking much older, he hardly resembled the carefree figure who'd sauntered into the White House only forty months before.

Things went from bad to worse on the tour. First, the president received distressing secret, coded messages from the capital about pending investigations of his cronies, including Daugherty. Then he suddenly suffered an acute attack of indigestion after eating apparently tainted crabmeat. Days later, following a brief recovery, he died at San Francisco's Cow Palace Hotel as his wife was reading to him.

His unexpected death caused a national outburst of mourning, but Harding wouldn't be allowed to rest in peace. The disreputable Means published a sensational exposé claiming that Mrs. Harding had poisoned her husband in order to prevent a possible impeachment over the sins of the Ohio Gang. Harding's untimely passing saved him, however, from the humiliation of learning how Daugherty and his henchmen would spy, cheat and eavesdrop to try and evade their final punishment. Most mercifully, he wasn't around for the sordid revelations of what became the crime of the century (up to that time), a rip-off that would be indelibly identified with his dishonored administration ever after.

This unparalleled cesspool of bribery and theft, commonly known as the "Teapot Dome" scandal, was the culmination of a generation of bitter struggle between conservationists anxious to assert more federal government control over public lands and development interests just as eager to retain a free hand to profiteer from millions of acres rich with timber and oil.

There was a large cast of characters in the drama, which played for almost ten years. The leading role was filled by Albert Fall, former senator from New Mexico and Harding's choice for interior secretary. Fond of Stetson hats, string ties and cigars, and speaking with a loud, distinctive drawl, the tanned, mustached Fall was the developers' dream. Land was for building and oil was for pumping out of the ground, and he had a frontierman's impatience for anyone who thought differently. "From his kind lynch law springs", wrote one correspondent of the self-assured senator, who once had been removed from the federal bench by Grover Cleveland for illegally joining a posse.

Harding had a lofty opinion of his old friend's intellectual capabilities and was happy to give him free rein on the simmering conservation controversy: whatever was put in front of him, he would sign. In the days before extensive background checks on White House nominees, the president had no way of knowing that Fall was desperately in need of cash by the time he joined the cabinet. His debts made him an inviting target for wealthy oilmen raking in unimaginable profits from petroleum strikes on undeveloped lands.

In 1909, President Taft had created three giant Naval Petroleum Reserves, located near Elk Hills, Nevada, Buena Vista Hills, California, and Teapot Dome, Wyoming, to safeguard against possible future shortages. The reserve around Elk Hills, the largest, is today worth billions of dollars. It was only matter of time before the oil companies found a way of tapping into the vast pools of black gold. In 1920, Congress passed the Oil Land Leasing Act, which permitted the leasing of drilling rights on government land to private developers.

To the collective delight of the oil barons, the three huge reserves were included in the legislation.

Albert Fall was no sooner in office than he launched an ambitious plan to wrest control of the petroleum reserve lands from the Navy Department. He encountered little resistance from Navy Secretary Edwin Denby, who apparently considered the administrative duties of his office a bothersome chore. Less than three months after assuming office, Harding signed an executive order, which Fall had shoved under his nose, giving the interior secretary the petroleum dictatorship he'd coveted. Unencumbered by legalities, Fall began awarding oil leasing contracts worth tens of millions of dollars to insiders.

Two who profited enormously were Edward Doheny and Harry Sinclair. An entrepenuer worth more than $100 million dollars, Doheny got the first Elk Hills leases. For those and later favors from his friend Fall, Doheny dispatched his son to the cabinet official with a $100,000 cash "loan." The kickback, large as it was, was a bagatelle for Dohney, who expected to make $100 million in profits from the contracts.

The fortunate recipient of the Teapot Dome contract was Sinclair, a wheeler-dealer who'd parlayed a small stake into an international fortune of an estimated $300 million. Fall hadn't selected the fabulously wealthy Sinclair out of the goodness of his heart. When the tycoon visited the interior secretary's struggling ranch in New Mexico, he gave him six heifers and a young bull after Fall remarked that he loved cattle but couldn't afford any. Never a cheap date, Fall wasn't about to hand over the leases for a few cows. A month after the agreements for Teapot Dome were signed in April 1922, Sinclair gave Fall's bagman Liberty Bonds worth almost $200,000. He later sweetened the pot with an additional $100,000 in cash. His investment was well-spent: Fall had the U.S. Marines sent in when business rivals attempted to drill at Sinclair's leasing site.

With characteristic bravado, Fall refused to hide his new-found wealth, and his hard-pressed neighbors couldn't help but notice a sudden, inexplicable prosperity at the Fall ranch, which previously had been flirting with bankruptcy. All his debts had been paid off, and he'd been buying additional land, evidencing a financial turn of fortune which didn't exactly jibe with his $12,000 cabinet salary; the same income had caused Wilson's secretary of state, the oratorically brilliant William Jennings Bryan, to begin lecturing at circus tents to supplement his take-home pay.

Experts with knowledge of the leasing arrangements begged the White House to investigate. Trusting as always, the president demurred. "If Albert Fall isn't an honest man, I'm not fit to be the President of the United States," replied Harding. In fact, even after newspapers had attacked Fall's actions and ethics, and he had resigned, claiming he'd done all he could in the job, Harding suggested appointing Fall to the Supreme Court. Perhaps fearing a tough Senate confirmation over his suspicious new fortune, Fall declined the honor.

Harding would know nothing of the eight-year investigation, which began just weeks after he expired, and would give his laconic vice president, Calvin Coolidge, months worth of headaches. Fairly or not, his tenure was stained with the misdeeds of the malefactors he'd put in positions of public trust. The sins of biblical Babylon, commented the famous Midwestern editor William Allen White, were a Sunday school story compared to the goings-on in Washington from June 1919 to July 1923.

*   *   *

I believe I can swing it," was the self-confident reaction of Harding's vice president, Cautious Cal Coolidge, upon learning of his ascension to the highest office. Characteristically, the unexcitable Coolidge disdained any highfalutin pomp when breathless officials arrived at his Vermont vacation residence on August 3, 1923, to convey the dramatic news of Harding's unexpected death. Almost off-handedly, he asked his father, a notary public, to administer the oath of office to him in the wee hours of the morning, and then went right back to sleep.

The uneventful first night of the new administration was vintage Coolidge. Initially, the nation didn't know what to expect from the relatively obscure former vice president. Well-known for tough strike-busting as the governor of Massachusetts, Silent Cal remained inscrutable to all but the few closest to him. Once, a chatty society dowager tested reticent Coolidge by informing him that she had made a bet that she could get more than two words out of him. "You lose," deadpanned Cal. His flinty personality and no-nonsense, puritannical outlook was the antithesis of the soft, permissive Harding persona, and the contrast seemed to promise major shake-ups for the scandal-tainted, disunited administration which he had inherited.

As an outsider to the Ohio Gang, Coolidge had sensed the larcenous shenanigans going on under his predecessor's nose, but had little idea of their real magnitude. "Get rid of Daugherty," was the terse advice offered by Idaho's powerful senator, William Borah, when asked to help guide the new president's initial steps. Coolidge moved at a snail's pace in carrying out any purges, however, fearing that abrupt dismissals might signal an admission of guilt from an administration in which he'd served and was now leading.

Abuse was heaped on the new president by the truckload during the opening months of his White House occupancy as the Teapot Dome relevations grew seamier by the day. If he thought Fall and the other light-fingered culprits were going to confess and quit in disgrace, he was mistaken. On the contrary, Fall boldly denied to a Senate committee investigating the oil leases that he'd taken any money from Doheny or Sinclair. For a short while, Coolidge's decision not to discharge the attorney general looked like a gutsy call. That's when the new president showed himself to be as bad a judge of character as his predecessor. True to form, Daugherty decided to play dirty, and turned loose gumshoes from the William Burns security agency on his Senate tormentor, Montana's Thomas Walsh, an austere progressive Democrat, who'd correctly surmised from the Interior Department's own records that he was on to one of the biggest scams of all time.

At the embattled attorney general's direction, federal agents opened Walsh's mail, dug into his past, and wiretapped his telephone. No creampuff himself, Walsh refused to back down, convinced that Fall had been bought off and had committed perjury. Under increasing pressure, Fall began to drink heavily and frantically scrambled to explain his financial windfall. He convinced a prominent financier, Ned McLean, to say that he'd loaned Fall $100,000 as a personal favor after Fall falsely claimed the money had nothing to do with the oil leases. An old Harding buddy, McLean had his own network of spies keep track of Walsh's investigation.

None of Fall's or Daugherty's subterfuges stymied the determined Walsh, who got Doheny to admit that he, not McLean, had given the dough to the former interior secretary. Fall turned into a broken, pathetic figure, who refused to answer further questions, took the Fifth Amendment, and sealed his doom.

His final, abject ruination, and the unfolding of the oil leasing scandal, was making mincemeat of the Republican party's reputation with the voters. Coolidge was forced to appoint two special prosecutors to show he meant business in cleaning up the Teapot Dome mess: he chose Pennsylvania lawyer Owen J. Roberts and former Ohio Senator Atlee Pomerene, who both later served on the Supreme Court. Belatedly, Cal also forced the resignations of Daugherty and Edwin Denby, the inattentive navy secretary who had inadvisedly permitted Fall to take over the leases in the first place. The investigations and civil suits over Teapot Dome would grind on inexorably for another seven years, culminating in a prison sentence for Fall in 1931.

Coolidge's unabashed admiration for the titans of industry caused several troublesome incidents for his administration, however, which weren't the result of any fallout from the sins of Harding's crew. His Treasury secretary, Andrew Mellon, got into a heated dispute with Republican Senator James Couzens over the implementation of Mellon's tax proposals. Couzens called for a probe of the Bureau of Internal Revenue, and records obtained with Mellon's grudging cooperation showed that the tycoon had financial interests in a number of corporations benefitting from his department's tax programs.

Incensed, Mellon rejected suggestions of conflict of interest and insisted that the inquiry be stopped; Coolidge came to his cabinet officer's rescue, trying to neutralize Couzens with an offer of an ambassadorship. When the stubborn senator persisted in going up against Mellon, he found himself accused of owing the Bureau of Internal Revenue ten million dollars from a stock sale years before. Only much later, in 1928, did an appeal board rule that Couzens had overpaid, rather than evaded taxes. Mellon's tax rulings were declared to be legal.

Auto magnate Henry Ford might have helped to ensure Coolidge's reelection in 1924 because of his lust for control of power sites and nitrate plants in the Tennessee Valley. Aching to gain ownership of the sprawling public tract in an area called Muscle Shoals, Ford had proposed leasing the rights to the Wilson dam for a hundred years, but although the self-serving deal gained support in some quarters of Congress, the proposal was denounced by Ford's detractors as a taxpayer-funded bonanza for him.

In December 1923, Ford was one of the most popular public figures in the Midwest and the western states. His well-pub-licized views against war profiteers and in favor of better conditions for workers, noted biographer Keith Seward, made the genius inventor a formidable potential candidate in his own right, despite his expressions of anti-Semitism. A *Collier's* magazine opinion poll showed him to be an over-whelming favorite of voters. That month Ford met privately with Coolidge in the White House. Not long afterward, in a message to Congress, the president recommended the sale of the Tennesse lands to private interests without mentioning Ford by name.

When Ford subsequently endorsed Cal's reelection ("I would never for a moment think of running against Calvin Coolidge for President on any ticket"), newspaper editorial-ists and at least one participant in the White House meeting came to the conclusion that a secret bargain had been struck— Muscle Shoals in return for the automaker's withdrawal as a possible candidate. Whether or not they had cooked up such a backroom plot, Coolidge won reelection, but Ford never got the coveted Tennessee lands; his repeated attempts were blocked by determined opposition in the Senate.

Ironically, in an era of prancing flappers and bathtubs full of bootleg gin, partying Americans were saddled with a presi-dent who neither drank nor chased women. The only time Coolidge publicly showed even a flicker of sexual pique was during a June 1927 vacation visit to the resort area of Black Hills, South Dakota. Hiking with a Secret Service agent named James Haley, First Lady Grace Coolidge innocently overextended a mealtime walk by ninety minutes and left the always-punctual president with a cold lunch. Headline writers had a field day with cleverly worded suggestions about Mrs. Coolidge's prolonged absence, and although he was blameless, the luckless Haley was removed as her bodyguard.

After his pithy retirement pronouncement, "I do not choose to run for President in 1928," Coolidge left the White House loaded down with gifts from admirers, presents which he carried home to Vermont.

*   *   *

Like the month of March in which he was inaugurated, Herbert Hoover went in like a lion and out like a lamb. One of the most capable public servants of his generation, Coolidge's secretary of commerce was, partly because of his humanitarian relief work in Europe, probably the best-known administration official except for the president himself. He overwhelmingly won the Republican nomination and then crushed the Democrats' candidate, "Happy Warrior" Al Smith, due largely to the anti-Catholic vote against the New York governor. "Hooverism" became a household word for waste prevention, and the campaign slogan "a chicken in every pot" symbolized the optimism that the gifted engineer and self-made millionaire carried into the White House. Four years later, he would leave office an unhappy and disillusioned man, not completely understanding the forces which transformed him from the harbinger of prosperity into one of the most unpopular men in the United States.

Hoover's reputation at the outset of his administration, in the words of pundit Walter Lippmann, was a "work of art." Crossing the threshold of the executive mansion was probably the worst thing Hoover ever did for that previously unsullied popularity. In forty painful months, he fell from public hero to President Reject, a victim of the tumultuous economic times as surely as Cal Coolidge had been the beneficiary of a more optimistic mood.

The punishing end of the somewhat artificial prosperity of the Twenties, six months after he assumed office, cut short any real chance Hoover might have had to implement the

far-reaching governmental reforms he'd planned. Unprecedented joblessness and hunger across the country altered
Hoover's image from that of a thoughtful, compassionate
progressive conservative into a hardcore reactionary. In conservation, civil rights and prison administration, Hoover had
proven to be a reformer with a workable program; but the
Great Depression, which grew steadily like a cancer on his
presidency, made him instead a scapegoat for a nation's misery.

Not all of his spreading unpopularity was his fault, to be
sure. William Doak, his second secretary of labor, earned a
reputation as a ruthless harasser of illegal aliens. Under the
dictatorial Doak, alien hunting and bashing "became a gladi-
atorial spectacle. No brutality or illegality stopped him,"
wrote columnist Drew Pearson. Hoover may have been ignorant of Doak's alleged jackboot tactics; but that's difficult to
believe, given press reports that aliens were being rounded
up and held for as long as eighteen months in Buffalo and
Cleveland.

After a while, Hoover just couldn't seem to do anything to
placate an increasingly critical press. Newspapers climbed all
over him, implying that he used taxpayers' money and soldiers' muscle to build a cozy Virginia summer retreat. Later it
turned out that the wealthy chief executive had put $114,000
from his own pocket into the project, and planned to donate
it to the state as a camp when his tenure ended.

There can be little dispute, however, that Hoover created
his own debacle during one of the most disgraceful spectacles
of the Thirties—the rout of protesting war veterans from their
Washington campgrounds. What had started as a ragtag
march across the country to protest Hoover's veto of a bonus
bill for war veterans swelled into an army of fifteen thousand,
who set up tents in the Anacostia section of the city.

Despite the president's personal inclination to seek a compromise solution, he unwisely allowed hard-line, communist-
baiting security and military aides to get his ear. With the
economy at its nadir and tempers frayed by the humid, swel-
tering summer heat, a bloody confrontation became almost
inevitable. The president delayed using force as long as he felt
he could, but finally made the fatal mistake of putting the

strutting, insubordinate General Douglas MacArthur in charge of crowd control.

Although under direct presidential orders to simply contain the bonus marchers, MacArthur, resplendent in full battle dress, personally led his troops into Anacostia on July 28 to attack the helpless protestors and burn their pitiful shantytown. More broken heads and bruises than fatalities resulted from the one-sided onslaught, but press accounts highlighted the dispersal of the hungry veterans in the shadow of the capital, and the death of an eleven-year-old child from tear gas poisoning. Just months before the national elections, Hoover was branded as an oppressor of the poor, after he had personally supervised more hunger relief during the war years than any other American. It didn't help matters when Attorney General William Mitchell issued a whitewash report on the affair, and War Secretary Patrick Hurley defended MacArthur's inexcusable defiance of his commander-in-chief's orders.

The fiasco helped nail the lid on Hoover's political coffin. "Hate Hoover" slogans and "Hooverville" ghetto-like encampments popped up all across the country. The 1932 campaign revealed the bitter personal enmity between Franklin Roosevelt and the incumbent president, who considered his successor a well-meaning but underqualified dilettante with little working knowledge of government. Out of this darker, more suspicious side of Hoover came the actions which made him the first president to surreptitiously record his White House callers.

In November 1932, just days after his decisive victory over Hoover, FDR telephoned the White House to arrange a visit. The fact that the president-elect called was no secret; it was front-page news. What wasn't known at the time (nor for years afterward) was that Hoover instructed a White House stenographer to listen in on the private conversation without Roosevelt's knowledge, and make a verbatim record for the presidential files. The chat was uneventful, with Roosevelt confessing he'd "been in bed for five days. I had a real case of the flu."

"That is too bad," sympathized his listener. Later in the exchange, Hoover suggested to his successor that he should instruct his aides to study the president's foreign policy briefs, for "I have a feeling we have to put up national solidarity." FDR readily agreed.

The chat wasn't the end of Hoover's covert transcribing. Angered by Roosevelt's remarks at a policy meeting following the telephone talk, he secretly recorded a second conversation on January 3, 1933. This time, the unsuspecting president-elect was calling to thank Hoover for the offer of a U.S. vessel for Roosevelt's upcoming European tour. FDR's comments were mudane, but the transcript showed the strain that four pressure-packed years had taken on Hoover; the idealistic humanitarian hero had turned into a distrustful eavesdropper.

Chapter 7

THE PRESIDENTIAL PLOTTER

Franklin Delano Roosevelt

March 1933—April 1945

Once dismissed as a playboy and a lightweight, Franklin Delano Roosevelt overcame the handicap of polio and the stigma of inherited wealth to become the greatest president of the twentieth century. The only man ever elected to the highest office four times, he was both the most loved and most hated man of his generation, the undisputed American leader through twelve turbulent years of social upheaval and armed conflict.

Although he had earned his stripes as a national campaigner during his unsuccessful bid for the vice presidency with running mate James Cox in 1920, Roosevelt had to overcome a reputation as a little-regarded "featherduster" to political observers and many who knew him personally. (Eleanor Roosevelt's biographer, Blanche Wiesen Cook, wrote that his female relatives joked that the initials F.D. stood for "featherduster.") Besides his role as the lower half of the doomed Cox ticket, the only high office the rich socialite and cousin of Teddy Roosevelt had on his resume was assistant secretary of state, a post which he'd held for eight years under President Woodrow Wilson.

When the aspiring 39-year-old politician contracted infantile paralysis (polio) the year following the 1920 election at his family's summer retreat at Campobello, Canada, and permanently lost the use of his legs, an astute oddsmaker would have been forgiven for writing off the jaunty New Yorker as a political powerbroker. But the chilly waters of New Brunswick's Bay of Fundy steeled rather than shattered the will of the future chief executive. "Franklin Roosevelt underwent a spiritual transformation during the years of his illness...The years of pain and suffering had purged the slightly arrogant attitude Roosevelt had displayed upon occasion before he was stricken. The man who emerged from the ordeal was more warmhearted, with humility of spirit and a deeper philosophy. Having been in the depths of despair, he understood the problems of people in trouble," wrote Frances Perkins, who became the nation's first woman cabinet officer as FDR's secretary of labor.

It wasn't an easy road back to public life. Initially, Roosevelt and his wife, Eleanor, a cousin whom he had married in 1907, feared that the disclosure of such a serious affliction would finish him politically. Only the closest members of the family were informed of the true severity of the attack. The press was initially told that the young heir had suffered a case of influenza.

His convalescence was a long, painful ordeal. Imbued with an unquenchable optimism, Roosevelt at first believed he would walk again. For seven agonizing years, from Harding's presidential debacles through Coolidge's largely paper prosperity, FDR's daily regimen was centered, not on national politics, but, towards physical rehabilitation. He tried every possible cure known at that time: massage, electric current, muscle training and ultraviolet light. The strength never returned to his legs, but he slowly learned how to get along without them and to make better use of his functioning muscles. The suffering of his fellow polio victims was greatly reduced through the time, effort, and money he devoted to the private foundation dedicated to rehabilitating others similarly afflicted, which he established at a resort in Warm Springs, Georgia.

"No sob stuff," he instructed a fascinated press as he began an almost unprecedented political comeback six years after his crippling illness had struck. Journalists, perplexed by the charming, multi-faceted Roosevelt personality, heeded the admonition, then and afterwards. For the rest of his career, few photographs were published of FDR in a wheelchair, and his handicap was almost never publicly referred to, even by the most malignant critics.

The media blackout on his health may have been the only free ride the future president received. His struggle against the paralysis in his legs certainly wasn't the only personal crisis FDR faced. Long before his climactic 1932 run for the presidency, FDR's marriage to Eleanor had disintegrated into a partnership in name only. Earnest, intense, sexually repressed, Eleanor had an inferiority complex a mile wide, and had thought of herself as an ugly duckling since her unhappy youth. The fact that she had snared her wealthy, handsome cousin didn't improve her self-image. Nor did five children solidify a marriage that was a physical and spiritual mismatch.

Lucy Page Mercer, Eleanor's lovely 22-year-old social secretary, a woman "with a hint of fire in her warm, dark eyes," tipped the delicate imbalance in the Roosevelt household in 1914. Feminine, with a voice having the "quality of dark velvet," Lucy possessed the sensuality that Eleanor lacked. She was even more attractive for her knack of bolstering a man's morale; in contrast, Eleanor felt compelled to compete with her outgoing, intensely ambitious husband. To add to the smoldering family chemistry, Eleanor could never get along with Sara Roosevelt, her domineering and interfering mother-in-law.

Combined with FDR's ingrained flirtatiousness, and his increasing dissatisfaction with his wife, the situation spelled domestic disaster. Eleanor's jealousy expanded by the month, and the Roosevelts' marriage, never communicative, became even more tense. Cousin Alice Roosevelt Longworth didn't help matters any by inviting Franklin and Lucy to dinner when Eleanor was out of town ("He deserved a good time. He was married to Eleanor"). Meanwhile, Eleanor's letters from her travels barely concealed her growing resentment of her husband's suspected infidelity.

In September 1918, as the rest of America was celebrating the end of the war, the Roosevelts were beginning theirs. Ill with pneumonia after a trip to Europe, Franklin stayed in bed while Eleanor tended to his mail. In the pile she discovered letters from Lucy which confirmed her worst fears; Franklin and Lucy were in love. It was showdown time. Crushed, Eleanor offered her straying spouse a divorce, a possibility which must have tempted Franklin, for he had talked to Lucy of ending his passionless marriage and beginning anew with her. But the drawbacks became quickly evident. First, divorce might have spelled the end of a promising political career. Untold scandal would be visited upon a family as socially prominent as the Roosevelts, if a man was seen leaving his wife and five children for her secretary. Second, being a very religious young woman, Lucy Mercer had serious reservations about marrying a divorced man. Third, and perhaps most importantly, Sara Roosevelt switched sides and came to the betrayed Eleanor's defense; if Franklin disgraced the family by deserting them, Mother would retaliate where it hurt—in the pocketbook.

Eleanor's gamble on a confrontation worked; Franklin agreed to stay home and stop seeing his young paramour. Lucy went even further, promising that she would never again allow herself to be unescorted when in the same room with FDR. Son Elliott Roosevelt wrote years later that although Eleanor agreed to a continuance of the marriage, the two no longer lived "as husband and wife."

Roosevelt was now as much a prisoner of his marriage as he soon would be of his wheelchair. And even worse for the awkward Eleanor, Lucy Mercer remained her largely unseen rival for the rest of her husband's life. Lucy married wealthy socialite widower Withrop Rutherfurd, who was thirty years her senior. She was out of sight but not out of mind in 1932 when FDR completed a startling political comeback, which had included two terms as governor of New York, by crushing the besieged and unpopular Herbert Hoover at the polls.

His first hundred days in office constituted a virtual revolution for the federal government. Drastic action had to be taken to shake the country out of the economic lethargy of the Depression, and Roosevelt turned loose a formidable gang of "braintrusters" to arm the federal bureaucracy for change. In a few scant weeks, FDR was moving on his inaugural call to action. The Agricultural Adjustment Act (AAA) was passed to bring farmers more purchasing power; the National Industrial Recovery Act (NIRA) represented perhaps the most ambitious attempt by the government to regulate private business ever proposed up to that time.

Roosevelt's cadre of reformers, mostly academics and lawyers, was just warming up. The dour, brilliant Harry Hopkins headed the Federal Emergency Relief Administration (FERA) to make direct grants to states for assistance to the unemployed. Millions of jobless youths were encouraged to join the new Civilian Conservation Corps (CCC), which refurbished parks, built roads and gave the hopeless a sense of civic purpose.

Not everyone was delighted, however. Conservatives suspicious about the increased intrusion of federal government into the private sector howled in protest. FDR, they grumped, was leading the nation towards socialism, an unthinkable sin. Dictator, communist, revolutionist, destroyer of capitalism, crackpot, unprincipled charlatan, weakling, were just a few of the more printable epithets hurled at the energetic, determined chief executive. No president since Lincoln had been the target of such vituperative slander. Roosevelt ignored most of the broadsides and unleashed additional ambitious government programs to spur economic recovery.

With billions of dollars being pumped into the economy from Washington, it was a minor miracle that Harding's halcyon days of fraud and bribery didn't reappear to stain Roosevelt's progressive experiment. In fact, relatively few instances of malfeasance were uncovered among the dozens of newly organized, federally funded agencies, even though Republican operatives tried hard to find them at election time. Attempted fixes weren't unheard of, though. Roosevelt adviser Louis Howe, head of the CCC, thought he was doing the Democrats a service when he steered an overpriced contract from his agency to an iron works in Maine, evidently hoping for future political gain in the state. But FDR, an old hand at contract shenanigans from his days in the Wilson administration's navy department, told Howe that the award to a high bidder would be "indefensible" and averted certain embarrassment.

The work relief agencies, actually, were the only programs which consistently came under the cloud of political favoritism. FERA, which took over from the short-lived Civil Works Administration, was vulnerable because its authority was divided between Washington and the states. FERA's irascible chief, Hopkins, tried to keep the agency non-political, but the huge funds and manpower reserves available to the local ward heelers and state politicians were too tempting. Several FERA administrators were accurately accused of using the agency's resources for political gain. One prominent FERA boss, Governor Martin Davey of Ohio, illicitly raised campaign funds through the FERA offices and was bounced from the post for the backdoor money-grabbing after a dressing-down from Hopkins, who also fired a couple dozen of Davey's political hacks.

When FERA became the larger Works Progress Administration (WPA), the problem worsened. One of the biggest bureaucracies in a city now full of them, WPA was a juicy plum for the Democrats because of the control that the party had over its management appointments. Critics lambasted WPA workers as lazy drones half-heartedly toiling at make-work projects. The WPA, cried detractors, was becoming a gigantic party employment machine, like the one New York Senator Roscoe Conkling had run in New York during the 1870s.

FDR left himself open to allegations of political manipulation concerning WPA when he instructed aides that "not one person is to be laid off on the first of October." Two years later, in the 1938 congressional elections, Republicans made the Democrats' use of WPA patronage a major campaign issue, and serious instances of pressure exerted on the votes of WPA recipients were proven in Kentucky and Pennsylvania. Interior secretary Harold Ickes noted in his private diary that "WPA is more than ever on the verge of an open scandal in so many places I wonder whether suppression will work in the long run." Congress later acted to remove WPA from the political arena, but only after two official investigations and reams of negative newspaper copy.

Much more serious than FDR's reluctance to police such favoritism was his habit of unleashing the tax hounds of the Internal Revenue Service on his enemies, an abuse he apparently considered quietly amusing. The most famous and troublesome target of such retaliation was the "Kingfish," the rabble-rousing Louisiana senator Huey Long. The virtual emperor of the Bayou State and a crowd-igniting demagogue, Long for a time posed a bigger threat to Roosevelt's reelection than any other politician in America. Huey's biggest problem was that he suffered from "halitosis of the intellect," quipped the sardonic Ickes, who detested Long's low-brow appeal.

Irritated that FDR had dared to bestow patronage on his opponents back home, the energetic agitator declared war on the administration and "Prince Franklin." Long took Roosevelt's governmental helping hand several steps further; he began a national "Share Our Wealth" movement, which proposed free homesteads and education, cheaper food and a guaranteed annual income. When Huey's noisy one-upmanship, and the opposition of nay-sayers such as Father Charles Coughlin, finally began to rankle FDR, he set federal tax men after the Kingfish. No less than fifty IRS bloodhounds were assigned to dig into Long's Louisiana fiefdom. Badly stung, Long struck back with accusations against Postmaster General James Farley, blasting the cabinet officer for allegedly giving out free stamps to friends and blocking an official investigation of another matter.

Only the Kingfish's assassination in September 1935 averted further malicious cross-fire beween the two heavyweight antagonists. Even after Long's untimely death, FDR showed himself to be a merciless adversary. He stepped up the IRS heat on the Lousiana political machine and Long's would-be successor, Gerald L.K. Smith, until the bosses caved in and pledged to stop thwarting the White House. "The Second Louisiana Purchase" was how columnist Westbrook Pegler contemptuously described this secret political surrender.

Long wasn't the only Roosevelt opponent to feel the hot breath of the IRS probers. Press baron William Randolph Hearst got under Roosevelt's skin with his media empire's incessant attacks on the president's programs, which he called "The Raw Deal." Hearst was declared *persona non grata* at the White House, and FDR finally decided to give the owner of San Simeon a little taste of presidential wrath. Tax agents were ordered to explore every nook and cranny of the vast Hearst financial holdings. Ickes, always the curmudgeon, had an even better idea—since the newspaper magnate lived on borrowed money to a large extent, why not pressure the California banks into calling in all of Hearst's loans? But FDR wisely stopped short of such a gross abuse of presidential power. Nothing particularly noteworthy was turned up against Hearst, much to the disgust of the White House inner circle, but Roosevelt had better luck with a third target, *Philadelphia Bulletin* publisher Moe Annenberg, another bitter critic. A close scrutiny of Annenberg's tax returns eventually landed the publisher in prison.

Near the end of his first term, Roosevelt's four-year campaign to revolutionize the government made him the national hero to millions of suffering Depression victims, but public enemy number one in the corporate boardrooms of Wall Street. To block further tinkering with the economy, a "whispering campaign" against the president and his family was started in 1935, producing ugly and fantastic tales about the first family. FDR was insane or senile, according to the milder stories which made the rounds in those days before television and instantaneous communications could immediately disparage such obvious lies.

The Lucy Mercer saga was dredged up and phony details were added out of whole cloth. Roosevelt's integrity was maliciously attacked; columnist Drew Pearson reported that high on the list of smears were charges that FDR was paying the rent for his Hyde Park estate in New York out of taxpayer funds. Down in the gutter, the most bileful haters spread false rumors that the president was impotent and sexually frustrated, due to his physical condition.

Eleanor, whose boundless energy and obvious sympathy for the plight of the poor and underprivileged won her countless friends, wasn't immune from critical blasts, either. Her fame had enabled her to earn a considerable outside income from the publication of magazine articles, a popular newspaper column called "My Day," lectures and radio broadcasts. One commentator, decidedly not an Eleanor fan, calculated that she made as much as three million dollars during her reign as first lady.

Fortunately for the well-loved Mrs. Roosevelt, the intimate

details of a possibly explosive sex scandal didn't surface until after her death decades later. Only those who knew the first lady personally could have suspected what her voluminous private correspondence revealed; that her long and loving relationship with journalist and administration aide Lenora Hickok could have been much more than a close friendship.

A South Dakota servant girl turned reporter, Lenora, or "Hick," as Eleanor fondly nicknamed her, met the First Lady while serving as part of the White House press entourage at the start of FDR's first term. Hick, who described herself as "square and stodgy," immediately became fast friends with the woman called "ER." Although Eleanor was nine years older, the two had similar outlooks. Both women considered themselves shy, and both had a passionate commitment to social change. Finding in Hick the soulmate she had always hungered for, Eleanor poured out her innermost thoughts and desires to her female companion in a way she had never dared with her emotionally distant husband.

To the understanding Hick, the first lady could unburden herself of her bitterness over FDR's affair with Lucy Mercer, which was still troubling her after fifteen years (probably because there was no one else to whom she could have talked about it before). She also confided her guilt over family divorces. "I don't seem to be able to shake the feeling of responsibility" for the marital problems of her children, she wrote. During the first term, Hick became a fixture in the White House, traveling and vacationing with Eleanor and other women and eventually giving up her promising reporting career to work for Harry Hopkins as a special field investigator for the scandal-plagued WPA.

Later, when Hick left the administration, her devoted companion wrote her daily—the FDR Library at Hyde Park contains more than two thousand letters from Eleanor to Lenora, and hundreds more weren't saved. Hick was almost as faithful a correspondent, and marked on her personal calendar every meeting with her beloved ER, recording whether or not it was a happy, uninterrupted visit. The tone of Eleanor's endearments raise questions about the real nature of the bond between the two famous women.

For instance, on Lenora's fortieth birthday, ER wrote,

"Hick, darling, all day I've thought of you & another birthday
I *will* be with you...Oh! I want to put my arms around you, I
ache to hold you close." On another occasion, when the couple had a jealous spat, Eleanor wrote plaintively, "I couldn't
bear to think of you crying yourself to sleep. Oh! How I
wanted to put my arms around you in reality instead of spirit.
I went and kissed your photograph instead..."

It must be remembered that these were the outpourings of
a lonely woman who craved the kind of intimacy that her
relationship with Lenora Hickok afforded. No observer ever
dared publicly suggest a sexual liaison while Eleanor lived in
the White House, but there was gossip about some of Mrs.
Roosevelt's supposedly "queer" friends. In August 1940, it
was reported that Eleanor kept her own cottage, called Val-
Kill, at Hyde Park, where she could be independent of her
domineering mother-in-law and receive her female friends, a
practice which stirred up more than a little idle speculation
about Mrs. Roosevelt's lifestyle and her strained relationship
with the president.

But, as Kansas governor Al Landon learned to his chagrin,
it took more than innuendo to stop the Roosevelt political
juggernaut. Alf managed to carry only Maine and Vermont as
FDR steamrolled the Republicans and swept into a second
term in 1936. His overwhelming victory (the electoral vote
was 523 to 8) was a sign to Roosevelt that he had the mandate
for additional New Deal programs. Unfortunately, the Supreme Court didn't see things FDR's way. His far-reaching
economic and societal projects recieved a series of devastating setbacks as the Court declared major pieces of New Deal
legislation unconstitutional, bringing the agencies which
funded them to a virtual halt.

The president was beside himself. He'd beaten the Republicans, Congress and Huey Long, and he wasn't going to be
stymied now by what he regarded as the asinine opinions of
a few reactionaries on the federal bench. As usual, he had a
closely held scheme up his sleeve to remedy the situation.
Thus the infamous "court packing" plan was born. In a January 1937 message to Congress, Roosevelt made perhaps the
boldest of all his extraordinary proposals; for every justice
who failed to retire within six months of age seventy, he

would be empowered to appoint another justice to a total of six, thus bringing the possible number of Supreme Court benchwarmers to fifteen. To his dumbfounded listerners, this seemed like an over-heated, spur-of-the-moment reaction to the Court's opposition to his programs, but in reality, he'd been brainstorming such a judicial coup in utmost secrecy for two years.

The court packing gambit was FDR's Waterloo, however, a one-man crusade doomed to failure by an unholy alliance of aghast conservatives and fearful liberals. The politically swashbuckling chief executive took a well-deserved licking for his brazen attempt to turn the Court's ideology towards his personal preferences, but not before the plan became the focus of a national controversy.

In fact, FDR should have stayed out of the judicial ballgame altogether in 1937. He almost got his fingers burned when he nominated Alabama Senator Hugo Black to the Supreme Court. To begin with, not even FDR thought Black was an outstanding jurist, and he privately confided as much to cabinet members. Black got the nod because he was relatively liberal, and if the president couldn't pack 'em in one way, then he'd try another.

What he didn't anticipate was the ruckus which would be raised when a Pittsburgh newspaper broke the story that Black had once been an active member of the Ku Klux Klan, the white-robed, night-riding racists who haunted the South. This unexpected revelation didn't do much for the reputation of a president who was supposed to be the champion of oppressed minorities. Nor did Black help his own cause when he declined comment on his alleged Klan past until after his confirmation. Afterwards, he took to the radio airwaves to admit that he'd been a sheet-wearer in his youth, but that it had been a tragic error. By then it was too late to derail the nomination, but the White House talent scouts who picked Black for the high court had egg on their faces.

The public brouhaha over Roosevelt's determination to bend the judiciary to his will cloaked a much more important series of actions which were to dominate the rest of this presidency, preparations for an "undeclared war," which occupied many of Roosevelt's waking hours during the latter stages of his second term. Even the most deferential reading of the president's actions demonstrated that he was less than candid about his true intentions concerning the growing world war in Europe. Under intense isolationist pressure and anti-war opinion in the United States, FDR pledged as late as September 1939 that "this nation will remain a neutral nation." At the same time, however, Roosevelt was making secret plans for a war he knew would ultimately involve the U.S. In June 1940, FDR and his cabinet made an historic and secret decision to depart from the "cash and carry" supply of weapons to the Western allies. Drastic new commitments of military equipment and supplies were made to these hard-pressed forces, but Roosevelt and his top advisers hedged repeatedly about those decisions during the campaign months of 1940. Later the president by-passed Congress to complete base transfers with the beleaguered British, covert arrangements about which he refused to comment in the press. Roosevelt was saying neutrality but thinking preparation, and quietly putting the nation on a war footing while cleverly holding the powerful isolationists at bay.

War was by no means the only topic on the Roosevelt agenda in 1940, though. Wendell Willkie stood between FDR and an unprecedented third term, and the Republican nominee from the heartland state of Indiana was very much a threat to Roosevelt, much more so than the hapless Landon had been. Secret tapes, recorded in the Oval Office during an eleven-week period in 1940, reveal FDR at his worst; a leader willing to spread scurrilous, sexual rumors about his opponent.

The White House tapes, the first of their kind, were made because Roosevelt was upset by what he considered inaccurate reports emanating from defense-related talks with congressmen inside his office in early 1939. After one particularly galling attack from isolationist senators displeased with presidential policy, FDR ordered White House stenographer Henry Kannee to find a method that would ensure accurate transcripts of such gatherings. The solution was provided by the RCA corporation's General David Sarnoff, who designed an elaborate recording machine to be installed in a concealed, padlocked space in the White House basement.

The covert recordings, made during the summer and fall of 1940, and recovered decades later by Professor R.T.C. Butow and Marc Weiss, showed Roosevelt at his most expansive and dramatic, holding forth on the increasing dangers of the European war and the Japanese threat in the Pacific. More interestingly, however, the transcripts bare FDR's willingness to descend to the gutter level of politics. The campaign that year was an especially difficult one for the Democrats, and by August, the president and his strategists were worried about Willkie, particularly since rumors had circulated that the GOP had obtained embarrassing information to use against the Roosevelt ticket.

FDR's running mate was the brilliant, controversial agriculture secretary, Henry Wallace. He had replaced the dour John Nance Garner, who during his four-year tenure as vice president had proven to be a nettlesome thorn in the president's side; the former Texas congressman had opposed virtually every major Roosevelt initiative. While Wallace was much more sympathetic to Rooseveltian goals, he was a poor campaigner; the progressive vice presidential nominee also had many detractors, including influential members of his own party. Worse still, someone had passed along to the Republicans letters he had once written to Nicholas Roerich, a White Russian mystic; the missives were addressed "Dear Guru," and were bound to prove humiliating to the Democrats.

Roosevelt's tapes showed that he intended to play his own brand of hardball to ensure that the Wallace letters remained suppressed. It was no secret to political insiders that Willkie, long separated from his wife, had a mistress in New York— this was the Achilles heel that the Democrats would expose and attack. "We can spread it as a word-of-mouth thing, or by some people way, way down the line...I mean Congress speakers, and state speakers and so forth. They can use the raw materials. Now, now if they want to play dirty politics in the end, we've got our own people...," said FDR on the White House tapes.

"Awful nice gal," continued the president, referring to Willkie's girlfriend. Roosevelt rambled on about how the former New York city mayor, the colorful Jimmy Walker, had once kept a mistress near the Roosevelt residence, and how Walker, a Catholic, had the audacity to "hire" his wife, from whom he had been separated, for $10,000, to live with him for a short time in Albany for political appearances.

Drawing a parallel between jaunty Jimmy and Willkie, Roosevelt observed, "Mrs. Willkie may not have been hired, but in effect she's been hired to return to Wendell and smile and make this campaign with him," confided FDR to aides. "Now, whether there was a money price behind it, I don't know, but it's the same idea," hinted the chief executive. Considering the sorry state of his own marriage, this kind of presidential plotting smacked of hypocrisy.

"What FDR did to Willkie made Watergate look like a tea party," claimed Sam Pryor, an octogenarian former political operative who forty years earlier had packed the galleys for Willkie at the 1940 Republican convention. Neither the Willkie gossip nor the Wallace letters were publicly used by the campaign combatants, perhaps because the unspoken threat from both sides got through to the right people.

The presidential spying didn't stop with a few locker room stories. At FDR's bidding, FBI agents monitored the telephone calls and movements of some of his isolationist critics in Congress and the press. *Washington Times-Herald* publisher Eleanor ("Cissy") Patterson and her chief editor, Frank Waldrop, both opponents of FDR's foreign policies, were bugged in this campaign.

Even after the Oval Office tape machines were turned off in late 1940, FDR continued to track suspected opponents and leakers with the use of intelligence agents, whom he recruited as presidential spies. Donald Nelson, who headed the War Production Board, was tailed constantly by FBI bloodhounds, according to the private admission of a top bureau official who is now deceased. Not that Nelson's patriotism was considered suspect—rather FDR found his lovelife fascinating and titillated himself with the reports of Nelson's amoristic conquests. Well into the war years, ranking intelligence officials watched their words at Oval office meetings, fearing that what they confided to the chief executive was noted by unseen stenographers or hidden electronic devices.

The sedentary president's secret information network

wasn't discovered for decades afterwards. He turned back the Willkie challenge and became the first president to win the highest office three times. Doubtful about his prospects for surviving the strain of another four years, he nevertheless pressed on with preparations for a war that he knew would soon involve America's soldiers as well as her weapons.

Secrecy surrounding the buildup led to the biggest unanswered question of the Roosevelt years—what did FDR know in advance about Japan's intentions to attack Pearl Harbor, and when did he know it? Historians and military experts have since argued about Roosevelt's role in leading the U. S. into World War II, with widely divergent conclusions. One fact seems inescapable; it seems almost inconceivable that FDR knew well in advance exactly when and where the Japanese would strike, or that he would deliberately sacrifice the Pacific Fleet and the lives of 2,400 men to force American participation in the war.

Nevertheless, Roosevelt's critics have suggested he knowingly helped invite a Japanese attack by imposing diplomatic and economic sanctions against Tokyo in 1940, including trade embargoes and aid to China. Furthermore, Japan's own diplomatic cables of November 1941, which U. S. intelligence intercepted, strongly suggested that retaliation would soon be forthcoming, assessments which caused Secretary of State Cordell Hull to warn a closed-door cabinet meeting on November 25 of a possible imminent military assault.

Most damning of all are allegations by naval officers serving in Hawaii at the time of the Pearl Harbor raid that FDR and the high command in Washington conspired to withhold vital military intelligence from subordinates just prior to the bombing. The interception and decoding of certain "hidden word" cables, in the Japanese "Purple" code, tipped off the American intelligence hierarchy that an attack was probable within a short period of time, and the Pacific Fleet was the probable target.

In response to coded messages, called "Magic," the Pentagon put the armed forces on a "war warning" footing on November 27, 1941, but the Hawaiian commanding officer, the highly regarded Admiral Husband ("Hubby") Kimmel, didn't view the order he received as unusual or an emergency directive. That apparent misunderstanding later led Kimmel and his immediate subordinate, Lt. General Walter Short, to be convicted of being derelict to their duty. Kimmel's counter-charges, that he hadn't been properly warned, triggered no less than eight official probes into the scenario preceding Pearl Harbor.

Whether critical information had been withheld or not, the "Day of Infamy" strike took Roosevelt off the hot seat. Instead of being accused of waging a "president's war," he had the almost unanimous support of an outraged public and Congress, which previously had opposed American entry into the conflict.

FDR's inner feelings that he might not survive his third term were wrong, but not by much. The combination of the war's incredible stress, together with his failing health, made him a fading chief executive, a physical shadow of the crippled but vital man who assumed office in 1933. That fact was largely concealed from an admiring public.

By late 1943, Roosevelt showed definite signs of chronic decline. After an attack of influenza, he recovered slowly and was plagued with fever, fatigue and a cough, nothing new for him but disturbing because he didn't recover quickly and remained under crushing stress. Over the next few months, presidential physicians diagnosed hypertension and related heart disease previously unsuspected. Complete bedrest and intensive medical therapy was what was needed, but the pressures of the highest office precluded the regimen of inactivity almost any other patient would have adopted.

In the months before the 1944 campaign, presidential doctor Ross McIntire insisted that his charge was "in spendid shape"; but although it was accurate that FDR had rallied from his low point the previous spring, commentator Walter Lippman struck closer to the truth when he later wrote that "the state of Mr. Roosevelt's health was a secret from millions of Americans" who needed the reassurance of his voice and commanding leadership. In a day when presidential candidates make their medical records public, it may be hard to believe, but Roosevelt's fourth presidential challenger, Thomas Dewey, made barely a peep about his opponent's declining condition in 1944.

Nor were armed conflict and mortality the only strains tugging at Roosevelt's weakening heart through the war years. Now almost totally estranged from Eleanor, who stayed away for long periods with female friends Nancy Cook and Marion Dickerman (and who frayed his nerves by arguing with him when she was around), FDR's thoughts turned back to the romance of his life. The elderly Winthrop Rutherfurd had died, leaving an older but still beautiful Lucy a suddenly available widow. Despite his promises of a quarter-century ago, he saw Lucy frequently.

In addition, he sought the companionship of other women. Crown Princess Martha of Norway had also caught FDR's roving, flirtatious eye, and during the war years she spent a good deal of time in the company of an admiring president. The obvious fondness between the two caused whispers about FDR's "royal affair," often at Eleanor's expense.

The end of the European war, perhaps not coincidentally, spelled the end for a president who'd lived with its constant nightmares for almost eight years. The conference at Yalta with Great Britain's Winston Churchill and the Soviet Union's brutal Josef Stalin, to decide the future of Europe, should have been a crowning political triumph. Instead, it was a wearing ordeal which the exhausted Roosevelt could barely tolerate.

Bone-weary and intent on avoiding any ugly scene with Eleanor, the president took his daughter Anna along so that he wouldn't have to include the first lady in the official traveling party. Mrs. Roosevelt concealed her disappointment at being snubbed for the historic journey, but years later, in private correspondence, Anna admitted that she was "pretty sure" her mother had been hurt at being left out. "I desperately wanted to go," Anna Roosevelt Halstead confessed, acknowledging that the fulfillment of her desire had meant further frustration for a mother who'd suffered through twenty-five years of personal slights.

Other top officials at the Yalta summit noticed the wan president's uncharacteristic lethargy and irritability, including the wily, implacable Stalin, who won concessions from the Allied leaders which he might not have gained if FDR hadn't been practically at death's door.

Knowledgable political observers didn't have to ask the

unspoken significance of Vice President Harry S. Truman's receiving round-the-clock Secret Service protection weeks later in March 1945, by which time insiders feared that Roosevelt wouldn't last more than a few weeks.

Incredibly, his almost indomitable spirit rallied briefly once again, upon returning to his beloved Warm Springs estate. But on April 12, 1945, in the company of a cousin and a portrait artist, the president clasped his hand to his head, muttered, "I have a terrific headache," and collapsed into a coma. Not until much later was it revealed that the long-loved Lucy Mercer had been with the dying chief executive, but had wisely departed before the anxious Eleanor could be rushed to the deathbed scene. The curtain had fallen on a unique, one-man era in American politics.

Chapter 8

TAKING HELL HARRY
Harry S. Truman

April 1945—January 1953

"Harry, the President is dead." With that simple declaration, Eleanor Roosevelt opened the Truman era, eight years of Cold War confrontation, communist-baiting hysteria and high-level corruption unmatched since Harding's disastrous tenure. Surrounded by Secret Service agents twenty-four hours a day for six weeks before FDR's sudden end in Warm Springs, Vice President Truman had suspected that his moment of truth might be forthcoming. Even during the 1944 campaign he had feared for Roosevelt's fragile health, and had been shocked to witness how close the sinking president was to death. Once during that fateful time, on leaving the White House, a friend told Truman to look back at the executive mansion. "That's where you're going to be living," he prophetically told the then-Missouri senator. "I'm afraid you're right," Truman had replied, "and it scares the hell out of me."

In contrast to the decisive "Give 'Em Hell Harry" image he would acquire later, Truman got off to a floundering start. The new chief executive told his cabinet that he saw himself as a chairman of the board who would be a majority of one and have the final vote on everything, but his lackluster choice of subordinates gave the first telling indication that his administration would be a "government by crony."

FDR had skimmed off the cream of the generation's intellects and placed them in creative competition with each other. Truman, a moderate conservative, disliked the New Dealers, considering them pointy-headed know-it-alls who tried to foist off unworkable, radical ideas on the American public. Being the product of an old-line political machine, he felt more at ease with the second-rate minds of hacks and ward heelers from his own social strata. Like Harding's thieving "Ohio Gang," Harry's "Missouri Gang" was an undistinguished collection of yes-men who saw Washington as a once-in-a-lifetime opportunity to make contacts and enrich themselves beyond their wildest dreams. As journalist I. F. ("Izzy") Stone wrote, "the New Dealers were replaced by the kind of men you met at county courthouses—big bellied, good-natured boys who spent as little time in their offices as possible. The Truman years became the 'era of the moocher'."

The decline of brainpower and integrity in the new administration was soon almost palpable, and it could be sensed not only in the bowels of the bureaucracy, but right at the top. Chief among Truman's inner circle of court jesters was a military officer named Harry Vaughan. He and the president had become fast friends while serving together in the Missouri National Guard. A jack-of-no-trades, Vaughan had spent the past ten years in a series of odd jobs, including tea salesman. Truman brought his blustering friend to Washington as an office aide in 1940, and when he became vice president, gave Vaughan the pretentious title of military aide, a curious post with vaguely defined responsibilities. When his buddy moved into the Oval Office, Vaughan became coordinator of Veterans Affairs, probably the least qualified person to hold such a position since Charley Forbes stole the military hospitals blind during Harding's term.

The blundering Vaughan soon became the standing joke of the administration. His frequent, shoot-from-the-hip oratories were a constant embarrassment; press secretary Charles Ross would just shrug his shoulders and say "Cherchez le Vaughan" (Look for Vaughan) when the general's oafish pranks gave the White House a black eye. He proved to be even more dangerous when operating behind the scenes. From his White House command post, General Vaughan started wheeling and dealing like Harry Daugherty had done twenty-five years before. Soon the word was out among the lobbyists and "five-percenters," who made their livings skimming off the cream of huge government contracts—Vaughan was the man to see for the favors.

He tried hard to live up to the flattering, word-of-mouth recommendations. A former Kansas City bootblack named Johnny Maragon, who one observer described as looking like a Prohibition gangster, got on a VIP travel list with Vaughan's assistance, so that he could set up an overseas business for a Chicago perfume manufacturer. Never one to turn down a friend's request, Vaughan also procured a job for Maragon in the American mission in Greece, so that he could collect two paychecks; one from his cologne cronies and one from Uncle Sam.

That was just the beginning of Vaughan's legal but ill-advised largesse. Another buddy of his, named Colonel J. V. Hunt (a five-percenter whose private diary showed he had been a White House guest no less than eighteen times in two years), paired up with Maragon to secure $150,000 worth of building materials in the scarce post-war housing market. When a federal housing expediter refused to play ball with the boys, they had Vaughan replace the meddling bureaucrat and quickly got their allocation permit. The nefarious duo also did some profitable favors for a molasses magnate who had trouble with government overseers. A few thousand dollars to the mysterious Maragon and the red tape miraculously disappeared, no questions asked.

To top it off, Vaughan, whose own political opinions could be described as reactionary, kicked up a minor storm by accepting a medal from Argentine dictator Juan Peron. None of this bothered his presidential patron. For daring to criticize Vaughan for implicitly conferring White House legitimacy on Peron's repressive regime, columnist Drew Pearson was labeled a "son of a bitch" by Truman, who added, "any S.O.B. who thinks he can cause any of these people to be discharged by making some smart-alecking remark over the air or in the paper, he has another thing coming." General Fix-it, in other words, had carte blanche from his poker buddy in the Oval Office.

The back-slapping chief executive might have had second

thoughts after Vaughan committed an embarrassing *faux pas* which would haunt the Truman administration. Up to this point, Vaughan's sole redeeming characteristic was his loyalty to his benefactor; reporters often joked about his favorite phrase, invariably uttered as he emerged from a private meeting with the president—"I'm still with ya, Chief." Political IOU's were the coin of Vaughan's transactions, later to be exchanged for generous contributions to the Democratic party.

On one occasion, though, Vaughan took one of the proffered gifts for himself, a new-fangled "deep freezer." Moreover, he arranged to have a half-dozen others delivered to the homes of administration officials, including one to First Lady Bess Truman in Missouri. The resulting uproar was deafening, especially when the press learned that the first family had accepted such an expensive gift from a lobbyist, David Bennett, who had entertained Truman and Vaughan aboard his sumptuous yacht.

Subsequent congressional hearings produced a plethora of humiliating headlines and Vaughan offered his resignation, but Truman, never more stubborn than when his personal loyalties were challenged, refused. "Harry," said the president, putting his arm around the sinning Vaughan's shoulders, "they're just trying to use you to embarrass me. You go up there [to Capitol Hill] and tell 'em to go to hell. We came in here together and Goddamn it, we're going out together."

Indeed, such unswerving loyalty was a hallmark of the Truman character. Never forget a friend or forgive an enemy—that was a Truman credo set in stone. He never forgave federal prosecutors for going after his Missouri benefactor, Thomas Pendergast. One of the first things he did after becoming president was to fire United States Attorney Maurice Mulligan, who had jailed the political boss for financial improprieties. Later, he refused to appoint Frank Murphy as chief justice of the Supreme Court, some said, because Murphy had been attorney general when Pendergast was indicted. Boss Pendergast was still his mentor, jailbird or not, and when the old man died, Truman thumbed his nose at the critics and went to the funeral, despite pleas from aides that he would be vilified in the newspapers. "He was used by people in an effort to discredit me," wrote the unrepentant president, who insisted that Pendergast's physical breakdown in 1936 had contributed to scrapes with the law.

Truman's unshakable faith in long-time friends and supporters seemed to influence his judgment in 1946, when he nominated California oilman and party fundraiser Edwin Pauley to the post of undersecretary of the navy. His name raised the conservation bugaboo that had haunted the Washington bureaucracy for forty years. The well-connected Pauley had lobbied hard and long against federal control of the oil tidelands, a subject dear to the heart of one of the greatest of Roosevelt's holdover braintrusters, Interior Secretary Harold Ickes. A zealous defender of conservation policies, Ickes didn't intend to let the seeds of any more Teapot Domes be planted while he was still breathing. The old curmudgeon gave the president a blunt warning—Pauley or me. To ensure that it registered, he went to friends in Congress to block Pauley, and publicly blasted the influential businessman for attempting to thwart his department's policies on the tidelands. Just as stubbornly, Truman, who was tired of Ickes' incessant complaining, chose Pauley and accepted the interior secretary's resignation. As usual, Harry had underestimated the opposition. Ickes' forced departure raised howls of protest on Capitol Hill and after much ado, Truman was forced to back off and withdraw Pauley's nomination, leaving him without an interior secretary or a naval undersecretary.

He didn't pick up the pieces of that fiasco too carefully, either. His good idea to get the distinguished liberal conservationist Senator William O. Douglas to replace the departed Ickes fell apart when Douglas wisely turned down the offer. Instead, Truman chose Julius ("Cap") Krug, a 260-pound man whose appetite for food, booze and lovely females matched his outsized girth. Reputed to be a capable engineer and generally well regarded when he came into office, Krug was less successful as a politician and administrator. He spent much of his time tasting the favors of the capital's generous lobbyists, and accepting invitations to fashionable soirees hosted by the likes of billionaire industrialist and film-maker Howard Hughes, where women and good liquor were in plentiful supply.

Newspapers reported him as involved in a $750,000 lawsuit, and Krug's name was discovered on the expense account of a lobbyist; he became a favorite target of Truman nemesis Drew Pearson, and his "Washington Merry-Go-Round" column. By 1948, after some particularly inept election-year politicking, Krug didn't pick up on an unsubtle hint to pack his bags. Truman was more blunt in a nasty letter berating the interior secretary on a minor matter, and practically invited him to leave.

Still, the antics of General Vaughan and Krug, and the flap over the Pauley appointment were small potatoes compared to what followed. At a time when Truman was publicly denouncing wide-spread speculation on the commodities markets, his personal physician, Dr. Wallace Graham, and the rejected Pauley (who had been shuffled over to the Department of the Army as a special aide) were implicated as profiteers in grain gambling. Pauley, who made almost a million dollars from his high-rolling, resigned his Pentagon post after a congressional inquiry into the speculations, which revealed that scores of federal employees had been playing at the same high-stakes game. Particularly galling to Truman was the fact that Graham initially claimed to have sold his holdings when the news broke in October 1947. Only under congressional scrutiny was it revealed that he had secretly retained his investment for an additional two months and reaped an extra profit bonanza.

The fun was just beginning. The next scam bagged a whole list of Truman intimates and hangers-on. RFC was the abbreviation for the Reconstruction Finance Corporation, but during the Truman years the acronym could more accurately have stood for "Really Full of Cash." Started under Hoover to bail out bankrupt firms during the Depression, and continued through the war years to stockpile scarce defense materials, the RFC had degenerated into a grabbag of speculation money for shaky ventures that private banks wouldn't touch. Truman's lieutenants turned the agency into a circus of shady deals and quickie loans. Knowledge of the pilfering became so wide-spread that a year-long congressional probe was initiated under Arkansas Senator William Fulbright.

Its progress was poky, but the committee's final report

raised official eyebrows. Foremost among the allegations was that Truman's patronage chief, personnel executive Donald Dawson, was lording it over RFC's appointed bosses, who owed their jobs to him. Dawson had been using the agency's resources for political purposes, dishing out loans to the Democratic National Committee and generally doing whatever struck his fancy. Investigators found that the RFC had become a dumping ground for political hacks. Bristling as always at the suggestion that one of his close aides might be involved in wrongdoing, Truman denounced the Fulbright report as "asinine." Fulbright countered by calling for public hearings and requiring Dawson's appearance before his committee. Stulbbornlly claiming executive privilege, Truman refused to allow Dawson to testify, but the reaction was loud and long, and the president was forced to allow his aide to face the music on Capitol Hill.

The tune that Dawson played before the Fulbright Committee was more sensational and damning to the administration than the original congressional findings. Under oath, Dawson admitted a host of abuses which implicated a handful of influential Missourians who had found a lucrative home at the mismanaged RFC. Examiner E. Merl Young had helped put through a $12,000 loan to the Lustron Corporation and then had the audacity to leave his job and go work for the company the day after the insider loan was approved. As a reward, he was also given a job working for Truman's 1948 reelection at the Democratic National Committee. Two paychecks evidently weren't enough for the hustling Young. Grateful Democrats saw to it that he got on the payroll of other companies which owed debts or outstanding loans to the RFC. The politicos also kept Young's wife happy by bestowing on her an $8,500 royal mink coat.

Former Truman secretary and paid confidante William Boyle, another active Democratic lawyer and powerbroker, was implicated in the RFC shenanigans as part of the Dawson cabal. To avoid a conspicuous conflict of interest, he had supposedly given up his law practice after returning to the White House payroll, but investigators discovered that Boyle had been using his executive connections to pad his client list. The tip-off came when Boyle rashly took a retainer of $8,000 to successfully push for an RFC loan for a St. Louis company which previously had been rejected by officials not in on the influence-peddling scheme. Characteristically, Harry backed his friend Boyle to the hilt, but the backlash was vicious, and the sinning Boyle was finally forced to resign "for reasons of health."

None of the sordid dramas of the Truman years were nearly as long-lasting or far-reaching as the decade of political and legal turmoil over the Teapot Dome, but in its shocking level of corruption and coverups, one scandal was reminiscent of the years-long flap over the naval oil reserves—the Internal Revenue Service debacle of 1950-1952.

Before it was over, top officials at the White House, the Department of Justice and the IRS had been fired and indicted for fixing tax cases and then obstructing investigations into executive malfeasance. The old saw that the only two things certain in life are death and taxes was temporarily suspended during the Truman years, at least in the case of the latter. An unusual nusmber of fraud cases were quashed when Harry Truman lived in the White House. Fixing tax hassles for big corporations and the well-heeled was nothing new in Washington; tax cheats had been bailed out during the Roosevelt administration and before. Truman's acolytes at the IRS and the Justice Department took the time honored practice to new lows. Tax dodging became as favorite a pastime as communist baiting during the early Fifties.

During Truman's second term, the revelations of these crimes and their coverup acquired a soap opera quality. They provided a daily melodrama at which onlookers could hardly wait to learn who would be fired, jailed or subpoenaed next. Big firms such as Midwest Petroleum and Guaranty Finance of Los Angeles successfully evaded tax bills, and IRS executives were seen fraternizing with highly dubious characters, including Mafia chieftain Frank Costello. Because tax cases came under the control of the Bureau of Internal Revenue of the Treasury Department and were prosecuted by the Justice Department, there were several stages at which a tax case could be sidetracked; by an IRS agent; his superior at the bureau; or by a politically ambitious U.S. attorney who might be willing to look the other way in return for a future favor or promotion.

Republican Senator John Williams of Delaware, a crusading veteran of congressional investigations, learned that all of the above methods had been used to subvert impartial enforcement of the tax laws. Closer scrutiny of the grossly misman-aged agency showed that the bureau was collecting taxes at a rate several times above the pre-war level despite being ham-pered by understaffing, antiquated systems and top officials with sensitive political ties. Williams documented a number of irregularities in the handling of the cases, but Attorney General J. Howard ("Mr. Bones") McGrath, a wily Irishman, and Treasury Secretary John Snyder, a former bank official from St. Louis, rushed to Capitol Hill to assure the doubting senator that all was well inside their fiefdoms.

Their testimony was highly suspect, as further congres-sional inquiries would soon reveal. Scores of federal tax col-lectors were caught with their hands in the till. In 1951 alone, no fewer than 166 employees of the Bureau of Internal Reve-nue resigned under fire, and nine of the sixty-four district directors were removed. One of the collectors, James Fin-negan of St. Louis, a crony of Truman and Snyder, had already been implicated in the RFC mess. He resigned after being accused of failing to act on tax fraud allegations referred to his office and was later indicted, convicted, and imprisoned for eighteen months for bribery.

As the scandal unfolded over a period of months, the cor-ruption was pursued to the highest levels and resulted in an impromptu housecleaning of unprecedented proportions. Commissioner of Internal Revenue George Schoeneman, while not personally implicated, resigned for "reasons of health." A few months later, Chief Counsel Charles Oliphant quit under a cloud of suspicion when his name was linked to a government shakedown operation related to the tax fraud ring. Schoeneman's predecessor, Joseph Nunan, was indicted and convicted for failing to report large amounts of income, and Assistant Commissioner Daniel Bolich got the same for pocketing $200,000 without telling the tax man.

Worst of all for the president, the conspiracy trail led right into the White House, tainting presidential appointments secretary Matthew Connelly. Truman had added the much younger Connelly to his staff years before, and he had followed him into the executive mansion, just as Vaughan had done. Of course, given General Vaughan's antics, it shouldn't have come as a complete surprise when Connelly embarrassed his long-time benefactor. He unsuccessfully tried to flex his political muscle in the tax case of administration friend Irving Sachs of St. Louis. For his trouble, Connelly was rewarded not with a deep freezer, but suits, a topcoat and oil royalties. He wasn't shy, either, about accepting the gifts right in the middle of the congressional probes in 1951 and 1952. Connelly was later indicted with co-conspirators inside the administration and spent a short time in prison.

Like the oil money of Teapot Dome, the stain of the tax coverup reached far and wide. A former assistant attorney general in charge of the controversial tax division, with the unlikely name of T. Lamar Caudle, was fired for his role in deliberately fumbling a tax prosecution (a congressional report later suggested that Caudle was personally honest, but naive.) Caudle, it was subsequently revealed, had been the subject of an FBI probe before being promoted to the tax job. It wasn't coincidental that he had gotten the justice plum after handling a politically-sensitive investigation of certain voting irregularities in Truman's home town of Kansas City, an inquiry which came out in favor of the president's men, despite what was reported to be a heap of evidence to the contrary.

Meanwhile, the savvy McGrath and his minions at the Justice Department were throwing everything but the kitchen sink in the way of congressional investigators. Under pressure to get to the bottom of obstructions of justice, Truman appointed a special prosecutor named Newbold Morris, but McGrath airily treated the newcomer like a subordinate, and finally fired him when he became too meddlesome. Morris' dismissal made Truman read the political writing on the wall and he finally gave McGrath his own walking papers and after dawdling for months, a delay which cost the Democrats dearly in the 1952 elections. The GOP made hay at the Justice Department's expense and cited that "Washington mess" in campaign slogans, a ploy which paid off at the polls.

With the RFC and IRS Justice Department scandals hanging

around his neck, Truman was conducting a United States "police action" in Korea, a skirmish which threatened to break out into another global conflict if one false move was made. Foremost among the president's Korean headaches was the insubordinate officer in charge, the jaw-jutting, pipe-smoking scourge of the Orient, General Douglas MacArthur. Far away from U.S. shores for over fifteen years, MacArthur remained every bit as headstrong as he had been in 1932, when he had defied another president's wishes and stampeded hapless protesting veterans a short distance from Herbert Hoover's White House.

This time the stakes were much higher. As a senator, Truman hadn't liked the pompous, egotistical MacArthur, and critical comments about the self-serving general were withheld from the Truman committee war report against his wishes. Yet the president, despite the bellicose reputation he'd so carefully cultivated, tip-toed carefully around the military's living legend. The hero of the Philippines had repeated his headline-grabbing exploits in September 1950 by counter-attacking behind North Korean lines and landing at Inchon, and was a more popular figure than his commander-in-chief, who not long before had achieved the dubious distinction of having the lowest public rating of any president of the century.

As the American military successes mounted during the initial stages of the Korean conflict, MacArthur pressured the Joint Chiefs back in Washington to allow him to push onward through North Korea and into Communist China. Such an invasion could have triggered World War III, for the Chinese repeatedly warned that there would be a limit to their patience with the American offensive—the 38th Parallel. Not as experienced a military commander as Roosevelt, Truman at first went along with what MacArthur and the Pentagon brass hats wanted. MacArthur's impatient, headlong march into North Korea ultimately landed him right in the middle of a trap and at the mercy of a seemingly endless horde of charging Chinese, and his disoriented, outflanked troops suffered one of the worst defeats in American military history near Yalu River. North Korea was again in the hands of the communists.

Such abject humiliation would have been the unhappy end of any other general's career, but MacArthur was as much a politician as a field strategist. Without batting an eye, he portrayed the rout of the United States' forces as a carefully executed, "brilliantly planned strategic withdrawal." With characteristic bravado, MacArthur laid the blame for the reversal on the namby-pambies in Washington who wanted to stop short of "total victory" over the godless Asian communists. Truman, an admirer of other generals (in particular, George C. Marshall), pondered what to do about MacArthur's exasperating insubordination.

By his own account, he took care of the problem at his only personal meeting with the general at Wake Island in the Pacific. Speaking bluntly as usual, MacArthur had said weeks before the meeting that "nothing could be more fallacious than the threadbare argument by those who advocate appeasement and defeatism in the Pacific that if we defend Formosa [Taiwan], we alienate continental Asia. Those who speak thus do not understand the Orient." Truman, in a "cold fury" after reading published accounts of the diatribe, forced the general to eat those words and decided that the unauthorized statement required a personal dressing-down as well as an official retraction.

By that time, Truman had concluded that "there were times when he [MacArthur] wasn't right in his head." The general's problem, according to Truman, was that he didn't have anyone on his staff who wasn't "an asskisser." Truman should have known, for he had plenty of them on his own White House staff. Actually, Truman wanted to fire MacArthur right there and then, and send the more sensible General Omar Bradley to relieve him, but his political aides, fearing a searing protest from Capitol Hill and MacArthur's adoring public, talked him out of it.

Their eyeball-to-eyeball confrontation at Wake Island was a dramatic scene, but accounts differ about what really happened. Some versions claimed that MacArthur tried to gain the upper hand right away by forcing the president's plane to land first and making the chief executive wait for him, but Harry would have none of that. "I'd waited 'til hell froze over if I'd had to. I wasn't going to have one of my generals

embarrass the President of the United States." When MacArthur finally made his overdue appearance, outfitted in his
customary field hat, sunglasses and unbuttoned shirt, Truman told him "I've come halfway across the world to meet
you...I just want you to know that I don't give a good Goddamn what you do or think about Harry Truman, but don't
you ever again keep your Commander-in-Chief waiting. Is
that clear?"

"It won't happen again. I've learned my lesson," the general contritely responded, according to Truman's later recollection of the climactic meeting.

But an entirely different scenario emerges from the transcripts made by a White House stenographer, Vernice Anderson. The once-classified conversations show MacArthur
charming his way into the good graces of all assembled, including several of his harshest critics. "There is little resistance left in South Korea," he boldly informed an attentive
Truman and the other conferees. "Those we do not destroy,
the winter will." Outlining his plan for returning Korea to the
Koreans, he continued, "I want to withdraw all troops as soon
as possible," a statement which apparently had the president
nodding his head in agreement. MacArthur seemingly dominated the meeting, and when he left, Truman concluded,
"This was the best conference I ever attended."

His award-winning performance allowed the general to
resume what he'd been spoiling for all along—total victory in
Asia, regardless of what the panty-waists at the capital were
saying. At last, on April 11, 1951, Truman lost his temper and
fired MacArthur, in his words, not "because he was a dumb
son of a bitch, although he was, but that's not against the law
for generals. If it was three-quarters of them would be in jail.
I fired him because he wouldn't respect the authority of the
President."

As expected, the backlash was fierce. At a meeting of congressional Republicans at Representative Joe Martin's office
the day after the sacking, Republican Charles Halleck demanded that the party press for Truman's immediate impeachment. Cooler heads dismissed the idea as ridiculous,
but nevertheless it wasn't unthinkable in the white heat of
MacArthur's disgrace. The Old Warrior came home soon af-

terward, but sentiment to turn the nation's best-loved soldier-hero into a political force died aborning. MacArthur had been out of the country for almost two decades, and was far from having his finger on the pulse of America—he was even out of touch with the Cold War, communist-fearing America of 1951.

There was another man who did know what Americans feared at that time, though: the balding, square-shouldered, sturdily-built junior senator from Wisconsin. His name came to represent, for a time, an aberration in American politics, a scoundrel time of suspicion, finger-pointing, and near-hysterical distrust. Joseph McCarthy became head priest and chief judge of an ugly witch-hunting cult which briefly won millions of converts. Ironically, Harry Truman may have been partially responsible for his emergence onto the national scene.

In 1946, according to the private correspondence of New Deal Braintruster Tommy ("The Cork") Corcoran, Truman and Democratic National Chairman Robert Hannegan pushed behind the scenes for Wisconsin Democrats to cross over and vote for Republican McCarthy in the Senate primary. The covert plot was spurred by a desire to oust liberal Republican incumbent Robert La Follette, who had refused Hannegan's entreaties to switch over to the Democrats. Truman and other party strategists thought McCarthy would be easy pickings for their candidate. Corcoran, then still a political powerbroker in his own right, opposed the unorthodox plan. He turned out to be right when "Tail Gunner Joe," as the newcomer brashly called himself, went on to victory in the primary and then crushed his Democratic opponent, Howard MacMurray, in the general election.

For his refusal to assist in the ill-conceived plan to boost McCarthy, Corcoran was treated to White House-ordered wiretapping and constant FBI surveillance. "I reaped the reward of 'effrontery' by having the FBI tap me for nearly four years," Corcoran wrote thirty years later. In fairness to Truman, while he probably sicced the FBI on the lobbyist and occasionally on newsmen who offended him, as a rule he detested using intelligence agents as private bloodhounds, unlike both Roosevelts.

"We want no Gestapo or secret police," he wrote in a private memorandum to himself in 1945. "The FBI is tending in that direction. They are dabbling in sex life scandals and plain blackmail when they should be catching criminals. *This must stop.*" True to his own warning, he refused to read confidential FBI files on the sex habits and financial improprieties of public figures which were sent over to him by Bureau chief J. Edgar Hoover, who was always seeking to curry favor with any president. Such wasn't the case with the other chief executives.

Harry Truman's reputation, both as a president and politician, has grown considerably in the forty years since he left office. British prime minister Winston Churchill, as Truman biographer David McCullough pointed out in a generally flattering treatment of the former president, praised the bantam weight Missouri native as being the man who did more than any other to save Western civilization with his bold, decisive leadership in the concluding days of World War II. Indeed, his basic forthrightness, decency and common sense have left Americans of this generation yearning for more men like him in political life.

However, Truman's stubborn reluctance to separate himself from some of the second-rate men who surrounded him, and took advantage of his admirable, but frequently obsessive loyalty, shouldn't be forgotten. As McCullough himself noted, Truman's own vice president, Alben Barkley, commented that "Mr. Truman was far too kind and loyal to certain old friends who took advantage of him, and whose actions sometimes were no credit to his administration."

Chapter 9

GIFTS FOR THE GENERAL

Dwight D. Eisenhower

January 1953—January 1961

To hear Harry Truman tell the story, he and General George Marshall secretly saved both the marriage and the presidency of Dwight David Eisenhower. During the war, the middle-aged military hero fell in love with a lovely, leggy former model and British Motor Transport Corps driver assigned as his chauffeur during his tour as commander of the American Allied forces in Europe.

At 32, Kathleen Helen McCarthy-Morrogh Summersby was as much an eyeful as her tongue-twisting name. The passion was reciprocal, according to Kay's own accounts. Although she was married (her beloved second husband, dashing pilot Dick Arnold, was killed in action while she was driving Ike around the European war front), Kay revealed a special affection for the man who would succeed Truman in the White House. "Yes, I loved this middle-aged man with his thinning hair, his eyeglasses, his drawn, tired face. I wanted to hold him in my arms, to cuddle him, delight him. I wanted to lie on some grassy lawn and see those broad shoulders above me, feel the intensity of those eyes on mine, feel that hard body against mine. I loved this man."

Transatlantic loose talk about the high-ranking romance wasn't lost on Mamie Eisenhower, a peppery, demanding former debutante who'd married Ike at the age of nineteen and followed him to an unappetizing succession of military bases between wars. Mamie, who'd adopted her famous bangs-over-the-forehead hairstyle only because her husband liked the look, was devastated by the constant, frequently vicious rumors about her husband's infidelity. Depressed, she sank into borderline alcoholism.

Enter Harry Truman (or so he claimed). "Right after the war was over, he [Eisenhower] wrote a letter to General Marshall, saying he wanted to be relieved of duty, saying that he wanted to come back to the United States and divorce Mrs. Eisenhower so he could marry this Englishwoman," recalled Truman. Harry's favorite general didn't let him down. "Marshall wrote back a letter the like of which I never did see. He said that...if Eisenhower even came close to doing such a thing, he's not only bust him out of the Army, he's see to it that never for the rest of his life would he be able to draw a peaceful breath [no matter] what country he was in." Marshall added that "if he ever mentioned a thing like that, he's see to it that the rest of his life was a living hell."

"I don't like Eisenhower...I never have, but one of the last things I did as President, I got those letters from his file in the Pentagon, and I destroyed them," the former chief executive concluded.

Other versions of the Eisenhower-Summersby liaison have surfaced, including testimony by former Eisenhower subordinates which directly challenge Truman's tale. Ike's former chief of staff, former NATO Commander General Alfred Greunther, has said: I knew Ike, and the story [about the romance] is totally false." Historian Forrest C. Pogue, who spent decades studying the lives of Eisenhower and Marshall, has declared that evidence of the affair is "slippery," and pointed out other instances of womanizing and drinking by Marshall's underlings in which the general acted far more charitably than he supposedly had toward Ike.

Others who served with General Eisenhower, while undecided about the truth of Truman's story, nevertheless believed that their commander did have a clandestine love affair with the comely Kay. In any case, whatever went through Eisenhower's mind at the end of the war, he went back to Mamie and his relationship with the statuesque Mrs. Summersby became a titillating footnote to history.

After the war, the scramble was intense to capitalize on Ike's comfortable style of leadership and fatherly appeal. Eisenhower felt most at home with the big business tycoons of the Republican party and became the GOP nominee in 1952: he got off on the wrong foot by timidly playing political patty-cake with the sinister forces of Senator Joseph McCarthy.

Publicly, Ike coddled the McCarthyites, while privately detesting them and the arch-reactionary attitudes they represented. Playing his star chamber role to the hilt, McCarthy held a series of intimidating loyalty hearings in the Senate and dispatched two eager young aides, counsel Roy Cohn and investigator David Scheine, to "inspect" American military installations and brand selected scientists and bureaucrats as disloyal. Even after one of McCarthy's devoted political disciples called the gifted General Marshall a "front man for traitors," Eisenhower the decisive war hero avoided a showdown with the cunning, witch-hunting Wisconsinite. While politically expedient, ducking the deliberate slanders was a cowardly performance and one of the lowest points in Eisenhower's public career.

But that wasn't the worst scandal of the election campaign. For Ike's running mate, the Republicans had chosen the man whose previous campaigns had shown McCarthy how to attract publicity for his vicious vendettas, California Senator Richard M. Nixon. He'd become a national figure in his own right during the Alger Hiss spy controversy, but it wasn't his outrageous red-baiting which made him a political liability to the Republican ticket. Barely seven weeks before the election, on September 18, 1952, the New York *Post* revealed in a sensational exposé, "Secret Rich Men's Trust Fund," that Senator Nixon had been dipping into a secret "slush fund" of more than $18,000, which had been bankrolled by a group of prominent conservative businessmen.

Overnight, the entire campaign hung in the balance. A cabal of GOP professionals, who had never liked Nixon in the first place, called for his resignation from the ticket, lest he ruin the Republicans' excellent prospects for recapturing the White House.

Ike found himself trapped in the backstage crossfire between hardline party warhorses like Senator Robert Taft, who insisted Nixon be backed unconditionally, and his own loyal friends like Bill Robinson, executive vice president of the New York *Herald-Tribune*, who called for Nixon's immediate resignation from the ticket following the disclosure. Faced with one of the most difficult decisions of his life, Ike wavered, hearing both sides out while waiting for Nixon to sink or swim on his own. Luckily for the general, the young senator bailed himself out of the jam with one of the boldest counter-attacks in American electoral history. His future hanging in the balance, the 39-year old vice presidential nominee went on national television, taking his case straight to the voters and over the heads of the quarreling party pols.

The result was the infamous "Checkers" speech, a masterfully maudlin, thirty-minute address to sixty million viewers, in which Nixon cleverly portrayed himself and his family as plain, simple people who had been unfairly maligned as scheming rich folk. Even that early in his career, Nixon had the cynical mastery of symbolism which would carry him through the rest of his long political life. Why, how could anyone charge that he was beholden to corporate fat cats when his wife, Pat, wore a worn cloth coat instead of a stole, and while the Nixon family lived in such a modest home, he asked plaintively? By the time Nixon had finished mentioning "Checkers," the family cocker spaniel, there was hardly a dry eye in the nationwide audience.

Corny, yes, but Nixon pulled it off. The outpouring of sympathy and support for "The Poor Richard Show" made Eisenhower's decision for him; cutting Nixon loose from the ticket after that *tour de force* would have been more disastrous than any allegations about slush funds. Although Eisenhower didn't immediately re-embrace his running mate, intimates believed that he made up his mind to retain Nixon the day after the broadcast, at a tension-filled meeting between the two in Wheeling, West Virginia.

If the duplicious Nixon was the whipping boy for critics of the Republican ticket, the presidential nominee himself got caught up in some questionable financial transactions during the course of the campaign. The incredibly popular general earned more than $600,000 on the publication of his wartime chronicles, *Crusades in Europe*. The book bonanza became even sweeter when Eisenhower received a favorable tax ruling on the publication's proceeds after writing a letter to Undersecretary of the Treasury Archibald Wiggins, a personal friend.

Eisenhower's almost unparalleled popularity, which made him a campaign manager's dream, together with his promise to clean up "the mess in Washington," carried the Republican ticket over the intellectual, principled (but uncharismatic) Adlai Stevenson, who was a tepid stumper. At last, Truman's cronies, whose sins had generated reams of negative news copy in 1952, would be replaced with a new team headed by the beloved military hero.

The actual result, unfortunately, was a far cry from the GOP's glowing expectations. The genial Eisenhower proved to be as blind to conflicts of interest as his combative predecessor. Despite the honors heaped on him by a grateful nation, tributes which included election to the highest office in the land, Eisenhower remained dazzled by wealth and titles even well into his late middle age. As famed muckraker Upton Sinclair noted, "Eisenhower grew up to have a great awe for wealth and to think of a millionaire as the most wonderful of God's creations. That is the dominating fact about his life— and about his Administration." His fascination with men of financial influence quickly became evident in his choice of advisers.

The confirmation hearings of Engine Charlie Wilson, chief officer of the General Motors Corporation, who had been nominated as secretary of defense, showed Ike's lamentable weakness for big business magnates. The amiable Wilson was shocked to learn from members of the Senate Armed Services Committee that he'd have to sell his considerable stock holding in G.M. to become Pentagon Chief. "My holdings [worth $2,500,000 at the time] may sound like a lot [but] as a percentage of General Motors they are less than one-tenth of one percent," Wilson protested lamely in his testimony, apparently not comprehending the glaring conflict of interest that G.M. would face by soliciting contracts from a Pentagon whose boss owned millions in stock and benefits in the auto giant.

Wilson confirmed his woeful lack of understanding when, asked if he would put his duty to his country ahead of his financial holdings, he replied memorably, "Yes, sir, I could," adding quickly, "But I cannot conceive of one [such situation] because for years I thought what was good for our country was good for General Motors and vice versa." Finally, after a week of indecision and a hard swallow, Engine Charlie caved in and told the committee that he could see his way clear to sell the stocks and give up his $600,000 salary and benefits package from G.M.

It wasn't that Eisenhower was personally unaware of these conflicts. On the contrary, having campaigned on the theme of corruption in government, the new chief executive was acutely sensitive to the public's perception of Washington's "buddy system." At the sixth meeting of his cabinet, in February 1953, he warned cabinet officials to watch carefully for signs of scandal and not to hesitate to call in the Justice Department when things began to smell suspicious. Never the political neophyte that some believed, the president realized that a large part of Harry Truman's problem had been his reluctance to take preemptive action against a number of his own straying appointees.

If his intentions were honest, however, the results made it clear that Eisenhower wasn't going to do much to remove the stench of cronyism from the business of government. Conflicts of interest propagated like weeds, and the only real change, if there was one, was that the press seemed to have a much more tolerant attitude toward Ike's foibles than they had toward Truman's. Corruption was just as bad if not worse, but reporters developed a blind spot to the kind of outrageous shenanigans for which Give 'Em Hell Harry would have been pilloried on the front page of every newspaper in the country.

For example, the five-percent shysters became bolder and greedier when Ike took office. An inflationary 10 percent suddenly became the standard for favors, graft and payoffs. During the same month that Eisenhower was chiding his cabinet about the need for careful watchdogging, one of the president's closest political intimates was setting new lows for conduct in office.

The culprit in the first important administration scandal was a Kansan named C. Wesley Roberts. Since he had opened and directed Eisenhower's Washington campaign office, it came as not great surprise when Ike gave his "hearty approval" to Roberts' nomination as National Chairman of the Republican party in January 1953. It took the fumbling Roberts almost no time to humiliate his patron. A long-time power in Kansas politics, Roberts apparently gave little thought to a cozy deal he made to serve as unofficial (and unneeded) broker for the sale of a privately owned hospital building in his home state. Just weeks after Roberts took office, it was revealed that he had received $11,000, or 10 percent of the total sale price appropriated by the state legislature, for insider activities which appeared to violate state lobbying laws. Howls of outrage greeted the exposé, yet Ike accepted Roberts' pathetic explanation that he had acted as a "private citizen," even though virtually everyone in Kansas knew of Roberts' considerable political muscle.

A state investigating committee uncovered fees paid in return for his insider contacts. Only an obscure legal loophole prevented him from being indicted for lobbying violations, and the resulting critical committee report caused Roberts to submit his resignation as GOP party boss after only two ineffectual months in office. Still, while Eisenhower lauded Roberts' decision to quit as "wise" for the party, he claimed the sinning chairman had resigned "on his own," suggesting that the White House didn't condemn his double-dealing.

Roberts' blunders were just the beginning. Ike's gut-level preference for private business over public administration triggered a scandal which Senator Estes Kefauver later characterized as "bad business, bad government, bad morals." The imbroglio was known as the Dixon-Yates case, named after the two businessmen, Edgar Dixon and Eugene Yates, who were central figures. Early in the administration, officials of the Atomic Energy Commission (AEC) decided that they needed more electricity to carry out their work. The publicly owned Tennessee Valley Authority (TVA) could have supplied the additional power if its facilities had been expanded, but Ike's big business buddies decided instead to put together a private coalition to construct a $100 million power plant near Memphis.

That move opened up a Pandora's box of conflicts of interest. Dixon and Yates, chiefs of the two private power companies, had combined to form the Mississippi Valley Generating Company to generate power to be "brokered" by the AEC, a dubious proposal which three of the five AEC commissioners opposed. Criticism of the questionable deal mounted until a Senate probe was launched, which uncovered the fact that Dixon's company, Middle South, had an unsavory history of excessive charges and dual bookkeeping. Despite months of outcry about what appeared to be a sweetheart contract for private power, Ike remained unperturbed, even after published allegations that he'd encouraged the deal to please well-connected friends such as golfer Bobby Jones, who was a member of the board of directors of one of the beneficiaries, the Southern Company.

The supporters of the Dixon-Yates scheme deflected all opposition until February 1955, when facts began bubbling to the surface which clearly indicated that the Eisenhower administration had been less than candid about the details of the initial contract. A man named Adolphe H. Wenzell caused the whole house of cards to begin tumbling down. Wenzell, a high-ranking officer of the First Boston Corporation, had been asked to serve as an unpaid consultant to iron out the "technical" details of the complex arrangement.

That might have seemed like a sound idea, except for the fact that the same First Boston Company was the financial agent for Dixon-Yates and was in charge of selling the plan's $120 million worth of securities. Wenzell, in other words, was holding closed-door meetings with Budget Bureau officials, advising them on Dixon-Yates, while his investment firm stood to make a huge bonanza from the private power plum. Wenzell's shaky ethical position didn't look any better after a confidential industry memo had spelled out the extent of his dual role by showing that the financial whiz had visited officials in the Dixon-Yates Washington office "about 5 P.M. when he had finished his day with the Budget Bureau people."

The Democrats had found a weak spot at last, and they

pounced with a vengeance, although it took months for the full story to unravel. Senate investigators learned that Budget Bureau employees had deliberately left Wenzell's name out of a Dixon-Yates chronology supplied to the press, and other federal officials had conspired to make Wenzell's role in the negotiations seem insignificant, when in fact he had been one of the key players. Southern state governors, suspicious of the deal in the first place, now had an excuse to refuse the power to be supplied by the expensive combine's plant. Following a highly publicized Senate probe, the AEC ruled that Wenzell's backdoor maneuver had voided the federal government's obligations to the contractors. That judgment prompted a long and costly lawsuit by the Dixon-Yates interests, who eventually received about half of what they claimed to have lost from the administration's abrogation.

The debacle caused some observers to wonder aloud for the first time if the president really knew what was going on inside his own administration. The skeptics didn't have to wait long for an answer; for soon other, more serious conflicts popped up, implicating high-ranking Eisenhower appointees. One which particularly troubled Ike involved Air Force Secretary Harold Talbott, with whom the president frequently had played bridge. Talbott, who apparently believed his government and business jobs were inextricably linked, took his cue from his boss, Defense Secretary Engine Charlie Wilson. A former chairman of the Republican National Finance Committee, Talbott, like Wilson, thought that what was good for business was good for the country; only in his case, it was what was good for *his* business that was paramount.

When he assumed office, he retained his partnership in the New York engineering firm of Paul B. Mulligan & Co. Shortly thereafter, Talbott began using his air force post to solicit contracts for the Mulligan firm—he even had the audacity to use air force stationery marked "Confidential" when writing letters on behalf of his company! Initially, the ploy worked—in his first two years at the Pentagon, he received more than $132,000 in profits from Mulligan's successes.

Talbott's cozy scheme was going along beautifully when a corporate lawyer had pangs of conscience about doing business with the controversial air force chief's firm. Talbott's

Waterloo came during hearings before the Senate Permanent Investigations Subcommittee. The whistle-blowing lawyer, Radio Corporation of America (RCA) chief counsel Samuel Ewing, testified that he had thought it improper for RCA, which held a number of defense-related contracts, to enter into any new agreements with Mulligan. After he had voiced this objection, he received a call from the air force's general counsel and then, incredibly, a man identifying himself as Talbott got on the phone and railed at Ewing for daring to act "so high and mighty"! The air force chief told the senators that he couldn't remember making such a call, but admitted unabashedly that he had helped the Mulligan firm, and he saw nothing wrong with lending a helping hand to his business.

It's unclear whether or not Eisenhower directly asked for Talbott's resignation, but he got it shortly after the official's public humiliation in the Senate. Since the air force secretary had been awarded the Medal of Freedom and the navy's Distinguished Public Service Award, however, it's obvious that the White House didn't consider Talbott a black sheep in the administration's political family.

The Talbott affair had hardly died down September 1955 when crusading columnist Drew Pearson revealed that Peter Strobel, the number-two man at the General Services Administration, was mired in a number of strikingly similar conflicts. Like Talbott, Strobel had maintained his connections with his company, an engineering consulting firm called Strobel and Salzman, after assuming office. Also like the disgraced air force chief, Strobel was in a position to pass judgment on hundreds of millions in government contracts—in his case, $346 million worth. A hard-driving immigrant, Strobel was outraged by charges that he had used his post to steer government contracts to his firm and to press his business' claims with federal agencies, most notably the Army Corps of Engineers. It wasn't a cut-and-dried case, for Strobel had given up a six-figure income to serve in a government job which paid only about one-sixth that. Nevertheless, the revelations and subsequent allegations led to an FBI probe of Strobel's behavior. When the Central Intelligence Agency had come to GSA for a new building, for example, eight of the fourteen firms which bid on the project had connections with Strobel's consulting company.

Strobel also permitted clients of his firm to bid on and receive GSA contracts, and on at least one occasion he actively sought business for his company while in office. His unswerving cooperation with a congressional investigation left legislators with the impression that Strobel truly believed that he had done nothing wrong, but his own testimony showed that he had placed himself in a hopelessly compromising position, and Democrats pressured the White House for action. They finally got it when the businessman resigned from his post just a few months after the Talbott fiasco.

Although hardly reflected in the news coverage of the day, it had become abundantly clear that there were just as many, if not more, conflicts of interest in high places in the Eisenhower administration as there had been when Harry Truman was being castigated for presiding over a government characterized by cronyism. By late 1955, Ike's business buddies had been given enough rope to hang themselves, and the extent of their collective naivete and greed was becoming a matter of public record. Worse yet, Ike and his White House aides were falling into the same trap that had clouded the integrity of other chief executives—administration officials were refusing to take decisive action concerning misdeeds by friends, even when the evidence against them was overwhelming. Not only did the White House drag its feet, but Eisenhower lieutenants used bogus claims of executive privilege to thwart investigations of malfeasance, something which the general had promised from the beginning would never happen.

Time and time again, Ike blindly accepted weak explanations of misconduct from his subordinates, and permitted them to sidestep proper congressional oversight with the claim this would not be "in the national interest." This patronizing attitude was used to block the General Accounting Office (GAO), the Congress's watchdog, from gaining access to inspector general reports on frauds hidden in air force contracts. Regulatory agencies whose businessmen-bosses had conflicts of interest began successfully using the "executive privilege" cover to shield themselves from scrutiny.

Toward the end of Eisenhower's first term, the Republicans' promised new era of openness and accountability in government had become little more than a memory. As in Harding's time, business and government had become one, and the problems created by such an ill-fated marriage grew more evident with each passing day. Back over at the Pentagon, the disgrace of Harold Talbott hadn't been enough to stop Assistant Secretary of Defense Robert Tripp Ross from turning his post into a free enterprise grabbag for his relatives.

Even before he got caught with his fingers in the government cookie jar, Ross got called on the congressional carpet for allowing an $834,150 contract for army trousers to be awarded to Wynn Enterprises, a firm headed by his wife, Claire Wynn Ross. Boldly, Ross claimed that he never discussed business with his wife. "I think it's bad enough to make a man sell everything he owns, but if he has to divorce his wife, too, that's going pretty far," he complained, alluding to Engine Charlie's earlier run-ins with the Capitol Hill overseers.

Taking the offensive against his critics didn't stem the tide for the free-wheeling Ross. He soon found himself charged with steering federal contracts to his brother-in-law Breezy Wynn, who'd received millions in government business despite being charged with repeated violation of federal labor laws by union officials. After winning a series of non-competitive contracts, Wynn's firm delivered fewer than 10 percent of the orders on time. Like Talbott, Ross apparently didn't realize, or care about, the impropriety of intervening on behalf of his relatives' financial interests. Disgusted congressional critics, by now growing used to seeing this kind of behavior in Eisenhower appointees, labeled the Wynn enterprise as little more than a "dummy" front corporation designed for the benefit of the Ross-Wynn filial partnership. Following one particularly ugly scene with congressional probers, Ross resigned his post and joined the burgeoning crowd of displaced Eisenhower office-holders.

None of these revelations should have come as a shock. The stridently pro-business attitude of the Eisenhower White House created a *laissez faire* atmosphere in the capital in which corporate America could do no wrong. If that harsh judgment seems a bit unfair, it should be noted that Ike was able to attract highly capable men into his administration, distinguished public servants of the caliber of Bernard Baruch and Tennessee Valley Authority chief David Lilienthal, among others. However, such dedicated, visionary public servants did not dominate the era.

The record speaks for itself; the fallen officials mentioned previously represented a tiny percentage of the guilty. Members of the Federal Communications Commission, for example, were so busy taking favors from the industry which they were supposed to regulate, that the agency became a rubber stamp for communications giants, which were just beginning to flex their formidable corporate muscle in the mid-fifties. FCC chairman John Doefer and his wife were treated to a free Caribbean vacation by a powerful broadcasting company which wanted favors; the couple also went on trips to golf resorts and began double-billing the government for their junkets. Fellow commissioner Richard Mack, not to be outdone, allowed his vote to be obtained on a crucial license when one of the applicants hired a crony of his to represent him. Over at the Federal Power Commission, Chairman James Kuykendall kow-towed to the oil barons by allowing a big price boost to Olin Gas Company after a hearing at which the corporation's representatives were the only witnesses.

Worse, the president permitted his top aides, especially the spare, forbidding chief of staff, Sherman Adams, to block congressional investigations when things got too hot for the White House. It's important to understand that the frequent episodes of malfeasance in high places wasn't some strange aberration—the favor-takers were following a lead which came straight from the Oval Office.

Indeed, it's impossible to comprehend the shortcomings of Eisenhower's two terms without reviewing the rise and fall of Adams, the president's most trusted aide and the man who ultimately caused him his greatest despair. A model of New England reserve, Adams, who could make decisions in an instant, became major domo for Ike, who disliked the presidency's administrative duties with a passion. Stern and business-like to the point of rudeness, Adams acquired a number of unflattering nicknames, noted Eisenhower expert David

Frier, among them "The Abominable Mr. No-Man," and "Rasputin," for his almost Svengali-like control over Eisenhower's executive decisions. Friends insisted that Sherman Adams had a warmer, human side to him, which he showed frequently in private. To those on the outside, however, Adams was the embodiment of what Arkansas Senator William Fulbright would term "the arrogance of power," a decade later. Adams' job was to play hatchet-man for the popular chief executive, and he didn't mind stepping on a few toes.

But the flinty White House aide, who was known to cut phone callers off in mid-sentence by slamming down the receiver, did far more than violate the courtly rules of Washington society; he terrorized the bureaucracy with a single-handed campaign of sheer intimidation. The rules were for others, and woe be to the foolish bureaucrat who questioned an Adams order. Virtually no important piece of paper passed out of the White House without the familiar notation "OK, S.A." The Adams mark was everywhere. He played a none-too-subtle role in the Dixon-Yates controversy, when he reportedly tried to oust Securities and Exchange Commissioner Paul Rowen from his post for opposing the private power scheme. At almost the same time, he was attempting to quash a probe of the New York Central Railroad and was pushing the Interstate Commerce Commission for a speedy resolution to a separate investigation of the Boston and Maine Railroad.

In effect, Adams became a one-man clearinghouse for favor-seekers from the corporate world who were distressed by the federal government's lame attempts to regulate the safety and health aspects of their businesses. Sherman was their tireless watchdog; or this case, lapdog. For years it was common knowledge that Adams was the president's "Mr. Fix-it," but no one dared challenge the personal power of the presidential gate-keeper, and it wasn't until Adams' arrogance and misjudgments became embarrassingly public that his star began to fall.

Ironically, it was a wealthy businessman who caused Adams' disgrace, a textile magnate named Bernard Goldfine, whose payoffs to Adams rocked the Eisenhower administration to its foundations and caused Ike his most painful moment in pubic life. Goldfine, a close friend of Adams, had been a frequent target of investigators at the Federal Trade Commission. When the FTC attempted to take Goldfine to task for a variety of alleged regulatory violations, the powerful Adams intervened, asking FTC Chairman Edward Howrey to see Goldfine personally. The boastful Goldfine was so confident of his connection at the White House that he placed a call from Howrey's office to Adams, telling his benefactor that he had been "treated well over here."

Other wool manufacturers alleged that Goldfine had managed to involve Adams in getting more protection against foreign textile imports, a move directly in opposition to the administration's publicly announced low tariff policy. According to one account, Adams even arranged for the opportunistic Goldfine to meet personally with Eisenhower about his problems, a tête-à-tête certain to have intimidated any regulator who had entertained thoughts of bringing tough action against the wool baron.

All these favors, of course, could have been excused as legitimate efforts on behalf of a friendly businessman, had it not come to light that the supposedly puritan Adams had accepted both favors and gifts from Goldfine for years. It wasn't any nickel-and-dime stuff, either. Goldfine had picked up the tab for many of Adams' well-tailored clothes, had given him expensive furniture, allowed him to haul liquor off by the vanful, paid $2,000 worth of hotel bills and provided him with a $2,400 Oriental rug. A costly vicuna coat, however, soon came to symbolize corruption in the Eisenhower White House as unmistakably as the $1,200 deep freezers given to Bess Truman and her husband's aides. Ike's inner circle of loyalists compounded their dilemma by lying and attempting to cover up for Adams, for all knew that the president considered the reticent former governor of New Hampshire as his most indispensable staffer. The deliberate obfuscation awakened a sleeping press, which after six years had begun to realize the full extent of ethical laxness inside the administration. The aloof Adams had made himself a host of bitter enemies in his search-and-destroy missions through official Washington. Once he began to bleed, the political sharks circled hungrily for the kill.

"What Sherman Adams did was imprudent, but I need

him," was the president's curt response to the legion of critics who pressed their demands for his chief of staff's resignation as the real meaning of Goldfine's influence-peddling surfaced. Beside the foreign policy calamities of the Cold War, the erosion of Adams' influence was probably the worst political crisis Eisenhower had faced. White House loyalists led by Press Secretary Hagerty, conducted a furious behind-the-scenes defense of Adams and Goldfine during the summer of 1958, while publicly denying that they were involved in any way. Finally, the heat from the combination of federal and congressional probes, plus the importuning of panic-stricken GOP party officials fearful of election year reprisals, became too much. By early September, Eisenhower's advisers had convinced the reluctant chief executive that his friend had to go. Ike couldn't bring himself to fire Adams face-to-face, and it's not clear whether he personally ordered his right hand man out.

In a televised interview with David Frost in the 1970s, Richard Nixon described Adams as a "man who had been totally selfless," and "honest in his heart." The former vice president recalled that Eisenhower "called me in [and] asked me to talk to Sherm" about resigning. That account, though, varies with others, which contend that Republican National Chairman Meade Alcorn gave Adams the bad news, and that Adams then agreed to quit, later claiming that "the President did not ask me to resign and neither did Alcorn or the Vice President."

The firing didn't end an intensive, years-long investigation into Goldfine's activities, though: federal sleuths working under the direction of Attorney General Robert Kennedy later discovered that Adams had long been receiving cash from Goldfine, as much as $15,000 in a single month and a total of perhaps $350,000 during their entire relationship from their days in New Hampshire through Adams' White House years. Only a personal plea from Ike to his White House successors John Kennedy and Lyndon Johnson kept Adams, who returned to New Hampshire to run a ski resort, from being prosecuted.

One might be tempted to feel sorry for the betrayed Eisenhower if it weren't for the fact that the gifts he accepted from

his political friends while in the White House dwarfed the
favors which disgraced the departed Adams. For openers, Ike
received from Goldfine one of the infamous vicuna coats. But
that indiscretion was small potatoes compared to the Midas
haul which was carted off to his Gettysburg, Pa., home during
his final years in the White House.

The president's grateful business buddies dumped expensive food, farm and household products on him as readily as
love-drunk disciples would bestow their worldly goods on
their spiritual guru. By the end of his presidency, at least
$300,000 worth of livestock, machinery and horticultural
products had been trucked up to Gettysburg. It was an amaz-
ing cornucopia: cattle, hogs, venison, chicken, hams, lobsters
and ducks. The farm lacked for nothing; even a greenhouse,
trees and two flower gardens were supplied, along with a
$3,000 putting green, a $4,000 tractor and other farm machinery. Inside, the Chippendale furniture, sterling silver and
new-fangled electric kitchen were ample proof that everything was first-class all the way. Perhaps most shocking, Ike
wasn't even paying for the property; it was secretly leased by
three wealthy oilmen, including Texan Billy Byars, who paid
all the expenses and claimed tax losses of half a million dollars.

To ease his personal workload, the president enlisted two
Filipino servants from the White House, and commandeered
government trucks to haul goods to Gettysburg. In fairness,
the Eisenhowers sank over a quarter-million dollars of their
own funds into the farm, enough to finance a highly comfortable retirement when bread was thirty cents a loaf, but it
didn't begin to pay for the royal comforts which they enjoyed.

The first lady wasn't left out of the corporate gratitude. One
of the most expensive single gifts accepted by the first couple
was the so-called Mamie cottage at the Augusta, Ga., golf
club, financed by grateful business interests. By the end of his
second term, Eisenhower's patrician lifestyle contrasted embarrassingly with Truman's spartan personal habits.

Knowledgeable experts estimated the Eisenhower personal
fortune at a million dollars. His oil industry friends, who had
contributed so much toward realizing his life-long dream of
wealth, didn't go away empty-handed; their friend in the

White House signed into law a controversial tidelands bill which benefitted the petroleum bosses immensely. He also stacked the Federal Power Commission to favor the oil and gas industries, and permitted a group of energy executives to write a gas bill, which he sent along to Congress almost exactly as they dictated. Only a whiff of a payoff scandal on Capitol Hill involving a South Dakota senator caused that legislation to be killed.

Ike's penchant for secrecy wasn't confined to his personal financial affairs—perhaps the best-kept secret of his administration was the fact that he surreptitiously taped dozens of White House visitors, including Vice President Nixon and members of his cabinet, for a five-year period between October 1953 and December 1958. Only a very few intimates, among them his personal secretary, Mrs. Ann Whitman, and Secretary of State John Foster Dulles, were aware of the covert recording system.

One impression that the confidential taped transcripts confirm was Eisenhower's apparent discomfort with Nixon. They reveal that on one occasion Ike admonished his vice president for publicly agreeing with Senator Joseph McCarthy, then in his communist-baiting prime. Noting that McCarthy had repeatedly labeled U.S. policy toward China as "twenty years of treason," Eisenhower warned Nixon, "that by no implication could [Nixon] be considered saying the same thing." Later, in a taped talk with the then-chief of Studebaker, Paul Hoffman, Eisenhower curiously left Nixon's name out of a long list of younger leaders who had the "energy and fresh ideas" to be regarded as potential future presidents. The private rebuff belied the public support Ike later gave to his two-time running mate's candidacy.

The tapes, the gifts and the entangling web of conflicts showed Eisenhower the president in a much different light than the fatherly, benign portraits of him painted by the generally uncritical press during his two terms. While confident of his own political acumen, Eisenhower as president seemed largely unaware of the personal shortcomings of those around him. His awe of money and the free-wheeling capitalists who made it was in tune with the times, but his blind spot for the necessary separation of public service and private commerce stained what was in many other ways a notable eight years.

Chapter 10

THE PLAYBOY PRESIDENT
John F. Kennedy
January 1961—November 1963

John F. Kennedy's adviser and intimate Theodore ("Ted") Sorensen (later Jimmy Carter's unsuccessful nominee for the Central Intelligence Agency directorship) was undoubtedly joking when he said that "this administration's going to do for sex what the last one did for golf," but it was a lot closer to the truth than staunch defenders of the so-called Camelot legacy would like to admit. The changeover in the White House palace guard during the chilled months of early 1961 could hardly have been more striking. Eisenhower, the aging military hero and grandfatherly presence of the comfortable Fifties, who had shepherded America through the Cold War, the hysteria of McCarthyism and the new technological era of the satellite, was replaced by young, dynamic John Fitzgerald Kennedy—the glib, boyishly handsome former senator and congressman from Massachusetts.

JFK, as he enjoyed being called in the newspaper headlines, impressed men with his quick, incisive intelligence and charmed women with an irresistible combination of virility and vulnerability. Together with Florida's "Gorgeous" George Smathers, another of the Senate's rakish ladies' men, the tousle-haired Kennedy had cut a wide swath across the cocktail circuits and bedrooms of the capital. "He had the most active libido of anyone I've ever known," confided one admiring fellow skirt-chaser. Beautiful women from every walk of life fell victim to the JFK mystique, including the lovely movie actress Gene Tierney, who reportedly had a brief affair with the wealthy bachelor in the late Forties. Gossip columnists could hardly keep up with the playboy legislator.

Usually discreet about his amorous trysts, which he didn't seem to take seriously himself, Kennedy rarely allowed his sexual adventures to spill over into his family or political life. On one occasion, however, he apparently got so carried away with a winsome brunette that he almost compromised the office of the presidency. The object of his affections was a striking, dark-featured, twenty-six-year-old divorcee named Judith Campbell. A party girl well-known in Las Vegas gambling circles, Judy Campbell met Jack Kennedy while he was still in the Senate, and they continued an affair through the fall of 1961 and the spring of 1962, even risking furtive meetings at the White House. According to her account, the president's chronic backaches worsened to the point that their lovemaking sessions in his bedroom were affected.

The revelation that the president of the United States was conducting an adulterous affair inside the White House under the first lady's nose was shocking enough, but Judy Campbell's other "friendships" were just as eye-opening. During the same period, she was also romantically involved with the notorious, powerful Chicago mob boss, Salvatore ("Sam") Giancana. Twenty years later, a remarried Judy Campbell, by then using her maiden name of Exner, would assert that her presidential paramour encouraged her sexual relationship with the brutal Mafia chief and used her as a courier to pass both intelligence messages and money to him.

Kennedy loyalists, including the president's longtime secretary Evelyn Lincoln, denied that they knew Judy Campbell, or that she ever got close to the president. The only Campbell he knew was chunky vegetable soup, scoffed Kennedy aide Dave Powers. As writer Anthony Summers discovered, however, Secret Service logs recorded as many as twenty visits and telephone calls by a "Judy Campbell" to the Kennedy White House in 1961 and 1962. These documents and other established details provide at least partial credence to her claim that there was some sort of dark, working relationship between the charismatic, popular young president and the organized crime *caporegime*.

Exner said that cash given to her by Kennedy during the 1960 presidential campaign was passed along to Giancana's henchmen for the purpose of buying votes. Skinny d'Amato, one of the mobster's legmen, stated that Giancana had sent him to West Virginia, one of the swing states in the election, "to get votes for Jack Kennedy." After he was elected, Ms. Exner contended, Giancana used to tease her by saying, "Your boyfriend wouldn't be president if it weren't for me."

When he learned of the illicit affair, FBI chief J. Edgar Hoover warned Kennedy at a March 1962 luncheon about the dire consequences of having his extra-marital lover linked with a dark liegelord of the underworld. No one knows precisely what the bulldog-like Hoover, who kept copious secret files on the sexual habits of famous and influential people, told the chief executive, but the telephone calls to his lovely playmate stopped shortly thereafter.

Another adulterous infatuation led to years of troubling whispers for both JFK and his brother Bobby. Since the Kennedy brothers were the most attractive and powerful political tandem of their generation, and their company was eagerly sought by the *glitterari* of Hollywood, it wasn't surprising when moviedom's reigning sex goddess, Marilyn Monroe, gravitated into their exclusive social circle. The link was Peter Lawford, a handsome, alcoholic actor with ties to Frank Sinatra's "Rat Pack" of Hollywood buddies and hangers-on. The suave, charming Lawford was also connected to the first family through his marriage to JFK's sister, Pat Kennedy.

There's little doubt that both brothers succumbed to Monroe's considerable, platinum-blonde charms, although their dalliances might only have produced titillating grist for the gossip mills if it hadn't been for Monroe's sudden, unexpected death in August 1962. Her demise at the age of thirty-six, apparently from an drug overdose, shocked a worshiping nation and gave rise to stubborn rumors that she had been murdered, either by Mafia assassins or intelligence operatives nervous about her escapades with the Kennedys. One Hollywood investigator, a friend of Marilyn's, claimed that she and Bobby Kennedy had exchanged angry words on the day of her death, and that a distraught Monroe, who apparently was enamored of the younger Kennedy, threatened to publicly reveal the details of their bedroom romps.

No solid evidence of any foul play has ever emerged; the cause of her death, in the official autopsy, was listed as "acute barbiturate poisoning, ingestion or overdose." Nevertheless, a number of baffling questions remained for two decades after the incident, and several writers and police officials have publicly suggested a coverup of more nefarious circumstances.

History professor Thomas C. Reeves, who described himself as a former Kennedy admirer, wrote in his 1991 book *A Question of Character: A Life of John F. Kennedy* that the president's adulteries, including the affairs with Exner and Monroe, "demeaned the Presidency." JFK's compulsive, reckless philandering, "have no doubt contributed further to the widespread public cynicism about the ability of politicians to sacrifice their personal indulgences."

If she suffered privately from her husband's perpetual infidelities, First Lady Jackie Kennedy rarely showed it. Perhaps getting back at him in one of the few ways she knew, Jackie instead enraged the young president by running up staggering bills on clothes shopping sprees. With an immense family fortune underwriting his wife's every whim, JFK didn't care about the money, and in fact was anxious about having his young wife dress properly for her White House duties; the first couple's almost royal appeal was gaining increasingly flattering television coverage. But the young chief executive fretted that it would be difficult for him to plead for anti-poverty funds in Congress while his wife was off buying racks full of the newest Parisian fashions.

It wasn't long, however, before the pipe-smoking director of the Central Intelligence Agency, Allen Dulles, and his Cold War crew at spy headquarters in Langley, Virginia, gave Kennedy something much more serious to worry about. CIA planners had been wringing their hands for two years over the successful communist coup in Cuba led by the crafty, bearded revolutionary, Fidel Castro. The intelligence spooks had no intention of permitting an armed communist outpost to prosper a mere ninety miles from Miami's sun-drenched beaches.

Plans were drawn up to back a U.S.-sponsored invasion of Cuba by rabid anti-Castro exiles eager for an armed confrontation with the socialist regime's forces, which had been hardened by years of living in the hills, hiding from the dictator Batista's soldiers.

The top-secret decision represented a political powderkeg, fraught with dangerous international repercussions. If the Soviets could prove that the U.S. was somehow behind a Caribbean brush war to oust Castro, then Moscow's aging, reactionary leaders might decide to retaliate in support of its puppet island government. The possible threat of nuclear holocaust or world war didn't deter the hardliners at the spy agency, though; they would convince their president of the wisdom of facing down the communist threat in Cuba before, as they fervently believed, it spread like a cancer to the rest of Latin America. The full extent of President Kennedy's knowledge of the CIA's intentions is still somewhat in dispute, but there's no question that he made the final, fateful decision concerning the invasion and the size of the armed force to be used.

Only a few days after his inauguration, Kennedy gave a conditional green light to the spymasters, reserving the right to cancel the clandestine foray at the last moment. Quarreling among the invasion leaders postponed the scheduled attack for three weeks in March 1961. During that time, the landing site was switched from Trinidad to the Bay of Pigs. The key to the success of the mission, stressed analysts, was U.S.-piloted air support for the invaders. Castro's air force must be neutralized or the beachhead charge might be quickly crushed. At a top-level cabinet meeting in early April, Kennedy hesitated. The use of U.S. air power might mushroom into a hemispheric conflagration if the Soviets decided that Castro's fall wasn't in their global interest. Suddenly, he backtracked, overruling the worried Joint Chiefs of Staff and prohibiting the use of any but Cuban-piloted planes, which would fly from bases in Guatemala.

His eleventh-hour compromise proved to be fatal for the invaders. After an initial success at the landing site, the refugees were cut off and repulsed in less than forty-eight hours, lacking the vital air support that they'd been promised by their American sponsors. The architect of the plan, CIA deputy director for plans Richard Bissell, begged Kennedy to relent and allow a U.S. air strike while there was still a chance of victory. Kennedy steadfastly refused and was forced to accept full responsibility for the debacle which followed, a humilation which included the death or capture of most of the CIA-trained anti-Castro force.

Privately, many of the spies thought their leader had looked the communists in the eye and blinked. For his part, JFK was furious about the hard-sell hustle he felt he'd been given by Dulles and his bureaucracy of paper-pushers. In a tirade, he threatened to "splinter the CIA into a thousand pieces and scatter it to the winds." Brother Bobby saw to it that the CIA advisory board's powers were diluted after the Bay of Pigs fiasco, which turned out to be a propaganda field day for the triumphant Castro.

Nevertheless, even with an outraged chief executive on their hands, the determined spies, disgusted with the Keystone Kops outcome of the carefully planned overthrow, weren't about to give up their obsession with regaining Cuba. Instead, the agency became an almost renegade force; CIA operatives, cooking up an unbelievable scheme, recruited Mafia chieftans to plot Castro's assassination. A chilling, unholy partnership was formed between the two most secretive organizations in the U.S.—the CIA and the Cosa Nostra. A variety of bizarre murder plots were hatched, to be carried out by organized crime's network of experienced hit men.

Fifteen years would pass before congressional investigators confirmed even partial reports that the CIA had proposed at least six separate assassination scenarios against Castro. The murder schemes had a James Bond flavor; in one instance, the would-be assassins considered slaying the bearded dictator with exotic, slow-acting poisons which would leave no trace.

Needing operatives with both political and intelligence connections, the CIA enlisted Robert Maheu, a former FBI agent who had worked previously for the spy agency as a freelancer. Maheu's choice to set up the unofficially sanctioned "Murder, Inc." was Johnny Roselli, a suave gambler and former movie industry hanger-on who had formidable ties to both the U.S. and Havana underworlds. To assist the odd couple, the CIA loaned two of its own operatives, William Harvey and James ("Big Jim") O'Connell. The pair went with Roselli to Miami to assemble a murder squad.

Even with the government's unofficial blessing, the resourceful Roselli needed more "juice," for he had no control over Cuba's criminal element. The only man in the United States who did was Miami's feared Mafia chieftan, Santos Trafficante. A numbers racketeer and extortionist, Trafficante hadn't had much use for Castro, as the 1959 communist revolution had cost the crime lord a fortune in Havana-based gambling "investments." Trafficante had once been briefly jailed by Castro, and would be only too happy to see him killed so that he could make Havana once more the tourist and gambling mecca it'd been during the previous decade.

The dapper Roselli, however, was too small a fish to ask for such a huge favor from Trafficante; the request had to come from the Chicago crime boss, Sam Giancana. Roselli convinced his mentor to fly to Miami and pow-wow with his fellow capo. Deciding that cooperation with the CIA to arrange Castro's demise would be in their mutual business interests, the mobsters went to work in earnest. First, Roselli smuggled poison pills to a contact who could get them close to the tightly guarded Castro, but that plot failed after initially encouraging reports that the dictator had fallen ill. In typical underworld fashion, when the subtle approach fell on its face, they went to more direct methods. In two speed boats, Roselli personally drove sharp-shooters equipped with high-powered rifles from Miami to the Cuban shore. The marksmen got on a rooftop within sight of Castro's lair, but didn't manage to squeeze off any shots.

After a half-dozen imaginative schemes flopped, and his contacts started mysteriously disappearing, Roselli theorized that Castro probably had been tipped off and had apprehended the traitors in his inner circle. Torture would have elicited answers about the identity of the plotters, but Roselli had been careful to cover the CIA's tracks, and even the would-be murderers didn't know who was funding their treacherous, unsuccessful activities. Later Roselli would confide to friends that he believed Castro had turned the tables on his American foes and sent Cuban assassins after JFK in retaliation.

For more than a decade afterward, Dulles' successor at the CIA, John McCone, vociferously denied that the agency had been involved in any such irresponsible, deadly shenanigans, but congressional committees finally got behind the official lies in the mid-Seventies, as part of a wide-ranging probe of CIA misdeeds. Older and balding, but still possessed of a rough-hewn sophistication, Roselli testified behind closed doors, but told his Senate interrogators little. Almost certainly because of his singular knowledge of the organization of the anti-Castro plots, he was murdered in July 1976. Strangled by unknown assailants, his legs were broken and he was dumped into Miami's Biscayne Bay, stuffed into an oil drum which unexpectedly floated to the surface sometime later.

How much did JFK know of the Castro murder plans and similiar, CIA-directed blueprints to bump off uncooperative foreign leaders, such as the Dominican Republic's Rafael Trujillo and South Vietnam's Ngo Dinh Diem? It's hard to believe he was totally in the dark, for brother Bobby was placed in charge of shaking up the CIA after the disastrous Bay of Pigs setback. The president's close friend George Smathers related that Kennedy once rolled up his eyes when asked about the assassination network, as if the idea were too wild to even consider. But Kennedy made it clear that he had suspicions about intelligence agents illegally conducting their own, free-wheeling brand of foreign policy, doubts which were later linked to his assassination in Dallas. In 1975, the Senate Intelligence Committee concluded that the plots were "incompatible with American principles, international order, and morality."

All was not well on the domestic political front, either. A Texas entrepreneur named Billy Sol Estes caused quite a ruckus in 1962, when he was indicted for fraud and conspiracy by a federal grand jury. The Lone Star State investigation soon sent tremors all the way back to Washington because it was disclosed that the enterprising Billy Sol had several ranking officials of the Kennedy Agriculture Department in his pocket. He'd built his West Texas financial empire mostly on fraudulent use of federal cotton allotments and lucrative

grain warehouse contracts. Highly placed Agriculture bureaucrats had done Billy favors in exchange for free shopping
trips, cash gifts and the use of Estes' telephone credit cards.

Initially, the revelations about the payoffs prompted calls
for the resignation of Agriculture Secretary Orville Freeman.
The president stood up for Freeman, though, insisting that
the corruption, while lamentable, was relatively minor and
had been nipped in the bud. Freeman cooperated with a
Senate probe, and although publicly embarrassed, kept his
job.

The president faced a much worse problem at the Pentagon. The award of the biggest military plane contract in history gave rise to political double-dealing and bureaucratic
lying which would stretch on for years and cost the taxpayers
perhaps hundreds of millions of dollars. "TFX" were initials
which became almost as famous as the president's, for a time.
They stood for a line of air force and navy fighter planes
whose development and construction contracts totaled $6.5
billion dollars, a plum which could keep any major defense
contractor's plants humming for a decade or more.

The coveted prize was urgently sought by two giants of the
defense industry, Boeing and General Dynamics. The immensely profitable bottom line made the award much more
than a routine procurement, which is why Pulitzer-Prize-win-
ning journalist Clark Molenhoff devoted months to the unfolding story. Thousands of present and future jobs were at
stake, and powerful politicians lined up behind the companies, each hoping to have a hand in directing the government's largesse to his home area. Since this single decision
would commit the Defense Department to an entire generation of fighter planes, the Pentagon's planners had exhaustive
studies performed to match the Boeing blueprints and test
models against those of General Dynamics.

Rumors of behind-the-scenes political pressure being applied from Texas surfaced during the months before the final
award was made, but few on Capitol Hill took the warnings
seriously. Nothing seemed amiss when Pentagon spokemen
announced in November 1962 that General Dynamics had
won out. That choice sent a shock wave through the Defense
Department, however; knowledgeable military analysts

knew that all their internal studies had showed Boeing's to be the cheaper, better plane by far.

Seattle-based Boeing's champion, Washington senator Henry Jackson, was told privately that four different studies had ended with the same verdict: Boeing's planes were superior, and their price was as much as $400 million dollars lower than General Dynamics'. The influential "Scoop" Jackson sicced his crack investigative staff on the Pentagon planners, and soon learned that internal documents proved what the critics had told him off-the-record—even the Pentagon source selection board, composed of nonpartisan experts, had chosen Boeing. Further sleuthing uncovered the fact that the bespectacled, intellectual secretary of Defense, former whiz kid Robert McNamara, had signed off on the controversial award for reasons which appeared to be almost nonsensical under close scrutiny. The slick-haired McNamara had earned a well-deserved reputation for being a determined, if not savage, cost cutter as a bigwig at General Motors. Why would he permit the virtually unanimous recommendations of his own blue ribbon plans to be ignored?

Disturbingly, Senate accountants found major errors in the documentation which McNamara had submitted in support of his decision. Classified data confirmed the growing suspicions; political influence or outright incompetence was at the bottom of this overturned rock. Hard-pressed by a usually fawning press corps, Kennedy assured questioners that McNamara had acted in the taxpayers' interest.

As it turned out, that wasn't true, nor was it all the tightly wrapped defense chief's fault. Two of his top subordinates had grossly violated conflict-of-interest laws which the president himself had instituted to prevent money-grubbing in high office, conflicts that had humiliated Eisenhower frequently. One of the culprits was McNamara's chief aide, Deputy Secretary of Defense Roswell Gilpatric. In and out of the revolving door between industry and government for years, the New York lawyer's firm had served as counsel to General Dynamics, which was in dire financial straits and desperately needed the TFX bonanza to avoid having to flirt with bankruptcy. Blithely ignoring the new ethics rules, Gilpatric, a key player in the TFX decision, convinced his boss to overrule the recommendations of no less than four selection boards, which were all in favor of Boeing, and grant approval instead to the more costly General Dynamics plane. Gilpatric then shamelessly pushed congressional committees for an immediate signing of the controversial contract, before the deal could be closely examined.

The conflict-of-interest was even more serious in the case of the second McNamara lieutenant, Navy Secretary Fred Korth, a Fort Worth banker and crony of Vice-President Lyndon Johnson. Korth's bank had loaned money to General Dynamics, and that should have raised a red flag right there. Like Gilpatric, Korth recommended that millions of dollars worth of in-depth analysis be ignored. Unlike his Pentagon ally, however, Korth also had the abysmally bad judgment to allow lobbyists for General Dynamics to visit his Pentagon office frequently during the months when the TFX contract was under completion. To top it off, Korth reportedly wrote letters on official navy stationery promoting the bank's business, *after* claiming he had severed the relationship. He'd also taken his bank's customers for rides on the navy's yacht *Sequoia*, congressional staffers discovered.

These embarrassing revelations forced the White House to seek Korth's resignation, which he tendered with the face-saving explanation that he had to attend to "pressing business affairs". Even then, Kennedy aides disingenuously sought to defuse the departure by leaking a story that Korth was quitting over a policy dispute on an unrelated matter. Gilpatric stayed at his post for a while, then left the government to rejoin his law firm.

Despite the flap, the iron-willed McNamara stuck to his original, unpopular decision to allow General Dynamics to build the planes. Years later, in the Johnson administration, it would become painfully apparent that the TFX boondoggle had more than doubled the cost to the taxpayers.

As hot as the TFX battle was in the summer and fall of 1962, it might have been bumped off the front pages if the public had come to know that JFK was secretly recording Oval Office visitors and as many as six hundred calls to and from the White House. An advocate of openness in government, Kennedy covertly taped private conversations for sixteen months.

Using a dictabelt activated by a button on the desk of secretary Evelyn Lincoln, the tapes were made between July 1962 and the president's death in November 1963, after which the system was quietly removed by dutiful Secret Service agents.

JFK taped everything from highly classified discussions with members of the White House National Security Council, to personal chats with First Lady Jackie. Few of Kennedy's aides were aware of the taping device. Ted Sorenson, one of the Kennedy's closest intimates during the White House years, claimed to be "dumbfounded" by the disclosure. Brother Bobby knew his older sibling's penchant for recording, for he used the tapes in writing his 1968 book *Thirteen Days*, concerning the Cuban missile crisis. At least one prominent political figure, Louisiana Senator Russell Long, a frequent visitor to the Kennedy White House, was outraged by the violation of personal privacy. "I consider it highly improper for anyone to record the conversations of a friend without informing the friend that a recording is being made," he snorted. It would be the final covert operation of Kennedy's life.

More has been written about the November 22, 1963, Kennedy assassination than any murder in history. Almost three decades later, dozens of investigations and millions of pages of testimony have produced myriad open questions and a major movie "JFK," challenging the findings of the official Warren Commission report. Mobster Johnny Roselli believed that the CIA plots to kill Fidel Castro backfired and that Castro subsequently had assassin Lee Harvey Oswald and perhaps others recruited to exact a terrible revenge. At least one extensive congressional probe gives credence to that theory: House investigators gathered evidence in 1976 that Oswald had conversations with personnel of the Cuban and Soviet embassies in Mexico City prior to the shooting in Dallas. The CIA concocted a phony story to hide that information, and even the Soviet KGB didn't believe that Oswald had acted alone, according to information released from its Moscow files in 1991.

There's little doubt that the FBI and the CIA both withheld vital details from official inquiries, including the Warren Commission. For example, Hoover's subordinates at the FBI had no less than sixty-nine reports concerning Oswald's pre-assassination activities; twenty-three of them were held back. After Hoover's death that it was learned that the FBI chief had lied about the bureau's knowledge of previous threats by Oswald against the president.

Certainly the CIA had a lot of dirt to sweep under the rug concerning the agency's repeated, blundering attempts to murder Castro and to destablize unfriendly governments by means outside their charter. Even more disturbingly, high-ranking law enforcement officials knew that a full disclosure of assassination evidence might provide harmful details about illicit, perhaps unauthorized CIA-FBI connections to the underworld; revelations of truces between spies, federal cops and the most notorious names in organized crime.

Suspicions of those links led a special House committee counsel to conclude that the Mafia had a sinister role in the killing of the president, and that reputed New Orleans gang-land figure Carlos Marcello was one of the primary suspects. A self-proclaimed tomato salesman, Marcello in reality was the overseer of both illegal and legitimate ventures worth almost a billion dollars, according to law enforcement esti-mates. His pet hatred was reserved not for JFK, but for Bobby Kennedy, whom he contemptuously referred to as "little Bobby son of a bitch." As attorney general, Bobby Kennedy had been responsible (or so the crimelord thought) for Mar-cello's sudden arrest and deportation to Guatemala in 1961, a temporary but humiliating exile which Marcello supposedly longed to avenge.

According to veteran investigative reporter Seth Kantor, Marcello presided over a meeting of ranking Mafiosa in Sep-tember 1962, during which he insisted upon blood-revenge against the Kennedy clan. Soon afterwards, it was reported that fellow capo Santos Trafficante had confided to Miami underlings that JFK was going to be killed. The House Select Committee on Assassinations subpoenaed Trafficante to tes-tify about his knowledge of the meeting and other plots against Castro. But the interrogation ran aground: the num-bers and gambling kingpin, who had feigned panic when served with a congressional summons, refused to answer any questions. His silence didn't stop many experts, including the chief counsel of the committee, G. Robert Blakely, from concluding that organized crime was probably behind the Kennedy assassination, and that the Warren Commission and subsequent probes had missed vital clues on the trail linking the Mafia to Kennedy's murder.

Reporter Kantor, who saw Oswald's assassin, Jack Ruby, on the fateful afternoon of the shooting, raised a host of revelant questions about the former nightclub owner. Far from being the patriotic avenger he was widely portrayed as at the time, Ruby had life-long underworld contacts and once had visited Trafficante in a Havana prison, according to a CIA document which the agency successfully hid for thirteen years. Oswald's possible co-conspirators, and Jack Ruby's true role are just a few of the many unanswered questions about the cataclysmic event which ended Kennedy's eventful Thousand Days—a brief, three-year presidency whose violent conclusion dramatically and unforgettably changed the political fabric of American life.

Chapter 11

TALL TALES FROM TEXAS
Lyndon B. Johnson

November 1963—January 1969

One of the most tragic days in modern American history, ironically, may have saved the long, checkered political career of Lyndon Baines Johnson. With the election still a year away in November 1963, whispers were circulating in Democratic cloakrooms that JFK intended to dump Johnson as his running mate for the 1964 reelection campaign. The young chief executive had reportedly told his vice-president that the rumors were untrue. "I know two states we'll carry; Massachusetts and Texas," Kennedy supposedly had said just before his assassination in Dallas.

Despite an outpouring of national goodwill toward the newly sworn-in president after the nightmarish murder in Texas on November 22, 1963, Johnson had serious personal and political problems to grapple with almost from the moment he took the oath of office. Intense speculation over whether there might have been a conspiracy to kill Kennedy, and who might have been behind it, was just one of the immense headaches facing a man who'd suddenly and tragically achieved his life's dream.

Moveover, a scandal from his tenure as Senate Majority Leader had followed Johnson to the vice-presidency and now took on heightened significance with his sudden ascension to the Oval Office. On the day of the assassination, a man named Don Reynolds was implicating Bobby Baker, Johnson's former chief aide in the Senate, in a tangled web of payoffs and kickbacks which would soon reach into the White House. An insurance salesman and former foreign service officer, Reynolds testified before a closed-door Senate committee concerning his knowledge of Baker's habitual influence-peddling. He wasn't the first to make accusations against LBJ's former right-hand man and errand boy. For months, newspapers and magazines had published a variety of investigative articles about the high-living Baker and his princely lifestyle.

Bobby Baker was literally a child of the Senate; he'd come to work as a page on Capitol Hill at the tender age of fourteen. From an impoverished South Carolina background, the hard-working, acutely ambitious Baker rose quickly through the ranks, and it wasn't long before he caught the eye of an older, powerful politician who undoubtedly saw in his pint-sized protege a younger version of himself. Johnson hired Baker as his secretary in 1955. The hustling congressional aide gained considerable influence when his mentor became the most powerful man in the U.S. Senate, a much-feared, lapel-grabbing, deal-making majority leader. Young Baker, said the autocratic Senate ruler, was "my strong right arm; the last man I see at night, the first one I see in the morning. If I had a son," he once told Bobby, "I'd want him to be just like you."

As LBJ's shadow, Baker became a formidable powerbroker in his own right within the confines of the Senate's prestigious corridors. Copying Johnson's carrot-and-stick approach, the precocious Baker became a staffer whom even Senators were reluctant to cross. He wasn't satisfied being a lackey, however; his friendships with Johnson and Oklahoma Senator Robert Kerr, a willing vassal of big oil companies, provided Baker with plenty of opportunities to cash in on his connections. His salary in 1955 was a modest $9,000, and he had a large family. Just eight years and a thousand favors later, though, his personal wealth had blossomed into a sizable fortune estimated at between one and two million dollars.

His ostenatious lifestyle and free-wheeling party-giving drew the attention of curious reporters; several wrote that Baker had put the squeeze on a Virginia aerospace contractor for a friend who wanted to sell vending machines. The friendly deal later went sour, and a lawsuit over Baker's unwanted interference produced headlines and additional stories about his considerable list of personal investments. Another, more sensational series of exposés about comely party girls at Baker's beck and call made an internal Senate probe almost unavoidable, since his former mentor had become Kennedy's vice-president. One of Baker's fun-loving companions, a twenty-seven-year-old German beauty, Elly Rometsch, was asked to leave the country after the FBI stumbled onto her indiscreet relationships with highly placed government officials.

The continuing Baker controversy was said to have secretly delighted Attorney General Bobby Kennedy in the summer of 1963; RFK detested his brother's running mate and though he might be able to wrap the sinking Baker like an albatross around L.B.J.'s throat and cast him off the Kennedy political ship in 1964. Although virtually everyone in official Washington knew the father-son relationship between Johnson and Baker, no evidence connecting the vice-president to any of Bobby Baker's get-rich schemes surfaced until Reynolds' confidential testimony on the hugely eventful day of November 22, 1963.

Actually, had Reynolds known that the president of the United States was dying at the very time that he was describing a series of kickbacks involving the Johnson family and directed by Baker, he probably would have kept his silence. Indeed, upon learning of the assassination just as he finished his tale, Reynolds attempted to recant his stories. "Giving testimony involving the vice-president is one thing, but when it involves the President himself, that is something else. You can forget I ever said anything if you wanted to," Reynolds implored the stunned senators.

What he'd told the closed-door committee was truly shocking. Through his acquaintance with Baker, Reynolds had sold $200,000 worth of life insurance to Lyndon Johnson in 1957 and 1961, with the premiums paid for and benefits going to the family's "L.B.J. Co." Soon after the sale, he found out that Johnson expected something in return for the investment. Reynolds said he got a telephone call from longtime Johnson aide Walter Jenkins, who suggested that Reynolds should buy advertising time on the Johnson-owned television station KTBC-TV, in Austin. Since his sales territory was in Maryland, the Texas advertisements would be virtually useless to him, but Reynolds understood the implied demand and purchased $1,200 worth of time, later selling it at a loss to a manufacturer.

Then in 1959, Baker had instructed Reynolds to send the Johnsons a stereo set, an order the insurance salesman again complied with, this time shelling out $542 from his own pocket. Reynolds wasn't exactly overwhelmed by gratitude from the Johnsons for his generous gift; Lady Bird complained that the entertainment set was larger than anticipated and didn't fit into her furnishing scheme. Baker and his cronies had also enlisted Reynolds' service as a bag man to deliver political kickbacks around Washington. The insurance salesman told the assembled senators that he'd acted as the "laundry man" for funds give to him by Baker; a lump sum would be divided up and slipped to the right people, while the rest of the boodle went as campaign contributions for Democratic candidates.

To the astonished senators, the devastating implications for the newly sworn president of the United States were obvious. Publicly, LBJ remained calm, downplaying his relationship with Baker and dismissing the charges as politically inspired. In answering questions posed by reporters, the president said that Baker was a "public employee" who had previously "exchanged gifts" with the Johnson family. He was confident that the Senate investigation would disregard "Republican criticism."

Behind the scenes, however, Johnson was in a state of near panic. His former aide could possibly end his presidency before it had really begun; the schemes of a lifetime were hanging in the balance. Beside himself with anxiety, Johnson barged into the office of House Speaker John McCormack and unburdened himself, according to the account of a Washington lobbyist who was present but unnoticed by the ranting president.

"John, that son of a bitch is going to ruin me," cried the chief executive, barely containing his near-hysteria. "I practically raised that m——, and now he's going to make me the

first President of the United States to spend the last days of
his life behind bars...we're all gonna rot in jail."

"Listen, Lyndon," responded the gentle, aging McCor-
mack. "Remember the sign Harry [Truman] had on his desk—
The Buck Stops Here...? Maybe he can make this buck stop at
Bobby."

"You've got to get to Bobby, John. Tell him I expect him to
take the rap for this one on his own. Tell him I'll make it worth
his while. Remind him that I always have," Johnson pleaded.

Following this desperate, private entreaty, LBJ went on the
offensive. Playing his own inimitable brand of Texas hardball,
he augmented its wallop with the awesome power of his new
office. Classified personnel files questioning Reynolds' integrity and testimony were leaked to journalists close to the
White House. For reporters who continued to write critically
of the Baker case, the price was high. On the sly, Johnson tried
to get at least one hard-nosed digger off the track, Clark
Mollenhoff of the Des Moines *Register and Tribune*, by going
over his head and trying to get him fired. Presidential pressure, never easy to resist, was exerted on the aggressive reporter's publishers, but it failed when the newspaper's executives hung tough despite Johnson's complaints that he was
being unfairly hounded by the bearish, boombox-voiced
Mollenhoff.

At the same time, Johnson called in political I.O.U.s in an
attempt to block further congressional probes of the Baker
affair. When the Senate investigation went forward in spite of
the roadblocks, the White House refused to allow testimony
by Walter Jenkins about his alleged pressure on Reynolds
over the television advertising time bought from the fabulously profitable, Johnson-owned station.

Trapped between loyalty to the man who'd boosted his
career and the threat of many years in jail, Baker refused to
answer questions put to him by his former Senate employers;
many of them owed the accused operator favors themselves.
A long list of Bobby's alleged misdeeds were paraded before
the committee, but the administration felt that publicity was
bearable as long as Johnson wasn't dragged any further into
the scandalous quagmire. Let the dirty linen be aired over on
Capitol Hill where it belonged was the prevailing attitude at

the Johnson White House. Ultimately, with Republicans crying whitewash and coverup, the Senate issued a report clear-
ing the president and Walter Jenkins while blasting Baker for
his finanical improprieties.

After the political furor died down, Baker was indicted by
a federal grand jury in 1966 on a variety of charges, including
fraud, conspiracy and income tax evasion. Convicted, he
spent three years in the Lewisburg, Pennsylvania, federal
prison. Bitterly estranged from his former father figure, he
did not meet Johnson again until six years later, just before his
former mentor's death.

Meanwhile, speculation over the true sources of Johnson's
immense personal wealth was yet another thorn in LBJ's side.
While the Baker issue was still in the news, *Life* magazine
published an in-depth examination of the Johnson family
holdings, estimating their fortune at fourteen million dollars.
Taking a page out of his Baker strategy, Johnson made
friendly calls to editors and tried to get them to kill the story.
Failing to block publication, the White House released an
incomplete and outdated account of the Johnsons' wealth
which placed the president's holdings at a small fraction of
other calculations.

The original base of the Johnsons' financial estate was an
Austin television station, which had an unusual monopoly; it
was the only station in the state capital, and continued to
dominate the electronic communications of Austin long after
its preeminence had become an embarrassing public joke.
Senator Barry Goldwater drew laughs on the 1964 campaign
trail when he wryly observed that, as a devoted amateur pilot,
he had never had any trouble finding Austin from the skies,
because it was the only town of that size in Texas with just one
large television antenna. The president's rehearsed reply to
questioners was that Lady Bird handled the family's finances,
and she had a Midas touch which had rapidly made their
dollars multiply.

While he'd discarded a sinking Bobby Baker to save himself, when it came to financial wheeling and dealing for personal gain, Johnson never forgot old friends. One of his most
longstanding personal relationships was with business magnate George Brown, head of the multi-billion dollar Brown

and Root construction conglomerate. Sweet George R. Brown, as Johnson's Senate staff had nicknamed the industrial tycoon, had been quite helpful to a younger, poorer Lyndon Johnson, and when the Texas politician, who'd once been a capable but dirt-poor teacher, found himself at the White House, he let his longtime benefactor know he wouldn't forget past considerations. Indeed, Johnson made certain that Brown and Root was at the top of the list for favors when it came time to dip into the burgeoning pile of federal contracts. In 1962, Brown and Root executives wanted a foothold in a $20 million National Science Foundation award known as "Project Mohole," a drilling expedition with inestimable potential benefits for oil companies. Although its bid was twice the next-lowest estimate, Brown and Root got the contract. After work commenced, the final estimate of cost was revised to $127 million dollars.

Even when U.S. involvement in Vietnam's military morass became a national obsession and threatened his grip on the Oval Office, Johnson took enough time off from meetings with Pentagon officials to see to it that Brown and Root got a generous piece of the lucrative construction awards being made for Southeast Asia. One such project, involving other prominent American firms as well, became a costly boondoggle.

The most damaging details of the president's finagling were never even suggested during his term of office, except in hushed, backroom whispers. Johnson's bootstrap emergence from a harsh backwater of Hill Country poverty made his thirst for money unslakable. The favors he handed out like candy from his first days in Congress weren't given for free; he looked upon the benefactions as investments, not outpourings of generosity or gratitude. By the time he'd reached the vice-presidency, his expectations for cash on the barrelhead were well known among the pin-striped movers and shakers of Washington. Lobbyists and other supplicants brought envelopes stuffed with cash to LBJ's offices, even after he was elected to the second highest office in the land. One oil company lobbyist told Johnson's incisive and tireless biographer, Robert Caro, that he alone had delivered fifty thousand dollars, in one hundred dollar bills and sealed in envelopes, to the vice-president.

Even the crushing responsibilities of the presidency didn't keep Johnson from overseeing his business affairs with the cold eye of an acquisitive board chairman. Lady Bird may have helped build the profitable family communications business, but it was her husband who ran the show. Specially routed telephone calls were placed from the White House to Texas so that the energetic chief executive could personally monitor his vast empire. His innate penchant for secrecy served him well, for during his lifetime no one was able to piece together the confusing puzzle of holdings. And a considerable bundle it was. Johnson's haste to counter *Life's* fourteen million dollar estimate may have been due to the fact, as is apparent in retrospect, that the calculation was too low, not ridiculously high, as the president then claimed.

Johnson's insistence on personal privacy didn't extend to others who came into his presidential orbit, however. Like a gossiping, teenaged girl, LBJ loved to know the latest, juiciest tidbit about everyone, whether friend or foe. If mysterious in his financial dealings, he was open to a fault in his social behavior. Fond of scatological humor, he delighted in summoning secretaries or stuffy, high-ranking officials to the presidential bathroom to take orders or dictation while he sat on the "throne." Completely uninhibited, he would drop his trousers on a sudden whim to show a White House visitor one of his surgical scars.

Among his favorite bedtime reading were top-secret FBI dossiers on a wide range of political and show business celebrities. Johnson would chortle with amusement on learning that a particular congressman was sleeping with his secretary or patronizing a house of ill repute. Just a hint of such knowledge could always prove useful if that legislator tried to withhold his vote on a key issue. J. Edgar Hoover's super-secret files on the famous and near-famous, which weren't uncovered until after his and Johnson's deaths, included many of the biggest names in politics and show business; and indeed, no president had been denied access to the files by an FBI director anxious to stay in favor at the White House.

With Hoover's willing cooperation, Johnson was kept informed of the minutest details of the private life of civil rights activist Dr. Martin Luther King, Jr., whom the FBI boss detested with a passion bordering on paranoia. In fact, one of Hoover and Johnson's most bitter personal enemies, Bobby Kennedy, made it possible for the bureau to spy on King. In October 1963, Attorney General Kennedy gave Hoover a memorandum authorizing the FBI to wiretap King's telephones.

The official justification for the government spying was to determine whether King had any ties to communist groups, a certainty as far as Hoover was concerned. The confidential FBI records show, however, that all the G-men got for their trouble was a sordid replay of King's active sex life. Once, eager agents bugged King's suite in Washington's elegant Willard Hotel, where the civil rights leader drank Black Russians, bragged about his sexual prowess, and then gave a demonstration of his lovemaking technique to a woman visitor. On another occasion, King allegedly became intoxicated and made passes at a woman in a New York City hotel. "King threatened to leap from the 13th floor window of the hotel if this woman would not say she loved him," reported the federal wiretappers solemnly.

The relentless Hoover, ignoring federal laws forbidding cooperative efforts with the Central Intelligence Agency, had raw, unverified reports forwarded to him from the CIA, which was monitoring King's "foreign affairs." While totally naked, King had chased a woman through an Oslo hotel during his Norway visit to receive the Nobel peace prize, according to the CIA spooks, who must have been having a slow week on the espionage circuit. These bedroom adventures, which obviously had nothing to do with King's political activism, were available to the president, who had an ace up his sleeve in case an emergency arose in dealing with the Alabama civil rights crusader.

Despite the mountain of intelligence information at his fingertips, Johnson either missed or failed to act on a background report which could have spared one of his most loyal aides from utter ruination. Walter Jenkins had served Johnson for twenty-five years by the time of the 1964 elections, and was one of the few men who seemed to have a real under-

standing of the multi-faceted Johnson pysche. There was virtually nothing Jenkins wouldn't do for his boss, as proven by
his shakedown of Reynolds for the advertising time. When
Jenkins' role in the Bobby Baker case made headlines, he
stood firm behind the White House phalanx and refused to
testify on Capitol Hill about his improper calls to the insurance salesman.

No one, though, not even the president, was prepared for
the events of October 7, 1964. Barely a month before election
day, at a YMCA mens' room just a block from the White
House, Jenkins was arrested, along with a pensioner in an old
soldier's home, for "disorderly conduct." That was a polite
way of saying that the police officers, who had staked out the
washroom because of complaints, had apparently caught the
two men in a compromising sexual encounter. Rumors about
the arrest of a top White House aide spread like wildfire, and
Republican party officials were only too happy to stoke the
flames by claiming that the incident had been covered up.
Almost frantically, White House advisers Abe Fortas and
Clark Clifford attempted to squelch the story, begging news
editors to consider the crushing effects which publicity would
have on Jenkins' career and family. The high-level pressure
worked for a week, but on October 14, United Press International broke the unofficial embargo.

Johnson was more worried about his political neck than the
fate of his friend of a quarter-century. The sordid revelation
caused election-week panic in Democratic circles, and the
concern doubled when it was learned that Jenkins had been
arrested for a similar offense five years earlier. No less a
journalistic luminary than James Reston of *The New York Times*
intoned gravely that there were national security implications, given Jenkin's lofty status. Why hadn't action been
taken before, asked Richard Nixon and a host of other political heavyweights? If the Soviets had known for years that
Jenkins was a closet homosexual, or bisexual, how may that
have been used to gain access to the nation's secrets?

As in the Baker case, the president was beside himself with
anger about the political backlash that Jenkins' behavior had
caused. Ignoring the human side of his aide's pathetic plight,
he ordered Hoover to find out if security had been breached

by the compromised Jenkins. Only after he learned on October 22 that the FBI had cleared Jenkins did Johnson issue a statement praising his employee for "personal dedication, devotion and tireless labor," and expressing the "deepest compassion" for his departed lieutenant. The sad incident had no discernible effect on Johnson's overwhelming reelection a few weeks later, but the professional life and career of the confused Jenkins had been ruined.

Whispers about the president's own sexual shenanigans had long been a topic of Washington's gossip mill. As insecure personally as he was bombastic professionally, Johnson loved the flattering attentions of attractive young women, and would frequently appear at capital soirees when Lady Bird was out of town with a lovely secretary or aide at his side, who he would introduce as his "date" for the evening. The first lady seemed to have infinite patience with her husband's wandering eye, for she knew that, despite his extramarital adventures, she was the center of his emotional life, his Rock of Gibraltar. After his death, in a televised interview, she said: "Lyndon was a people lover and that did not exclude half the people in the world—women. Oh, I think perhaps there was a time or two...," she broke off, later adding, "If all these ladies had some good points I didn't have, I hope I had the good sense to learn a little bit from it."

Lady Bird wasn't the only person close to the president who experienced both the rewards and punishments of not being able to resist the almost gravitational pull of Johnson's strong personal magnetism. The brilliant attorney Abe Fortas was owed a large debt of gratitude by his Texas friend. As one of Franklin Roosevelt's New Deal braintrusters, Fortas had held a variety of ranking government posts; at the tender age of thirty-two, he'd been undersecretary of the interior. Later he started the law firm of Arnold and Porter, one of the country's most powerful and prestigious legal partnerships.

Most importantly, he'd saved Lyndon Johnson's hide during the most critical months of his political life; Johnson had hired Fortas to represent him in a 1948 court fight stemming from the Senate primary election which writer Caro and others showed was stolen from his opponent, Coke Stevenson. Fortas smoothly negated a challenge to Johnson's candidacy in the general election and he won easily; otherwise, LBJ's career in politics would almost certainly have come to an end. The able Fortas was called upon to pull Johnson's chestnuts out of the fire on many other occasions afterward, including the Baker affair and Jenkins' callously handled departure.

When a seat opened up on the Supreme Court in 1965 with the retirement of Justice Arthur Goldberg, Johnson nominated Fortas, who at first resisted. Finally giving in to the president's legendary powers of persuasion, Fortas acquiesced and served capably on the high court for four years, voting with the majority on landmark civil rights cases. The president had no reason to regret his choice, until suspicions of a conflict of interest arose in 1968. Allegations that Fortas had taken fifteen thousand dollars from donors hoping to sponsor a program of university seminars by him blocked his rise to the chief justice's chair.

What the public wouldn't know until after LBJ left the White House was that Fortas had accepted twenty thousand dollars from a foundation headed by financier Louis Wolfson; that revelation, by *Life* magazine, caused a rare whiff of scandal to emanate from the stately corridors of the Supreme Court. Wolfson, who was later convicted and sentenced to prison on charges of violating federal securities regulations by manipulating stocks, had given Fortas the money just months after the former Johnson adviser had assumed his seat on the court.

While the exchange wasn't illegal, Wolfson dropped Fortas' name in "strategic places" as part of his efforts to stay out of prison on criminal charges. The fact that he used the justice's name without his permission or knowledge didn't lessen the embarrassment for the Court, nor the public outcry when Fortas subsequently admitted that the foundation arrangements provided him with twenty thousand dollars annually for life, payable to Mrs. Fortas in case of his death.

Fortas had seen nothing wrong with attempting to supplement his annual court income of $39,500; he and his cultured wife enjoyed the finer things in life, and the powerhouse laywer had been earning as much as four times this salary before his appointment. Nevertheless, less than two weeks after the disclosures Fortas resigned, the first Supreme Court justice to leave under pressure.

The most far-reaching contretemps of the Johnson White House years, in terms of human suffering and government deception, related to the conduct of the Vietnam war, a devisive conflict which doomed LBJ's otherwise largely successful presidency. A master deceiver and manipulator, Johnson had the tables turned on him and was sold a bill of goods by his military advisers. That bill came due in the turbulent year of 1968, when after months of private anguish, Johnson finally realized that he would have to leave the White House in order to avoid a humiliating defeat at the polls or a full-scale national upheaval. What worse scandal could befall a country than having a president who was unable to safely speak at public gatherings? The entrenched resistance to his Vietnam policies had made Johnson a prisoner of the White House he had so long coveted.

The official lying continued well past his presidency; in 1971, a ton of classified Defense Department documents, dubbed "The Pentagon Papers" by the media, spelled out in gruesome, overwhelming detail the true magnitude of the federal government's deceit about the United States' role in Southeast Asia.

The secret Pentagon files, whose publication caused a landmark court confrontation between the federal government and the media, related Johnson's role in full. During the Vietnam peace negotiations, for example, LBJ alternately suspended and escalated bombing raids in what amounted to a macho effort to intimidate the men across the bargaining table. I'll keep pounding you until you come to heel, Johnson seemed to be saying to the implacable communist foe. Unfortunately, the presidential strategy had the opposite effect on Hanoi; the harder the U.S. bomber planes hit North Vietnam, the more reluctant the communists were to attend the peace talks.

As Soviet ambassador Anatoly Dobrynin told Secretary of State Dean Rusk when peace messages being exchanged through the Poles were abruptly cut off after a series of December, 1966 bombing raids: "The bombing was just before that; the U.S. thought it could pressure Hanoi to talk."

When Johnson doggedly tried the same tactics the following August, North Vietnam's Mai Van Bo replied icily, "The bombing of Hanoi at the same time as the sending of the August 21 [peace] message constitutes a pressure." Only the next year, his forty-year political career in shambles, did the lame duck president realize the futility of bombing diplomacy.

However, in fairness, even the national nightmare of Vietnam, with its toll of 55,000 dead Americans, could not erase the compelling vision of Lyndon Johnson's Great Society or the herculean strides made in civil rights under his courageous and occasionally titanic leadership. But the quicksand in Southeast Asia put a slow, strangling end to his presidency, much more surely than his greedy wheeling and dealing for personal gain, or the sins of Baker, Jenkins or Fortas.

Chapter 12

HIGH CRIMES AND MISDEMEANORS

Richard M. Nixon

January 1969—August 1974

On June 17, 1972, a team of ex-patriate, anti-Castro Cubans, led by a shadowy Central Intelligence operative named E. Howard Hunt and an overzealous Treasury department gumshoe, Gordon Liddy, executed a failed midnight break-in against the offices of the Democratic National Committee at the fashionable Watergate complex in southwest Washington. A piece of tape carelessly left on a door led to their detection by an alert security guard named Frank Willis. Although only a handful of men knew it at the time, the arrest and subsequent criminal prosecution of the motley crew of Watergate burglars was much more than what presidential press secretary Ron Ziegler contemptuously termed a "third rate burglary." Over the next 26 dramatic months, the sloppy crime would lead to an almost unbelievable series of payoffs, coverups and other felonies by top government officials, and ultimately would result in an unprecedented action—the forced resignation of a president of the United States. Two young, intrepid reporters from the *Washington Post*, Bob Woodward and Carl Bernstein, played a pivotal role digging out the multi-layered, shocking story behind the break-in and changed the face of both American politics and journalism in a most profound way.

Perhaps only the years-long Teapot Dome ripoff of President Warren Harding's troubled tenure is a worthy rival to Watergate for the unenviable title as political crime of the century. When Richard Milhous Nixon left the White House aboard a military helicopter after a teary-eyed farewell to his staff on August 9, 1974, and flew into a lonely San Clemente, California exile, he did what no president before him had ever done: he resigned and fled Washington to avoid being impeached and removed from office. In accepting what he later termed "voluntary impeachment," the thirty-seventh chief executive surpassed even the ignominious sins of the Buchanan, Grant and Harding administrations.

The tense, slowly unfolding Watergate drama broke the mold of scandal in the Oval Office, for the president himself was accused of participation in a series of felonies to cover up the original misdeed, an almost laughable piece of political espionage which by itself almost certainly wouldn't have brought down the Nixon White House. Many of Nixon's predecessors had been accused of having crooks or incompetents in their employ, but the drumbeat of the Watergate revelations made it, in Nixon's own pet phrase, "perfectly clear" that he was an unindicted co-conspirator in the crimes.

Watergate gave our constitutional system its gravest test of the modern era. But the sordid saga, as some (most notably author Stanley Kutler) have accurately observed, was by no means an aberration or an isolated event for the Nixon team. In fact, Watergate was the culmination of five and a half years of government by deceit and manipulation. For Richard Nixon, it was the almost inevitable outcome of thirty years of political chicanery and lying.

Having been bitterly disappointed by a razor-thin loss to John F. Kennedy in 1960, an election which might have been stolen from him, Nixon and his cadre of true believers lost no time in showing their win-at-any-cost intentions during the heated presidential campaign of 1968. For starters, the Nixon camp hired a former news editor to act as a "plant" inside the campaign of the Democratic candidate, Vice President Hubert Humphrey. Seymour Freiden filed surveillance reports as often as three times a day with the office of longtime Nixon confidante Murray Chotiner, who forwarded the edited intelligence tidbits to campaign aide H. R. ("Bob") Haldeman.

(Freiden later denied that his activities for the Nixon camp amounted to spying.) Other copies of the covert digests, which were mainly news reports of Democratic activities, were hurriedly copied and provided to Nixon's campaign manager and former law partner, the stoic, pipe-puffing John Mitchell.

Neither this nor similar behind-the-scenes shenanigans caused the Republicans any serious trouble during the presidential race, however. Nixon's narrow election victory capped off the tumultuous year of 1968, which had already seen the assassinations of Robert Kennedy and Martin Luther King, Jr., the humiliating departure of President Lyndon Johnson from a Vietnam-wracked White House, and a head-cracking police riot at the Democratic National Convention in Chicago. These events, coming in quick succession, shocked the nation.

The obsessive paranoia which was to dominate the Nixon White House didn't take long to surface. Haldeman, the crew-cut California advertising executive who became the president's chief of staff, was convinced that outgoing chief executive Lyndon Johnson was bugging the temporary office of the president-elect. Eager to curry favor with the incoming chief executive, FBI chief J. Edgar Hoover endorsed this suspicion and privately warned Nixon not to use the White House switchboard during the transition period. Haldeman, meanwhile, summoned the head of the White House communications agency, Jack Albright, and confronted him with the wiretapping allegation, which the expert immediately branded as a lie. In disbelief, Haldeman dispatched his own de-bugging sleuth to double-check; a thorough combing of the White House turned up nothing unusual. Nevertheless, Nixon aide Melvin Laird had the Secret Service remove the bugging apparatus currently in the Oval Office and replace it with another system. Ironically, that action was later a decisive element in Nixon's downfall.

Just a few months later, in March 1969, White House officials were busily planning to punish opponents of administration policies. Beetle-browed, stern-faced Nixon aide John Ehrlichman, who would soon be known, along with the dour Haldeman, as the White House "Prussian Guard," hired former policeman Jack Caufield to investigate the president's political enemies. Their voluminous hate list later included as many as eleven hundred prominent names from virtually every walk of life: politicians, actors, labor leaders, writers, businessmen, and celebrities as politically negligible as football hero Joe Namath. In turn, Caulfield recruited a retired New York undercover cop named Anthony Ulasawicz, whose varied assignments included digging up dirt on Democratic campaign contributors and candidates in more than twenty states.

Perhaps most disturbingly, the anti-war, counter-culture social activitism of the era grated on Nixon's stiff, button-down management team so much that chilling, even Orwellian, measures were authorized to beef up internal surveillance of enemies of the White House, who were seen to be everywhere. Under the enthusiastic guidance of a previously unknown aide named Thomas Charles Huston, a secret plan was drawn up to permit the National Security Agency to intercept the correspondence and cables of Americans abroad. In addition, all intelligence agencies were permitted to open the mail of anyone whose loyalty was suspected for any reason.

Incredibly, the so-called Huston Plan even legitimized government agents breaking into private homes on grounds of national security. At 29, Huston was placed in charge of what presidential scholar Theodore H. White called the "super-police." Fortunately, Huston made one huge mistake; he tried to go around the bulldog Hoover, one of the toughest bureaucratic gut-fighters of his or any other time. Hoover prevailed on Mitchell, then serving as attorney general, to convince the president of the plot's blatant illegality and unconstitutionality. Within days, all but a few copies of the aborted plan were recovered from the agencies to which they'd been sent, and the suddenly powerful Huston fell from grace, convinced that he'd been done in by weaklings and wastrels in the president's inner circle.

As much as he relished dispatching his detractors in the fierce give-and-take of election campaigns, Nixon's favorite pursuit had long been foreign affairs, and it was in this area that the president and his chief foreign policy guru, national security adviser (later secretary of state) Henry Kissinger, sowed the seeds of their grandiose global ambitions. The specter of a Marxist government in Chile was one of the foremost targets of their designs for covert action. Executives of American-based conglomerates were appalled at the election of socialist Salvador Allende Gossens, fearing that his plans to nationalize the country's industries would cost them hundreds of millions of dollars in lost investments.

Leading the corporate charge against Allende was the International Telephone and Telegraph company (ITT). Aided and abetted by the Central Intelligence Agency, the multi-national corporation spent a king's ransom in an unsuccessful bid to derail Allende's popular 1970 campaign. When their meddling failed, ITT representatives went to the White House with offers to "assist financially in sums to seven figures" in Allende's defeat, according to documents from the company's own files. White House, State Department and CIA bureaucrats were called or visited in an extraordinary lobbying effort.

One knowledgeable source close to CIA Director Richard Helms charged that Nixon "specifically ordered the CIA to get rid of Allende"—which some interpreted as a mandate for the Chilean leader's assassination, according to a detailed account by veteran investigative journalist Seymour Hersh. At the very least, the CIA financed a well-organized propaganda campaign against Allende, and later the agency covertly participated in plots with Chilean right-wing politicians and generals to keep Allende from assuming office. Their aims were belatedly realized when Allende's government was overthrown by an armed coup and he was killed in September 1973. Years of repressive military rule by the dictator General Augusto Pinochet followed.

South America wasn't the only part of the world where Nixon and Kissinger were making mischief, unauthorized by Congress or the American voting public. When a border dispute between India and Pakistan escalated into an ominous regional war in 1971, Nixon publicly stated that the United States would remain neutral. That was an outright lie. Top-secret national security documents revealed that the president was "tilting" toward Pakistan, and that he had ordered

Kissinger to facilitate the provision of U.S. arms and other aid to India's foe. "I am getting hell every half hour from the President that we are not being tough enough on India," the harried national security adviser's aides heard him wail when Nixon felt Kissinger wasn't moving far or fast enough in Pakistan's direction.

With evidence mounting that the Pakistanis were bombing civilian positions, State Department analysts suggested in eyes-only cables that the president's faith might be misplaced and could generate a backlash of resentment against the U.S in Southwest Asia. Opposition from a foreign service bureaucracy which he despised served only to stiffen Nixon's determination. Stubbornly, he dispatched the navy's Task Force 74 to confront the growing Soviet naval presence in the war zone. After a last-minute plea for a cease fire, the beleaguered Pakistanis' military commanders halted the successful Indian offensive and averted a possible eyeball-to-eyeball confrontation between the superpowers.

While making their mark on conflict and intrigue in virtually every corner of the world, Nixon and his Metternich, Kissinger, saved their most duplicitious sleights-of-hand for the continuing heartache in Vietnam, which had driven his predecessor Lyndon Johnson from office. The president was determined to go down in history for delivering a "generation of peace" to Southeast Asia; to achieve that lofty goal, he was prepared to bomb military and civilian targets alike without congressional authorization. In the spring of 1969, when the North Vietnamese were dawdling over the terms of peace negotiations, Nixon ordered the Pentagon to begin a massive secret bombing campaign in neighboring Cambodia, in the hopes that the wholesale destruction might disable the supply lines of his communist foes and accomplish through intimidation or sheer destruction what diplomatic posturing had not.

The provocative tactics backfired; the greater the tonnage of bombs rained on Cambodia, the more intransigent the North Vietnamese became. Nixon's Cambodian escapade prolonged, rather than shortened the U.S. stay in Vietnam. (Years afterward, he obstinately insisted that he should have begun the unprecedented and illegal air assault earlier.)

More significantly, the revelation of the B-52 bombing triggered a fatal domestic policy decision, which ultimately damaged the Nixon White House just as much. In May 1969, press reports detailing the super-sensitive Cambodian operations, the first of which were written by William Beecher of the *New York Times*, so infuriated Kissinger that he swore to "destroy whoever (leaked the national security information) if we can find him, no matter where he is," according to an FBI memo of a conversation with agency director Hoover.

Kissinger's angry tirade set the stage for a covert wiretapping program directed against the White House's own staff, and the reporters who spoke to them. The two years of telephone tapping ("special coverage" as the president euphemistically referred to it) provided insight into the paranoia and self-delusion growing like a cancer inside the Nixon administration. Kissinger even approved (if he did not personally order) the wiretapping of the home phones of members of his own National Security Council staff. The electronic surveillance was also extended to track Air Force Colonel Robert Pursley, the top aide of Defense Secretary Laird, who reportedly was regarded with scorn and distrust by both the president and Kissinger.

The spying only finally came to an end at a July 12, 1971, retreat at the presidential residence at San Clemente, California, when Nixon ordered the destruction of all White House logs and wiretap summaries. The purging of the files didn't satisfy the Nixon crew's hunger for blackmail information on media figures whose sympathies were regarded as unfair or anti-Nixon (the terms being synonymous at the White House). When syndicated columnist Jack Anderson became particularly nettlesome in 1971, Nixon had a special internal security team, informally known as the "Plumbers," track the newsman and his staff twenty-four hours a day, including their journeys to work and trips to the supermarket. Codenamed "Operation Mudhen," the enterprise was a Keystone Kops comedy. Bird-dogging the pestering pundit must have been a boring assignment for the highly trained government gumshoes: Anderson was a teetotaling, pot-bellied Mormon who sneaked chocolate-covered macadamia nuts out of his desk drawer, rarely socialized, and whose idea of an exciting evening was watching television with his wife, Olivia.

The infamous Plumbers unit had grown out of the larger wiretapping investigation. As Nixon scholar Stephen E. Ambrose noted, the president himself ordered the creation of the Plumbers unit because he was growing increasingly exasperated by leaks originating from the White House. Ehrlichman was told bluntly by an irritated chief executive: "If we can't get anyone in this damn government to do something about [leaks], then, by God, we'll do it ourselves. I want you to set up a little group right here in the White House. Have them get off their tails and find out what's going on and figure out how to stop it."

Operating out of a barren office in the White House basement, the Plumbers had a wide variety of clandestine activities. Besides spying, their operations included a 1971 attempted burglary, which Ehrlichman contended was personally ordered by Nixon, into the office of the psychiatrist treating Daniel Ellsberg. A Rand corporation employee, Ellsberg was a brilliant, obsessive intellectual whose disaffection with the administration's Vietnam war policies led to the leaking and subsequent publication of the so-called Pentagon Papers, classified studies outlining years of duplicity and self-deception in Southeast Asia.

Meanwhile, Nixon and Kissinger pursued their ambitious foreign policy to establish American hegemony by setting the stage for billions of dollars worth of price gouging by the international oil cartel. The most important economic stories of the early 1970s centered around oil and its tactical use as a weapon by petroleum-rich nations. The skyrocketing price policies of the Organization of Petroleum Exporting Countries (OPEC) forced frustrated Americans to wait in long gasoline lines, sent entire nations into economic panic, and caused spiraling international inflation which stymied even the combined leadership of the western oil-consuming countries. But locked in the files of the CIA was evidence that the Nixon White House, far from fighting the catastrophic price hikes, had deliberately allowed the American public to be overcharged.

The shah of Iran, Mohammed Reza Pahlavi, was described

as unstable, weak and capricious in secret CIA psychological profiles (despite the fact that the agency had helped install him on the Peacock Throne in 1953). The Iranian leader had an all-consuming dream: he was determined to drag his technologically backward nation into the twentieth century, while remaining a bulwark of anti-communist stability in the Persian Gulf. Such grandiose plans fit perfectly into the Nixon-Kissinger blueprint for the region, and in July 1972, orders were issued giving the shah a virtual *carte blanche* to purchase whatever U.S. weapons he wanted. Needless to say, military contractors were delighted, eagerly scrambling aboard planes to Teheran in order to display the latest in electronic warfare gadgetry to the receptive Iranian ruler.

The shah's appetite for advanced technology seemed boundless, despite increasing internal opposition to his free-spending, Westernized regime from fundamentalist Islamic leaders. However, he realized that in order to transform his nation into a world power in a generation, he would need more dollars, a conclusion which convinced him to jump onto OPEC's budget-busting oil price bandwagon. CIA analysts noted in a secret summary: "The largest oil price increase in history took effect...as a result of decisions made at a December [1973] meeting of OPEC ministers in Teheran. The increase in the posted price—$5.04 to $11.65 (per barrel)—came primarily through the efforts of the Shah of Iran.

The shah, in need of money for his development and military programs, argued that the price of oil should rise because (a) such a move would immmediately improve the revenue and balance of payments positions of OPEC members, (b) oil was being wasted by consuming countries at prices then prevailing and (c) oil is a nonrenewable resource that would soon run out.

Saudi Arabia, however, recognizing the potentially disastrous inflationary and trade implications of sudden price hikes, resisted the cartel's advances. Behind the scenes, the Saudi princes implored Washington officials to pressure the shah to hold down oil prices; only with the Iranians' cooperation, they insisted, could they break the OPEC stranglehold. But Nixon and Kissinger ignored their repeated entreaties. Alarmed, King Faisal told Secretary of the Treasury William

Simon that he would help force prices back down by increasing the formidable Saudi oil production, if the U.S. would enlist the shah's support. To show their good faith, the Saudis promised to sell a large volume of oil at public auction, thus cutting world demand and putting a lid, if only temporarily, on the spiraling petroleum prices.

Returning to Washington, Simon met privately with Nixon and thought that he had impressed the president with the urgency of the situation. Nevertheless, no effort was made subsequently to convince the shah that he and his OPEC cohorts might devastate the economies of the U.S. and Latin America. Besides, the Saudi auction, reported the CIA, "never materialized." Characteristically cautious, the Saudis' arch-conservative ruling families were unwilling to stand alone against the other Arab oil-producing nations. Even after prices increased four-fold and the world economy was reeling from the shock, the shah was unsatisfied with his cash flow and sought further hikes; his ministers launched an intensive lobbying campaign which resulted in another 10 percent boost in OPEC prices.

At the same time, the arms-hungry shah was circulating rumors that the U.S. leadership privately supported the price hikes. The U.S. ambassador to Saudi Arabia, James Akins, reported in a confidential diplomatic cable that, "the Iranians had told [the Saudis] that we were completely unconcerned about any price rise. The Shah has also told this to numerous oilmen as proof that the U.S. is at least indifferent to an increase in oil prices."

Whatever the U. S. government's intentions, the hundreds of millions in additional oil revenue amounted to a direct subsidy to the shah, who used the booty to buy even more U.S. military hardware. Yet, the weapons bazaar did little to prevent his repressive regime from being subsequently overthrown by Islamic radicals, and he ended his life as a lonely, sick exile. The shock waves from this foreign policy fiasco would reverberate for years; the fundamentalist takeover and subsequent seizure of American hostages in Iran would later undermine the presidency of Jimmy Carter.

While this economic and foreign policy disaster was slowly unfolding, Vice President Spiro ("Ted") Agnew, a former

Maryland governor whom Nixon had plucked from relative obscurity and transformed into an eager point man for the administration's strident campaign against its detractors, was aggressively attacking the president's perceived enemies in the media, academia and Congress. He also verbally assaulted faint-hearted officeholders from his own party who, by White House standards, weren't hewing closely enough to Nixon's policy pronouncements.

Speaking up for what he called America's voiceless "silent majority," Agnew let loose with the tongue-tripping broadsides which Nixon loved, but felt he couldn't utter personally. His headlined railings against the "nattering nabobs of negativism" and other alliterative malapropisms made fascinating news copy and created a hardcore fan club, which soon included politically conservative Hollywood luminaries, such as Frank Sinatra and Bob Hope. As Agnew successfully, if crudely, articulated the prejudices and frustrations of middle and working class Americans dazed by the confusing social upheavals of the era, Nixon's lieutenants quietly congratulated themselves on finding such a useful lightning rod to take the heat off the "Old Man," as they irreverently referred to the president behind his back. Agnew's ability to draw some of the fire away from Nixon may not have been simply political; according to Kissinger, Nixon believed that his vocal vice president also provided assassination insurance for him by providing a more accessible and attractive public target.

Agnew eventually would prove to be more of an albatross than a harbinger of good fortune. In his highly publicized speeches, he was sharply critical of "affluent, permissive, upper class parents who...threw discipline out the window when they should have done the opposite." Yet it was clear that Agnew couldn't handle his own family crises. His son Randy had been arrested for maintaining a "disorderly house" and for marijuana possession, broke up with his young wife and moved in with a male hairdresser while his father was lecturing millions of Americans on the sanctity of traditional family values, according to the revelations of syndicated columnist Anderson.

Financial propriety wasn't one of Agnew's strong points, either. As governor of Maryland, a state with a murky history of political corruption, he had accumulated a closet full of skeletons. Nixon's background-checkers hadn't ferreted these out when they picked him as second banana for the 1968 ticket, but they began to come to light even before the Republican team won at the ballot boxes. For instance, it was revealed that the vice presidential nominee had been a director and stockholder of a bank which held $200,000 in state funds, while at the same time administering Maryland's banking laws. He'd also bought land which, as governor, he later helped select as an approach to a bridge; the tract's value, of course, skyrocketed.

Agnew's ethical compass hadn't gotten any closer to course in the summer of 1968 when he became a vice presidential candidate. He boastfully promised a group of admiring Texas oilmen that the administration would block the construction of a refinery they opposed, *if* they anted up sufficient campaign contributions for the GOP ticket. After the election, Agnew didn't shrink from using his influence to cadge favors and federal contracts for business friends.

Nixon seriously considered replacing his controversial vice president on the 1972 ticket with the man he wanted to replace him as president after his second term—former Texas governor and Treasury secretary John Connally. Agnew's enthusiastic following among diehard conservatives, however, made him practically impossible to drop, so Nixon did the next best thing; he kneecapped him. Less than a week after the election, he summoned Agnew to the presidential retreat at Camp David for a brutally frank message; thereafter, the reelected president told his stunned running mate, the White House staff would run the vice president's office. Presidential aides would decide whom Agnew could hire and fire, where he would travel and how much money he could spend.

Ultimately, whispers that, as governor, Agnew had accepted kickbacks from Maryland state contractors spilled out into the open; federal prosecutors secretly assembled evidence from witnesses who claimed to have paid cash bribes to him. One informant charged that he had continued to make payments even after Agnew ascended to the vice presidency.

In April 1973, Agnew learned that a federal grand jury was hearing evidence against him. Nixon kept his outspoken vice president at arm's length for months during the headlined investigation. Over a period of months, Agnew the lightning rod became Agnew the political deadweight. Finally, in September, the White House suggested to Charles Colson, who'd left the administration and was helping Agnew as a private attorney, that the vice president ought to consider resigning. "I am innocent. I am going to stick it out," Agnew vowed defiantly.

White House officials had no intention of backstopping a vice president who was on a beeline to federal indictment. A laboriously worded arrangement was worked out, and on October 10, 1973, in a crowded Baltimore courtroom, Agnew quietly agreed to the conditions of his resignation. Soon afterward, the ex-vice-president pleaded no contest to charges that he hadn't paid taxes on $10,000 in income. Nine years later, in January 1983, Agnew was ordered to pay the state of Maryland more than $268,000 in fines and interest relating to the kickbacks which he allegedly had received while governor.

Under more normal political circumstances, the humiliating, forced resignation of a vice president would have been one of the worst calamities which could befall a sitting chief executive. But Agnew's agonizing public ruination wasn't foremost in Nixon's mind after his reelection, for he had his own problems. First of all, the 1972 campaign had been probably the dirtiest in modern history; although he didn't realize it at the time, it had set the stage for Nixon's ultimate downfall. Nixon had spent a lifetime fighting for the ultimate prize of the presidency, and he had no intention of serving only one term. Two years before his reelection race, he had mercilessly set out to disrupt the plans of his potential Democratic adversaries, and now the over-zealous activities of his White House-directed fanactics had come back to haunt him.

Nixon and other Republican candidates, most notably Arizona Senator Barry Goldwater, had been bedeviled by the Democrats' unofficial political prankster, Californian Dick Tuck, for years. Once, Tuck supposedly had arranged to sneak a young female spy onto Goldwater's presidential campaign train; she'd distributed copies of an amusing but phony newsletter ridiculing Goldwater before she was caught by press aide Vic Gold and was unceremoniously kicked off the train in Charlestown, West Virginia. The imaginative Tuck had also been credited (perhaps overcredited) with hounding Nixon with a variety of imaginative and embarrassing tricks.

For instance, political lore has it that once, when Nixon was giving a campaign speech from a train caboose in California, Tuck was dressed as a conductor and tried to get the train to pull out of the station. Another time, Tuck and his cohorts bedeviled a Nixon appearance in an Asian district with signs in Chinese which said, "What about the Hughes' loan?" referring to a controversial $205,000 loan provided by tycoon Howard Hughes to Nixon's brother, Donald.

Now it was get-even time. The White House campaign team hired a baby-faced, thirty-year-old lawyer named Donald Segretti (whose surname, ironically, means "secrets" in Italian) to help sow discord in the enemy camp long before it was even clear who Nixon's opponent might be in the 1972 presidential election. In words of Ehrlichman, Segretti would be "our Dick Tuck."

Nixon's minions had far more in mind than a few innocent pranks, although the secret operation produced several sophomoric stunts which were nasty, but fairly harmless. Working with fellow University of Southern California alumnus and Haldeman aide Dwight Chapin, Segretti established political operatives in as many as seventeen states. Their mission was to undercut the Democrats by whatever means possible: the schedules of Democratic candidates were thrown off by calls from GOP mischief-makers; unwanted pizzas and office equipment were ordered and billed to clueless campaign aides; false statements were given to the press; hecklers were hired to harass opposing candidates and their wives; offices were trashed or otherwise disrupted; and forged letters containing bogus claims about Democratic office-seekers were circulated.

Spies were also utilized to eavesdrop or steal information from several prominent Democrats who were regarded as potential threats to Nixon's reelection. The White House planners initially were most concerned about a challenge from an articulate, statesmanlike Democratic senator from Maine, Edmund Muskie. As part of their secret, ominously-titled "offensive security program," the White House's naughty boys recruited a taxicab driver to serve as a plant inside Muskie's campaign headquarters. Elmer Wyatt portrayed himself as an eager volunteer for Muskie while earning five hundred dollars a month from the other side to smuggle out memos and schedules. He delivered them to an ex-FBI agent named John ("Fat Jack") Buckley, who in turn obligingly handed them over to Nixon campaign aides Jeb Stuart Magruder and Bart Porter.

Segretti's team of youthful miscreants also arranged for a private detective to shadow Muskie in California, and hired accomplices to break into Muskie's Florida headquarters and plant a stink bomb. In addition, they concocted a phony flyer on Muskie stationery, which wrongfully accused fellow Democratic senators (and presidential hopefuls) Henry ("Scoop") Jackson and Hubert Humphrey of sexual and drinking misdemeanors, a missive Segretti later described as "scurrilous."

In covert operations codenamed "Ruby I" and "Ruby II," the White House-directed Plumbers stole confidential documents from Muskie's headquarters in Washington and passed them along to the Republican Committee to Re-elect the President (known by the apt acronym of "CREEP"). Haldeman even suggested that Ruby II's operatives electronically bug the offices of South Dakota Senator George McGovern, but he was overruled.

"Sedan Chair," named after a military exercise, was another plot, aimed at the campaigns of Senators Humphrey, Muskie and McGovern. This two-phase sabotage effort was just as underhanded but somewhat less successful, according to the later account of its manager, the weak-willed Jeb Stuart Magruder, who served as CREEP's deputy manager during the campaign. Another young Californian, Roger Greaves, was hired to do spying chores, but soon quit because he disliked the work. A private detective from Kentucky was then retained as part of "Sedan Chair II," to infiltrate Humphrey's Pennsylvania campaign. However, Magruder found that Humhprey's effort in that state was a "disaster," with few volunteers and no organization, and concluded that throwing a monkeywrench into it was totally unnecessary.

That scheme was written off as "comic relief" by Magruder,

who may have had a rather twisted idea of what was funny. More seriously, in 1969, the young, ambitious White House aide had suggested in writing to his White House superiors that they utilize the Internal Revenue Service "as a method to look into the various organizations that we are most concerned about. Just the threat of an IRS investigation will probably turn their approach"—this from a man who became a Presbyterian minister some years after serving seven months in jail for Watergate-related offenses.

Perhaps the most telling incident presaging the Watergate burglaries and bungled cover-up, though, was a January 1972 briefing for Attorney General Mitchell concerning the Nixon campaign's gameplan for covert intelligence-gathering and convention security. Conducted by G. Gordon Liddy, a Justice Department lawyer and former member of the Plumbers' unit (which was disbanded in 1971), the presentation raised the eyebrows of even the hard-bitten Mitchell, who certainly was no stranger to political hardball. The mustached Liddy, whose bearing and attitude more closely resembled a soldier of fortune than a government bureaucrat, liked to get attention by holding his hand over a candle to display his physical courage. Some of his CREEP colleagues regarded Liddy as a bit odd, but a reliable go-getter; others thought he was just plain nuts.

"Operation Crystal" demonstrated Liddy's mindset. It called for extensive electronic surveillance of the political opposition, including a "chase plane" to tail the Democrats' campaign plane and make transcriptions of all airborne communications. Wiretaps were also to be part of the unprecedented preelection spying operation.

That was just a prelude to what Liddy had in mind for the Democratic convention site, according to the accounts of those present at the briefing, including Magruder and presidential counsel John Dean. "Operation Sapphire" detailed proposals for kidnappings, blackmail, and the use of high-priced prostitutes ("only the best," intoned Liddy solemnly) against the Democrats. Nixon's unleashing of the Plumbers had allowed the paranoia of Liddy and other true believers to reach new heights. A stickler for detail, Liddy even had contingency plans to sabotage the air conditioning system inside the convention hall, so that the assembled delgates would sweat and swear for the television cameras.

"Well, Gordon, that's all very intriguing, but not quite what I had in mind," said Mitchell weakly, appalled both at the audacity and the cost of the ambitious paramilitary scheme. Despite Mitchell's veto of activities he later described as "beyond the pale," another, slightly toned-down version of the bizarre battle plan, this one codenamed "Gemstone," was approved only weeks later, and led directly to the Watergate break-in during June, six months after Liddy's harebrained lecture.

Why did the bumbling gang of Watergate burglars sneak into the Democratic headquarters in the first place? Theories have been offered, although none has answered all the hundreds of questions. One widely accepted explanation was that Democratic party boss Larry O'Brien, a long-time Nixon nemesis, was the target. Hunt, Liddy and their cohorts were searching for derogatory information on O'Brien, who was probably near the top of Nixon's hate list. Or, perhaps they were hunting for any information that O'Brien and his aides might be hoarding to use against Nixon and his fellow Republicans.

O'Brien had driven Nixon to distraction for more than a decade with allegations that billionaire industrialist and movie tycoon Howard Hughes had given the president's brother, Donald, a $205,000 loan under suspicious circumstances. The circumstances surrounding the loan had been a campaign issue in Nixon's 1960 run for the presidency, and were still largely unresolved a dozen years later. There's considerable evidence to show that the Nixon White House feared an attempt by O'Brien and the Democrats to resuscitate the controversy as part of a campaign attack on the president's personal finances, about which many questions had also been raised. Moreover, Nixon was livid that so little had been made of O'Brien's own acceptance of a retainer from the fabulously wealthy Hughes.

Nixon's almost obsessive preoccupation with O'Brien was revealed in a January 14, 1971, memo dictated from Air Force One, suggesting to H.R. Haldeman that "it would seem that the time is approaching when Larry O'Brien is held account-

able for his retainer with Hughes." The memo seemed to
suggest that the president was trying to get even with the
Democratic party chief by ordering an extensive probe of his
activities and financial records. Indeed, the espionage plan
ultimately approved by Mitchell, Gemstone, had as its two
primary targets O'Brien's safe at the Democratic headquarters in Washington, and the safe of Las Vegas publisher and
Hughes-watcher Hank Greenspun, who was thought to have
documented information relating to the O'Brien/Hughes
connection.

This was, in part, the thread that the *Washington Post's*
investigative duo, Woodward and Bernstein, followed in a
three-year series of Pulitzer Prize-winning stories. They doggedly traced the questions raised by money found in possession of the Watergate crew, which eventually led to its origin
with the CREEP committee and payoffs to buy the burglars'
silence.

Others with a more conspiratorial frame of mind believe
that the U.S. military intelligence establishment felt betrayed
by Nixon and wanted him destroyed. Adherents of this interpretation point to Hunt's life-long ties to the Central Intelligence Agency, and the involvement of the Cubans. Several of
the Cuban burglars recruited by the shadowy Hunt were
veterans of the ill-fated Bay of Pigs invasion, which was
botched by the CIA and resulted in a decade of angry recriminations within the spying community. The authors of *Silent
Coup*, Len Colodny and Robert Gettlin, detail spying against
the Nixon White House and the theft of classified documents
by the military intelligence network. Their analysis further
asserts that, rather than being merely a participant in the
coverup, presidential counsel John Dean was the instigator of
the break-in *and* its coverup, because the Democrats' files
supposedly contained explosive information on a criminal
prostitution investigation relating to his wife, Maureen, and
several of her friends. Dean called the charges "absolute gar-
bage."

Whatever really lay behind the break-in, the evidence
gleaned from two extraordinary congressional investigations
and the independent probe of special prosecutor Leon Jaworski, clearly demonstrated that, rather than admit publicly that

his cadre of spies and dirty tricksters had careened out of control, Nixon chose to orchestrate a determined cover-up of his knowledge of the incident almost from its discovery. The single most telling piece of proof is contained in the so-called smoking gun tape of a White House conversation recorded on June 23, 1973, less than a week afterwards, which revealed that the president illegally authorized the CIA to block further FBI investigation of the Watergate controversy.

The FBI had traced some of the money recovered from the burglars back to CIA connections, and Mitchell recommended that CIA deputy director Vernon Walters be encouraged to tell FBI director L. Patrick Gray III to "stay the hell out of this." On the fateful tape, Nixon ordered Haldeman to call the CIA hierarchy and warn them that further interference might lead to the "whole Bay of Pigs thing." The CIA should tell the FBI "Don't go further into this case[,] period!"

The obedient Walters, after assuring Haldeman that there was no CIA involvement in the Watergate break-in, visited Gray promptly. "I reported," Walters recorded in a June 28, 1972 memo, "that if the [Watergate] investigation were pushed 'south of the border,' it could trespass on some of our covert projects, and in view of the fact that five men involved were under arrest, it would be better to taper the matter further." The pliant Gray responded, according the memos, that "this was a most awkward matter to come up during an election year, and he would see what he could do."

The Watergate tapes also revealed that Nixon knew that it would be fatal to have it revealed that his concern with the break-in was with the political rather than criminal aspects of the case; but from that critical moment the president of the United States was the orchestrator of a criminal cover-up. When this fact was made public almost two years later, even some of Nixon's most diehard supporters were forced to realize that his presidency was doomed. The president had been unmasked as a duplicitous liar, to his own lawyers and aides as well as to the nation.

Ironically, the unraveling of the tapestry of falsehoods during two years of torturous investigations exposed Nixon to many more humiliations than he would have had to endure if he'd merely thrown himself on the mercy of a largely adoring

public in 1972 and confessed to what might have been regarded as minor indiscretions, or perhaps even "politics as
usual." The Senate's special Watergate committee of almost
100 employees, headed by North Carolina's folksy Sam Ervin,
and the House Judiciary Committee, chaired by New Jersey
Congressman Peter Rodino, initiated months-long probes
(the Senate's covered by live television broadcast) which uncovered the sordid details of five years of government by
deceit. Ultimately, after much wrangling, Rodino's colleagues
recommended impeachment proceedings against the president before the full House, the first such recommendation
since Andrew ("King Andy") Johnson's climactic confrontation with Congress, 106 years before.

Nixon's ill-advised move to fire special prosecutor Archibald Cox (he was replaced by Houston attorney Jaworski),
and the resulting resignations of Attorney General Elliot
Richardson and his deputy, William Ruckelshaus, in the infamous "Saturday Night Massacre" was another milestone in
the unsuccessful attempt to prevent outside ears from hearing
the damning words of the tapes in full, and proved yet another nail in the president's political coffin.

Nixon's repeated use of the Internal Revenue Service to
punish political opponents (he once proposed that IRS audits
be directed at every member of Congress and, on the Watergate tapes, threatened to replace IRS commissioner Johnnie
Walters with "a man," because he wasn't bending to White
House suggestions to utilize the agency as a political weapon)
might never have surfaced except for the Watergate inquiries.
In all likelihood, the payoffs to the Watergate conspirators,
the excesses of the Plumbers unit, the wiretaps against reporters and administration employees, the revelations that Nixon
had grossly underpaid his personal taxes by almost half a
million dollars, and the campaign crimes of CREEP—would
have remained unknown to the public had it not been for for
the accidental apprehension of the Watergate burglars and the
two-year, clandestine effort to buy their silence.

The March 21, 1973, tapes revealed that the president knew
of threats by Howard Hunt to blackmail the White House, and
that he approved of efforts to raise hush money for the Watergate burglars. But he might have survived even the revelation

of his complicity, had it not been for his clearly illegal decision, the week after the break-in, to order the CIA to block the
FBI probe of Watergate. Once he had committed the unmistakable crime of obstruction of justice, not even his most
ardent defenders on Capitol Hill could save him.

Eight years after the unprecedented events which led to the
resignation of an American president, Nixon conceded to
interviewer David Frost that events had "snowballed. It was
my fault. I'm not blaming anyone...I brought myself down."
Even then, however, Nixon stubbornly argued that "technically," he hadn't committed a crime, but that his actions had
given his enemies a "sword" and "they twisted it in." Reveal-
ingly, he concluded, "I guess I would have done the same
thing."

Chapter 13

FORD'S FOLLIES

Gerald R. Ford

August 1974—January 1977

"If Jerry Ford saw a hungry child, he would give the kid his lunch. But he can't see that voting against the school lunch program is depriving millions of kids of food." That revealing comment, from Democrat A. Robert Kleiner of Gerald Ford's former congressional district, goes a long way towards describing the dichotomy of Ford the man versus Ford the politician. Personable, with an affability which endeared him to political foes as well as Republican allies, Jerry Ford was the kind of man anyone would want as a next-door neighbor.

In many ways, he was the quintessential all-American boy—a blonde, handsome, celebrated college football hero who went on to considerable success, but remained humble, decent and public-spirited. He and his wife, Betty, an attractive, intelligent divorcee whom Ford married in 1948, raised a quartet of good-looking, well-adjusted children. The young Michigander won a seat in Congress and took his unvarnished Midwestern values to Washington, where he displayed traits of loyalty and industriousness, if not originality. Ford as politician gradually became much like the position he played so well in college—a center; the solid, dependable team player who would unselfishly lead the way for others to score points.

His cautious, hard-working, responsible approach served him well during his quarter-century on Capitol Hill. Put suc-

cinctly, Ford followed the often-repeated maxim of the cantankerous, legendary Speaker of the House Sam Rayburn:
"Go along to get along." A key figure in organizing Republican opposition to the Great Society programs of social legislation proposed by Lyndon Johnson, he was skillful enough to
cause LBJ to grouse to amused newsmen, "Jerry Ford is a nice
guy, but he's played too much football with his helmet off."

All in all, the congressional life was a good one for Ford,
albeit with a few rough spots. He was grieved by accusations
that, as a member of the Warren Commission investigating
the assassination of John F. Kennedy, he had been part of a
massive coverup of evidence which suggested a conspiracy
during the November 22, 1963, shooting of the president in
Dallas. More embarrassingly, his unrestrained partisan zeal
helped give him a black eye in 1970, when he led an ill-advised effort to impeach Supreme Court Justice William O.
Douglas, as part of Richard Nixon's drive to halt what he
regarded as the legislating of liberal social policy from the
bench.

Three years later, the failing political fortunes of the Water-
gate-tainted GOP had Ford considering whether his future
lay outside the Congress he had served for most of his adult
life. Fate and the sins of Vice President Spiro Agnew intervened, however, and Ford the loyal foot soldier and party
leader was tapped for the most demanding assignment of his
life. To replace the disgraced and departed Agnew, Ford had
to undergo a grueling background check by the FBI and the
Senate Rules Committee; few, if any, public officials ever received this level of painstaking scrutiny.

Anyone who had a bad word to say about Gerald Ford or
his public career was interviewed at length and their allegations cross-checked. Investigators talked to former college
footballers whom Ford had scrimmaged against 35 years earlier to determine whether he had been a clean player on the
gridiron. Charges that Ford had been the bagman for millions
in secret milk fund money for the Republican party were
examined and discounted, as were dubious charges by a former Washington lobbyist that the congressman was a willing
participant in a series of under-the-table deals with big business magnates.

One political sore spot that was rubbed hard was an allegation that Ford had actively sought to block one of the original Watergate probes. The investigation in question, initiated to trace how Watergate-related money had been laundered in Mexico, was conducted by the chairman of the House Banking Committee, Democratic Representative Wright Patman, a staunch, unabashed Texas populist and sworn enemy of the Nixon White House.

Patman had lost no time going after the trail of Watergate greenbacks; he'd smelled a skunk in the Nixon campaign woodpile even before the president's 1972 reelection victory. His staff's dogged snooping had White House officials nervous, and they pulled out all the stops to short-circuit the inquiry before the real implications of the money-laundering scheme could be uncovered. Patman's plans to take a committee vote for subpoena power to pursue the line of questioning had Nixon beside himself with anger. As a Republican leader, Ford admitted that he had opposed the Patman investigation, but denied that his footdragging tactics were orchestrated from the White House.

Given his sterling reputation, he was believed, but the Watergate tapes, released years later, suggest that the Nixon White House had had different ideas about utilizing the Michigan congressman to thwart the hated Patman. On September 15, 1972, in discussing Patman's plans to White House aides, Nixon stressed, "Jerry has really got to lead on this...Ford should be told, emphasized Nixon, "Now, goddamn it, get the hell over with this" [Patman probe]. On another occasion, the beleaugered chief executive ominously wondered aloud whether Ford could "do anything with Patman....The game has to be played awfully rough." Nixon wanted Ford to bolster the confidence of wavering Republicans on the committee who might be tempted to side with Patman. One of them was New Jersey Representative William Widnall, the ranking Republican member of the banking committee. Nixon apparently regarded Widnall as too weak to play hardball for the White House's cause, for he suggested on the taped transcripts that "Jerry should talk to Widnall and, uh, just brace him."

The two men chosen to deliver the message from Nixon to

Ford were White House aides Richard Cook and William Timmons. Former presidential counsel John Dean, who was privy to most of the Watergate coverup scenarios, claimed that Timmons and Cook met with Ford to discuss derailing the pestering Patman. Both aides denied that they spoke to Ford about aborting the probe, and the congressman insisted he acted on his own. Whatever the reason for Ford's meddling, it was effective, for Patman was defeated in a committee vote of 20-14, and an early opportunity to uncover a key part of the truth behind the Watergate break-in was sacrificed.

By July 1974, Nixon was damned by his own words on the Watergate tapes; when he was told by Alexander Haig and others that he would almost surely be impeached if he remained in office, he abdicated the presidency by helicopter and retreated into exile in his home state of California. Suddenly, a bland-looking former congressman unknown to most Americans became their leader.

Ford's first thirty days in office were greeted with an unprecedented outpouring of good will and overwhelming public support. Temporarily dropping their Watergate aggressiveness, reporters marveled at Ford's casual accessibility, his becoming modesty, the pedestrian touch he showed at buttering his own English muffins for breakfast at his Alexandria, Virginia, home. Here at last was a man to restore faith in honest and open government. Past political controversies were quickly forgotten in a concerted effort to awaken Americans from the national nightmare of Watergate, and to celebrate that the democratic system had somehow survived intact.

The honeymoon lasted almost a month to the day. On September 8, 1974, with a few quick strokes of his presidential pen, the new chief executive cut short the brief summer truce and brought the renewed wrath of the press and much of the American public down on his bald head with a fury he never anticipated. He pardoned his predecessor, Richard Nixon, who had not been formally charged with any crime, and caused his personal popularity to take a precipitous, overnight nosedive of more than twenty points. With a stiff formality uncharacteristic of the casual Ford, he announced that he had decided to use the powers of his office to grant a "full, free and absolute" pardon to Nixon.

Although he had realized his action would be unpopular ("I don't need the polls to tell me whether I'm right or not," he grumbled at aides who sought to dissuade him or delay the decision), even this seasoned politician familiar with the capricious nature of public opinion didn't anticipate the deluge of anger and resentment which reverberated across the country. Polls reflected a disapproval of his pardon by almost two to one, and many of the same legislators who had pledged their fealty to the Ford regime were now fuming about rumors of a secret deal between Ford and Nixon's retainers, closeted at San Clemente, California, three thousand miles from Washington.

True, Ford had hinted earlier, in response to reporters' questions, that he was "not ruling it [a pardon] out." But, usually the ultimate team player and conciliator, he kept the decision to himself and a few trusted staffers until just prior to the public statement. The Watergate special prosecutor, Leon Jaworski, wasn't told, although he was ready to seek a federal indictment against Nixon "within a matter of weeks" if the pardon hadn't intervened, according to those familiar with the Texas lawyer's plans. Jaworski believed that he had an "iron clad" case against the former president, based largely on the hundreds of hours of White House tapes.

Jaworski wasn't the only one left in the dark. Presidential press secretary Jerry TerHorst, a respected Detroit journalist and longtime close personal friend of Ford, and who'd been at his job only a month, couldn't reconcile himself to his employer's controversial decision. Not wishing to embarrass a man he'd admired for many years, TerHorst nonetheless spent the night before the formal press briefing drafting a letter of resignation in protest. "Try as I can," TerHorst wrote to Ford, "it is impossible for me to conclude that the former President is more deserving of mercy than persons of lesser station in life whose offense had far less effect on our national well-being."

Ford asked aides to press TerHorst to put off quitting so that the next day's headlines wouldn't reflect an internal split on the pardon so close to the Oval Office. The conscience-stricken press secretary waited a few hours, but his hasty exit temporarily placed a severe strain on his personal friendship with the president.

For weeks, speculation centered around the question only the president could satisfactorily answer—why had he jeopardized the entire future of his administration to pull Nixon's legal chestnuts from the fire? His predecessor's health was obviously on Ford's mind. Nixon had been described as "weary, depressed and completely despondent" by those who had seen him at San Clemente. The nagging phlebitis in his leg had flared up again, his skin looked gray and he'd lost a noticeable amount of weight. Most troubling, Nixon's normally piercing mind seemed to wander in conversation.

It's likely, however, that Ford's real motive was more selfish and practical. He had to get out from under the constant tug-of-war for the tapes and other evidence against Nixon and his collaborators. Sitting in the Oval Office for just a few short weeks had taught him to look ahead, and all he could see before the granting of the pardon was having his administration indefinitely tied up in legal knots over the possible criminal prosecution of a once-popular chief executive. Ford wanted no part of protracted wrangling, nor did he desire to listen to the daily pleas from Nixon loyalists who lobbied strenuously on his behalf. If Ford was going to have to do this job, then he'd take decisive action and put his own personal stamp on the presidency.

With all that in mind, he sent 36-year-old attorney Benton Becker out to the Nixon compound in San Clemente to negotiate a complex agreement over the acquisition of the tapes. Becker was instructed to tell Nixon and his representatives that a pardon was just a possibility, not a foregone conclusion. The young lawyer showed a draft of the pardon statement that he was told Ford might deliver to Nixon's personal lawyer, Herbert ("Jack") Miller, and former presidential press secretary Ron Ziegler. After lengthy discussions over administrative and legal details, Becker was ushered in to see an alert but tired Nixon. "Thank you for being fair...You're a fine young man," Nixon blurted to the startled Ford emissary.

Fifteen months later, in December 1975, the *Washington Post's* investigative duo Bob Woodward and Carl Bernstein reported that Ford had given Haig "private assurances" that a pardon would be granted, almost two weeks before the president made his decision public. From his post as U.S. Ambassador to the North Atlantic Treaty Organization (NATO), General Haig confirmed that discussions did take place about that time, and it was no secret that Haig and other Nixon diehards, such as speechwriter Ray Price, tried to win Ford over to the idea of an unconditional pardon from the first day of his presidency.

The resulting hubbub caused a congressional panel to submit written questions to Ford concerning the events surrounding his momentous, unilateral decision. To the surprise of the House Judiciary subcommittee and its chairman, Representative William Hungate, Ford disdained the formal exchange of written communiques and offered to answer the questions in person. In an almost unprecedented action, Ford fielded inquiries from the panel on Capitol Hill for two hours on October 17, 1974.

"In summary, Mr. Chairman, I assure you there never was at any time any agreement whatsoever concerning a pardon to Nixon if he were to resign and I were to become President," Ford told the committee members, realizing that a significant number of people, in Washington and around the country, no longer believed him.

With the pardon backlash still ringing in his ears after barely two months in office, Ford could have been forgiven for hoping for a little smoother sailing. No such luck. Nelson Aldrich Rockefeller, whom Ford had decided to nominate to fill the vice presidency that he had left vacant, was his next unexpected headache. Stupefyingly rich and ambitous, the former New York governor had made an illustrious career from understanding and playing upon the symbiotic relationship between immense wealth and political power. Active in national politics since Franklin D. Roosevelt's New Deal days, Rockefeller had failed to capture the top rung on the political ladder largely because the conservative members of his own party distrusted his motives and his family's clout in international finance. His divorce and remarriage to his second wife, "Happy," hadn't helped his prospects, either, in an era when divorce frequently meant the end of a promising political career.

The choice of the raspy-voiced tycoon politician prompted howls of outrage from disappointed arch-conservatives, suspicious of allowing any member of the hated Rockefeller clan so close to the Oval Office. These objections notwithstanding, a Senate weary of controversy was in no mood to deny Ford his choice for any major post, and Rockefeller's record of public service to country and party should have made his confirmation a foregone conclusion.

Unfortunately for the Ford White House, Watergate had changed the rules of the game. The last thing Ford needed in the fall of 1974 was another public airing of dirty linen. That's exactly what the White House got when extensive FBI and congressional background investigations uncovered the fact that Rockefeller had given large sums of money to former employees and public servants, including some who were among the cream of the political establishment.

For example, Secretary of State Henry Kissinger, who had been invited to remain in the Ford cabinet, had received $50,000 from Rockefeller in 1969. The nominee and his brother David, chairman of Chase Manhattan Bank, had long been the diplomat's patrons. L. Judson Morhouse, former chairman of the state Repubican party organization, got $86,000, and William D. Ronan, chairman of the New York and New Jersey Port Authority, had been granted no less than $550,000, presumably because Rockefeller felt he was a dedicated public servant. Naturally, congressmen then earning a little more than $40,000 annually felt obliged to inquire as to whether such lucrative tributes might not also buy influence. Ford, like Eisenhower, was in awe of men with tons of money, and dismissed the criticism. Belaboring the obvious to the point of embarrassment, the president noted that Rockefeller was a "very, very wealthy" man, and his generosity was merely the normal expression of gratitude to public-spiritedness.

The uproar over elevating Rockefeller to the second highest office didn't end there. It seemed that, like his friend Jerry Ford, Rockefeller had a barracuda's taste for distinguished jurists. Just as Ford had attempted to slam Justice Douglas, Rockefeller had a favorite Supreme Court target—former Justice Arthur Goldberg. However, Rockefeller was a bit more discreet about putting the knife into his victim. Rather than denouncing him directly, Rockefeller bankrolled $60,000 toward a decidedly unflattering biography of Goldberg, written by conservative curmudgeon Victor Lasky and entitled *Arthur J. Goldberg: The Old and the New*. The covert funding of the scurrilous attack was only half the story; the book had been published during 1970, when Goldberg had campaigned against Rockefeller for the governorship of New York. Senators sitting in judgment on the confirmation were surprised to learn that the nominee's gubernatorial campaign had received 100,000 copies of the anti-Goldberg diatribe to distribute to voters.

The plot thickened further when Rockefeller and his phalanx of public relations sycophants were accused of making misstatements about the Goldberg affair. Soon the mystery over who had actually paid for the anti-Goldberg book took on greater significance than Rockefeller's habitual gift-giving. Initially, Rockefeller stated that his brother Laurance had put up the dough for the attack on Goldberg, but it soon became apparent that he had let his sibling take the fall for the dirty tricks campaign planned, financed and executed by Nelson's own team of political men-in-waiting. Attributing his earlier version of events to a faulty memory, Rockefeller finally confessed after it became clear that House investigators decided that his aides had possibly lied, and that his once-unassailable nomination might be in danger if the charade continued. None of the congressmen passing judgment, however, were anxious to create another political showdown by denying Ford his choice for vice president, especially just a few months after the resignation and pardon of a disgraced president. Only a handful of anti-Rockefeller conservatives and a few outraged liberals voted against the nominee.

There was to be no rest for the weary. Yet another brouhaha, one of the most serious and far-reaching of Ford's term, literally hit the headlines on December 12, 1974, when *The New York Times* began a critical, front-page investigative series by their ace reporter, Seymour Hersh, on the past sins of the intelligence community. The Central Intelligence Agency, charged Hersh, had engaged in wholesale illegal domestic spying and mail-opening during the 1950s and 60s, and had kept thousands of secret files on antiwar dissidents. Predictably, the revelations created a furor, with other major news organizations scurrying to catch up to Hersh's months of determined digging.

Ford, worried that a scandal could cripple the intelligence agency and its ability to gather information, was assured by CIA director William Colby and Henry Kissinger that no such programs existed in *his* administration. The bespectacled Colby conceded that there had been some abuses in the past, however. The CIA's illicit shenanigans had been chronicled in what was known inside the spy world as "The Family Jewels," compiled on the orders of the organization's director in 1973, James Schlesinger.

When he got a close look at the "Jewels," Ford agreed to a full-scale investigation. The president was stunned and dismayed by all that the list revealed: among other plots, were details of past assassination schemes aimed at unfriendly leaders, including Cuba's Fidel Castro. Trying to head off accusations of a coverup, Ford appointed a special commission, headed by Vice President Rockefeller, to plumb the CIA's inner workings.

With an emboldened, post-Watergate press breathing down its neck, Congress lost no time getting into the act, and two separate investigations were formed, chaired by Democrats Frank Church in the Senate, and Representative Otis Pike in the House. Top-ranking CIA officials at the agency's Langley, Virginia, headquarters had no intention of becoming scapegoats for journalistic or political headhunters. Colby pledged his full cooperation, but the intelligence agents, in the view of congressional probers, stonewalled and obfuscated every step of the way, citing "national security" as the overriding reason for withholding vital files.

Gregory Rushford, then a staffer on the House Select Committee on Intelligence, which looked into the allegations, said that the CIA "used every executive branch tactic to frustrate our investigation." Colby's idea of revealing testimony, charged Rushford, was "little lectures on the evils of communism; banal, condescending trivialities," which prompted one member of the Pike committee, Representative Philip Hayes, to complain that he was tired of hearing "appeals to a very low level of sophistication."

Meanwhile, the president had promised the congressional committees unrestricted access to the files opened up for the Rockefeller Commission, "plus any other material that is available in the executive branch." Yet it took the Pike committee months to obtain an unexpurgated version of the "Family Jewels," and that only after the disgusted New York congressional chairman threatened to cry coverup. According to Rushford, the CIA's real reason for withholding documentation was "bureaucratic self-protection." Pike and Church staffers received copies of "Top Secret" intelligence reports which contained only those words, and were otherwise blanked out by CIA censors for page after page. Government experts at the CIA and State Department, when scheduled for interviews by the Pike committee, were ordered not to talk to congressional investigators. When an analyst was made available, the spy agency's bureaucrats insisted on having a "monitor" present to eavesdrop on the interview and interrupt it if anything deemed sensitive was broached by Capitol Hill interrogators.

One fact became apparent—the CIA had its share of foibles under Presidents Eisenhower, Kennedy, Johnson and Ford, and was no stranger to petty in-fighting, sloppy analysis and occasional incompetence. Like every bureaucracy, the CIA was self-serving and self-perpetuating, but it possessed shady resources which frightened even presidents.

The ongoing probes were disturbing the daily routine at the White House. So many requests for documents were coming in to the National Security Council and the White House that Ford had to appoint a special top-level committee, headed by aides John Marsh and Mike Duval, to handle the paper traffic.

Fat was added to the fire in March 1975 when syndicated columnist Jack Anderson broke a story which had been supressed for months by other news organizations. The CIA had secretly slipped $250 million to tycoon Howard Hughes for an extraordinary "deep cover" project. Hughes' organization had built a unique deep-sea exploration ship named the *Glomar Explorer*. The intelligence operatives had an ulterior motive for stealthily sharing so large a chunk of the taxpayers' money with the brilliant but unpredictable Hughes. In August 1974, the *Glomar* had recovered part of a Soviet missile submarine which had sunk in 1968, hundreds of miles from the Hawaiian coastline.

Snippets had been leaking out for months. The *Los Angeles Times* had pieced together the essential facts, but Colby had managed to block publication by going over the reporters' heads and pleading to editors that the remainder of the sub, purportedly an intelligence goldmine, could never be retrieved if the account came out. Calls from the persuasive Colby had put the lid on the story all over the capital, until Anderson, a long-time Hughes-watcher, got wind of it. When Colby heard that the columnist was also on the trail, he placed a personal, late evening call to his office.

With a firm tone in his voice, the CIA boss tried to convince Anderson, as he had others, that publication of the *Glomar* details would strike a fatal blow to an important government intelligence project. Doodling on a nearby pad, Anderson listened politely to Colby's well-rehearshed pitch, reassuringly replied that he had withheld stories in the past for legitimate reasons of national security, but made no commitment to the spy chief. Almost immediately after hanging up the phone, Anderson broke the explosive story on his national radio show, fearing that if Colby was lobbying with such determination, it was going to become public soon, anyway. The rest of the recovery mission was scrubbed as a result of the nationwide publicity which followed.

By the next month, the Rockefeller Commission had finished its lengthy investigation, and the results were made public after a brief flap in which Ford administration officials were accused of sitting on the potentially damaging findings. As Hersh had reported, the agency had indeed been guilty of opening the mail of American citizens, and of wiretapping the telephones of antiwar protestors and federal tax evaders, in direct violation of the agency's charter and mission. Worse yet, CIA officials had inexplicably administered the hallucinogenic drug LSD and other mind-bending substances to unwitting experiment subjects to test them for possible use in intelligence and military operations. The lives of several unsuspecting victims were ruined by exposure to experimental narcotics whose effects were at that time unknown and unpredictable.

The Church and Pike committees received sworn testimony that the CIA had been involved with other plots against the lives of foreign leaders unfriendly to the U.S., such as the Congo's Patrice Lamumba, South Vietnam's Ngo Dinh Diem and Haiti's notorious Papa Doc Duvalier. The Rockefeller commission's gumshoes also learned that the Soviet Union had installed sophisticated electronic eavesdropping equipment at its embassy to listen in on White House conversations only a few blocks away. When Henry Kissinger objected to the publication of such an alarming discovery, the offending passage was watered down for the public report, according to Ford's second press secretary, Ron Nessen.

Months of headlines and television interviews with outraged congressmen made it inevitable that the CIA, which many thought had become a rogue elephant, would have to be restrained in some fashion. New laws were promulgated, forbidding certain types of covert activities without the express knowledge or consent of Congress. Intelligence officials protested vehemently that their legitimate information-gathering networks would be completely hamstrung by the restrictions, but the thunderous public pressure was not to be denied. The shakeup rocked the agency for over five years.

The most humiliating flap involving a cabinet official during the Ford era was centered around an unlikely figure for scandal, Agriculture Secretary Earl Butz. A well-regarded administrator, Butz was popular in Republican circles despite a frequently abrasive personality. Ironically, his downfall occurred not over his farm policies or the administration's controversial wheat sales to the Soviet Union, but because of a thoughtless, coarse joke he told aboard an airplane whose passengers also included show business celebrities Sonny Bono and Pat Boone.

Having just attended the Republicans' 1976 convention in Kansas City, where he had noticed a dearth of African-American conventioneers, Boone, a staunch GOP loyalist, innocently asked Butz why the GOP couldn't attract more black voters. Always possessed of a sharp tongue, the agriculture secretary answered before he thought: "I'll tell you why you can't attract coloreds...because coloreds only want three things...first, a tight pussy; second, loose shoes; and third, a warm place to shit. That's all."

The straight-laced, deeply religious Boone was no doubt shocked by Butz's crass locker room reply, but it was former Nixon counsel and Watergate tattletale John Dean who reported the incident in *Rolling Stone* magazine, having overheard the cabinet official's off-hand remark.

Dean didn't identify that agriculture secretary by name, but it didn't take long for campaign reporters familiar with Butz's taste for off-color humor to figure out who had uttered the slur. Republican cronies rallied to defend the free market advocate. However, Butz's remarks had been too racist and graphic to be ignored, even in jest, so close to election time. He was forced to resign, almost in tears over the ignominious end of his distinguished public career.

Butz's indiscretion wasn't the only gaffe by the Ford camp in the campaign against former Georgia governor and born-again Christian Jimmy Carter. Ford's vice presidential running mate, Kansas Senator Robert Dole, was accused of pressuring the Nixon White House on behalf of the dairy industry to accept two million dollars in milk money for GOP campaigns.

The milk scandal temporarily stained former Treasury Secretary and Texas governor John Connally's image (although he was acquitted in a jury trial) and sullied reputations on both sides of the political fence. Internal White House memos dated February 1971, from Nixon chief of staff H. R. ("Bob") Haldeman to Charles Colson, revealed that the dairymen had leaned on Dole to lobby the White House for higher price supports for milk. At a secret White House meeting, Nixon had indeed decided to reverse a ruling against the subsidies increase. Dole's office conceded that he had made a few appeals to the White House, but they insisted that wasn't part of the decision-making process at the executive branch.

Dole's alleged role in the milk industry controversy didn't do as much harm as his frontal assaults on the administration's critics, which attracted a floodtide of criticism for the Ford ticket. At least the acerbic senator attacked his opponents out in the open; the same couldn't be said for his running mate. Ford's staff leaked unfounded rumors that Carter had had extra-marital affairs with several women. The dirty trick backfired when the allegations against the clean-living Baptist candidate were traced back to their presidential sources.

A slumping economy and the promises of a Southern-bred, anti-Washington populist frustrated Ford's hopes to be elected to the highest office on his own merits. Bitterly disappointed by the close defeat, he left the White House with a touch of class, his head up, knowing that he had played the key role in rescuing America from an especially stormy constitutional and political period.

Chapter 14

THE PEANUT PREACHER

James E. Carter

January 1977—January 1981

Jimmy Carter, as a presidential candidate, was neither ahead of nor behind his time in 1976: the former Georgia governor was the perfect remedy for the post-Watergate era, for an America sick of official Washington, high-level lying, grand jury indictments and screaming headlines. His toothy grin and soft-spoken, down-home populism was an exilir for the voters' woes. A compulsive planner with a formidable intelligence and an iron will, Carter correctly surmised that a national candidate who emphasized personal honesty and openness over ideological purity on the issues would be the man to win.

Just as they had fawned over Jerry Ford's self-effacing manner and modest habits, reporters and commentators made an overnight hero of the Peach State peanut farmer, praising his every pronouncement and offering only a cursory examination of his record as a public official. His brash, callow "Georgia mafia" were hailed as a welcome change in stuffy Washington, and expectations were raised to a level unequaled in the capital since the charismatic John F. Kennedy had captured the imagination of the entire nation.

If Carter's rise was meteoric, his fall and the disillusionment it created were all the more swift and tragic. His one-term presidency was viewed by many observers as a bold experiment that failed. It wasn't for lack of ability; Carter's intellect was as rarefied and exceptional as that of Nixon or Kennedy, and he worked as hard as any chief executive of the modern era. However, his annoying penchant for moral posturing, and a tendency to be preoccupied with mundane details, rather than the big picture, caused some to question his executive leadership abilities. While his personal probity was unchallenged, Carter surrounded himself with an inner circle of inexperienced cronies who could not or would not subjugate their narrow-minded parochial interests, or their collective desire to publicly humiliate their enemies, real and imagined alike. The most talented men in his administration, such as the universally respected secretary of state, Cyrus Vance, were rarely the real decision makers.

To be sure, Carter's four years did feature some notable and under-recognized achievements: the historic Camp David peace accords for the Middle East, the beginnings of a rational energy policy, the necessary and difficult passage of the Panama Canal treaty—to name just a few. A closer look at the record, however, shows a president who, for all his powers of intense concentration and good intentions, never gained full control of careless aides, blundering family members or an entrenched bureaucracy which ill served him. Scandal was no stranger to the Peanut Preacher who in Biblical terms, could always see the speck in another's eye, but never the log in his own.

It didn't take long for trouble to start brewing in the Carter White House. In fact, just days before the inaugural, it was revealed that the president-elect's son, Jack, had been less-than-honorably discharged from the Navy as a result of a drug bust by naval agents in Idaho. It was a minor, one-day flap, but a disturbing harbinger of what was to come; as the incident demonstrated, things were not always as advertised in the Carter camp.

Just weeks into the presidency, Carter learned that the turmoil inside the intelligence community hadn't died down, even after three official investigations and a host of new restricive regulations had been imposed upon the spy world. On February 18, 1977, the *Washington Post* splashed a Bob Woodward scoop across the front page: "CIA Paid Millions to Jordan's King Hussein." Operating under a clandestine program called "No Beef" since the mid-1950s, the CIA had been funneling millions of dollars to Hussein, a bearded, diminutive monarch who'd survived more than fifteen assassination plots.

A lover of sports cars and beautiful women, Hussein apparently had been a willing recipient of the U.S. taxpayers' largesse. What only a handful of people knew at the time was that Carter had made his first attempt at media censorship: he'd tried to kill the story with a personal appeal to *Post* executive editor Benjamin Bradlee, who had listened attentively but remained unmoved. The timing of the revelation put Secretary Vance in an awkward position, as he was scheduled to meet with the Jordanian leader the day the story was published.

The next administration misstep was far costlier. Carter personally set the stage for a major fiasco by appointing his bosom buddy T. Bertram Lance, a millionaire banking executive with no experience in federal fiscal policy or budgets, as his director of the Office of Management and Budget. A bearish, convivial back-slapper, Lance had used his banking connections in Georgia to raise campaign funds for Carter's previous races (he had tried to succeed Carter as governor but finished a dismal third in the balloting). He was a confidant with whom the president felt comfortable praying in the Oval Office. "He was the first person I thought about when I was finally sure I would be elected President," Carter had said.

Greenbacks as well as camaraderie bound the two expatriate Georgians together. The Carter family's peanut warehouse ran up loans of $4.7 million (some of it at preferential rates) at Lance's National Bank of Georgia, making the first family the institution's biggest borrower.

Initially, the country banker from Calhoun was given red carpet treatment at his nomination hearings by a cordial bipartisan group from the Senate Governmental Affairs Committee. The office of the Comptroller of the Currency at the Treasury Department had investigated overdrafts at Lance's Calhoun bank, but acting director Robert Bloom passed over these irregularities. In a report to the committee, he instead praised the bank's rapid growth, pronouncing Lance "well qualified" to be the nation's budget chief. After being virtually rubber-stamped into office, Lance consolidated his position as the second most powerful man in the administration, for with the exception of First Lady Rosalynn Carter, he became the president's most trusted adviser, as well as his fiscal policy manager.

Despite the toothless Senate inquiry, rumors persisted concerning Lance's financial background, which several enterprising reporters, including Philip Taubman of *Time* magazine and former Nixon speechwriter and pundit William Safire of the *New York Times*, began to examine in detail. The truth behind Lance's dubious bank dealings was a shocking tale. In addition to allowing his wife, LaBelle, and relatives to routinely overdraw accounts at his Calhoun Bank, the budget boss had used the same bank stock as collateral for two different loans, a practice generally regarded as a violation of banking ethics.

Far from being a cautious investor, Lance was revealed to be a free-"lancing" wheeler-dealer who was more heavily in debt than he had previously admitted. Worse yet, the value of his stock in the National Bank of Georgia, of which he had become president after his tenure at Calhoun, had fallen so low that a good deal of his personal financial assets would have been wiped out if he had sold them, as he was required to do under the federal conflict-of-interest regulations.

The weak-willed Bloom's replacement, John Heimann, launched his own probe into the burgeoning Lance affair, which by this time was generating a lot of heat for the Carter White House. The result was a laborious, 403-page official report which, while not recommending any criminal action or official sanction against the OMB director, disclosed a significant number of "unsound banking practices" in violation of federal regulations.

Incredibly, the president treated this scathing document as a total vindication of his Georgia pal. "Bert, I'm proud of you," Carter intoned, beaming at Lance as the two of them stood side by side at a press conference to discuss Heimann's findings. The man who had promised the highest standards of integrity in goverment turned a blind eye to solid evidence that his best friend was fiscally reckless at best, and perhaps criminally negligent.

Carter's Panglossian attitude didn't make Lance's troubles disappear. On the contrary, the Heimann report touched off a new avalanche of criticism directed at the White House. There was a another, darker side to the story: a Justice Department inquiry into Lance's activities had been quietly terminated in December 1976. The former U.S. attorney who had been in charge of the case, John Stokes, Jr., maintained that he had acted properly and in good faith, but claimed that the administration had withheld from him an FBI report critical of Lance's tangled financial background.

That was too much for several senators, who had already been embarrassed by the budget chief's sloppy confirmation. They went to the White House to pressure the president for Lance's immediate resignation. Both Carter and Lance refused to budge, however, and the demand caused presidential press secretary Jody Powell to unleash a nasty little piece of attempted revenge. Irked by the turnaround on Lance of Republican Senator Charles Percy, he leaked a phony story to reporters that in a 1972 election campaign, Percy had improperly used an airplane belonging to the firm he had helped to start, Bell & Howell. When the underhanded ploy was traced back to a sheepish Powell, it only added fuel to the Lance controversy and brought new suspicions that the White House had something to cover up.

A fresh round of Senate hearings was convened, with the inquiring legislators determined not to look foolish again. Still the picture of affability and innocence despite the furor, Lance spent long hours with Washington superlawyer Clark Clifford and other top legal talent in an effort to organize a defense and deflect the torrent of criticism awaiting him on Capitol Hill. His performance was impressive, considering the circumstances, and Carter loyally stuck by his friend; but by this time, half a dozen federal investigations were pending against Lance, including probes by the Internal Revenue Service and the Securities and Exchange Commission.

Deeply religious, like his presidential patron, Lance had dropped by the Oval Office for a daybreak prayer session with Carter preceding the Senate grilling. He had selected three Bible passages, which he read aloud to the born-again president. Nothing could save his job, however; the political heat had gotten too intense for him to remain in the administration. So, on September 21, 1977, Carter reluctantly announced that he had accepted a letter of resignation from his beleaguered friend.

"I was talking the other day, with just a group of us who had been close, and we all decided that if we could have named 2,000 different things that might have caused me any problem or any embarrassment, that Bert Lance's character would have been the last thing we would have guessed about," the dejected chief executive mused.

Leaving government service didn't end Lance's woes; in fact, they were just beginning. Months later, federal investigators discovered possible evidence of an improper one million dollar loan to the Carter family's peanut business. A federal grand jury in Atlanta called the President's irrepressible brother Billy to explain his role in arranging the suspect loan, which apparently was not fully secured by bonded commodities (in this case, peanuts) as required by law. Defiant as usual, Billy took the Fifth Amendment and refused to testify, on the grounds that the grand jury hadn't produced the warehouse's financial records for him to study first. The president, who was the majority stockholder in the family corporation at the time, had a hand in arranging the controversial loan.

So many questions were raised about the Carter brothers' handling of their warehouse finances that a special federal prosecutor, Republican attorney Paul Curran of New York, was appointed to investigate suspicions that funds might have been illegally diverted from the business to Carter's campaign. After a six-month probe, Curran declared on October 16, 1979, that "every nickel and every peanut has been traced," and cleared the Carters in a 180-page report. During the course of the investigation, which cost $360,000, FBI agents and investigative accountants poured over 80,000 bank documents and papers, and Curran took four hours of sworn testimony from President Carter. The special prosecutor found overdrafts, inadequate bookkeeping and payment errors in the warehouse records, but his bottom-line conclusions quieted most of the storm of controversy.

The termination of the peanut probe didn't get the long-suffering Lance out of hot water, though; he was indicted by a federal grand jury in Atlanta for banking irregularities. Although finally acquitted in April 1980 on nine counts of bank fraud (a mistrial was declared on three other criminal counts), Lance was emotionally wrung out and considerably poorer at the end of his ordeal. Ironically, none of these contretemps would ever have happened had his buddy, the President, not sought to thrust the good ole boy banker into the national financial spotlight.

Peter Bourne, a dapper Englishman, was strikingly different from Bert Lance. Urbane, highly educated, Bourne and his wife Mary King had helped to introduce the Carters to Washington's wealthy and powerful "green book" society during the pre-election days, when the future president was still regarded as "Jimmy Who?" in the fashionable drawing rooms of Georgetown and Capitol Hill. Their blueblood society contacts made it possible for the Carters, then outsiders to the capital and its cliquish ways, to gain influential fundraising, door-opening friends.

Both Bourne and his well-coiffured wife had hoped for plum appointments as their reward after the Carters moved into 1600 Pennsylvania Avenue, but as part of Washington's upper crust, they were regarded as outsiders themselves by the inner circle of Georgians who took command of the White House. Mary King was appointed deputy director of the social welfare ACTION agency, which was under the leadership of former antiwar activist Sam Brown, and Dr. Bourne was offered the post of presidential drug adviser. In their own way, each appointment turned out to be mildly disastrous for the administration. Perhaps unfairly, King was viewed as an imperious social climber, and her motivations were widely distrusted by the dedicated anti-poverty activists who dominated ACTION. Survivors of the Nixon administration's attempted dismantling of the agency worked hard to thwart her, and leaked gossipy and possibly exaggerated stories about her fussy grooming habits and her supposed junketing at agency expense.

The ugly infighting that King's presence caused at ACTION, though, was a minor inconvenience compared to the commotion her husband's careless blundering caused. The drug adviser's problems started early in July 1978, when

Bourne aide Ellen Metsky complained to her boss that the stresses of her White House position were straining her ability to cope. Sympathetically, Bourne suggested counseling. When Metsky reportedly rejected that advice, Bourne wrote out a prescription for Quaaludes, a tranquilizer popular with the drug subculture. For reasons known only to the good doctor, he used the ficticious name "Sarah Brown" on the prescription.

Little did Bourne realize that his well-meaning action was the beginning of the end of his short-lived career as a presidential appointee. When a friend of Metsky tried to get the prescription filled in a suburban drug store, a state pharmacy board investigator, who just happened to be in the shop, asked the purchaser for identification. Having nothing in the non-existent name of Sarah Brown, she was arrested and forced to admit that the Quaaludes were for someone else—a someone who worked at the White House.

Revelation of the incident by the *Washington Post* set off emergency meetings at the White House over what to do about Bourne's thoughtless folly. He was, after all, the president's chief drug adviser, and writing a presciption for what were popularly regarded as "downers" under questionable pretenses would do nothing to raise his standing in the drug enforcement community. Powell and strategist Hamilton Jordan, after discussing the situation with Carter legal counsel Robert Lipshutz, decided that Bourne would have to be suspended with pay until the matter could be investigated and its political ramifications analyzed.

If the controversy had ended there, Bourne might have survived the few days of critical headlines, since it became clear that he had been acting out of concern for an emotionally distraught assistant who had come to him for help. His forgery was ill-considered, but perhaps forgivable considering the circumstances, his defenders hopefully maintained.

But Bourne was about to receive a lesson in the competitive, highly charged world of White House media coverage. Stories such as Bourne's usually came in twos and threes; once an official of his rank admitted an indiscretion, a ratpack hunt of his entire personal and professional history was al-

most sure to follow. With blood in the water, the press corps
piranhas circled for the kill.

As might have been predicted, Bourne's indiscretion
brought down another, far more serious charge against him
which had been circulating as rumor for weeks at cocktail
parties and in newsrooms—that he had not only prescribed
drugs illicitly, but he had used more potent narcotics himself,
including cocaine. Columnist Jack Anderson's reporter Gary
Cohn, a tow-headed, frenetic young journalist, had personally attended a large party where cocaine had been passed
around. That in itself was not remarkable for a capital soiree
of that period, but it hardly inspired confidence that the president's chief narcotics adviser had allowed himself to be seen
at a social function where cocaine was being used, even if he
didn't know it. Even worse, several guests told the blue-
jeaned Cohn that Bourne had put a little of the white powder
up his nose in front of witnesses.

No one had made any public statement about Bourne's
alleged drug use so far because they didn't want to be accused
of hypocrisy or a partisan political attack. Now that the besieged drug adviser had revealed himself as fair game with
the admission of the prescription forgery, however, all bets
were off. The aggressive Cohn, whose contacts in the pro-
drug lobby seemed to regard Bourne as a hypocrite, moved
quickly. His boss, Anderson, broke the details of the coke
incident on national television the morning after Bourne was
suspended in the prescription incident. What had been a man-
ageable flap was now a full-fledged drug scandal. Despite
Bourne's repeated denials, others charged privately that they
had seen him inhaling cocaine, and his resignation became a
foregone conclusion. "Though I make mistakes...I have never
intended to do anyone harm," an emotional Bourne wrote to
his former dinner partner Jimmy Carter in his resignation
letter. For the second time, an administration official hand-
picked by Carter self-destructed right before the president's
eyes.

Lance and Bourne weren't the only people causing grief for
Jimmy Carter. Members of the Carter clan, warmly presented
as colorful, fun-loving figures during the campaign and first
months of the adminstration, were increasingly caricatured as

loutish, presumptuous outsiders who were heaping disgrace on the office of the presidency. The president's rambunctious kid brother, Billy, the opposite of his accomplished sibling in many ways, seemed to relish poking fun at Jimmy's religious convictions and deeply driven ambition. "There are more beer drinkers in America than there are born-again Baptists," he said with a smirk in October 1977, commenting on the initially thriving sales of the inferior "Billy" brew, which sought to capitalize on his demonstrated fondness for the suds. Swilling beer, urinating on airport runways (as he once was reported to have done in Atlanta), and speaking his mind to anyone who would listen, the pot-bellied Billy made White House aides grimace with fearful anticipation every time he opened his mouth, which was often.

At the same time, the president's sister, evangelist Ruth Carter Stapleton, who brought Jimmy back to the Lord after his crushing depression following an election defeat, also roused critics with her holy-roller style of impromptu preaching and her unwelcome meddling in the maelstrom of Middle East politics.

Like the Ford children who preceded them in the White House, the Carter offpsring found themselves drawn into the celebrity social circuit. Partying long and hard with, among others, pop singer Linda Ronstadt, the president's affable son, Chip, saw his marriage begin to crumble in the merciless fishbowl of publicity surrounding the White House and the entire Carter family. The worsening split bothered the president immensely, for he believed deeply in the sanctity of marriage and reportedly had lectured his aides about legitimizing several out-of-wedlock living arrangements.

Carter's image problems were compounded, fairly or not, by political honcho Hamilton Jordan, the 33-year-old *wunderkind* campaign strategist whose lengthy and insightful memo had laid the groundwork for Carter's surprisingly successful grassroots campaign of 1976. Unwilling to play by the rules with Washington's established movers and shakers, Jordan found himself the target of a spate of cruel social gossip. One over-publicized story claimed he'd looked down the bodice of the Egyptian ambassador's well-endowed wife and cracked, "I've always wanted to see the pyramids." Others present at the dinner protested that Jordan's behavior had been impeccable.

On another occasion, Jordan stepped into a thicket of unnecessary controversy at Sarfield's bar in Northwest Washington, an unofficial Carter administration hangout, when he allegedly got into a heated argument with a female patron and supposedly spat his drink of Amaretto and cream down her blouse. Jordan wanted to shrug off the report as part of the price of being in the public eye, but White House aides over-reacted in grand fashion and produced a 33-page official "white paper" on the incident, refuting in unbearably painstaking detail claims that the presidential aide had spit at anyone at all. The administration's ridiculously portentous tone served only to magnify the social flap still further, and the infamous Amaretto and cream drink was thereafter christened "Jordan's Lotion."

The rumpled casualness and youthful cockiness of Jordan, Powell and other thirtyish Carter functionaries led many to believe that Peter Bourne and Jack Carter weren't the only two close to the president who stood accused of experiementing with drugs. While they were plea bargaining a tax evasion with federal authorities, Steve Rubell and Ian Schrager, the co-owners of Studio 54, a trendy New York disco, claimed that they had information relating to an allegation that Jordan had sniffed cocaine at their exclusive establishment, where undisguised narcotics consumption had been regularly observed.

Jordan vehemently denied the charges, but socialite Barry Landau gave authorities a five-page, handwritten statement supposedly corroborating them. According to celebrity hound Landau, Jordan "said he wanted to see where the famous basement caves [inside Studio 54] were and if he could obtain some cocaine."

Another witness in the ensuing probe, businessman Leo Wyler, added fuel to the fire by describing a West Coast party attended by Jordan and Carter aide Tim Kraft, at which he claimed coke and girls were passed around in a bawdy fashion, although he admitted that he didn't actually see either man do any "tooting" of coke. The incident disturbed Wyler enough that he complained to a politically well-connected friend, who reportedly passed the objections along to the administration.

These allegations, and the mention of a mysterious cocaine dealer known as "Johnny C", caused the FBI and a special federal prosecutor, Arthur Christy, to get into the act. While Christy spent a good deal of time trying to learn who was leaking information to the media, a federal grand jury was convened, but declined to indict Jordan after hearing the arguments, stating that "there is no evidence whatsoever" that he used drugs or tried to buy them. Indeed, Jordan's only sin on this occasion might have been his bad judgment in even being seen in such an establishment. His final vindication from the grand jury didn't come until May 28, 1980, however, following months of headlined speculations, adverse publicity for the White House, and thousands of dollars in legal bills for Jordan, who was obliged to hire former Watergate prosecutor Henry Ruth and former Justice Department attorney Steve Pollack to defend him.

Since his days as Georgia's governor, Jimmy Carter had promised to organize an administration that would be judged not by "how popular it is with the powerful and privileged few, but how honestly and fairly it deals with the many who must depend on it." Yet it was in this area of administering fair and impartial government that the Carter record was found most wanting.

For instance, confidential White House minutes from the spring of 1979 indicated that Carter and his energy secretary, James Schlesinger, may have misrepresented the true nature of a gasoline pinch being felt by consumers. At that time, the United States was cutting its oil imports, a drop which "will create constraints in oil supplies," stated the eyes-only, official record of a Cabinet meeting on the subject. During a White House session in April, Carter informed his cabinet that "the Secretary indicated that, in general, we will meet our goal of reducing overall demand in the United States by about five percent."

Yet, because of his cutback, the president warned, "gasoline demand remains high, and a tight supply situation is expected this summer." That's not the message the pipe-puffing, professorial Schlesinger related to reporters some weeks later; "Gas lines should end around the country...There should be no generalized shortages." Neither Carter nor Schlesinger did anything to correct the shortfall which they had apparently misrepresented until there was an angry backlash over the rising prices and persistent lines at gas stations nationwide. In fairness, Carter did more than his predecessors to move toward a rational national energy policy, but the White House minutes showed that, as in other areas, Carter's management style and ability to communicate his ideas directly to the public were lamentably weak.

The General Services Administration, Uncle Sam's warehouser and supplies purchaser, had been a cesspool of corruption, contract shenanigans and favoritism long before Carter moved into the Oval Office. It was one of the obvious targets of the president's pledge to clean up government mismanagement. The five-billion dollar agency was losing more than sixty million annually through employee incompetence and theft, according to its own estimates. Fraud was rife at GSA, which had become a grabbag for influence-peddlers and the politically connected.

A couple of decades worth of pilfering exploded into a major scandal in early 1978 when the *Washington Post*, the *Boston Globe*, and other media outlets reported allegations of widespread cheating and stealing inside the agency. Worse, the few employees honest enough to come forward with the inside story charged that their superiors had systematically condoned the chicanery and punished them by shipping them off to bureaucratic Siberias or stripping them of their duties.

Carter started off on the right foot by appointing Jay Solomon, a prominent Nashville, Tenneesee, business executive, as GSA administrator, to root out the malefactors. Taking the chief executive at his word, the straight-forward Solomon hired a number of top-notch investigators, including as his deputy Vincent Alto, a former Justice Department organized crime strike force official. But the White House was apparently only willing to stand firm as long as lower-echelon workers were being implicated. GSA's number-two man, Robert Griffin, a close personal friend of the burly, white-maned Speaker of the House, Thomas ("Tip") O'Neill, had been at the agency for almost twenty years. Solomon and Alto soon realized that, even in a worst case scenario, Griffin should have been aware of the gross mismanagement going on around him, and they concluded that he would have to be removed if a thorough housecleaning was to take place.

That meant stepping on some powerful toes, however. As soon as he learned that his buddy Griffin was about to be forced out, O'Neill contacted the White House in a rage, demanding an explanation from Jordan, whom the speaker privately referred to contemptuously as "Hannibal Jerkin," due to the young chief of staff's perceived lack of respect for his elders on Capitol Hill. Worried about alienating the immensely powerful speaker, White House officials caved in. Democratic leaders, including Vice President Walter Mondale, hastily assured the unhappy O'Neill that a proper title and position would be found for Griffin, who was then transferred to the office of the president's special trade representative.

From his new office at the White House, Griffin reportedly proceeded to block Solomon's internal probe of GSA by denying him access to his records, for the files of the former deputy administrator were crucial to tracking down the sources of the waste which had built up over two decades.

Soon Solomon's persistent digging, along with a brace of favorable publicity it was bringing the previously unknown businessman, began to rankle White House aides. Before long, Solomon's constant calls to presidential assistants were going unreturned, and he learned from reporters that he would be replaced. His unrestrained zeal for unearthing GSA cronyism and fraud was causing a lot of backroom pressure for Carter from Democratic beneficiaries of GSA's largesse.

Finally, in March 1979, Solomon realized that he'd been left hanging in a bureaucratic no-man's land, and by the very administration officials who'd welcomed his no-holds-barred enthusiasm less than a year before. Solomon's forced resignation put to rest the canard that Jimmy Carter was a crusading reformer, a white knight tirelessly fighting the entrenched bureaucracy. His surrender to political pressure in the GSA mess demonstrated that he was willing to place politics ahead of the public dollar. In fairness, reforms were made, and dozens of low-to-mid-level GSA workers, supervisors and contractors were indicted and prosecuted for corruption. But the big ones had gotten away, in the view of congressional investigators, causing a host of GSA-connected politicians and businessmen to breathe a huge sigh of relief.

A more subtle failure occurred inside the Carter Justice Department. Time after time, Carter and his appointees lost opportunities to restore the public's confidence in this Department, which had been shaken during the Watergate fiasco and was never completely resuscitated under President Ford.

As with GSA, Carter showed a willingness to put politics ahead of reform. During his first year in office, for example, he stumbled badly in what came to be known as the "Marston affair." David Marston was a young U.S. attorney in Philadelphia who'd had notable success prosecuting official corruption and white collar crime, with the assistance of the FBI and one of its toughest headhunters, special agent Neil Welch.

Marston had one shortcoming, however, at least in the eyes of those controlling political appointments—he was a Republican, and the Carter White House, despite a pledge to remain non-partisan in its appointments, was under enormous pressure from party officials to staff sensitive prosecutors' slots only with those who could pass the Democratic litmus test. Marston compounded his problem when he showed no reluctance to take on a powerful Democratic congressman, Representative Joshua Eilberg, who had been accused of accepting money to help obtain a multi-million dollar contract for a Philadelphia-area hospital.

Placing a call to Carter at the White House, the congressman reportedly insisted that the president speed up his replacement of the crusading Marston, who was seen by some to be on a partisan witchhunt. Carter did just that, calling the Justice Department and ordering them to get the ball rolling. Neither Carter nor his attorney general, Griffin Bell, was prepared for the political donneybrook which followed the announcement of Marston's canning in January 1978. All hell broke loose. Angry Philadelphians stood in line in fifteen-degree weather to sign protest petitions. Thousands of people flooded the White House with letters, telegrams and phone calls complaining that the dismissal looked suspiciously like a fix. The eager, ambitious Marston didn't make it any easier for Bell or the White House; he publicly charged that he was being removed because his probes were getting too close to friends of the administration, and a significant percentage of observers agreed, including a number of editorialists.

When a federal investigation followed the telltale signs of obstruction of justice, a top Justice Department official suppressed the FBI's report on the timely telephone call from Eilberg. Instead, Justice officials claimed that President Carter had been "exonerated," presumably because of his contention that he didn't know Eilberg had been a candidate for official scrutiny when he called. Eilberg subsequently pled guilty to accepting an illegal gratuity and was fined. Marston became a minor political celebrity for a time, and the Carter Justice Department took the first of its several black eyes.

While that flap could have been partially excused as an exercise in political hardball that backfired, no such explanation sufficed for the highly unusual circumstances surrounding the Carter White House's entanglement with the world's most notorious financial fugitive. Robert Vesco was the ultimate snake oil salesman. Any informal poll ranking the canniest con men of the generation would have had his name at or near the top. That selection would have been by acclamation if the vote had been taken at the Securities and Exchange Commission. SEC investigators had been trying to unravel the freebooting Vesco's labyrinth of phony stock deals for more than a decade. The mustached money manipulator had ripped off more than $220 million from a mutual fund he'd controlled, Overseas Investment Services. He'd added to his felonies by giving an illegal $200,000 cash contribution to the Nixon presidential campaign in 1972. When the authorities closed in, Vesco took his sizable fortune out of the country, and set up house in secluded splendor in Costa Rica, until President Rodrigo Carazo kicked him out in 1978. Like the late Howard Hughes, Vesco then became even more reclusive, rumored to be hiding away on a yacht in the Caribbean and fighting U.S. attempts to extradite him for trial.

With the Republicans out of the White House in 1976, the wily Vesco apparently saw a ray of hope. The finagling financier desperately wanted to return to the U.S., but not to spend the rest of his life in court and prison, which was the fate the

FBI had planned for him. His only way out was to buy influence, a tactic at which he was an acknowledged master. Operating from his sumptuous Costa Rican outpost, he began to do just that, beginning as soon as Jimmy Carter won the 1976 election.

Vesco's complex scheme, according to news reports and other accounts, started with a bankrupt businessman named R.L. Herring, who saw a fortune in helping Vesco get a message through to high levels of the Carter administration. Herring managed to establish an indirect line to the White House when he was introduced to Spencer Lee IV, a chum of Ham Jordan since childhood. Herring made it clear to Lee that Vesco would make it worth their while to serve as his unoffical messenger boys. The pair flew to Costa Rica on January 14, 1977, just days before the Carter inaugural.

According to Herring's later account, Vesco outlined one of his patented, convoluted paper pyramid transactions which would transfer to them valuable paper stock in a dummy corporation called Southern Ventures, Limited. Their job was to pass the word to the White House to quit trying to extradict him. For once, according to the later statements of Herring, the inscrutable, moody Vesco kept his word, and began a series of moves to transfer millions of dollars worth of stock to his visitors.

Lee later admitted visiting Vesco, although he denied that Jordan's name came up during the conversations. But he did go to Washington a few weeks afterward and had a chat with presidential assistant Richard Harden about Vesco's rather unusual approach to public relations. Harden, a former accountant, heard details of a possibly explosive influence-peddling scheme being masterminded by the nation's number one fugitive. Yet he waited a week before he told his boss, the president, that his White House was the target of a bizarre request from the man whom the administration's law enforcement officials wanted more than any other criminal. It couldn't have been because of the source of the information; both Harden and Carter knew Lee personally, and were well aware of his close friendship with Jordan.

Carter reportedly was nonplussed when informed of the supposed plot. Neither he nor Harden notified the Justice

Department about the alleged backdoor approach by Vesco. Instead, the president scribbled a note to Attorney General Bell, urging him to "please see Spencer Lee of Albany [GA] when he requests an appointment."

The Justice Department was forced to examine Vesco's imaginative fishing line to the White House when it was revealed eighteen months later by columnists Jack Anderson and Les Whitten, who had interviewed Herring and others knowledgeable about the contacts. Harden asserted that he had talked Lee out of participating in the scheme, and the White House insisted that the administration's decision not to pursue Vesco's extradition was coincidental and had nothing to do with Lee's visit.

True, there were some holes in the story: it was subsequently shown that some of Anderson's information had been "reconstructed" on tapes that Herring had turned over. But nevertheless, the Carter team's categorical denials lacked credibility in several key areas. Jordan declared that his friend Lee had never mentioned the Vesco offer to him, although Lee admitted he'd accepted $10,000 to act as a go-between with his childhood buddy. The chief of staff's case looked even weaker when he lamely admitted he'd forgotten being interviewed by FBI agents about Lee and Vesco.

Harden at first insisted he'd told no one about Lee's revelations concerning Vesco. Afterwards, he admitted telling the president a week later, which cast some doubt on his credibility. Lee steadfastly agreed with Harden's version of events, but both reportedly failed lie detector tests on the details.

Moreover, Ralph Ulmer, the foreman of the grand jury investigating the alleged payoff scheme, attempted to resign his post after ten months, charging the Justice Department with "duplicity" and "manipulation." Angrily, Ulmer wrote to presiding judge William Bryant that "coverup activities are being orchestrated within the Department of Justice under the concept that the administration might be protected at all costs." Ulmer asserted that the prosecutors conducted the investigation in a haphazard manner, impeding the grand jury's access to key evidence and pressuring jurors to sign writs which would have blocked indictments. A Senate staff investigation later confirmed the thrust of some of Ulmer's allegations.

Although he never set foot inside the U.S. during Carter's term of office, Vesco also figured prominently in the so-called Billygate caper, which involved one of the earth's foremost supporters of international terrorism, Libyan dictator Muammar Quaddafi. The firebrand North African leader had sponsored acts of violence and death against the U.S. and its allies throughout the world, and contemptuously regarded all Western societies as enemies of his radical brand of Islamic fundamentalism. Nevertheless, he admired advanced U.S. technology, and during Carter's tenure he sought to reverse a State Department ban on the export of Lockheed C-130 and Boeing 727 aircraft that his oil-rich government had purchased earlier, but couldn't get delivered due to the embargo.

Vesco had a secret relationship with Quaddafi and knew that the single-minded colonel would pay millions of dollars to get the planes released and flown to Libyan soil, no questions asked. At roughly the same time as he was trying to grease the skids for himself at the Carter White House, he had a parallel scheme cooking to bribe the planes loose from the State Department and rake in as much as $20 million from his grateful Libyan friends.

His efforts to recruit a couple of greedy conspirators triggered a Justice Department investigation, which was characterized by a notable lack of cooperation between the Department officials and the FBI; each agency apparently had informants that the other knew nothing about. A later Senate Judiciary Commiteee report called the turf fight a "shame and a disgrace."

Despite the problems, the FBI was able to monitor a supposedly casual meeting between Democratic National Chairman John White and Libya's United Nations ambassador, Mansur Rashid Kikkia. That meeting, and White's followup calls to three high-ranking State Department officials about the grounded planes coveted by the Libyans, were examined by a federal grand jury in New York. White stoutly denied that he'd had any hand in lobbying the State Department. But a Senate report cited "serious inconsistencies" in his grand jury testimony. "There is no doubt," stated the September 1982 Senate document, "that he [White] got special treatment" from the Justice Department during the course of its investigation.

The wisecracking Billy Carter liked the volatile Quaddafi's countrymen and their money. The Libyans "are the best friends I have in the world right now," Carter said only half-jokingly in early 1979. Billy's idea of Libyan-American friendship was taking an entourage of Georgian businessmen and state legislators, headed by real estate developer Mario Lianza, to the Libyan capital of Tripoli for an all-expenses-paid junket which served only to show what a buffoon the president's younger brother was.

The Libyans spent at least $50,000 to wine and dine Billy and his buddies. The generous hosts wished to take some of the sting out of news stories detailing Quaddafi's brutal terrorist excesses. Lianza, stated an internal report by the Justice Department's Office of Professional Responsibility, "was present when the C-130 issue was raised at a dinner reception during which Billy Carter promised to obtain aircraft for Libya." Other witnesses admitted that they overheard Libyan officials promise an upgrade in chilly U.S.-Libyan relations if the banned planes were delivered.

On their return to the U.S., Billy and his Georgian traveling partner Randy Coleman "asked goverment officials about the release of the aircraft to Libya," said the Justice Department's findings. In January 1979, Billy hosted a large reception at the Atlanta Hilton hotel for his Libyan friends, a party which his mother, the inimitable Miz Lillian, and sister Ruth Carter Stapleton attended. A charter declaring a "Libyan-Arab-Georgian Friendship Society" was signed, a highly publicized action which no doubt caused a number of tension headaches at the White House. Two days later, Billy expounded on his rather curious preferences by exclaiming, "There's a hell of a lot more Arabians than there is Jews."

What only family and close friends knew at the time was that there was a good reason why Billy's behavior was even more erratic than usual; he was speaking through a haze of booze. Less than a month later, he committed himself to a rehabilitation program for alcoholics at the Long Beach Naval Hospital in California, where he conveniently remained incommunicado for six weeks, probably the happiest period ever for Carter aides weary of explaining his latest shoot-from-the-hip pronouncements.

Drying out didn't get the Libyans or their petrodollars out of Billy's system. His partner, Coleman, reportedly continued to meet with the Libyans, who were still anxious to enrich the president's brother with generous oil contracts for which he would have to do next to nothing. A deal involving Charter Oil Co. was discussed in which the Libyans would supply the oil and Billy would get a commission on every barrel. Among other inducements, Billy would receive a $500,000 loan.

Meanwhile, the Justice Department official in charge of registering foreign agents bravely determined that Billy had not registered properly and that repeated attempts to encourage the younger Carter to comply with the law had been to no avail. The official, Joel Lisker, sought an interview with Billy on this matter and to inquire about allegations that he had accepted expensive gifts from his Libyan hosts, including a silver-threaded saddle.

After grilling Billy about the gifts and his contacts with administration officials about Libya, Lisker told the White House that he had found no reason to prosecute Billy and that the matter would soon be closed. He didn't know then that Billy was continuing to push the Libyans for six-figure loan money and the promised oil allocations for Charter.

Even in early 1980, months after the seizure of the U.S. Embassy in Teheran by Islamic radicals, Billy was negotiating his private business deals with a Libyan government which was in sympathy with the Iranians holding 52 American hostages.

In April 1980, he got a $200,000 check from his Libyan contacts, delivered by an associate who had traveled yet again to Tripoli. The discovery of the payment, and of a private telephone conversation on the subject of Libya between the president and his brother, helped trigger a criminal investigation and an internal inquiry at the Justice Department.

Billy was again questioned by Lisker, but the interview was interrupted, and he later refused to continue it on the advice of attorneys. Despite all the hoopla, Billy did not register with the Justice Department until July 14, 1980, the same day the

Department filed a civil suit against him for his failure to comply.

"Billygate," as it was dubbed in news accounts, finally got Attorney General Benjamin Civiletti, who had succeeded Bell, into hot water. Responding to press inquiries, Civiletti denied that he had talked to the president about Billy's problems at the Justice Department. When the chief executive's personal logs were shown to admit that "he [Civiletti] told me that Billy ought to acknowledge if he were an agent of Iraq (sic)," the law enforcement chief was caught in an embarrassing conflict. His rather feeble attempts to explain the discrepancy caused even his Justice Department subordinates to "conclude that the Attorney General's answer was not the truth and that he knew he was dissembling as he was answering" queries about his private talks with Carter.

As for Billy, his refusal to file as a paid agent of the Libyans was "reprehensible," admitted Justice officials, who added that the presidential sibling "lied under oath" not once, but on successive occasions, when questioned about the source of his sizable loans.

Briefly stated, the president's brother enriched himself by accepting payments and valuable gifts from a country hostile to U.S. interests, and it took the Justice Department almost two years to piece together his brazen influence-peddling.

In fairness to Jimmy Carter, rampaging inflation and the hostage crisis in Iran, over which he had little real control, did much more damage to his chances of being reelected than Bert Lance's tangled finances or Billygate. And to his credit, he's proven to be the most industrious and charitable ex-president of modern times. He's built housing for the disadvantaged with his own hands, and loaned his expertise and public reputation for a wide variety of worthy projects, while former chief executives such as Ford and Reagan have distinguished themselves mainly by the size of fees and corporate board payments they've accepted. Carter is a man who matured in the most demanding job in the world, but perhaps a little too late to have made his presidency the overall success it could have been.

Chapter 15

THE TEFLON PRESIDENT

Ronald W. Reagan

January 1981—January 1989

"Mr. Norm is my alias...Nothing about me to make me stand out on the midway...Average will do it." That modest, self-effacing description of himself was written by Ronald Reagan fifty years ago in August 1942, and unearthed by biographer Lou Cannon, a veteran *Washington Post* reporter who's been close to the Reagan inner circle since the former president's two terms as California governor.

There's little doubt that Reagan sincerely believed that humble self-portrait just as much on January 20, 1981, when he took the oath of office as the fortieth president of the United States, as he had half a lifetime before when he penned the phrases for *Photoplay* magazine in a profile presenting him as one of Hollywood's stable of young male movie stars under contract. Affable, optimistic almost to a fault, yet capable of coarse political rhetoric in private, Reagan's polite, easygoing manner usually charmed even the most skeptical when they met him face-to-face.

However, the man behind the amiable facade was much harder to read or know, even for those who'd been around him for decades. Reagan's official biographer, the Pulitzer-prize winning Edmund Morris, who was granted extraordinary personal access to Reagan during his presidency, described him as "the most mysterious man I've ever confronted. It is impossible to understand him."

307

A child of hard times who'd suffered a tough childhood with an alcoholic father, young "Dutch" Reagan struggled for an education and prospered as a result of a handsome face, sturdy physique, sunny personality and bit of Irish good luck. His eventual rise to fame in the Hollywood of the forties and his later acquisition of corporate-sponsored wealth gave him an unshakable faith in American democracy and limitless rewards of the free enterprise system. If a poor boy like him could scramble to the top of the economic and social ladder, then surely anyone who wanted a better life could do the same, he firmly believed. The system worked for those who learned how to use it; that was the message Ronald Reagan brought with him into the national political arena in the sixties, and his credo contained the same, unvarnished set of values he carried into the White House with him more than fifteen years later.

He hadn't always had the same evangelical fervor about the merits of self-sufficiency and laissez-faire economics. On the contrary, the young Ronald Reagan had been an ardent joiner and organizer, and had enthusiastically led a number of crusades against the status quo. As a student at Eureka College in Illinois, he had been at the forefront of a student protest against faculty layoffs in his freshman year. Later in Hollywood, where his All-American features and athlete's body landed him a series of undemanding movie roles, he became as well known for his activism as president of the Screen Actors' Guild as for his generally mediocre acting.

Entertainer Sheila MacRae, who worked with Reagan then, once described him as the "Warren Beatty of his day." The younger Beatty's activist, liberal politics were anathema to the septuagenarian Ronald Reagan of the White House years. Nevertheless, during the 1940s, Reagan supported several left-leaning causes, and performers who were having trouble with the film establishment's feudal management policies knew that they could turn to the articulate, energetic actor for assistance. His soap-box enthusiasm for causes was so intense that it placed an additional strain on his unsuccessful first marriage to actress Jane Wyman, who grew tired of his endless politicking and divorced him, much to Reagan's surprise and dismay.

What happened to transform the amiable celluloid celebrity from a liberal lion into an equally determined defender of conservative causes? His longtime friend, former movie dancer and U.S. senator George Murphy, thought it was Reagan's dread of Communism. "We had discussions about the communists," said Murphy, who in 1976 told an interviewer he'd warned his younger friend that leftist radicals were infiltrating the movie union Reagan was then leading. "Ronnie didn't believe me at first," Murphy recalled thirty years later. But the former film hoofer was convinced that the Cold War years and the McCarthy-era blacklisting of Hollywood writers and actors finally caused Reagan to see the light, and it was red.

The fact that the General Electric corporation signed Reagan to a contract in 1954 for lucrative television advertising and lecturing roles didn't do anything to dim his new-found fondness for the ample rewards of capitalism, particularly since by then his steady if unspectacular film career was floundering. Besides, he had a growing family to worry about after making petite actress and one-time co-star Nancy Davis his second wife.

Reagan's undeniable, natural gift for communicating through the camera lens gave him a new career in the fledgling television medium. The national exposure and his unflagging drive to speak out publicly on various political and social issues, from taxes to student revolt, made the former film star one of the unelected leaders of the country's conservative true believers over the next decade. Gradually, with the eager financial assistance of corporate executives such as Justin Dart and auto dealer Holmes Tuttle, he gathered around himself a loyal brain-trust of well-heeled businessmen and conservative activists. Eventually, the informal group became known as "The Kitchen Cabinet," and their task would be to give tangible political form to their spokesman's inspiring paeans to "standpattism."

In 1966, the Reagan team began eight years in California's governor's mansion, but even then some insiders were focusing on larger political horizons in Washington. It took eight more years of organizing, speech-making, backroom plotting and an unpopular Democratic president; but in November

1980, Reagan completed his long, winding life's journey from sportscaster, actor and television host and governor to Chief Executive when he defeated the incumbent president, Jimmy Carter. A revolution, with his name attached to it, would blossom in the decade of the eighties and literally transform expectations of what the federal government could and would do for its citizens. In his two terms of office, however, Ronald Wilson Reagan remained an enigma, causing endless debate over whether he was a detached, hands-off chief executive, or a bold, activist leader whose greatest gift was in leaving no fingerprints.

Just as Carter's so-called Georgia Gang before them, Reagan's Republican aristocracy lost no time making their mark in social Washington. California chic quickly replaced Southern country among the stylemakers of the capital's dinner party circuit. At his inaugural, Jimmy Carter had set the tone for his term of office by walking down Pennsylvania Avenue hand-in-hand with his wife Rosalynn. By contrast, the Reagan inaugural was, in the phrase of one capital correspondent, "a bacchanalia of the haves," a shimmering procession of sleek limousines, diamonds and designer gowns. Ostentation was in. After four years of relative austerity in the White House, it was again all right to be rich.

The tanned, moneyed elite of Palm Springs and Beverly Hills poured into Washington, and it wasn't long before this newly established Hollywood connection caused a publicity headache for one of the new president's closest personal friends, William French Smith. A white-haired, pleasant yet private man whose distinguished appearance fit his role as a highly paid corporate lawyer, Smith had been Reagan's legal counsel and dinner companion for almost thirty years. On December 11, 1980, Reagan rewarded Smith's friendship and loyalty by announcing his nomination for attorney general of the United States.

It took the naive Smith, uninitiated in the fishbowl ways of the capital, just days to get himself into hot water. The attorney general designate attended a party in honor of entertainer Frank Sinatra, a longtime friend of the Reagans. Back in the familiar environs of Los Angeles, no one would have raised an eyebrow. But rumors that the aging crooner's name had

surfaced in a federal grand jury probe involving profit-skim-
ming at a New York theater caught the attention of *The New
York Times* columnist William Safire. Always ready to point
out the appearance of impropriety to public officials too unschooled or lazy to see it themselves, Safire blasted Smith's
elbow-rubbing at the Sinatra party as a "deliberate affront to
(the) propriety of the Reagan Administration."

Enraged at what he regarded as an assault on his personal
integrity, Smith called Safire's criticism a "cheap shot," but
other published reports took note of the fact that the Justice
Department had thousands of pages of files on Sinatra and his
alleged links to organized crime figures. In addition, Sinatra
representatives were trying to obtain a license for casino operations in Nevada, a prospect which generated little enthusiasm among law enforcement and gambling authorities. When
questioned concerning "Old Blue Eyes'" suspected links to
organized crime figures, President Reagan was quoted as
saying: "Yeah, I know...we've heard these things about Frank
for years, and we just hope none of them are true." The
revealing comment showed that Reagan didn't seem to grasp
that as president, his official duties and personal friendships
wouldn't always comfortably coincide. Smith's reaction demonstrated that he didn't get the message, either.

That impression was reinforced when the mild-mannered
Smith got himself into a second ethical imbroglio by accepting a $50,000 severance payment from a California firm for
which he had performed legal work. After reports of the
controversial payment surfaced in the media, Smith returned
the money. A Justice Department inquiry closed in 1982 concluded that Smith hadn't violated any department rules or
guidelines, but again he was pictured as a high-ranking Reagan official who couldn't keep his public responsibilities
separate from his private business.

Meanwhile, a louder howl of protest was being heard about
the Reagan administration's cozy relationship with the Teamsters' union, which was no stranger to corruption and controversy. Once it would have been unthinkable for a big labor
union to back any Republican candidate, but the continued
legislative protection of the Teamsters' government-sheltered
tranportation cartel put expendiency above political loyalties.

For more than a year before the election, Teamsters' executive Jackie Presser had aggressively pushed Reagan's candidacy to board members in closed door meetings. When Reagan got the coveted Teamsters' endorsement and won the election, the rotund Presser was rewarded with an appointment to the administration's labor transition team.

That surprising selection sent shock waves throughout the law enforcement and labor communities. Internal Justice Department files revealed that Presser had a history of "organized crime associations" which, said one analysis flatly, "are a known fact." Presser's meaty fingers, according to another Justice Department study, were "out to pick whatever pockets he can." Presser called the Justice Department's official conclusions "absolutely false," but his denials didn't allay the suspicions of knowledgeable industry insiders, who viewed Presser's appointment as a sign that a darker side of the labor movement was muscling into the Reagan administration.

The doubts about Presser (who later was revealed to have been a government informant for both the FBI and the Internal Revenue Service) were minor compared to the political flap Reagan created when he nominated a little-known New Jersey construction executive named Raymond Donovan to be his Secretary of Labor. Unlike several of his other cabinet nominees, who were personal friends, Reagan barely knew the bespectacled Donovan, but Republican party fundraisers were fond of the construction magnate. Donovan had collected over $600,000 for the Reagan campaign, which included proceeds from a gala party hosted by Donovan and attended by the candidate and his wife. Labor and union heavyweights pushed Reagan transition officials to return the favor by giving Donovan, a former Roman Catholic seminarian, a job in the president's cabinet. To their later regret, Reagan's talent scouts capitulated to the entreaties and Donovan was nominated to the top labor job. The subsequent brouhaha displayed Reagan's lamentable tendency to delegate important decisions to subordinates and remain largely uninvolved in the messy business of political appointments.

Trouble brewed as soon as reporters stopped saying "Ray who?" and started looking at Donovan's controversial background. By the time Donovan arrived at his nomination hearings at the Senate Labor and Human Resources Committee, a host of serious allegations awaited. Even though its background check of Donovan had been hurried, the FBI had uncovered witnesses who'd sworn that the nominee's company, Schiavone Construction, was "mobbed up", and that the firm and its executive vice president, Donovan, had engaged in a number of unsavory and perhaps illegal labor practices.

At least a half dozen informants, most of them with shady backgrounds, told FBI agents that Schiavone executives had made payoffs to union officials to "buy" labor peace and to prevent strikes from occurring at the firm's construction sites. Irate, Donovan vociferously denied any knowledge of either of the questionable schemes, but his claim of ignorance led some of the perplexed questioners to wonder just how much control the building executive had over his own company.

The plot thickened when FBI official Francis "Bud" Mullen told the committee that the Bureau had been unable to substantiate any of the allegations made against Donovan or his firm, and therefore gave him a clean bill of health. Inexplicably, Mullen didn't tell the committee that he (and at least a half dozen other FBI officials) had seen an internal Bureau memo which stated: "Two independent sources of the New York Division have advised that the Schiavone Construction Company is 'mobbed up.' One source indicates that the upper management of Schiavone is closely aligned with the Vito Genovese family of LCN (La Cosa Nostra)...and its contracts with Jopel Construction headed by William Masselli, who is an alleged soldier in the Genovese family." Senate investigators and reporters unsatisfied with the Bureau's representations learned that federal authorities had failed to follow up interviews on key allegations concerning Donovan's alleged relationships with organized crime figures who were under FBI surveillance.

Labor Committee Democrats, led by ranking member Senator Edward Kennedy of Massachusetts, demanded that Republican committee chairman Orrin Hatch of Utah reopen the Donovan probe and examine the testimony of an "extremely reliable" informant named Patrick Kelley, who had alleged that Schiavone "had a reputation of having ties with the

Genovese crime family." Kelley, who was being held in the Department's witness protection program, had also told authorities that he had heard Donovan's name mentioned "in a conversation by a contractor who obtained state contracts by bid rigging on behalf of the Schiavone company."

"The FBI had conducted no investigation of these allegations," stated the committee's minority report by the Democratic staff, which recommended further digging. The critical blast didn't shake Mullen, the FBI official in charge of the Donovan background check. Exasperatedly, he shot back, "It has to stop somewhere." Donovan's indignant denials and the Bureau's assurance that every allegation had been fully explored convinced the majority of Democratic Senators, and Donovan was confirmed 80-17 after intense White House pressure on Senate Republicans to back the nomination.

Like a dripping faucet, however, additional charges against the new labor secretary slowly leaked out of the Justice Department in the months following his confirmation. Fairly or unfairly, the innuendos, rumors and allegations made it all but impossible for Donovan to be an effective cabinet member. No favorite of the Labor Department's entrenched bureaucracy, he grew increasingly isolated, and his penchant for attracting adverse publicity made image-conscious administration officials nervous.

Four months after Donovan took the oath of office, two New York investigators for the Justice Department's Organized Crime Strike Force named Michael Moroney and Edward Barnes came upon potentially explosive new charges against Donovan. In the course of an investigation into Schiavone's role in New York City subway construction, the pair interviewed a former official of the the New York City Blasters' Union, Local 29. His name was Mario Montuoro, and he told the investigators that he had been present at a 1977 luncheon at which an envelope containing $2,000 had been passed to the president of the union by a Schiavone official. Nothing had been done to follow up on Montuoro's tale at the time of the confirmation, because he had been serving as a witness in a Justice Department trial on another, unrelated matter.

When the Montuoro accusation was headlined in the press in December 1981, Attorney General Smith had no practical choice except to call for yet another FBI investigation of Donovan. This time it was decided that the services of a special prosecutor would be required. In 1978, Congress had legislated a new category of prosecutors, known as "independent counsels," to insulate politically-sensitive cases from charges of interference or conflicts of interest by administration officials.

Leon Silverman, a well-known, cigar-chomping New York attorney, was appointed independent counsel to get to the bottom of the allegations swirling around Donovan once and for all. He began a comprehensive, six-month investigation which included the convening of a federal grand jury. At about the same time, Senator Hatch called Labor Committee hearings to determine the possible culpability of the FBI in the Donovan background investigation, which by that time was considered a fiasco in many quarters of official Washington.

By the spring of 1982, with the Silverman and Senate inquiries in full swing, the protracted Donovan probe took on an ugly undertone. Nat Masselli, the 31-year-old son of an alleged mobster who reportedly had connections to Donovan, was shot in a gangland-style execution slaying. Silverman believed that young Masselli had been killed for reasons unrelated to the Donovan grand jury, but no one could be certain at the time. Later, a former Mafia courier named Fred Furino, who repeatedly failed lie detector tests concerning whether he knew Donovan, was found murdered in the trunk of his car. Furino's slaying left federal gumshoes wondering if there might possibly be a connection to his previous questioning by law enforcment officials.

Over in the Senate, meanwhile, Hatch investigator Frank Silbey, a balding, tough-talking Labor Committee staffer, reported that he'd received a telephone call at his office threatening deadly reprisals if he didn't "lay off" Donovan. An anonymous male caller reportedly told Silbey that "if you keep messing with" the Cabinet nominee, "your wife and children" would "end up in pine boxes." Already fuming about the FBI's ineptitude and constant pressure from the White House to wind up his committee's renewed investigation, Hatch became even more upset when he learned that the

Schiavone firm had hired private detectives "on behalf of the company and its employees" to do some snooping of their own against Senate staffers, including Silbey. Donovan denied authorizing the hiring of corporate-paid spies, but let it be known that he had no special affection for Hatch's minions. "We'll see who's immoral on Capitol Hill and who isn't," he was reported to have said during a visit to the White House to discuss his continuing troubles.

A public flogging in the press over the Bureau's handling of the Donovan probe didn't dissuade FBI officials from withholding secret tape recordings of a telephone conversation in which the elder Masselli discussed "washing" money through the accounts of Donovan's Schiavone firm by means of vouchers ranging from $10,000 to $50,000. The tapes also revealed details of entertainment provided to Schiavone executives at the 1979 Super Bowl in Miami. An in-depth report on the tapes in a *Fortune* magazine article alleged that a federal official had confirmed that Donovan personally met with Masselli during the raucous social weekend. Party girls and liquor were provided for the enjoyment of the construction executives by figures who government officials said had organized crime connections.

Other raw FBI data, which had also been withheld from Senate, alleged that Donovan had repeatedly been out on the town with Salvatore "Sally Buggs" Bruguglio, a New Jersey Mafia boss who'd been gunned down on a New York street in 1978. During the late 1960s and early 1970s, the labor secretary and the notorious Bruguglio "took various pleasure trips together," stated a secret FBI memo dated February 2, 1981 (the day before Donovan was confirmed in the Senate).

Summoned into Silverman's presence, Donovan spent five hours answering questions on these and other matters before the grand jury. Smiling broadly as he exited from the session, Donovan professed his innocence. He refused to capitulate to intense pressure for his resignation from many top political and labor officials, and his continued bravado in the face of months of accusations was winning him public sympathy. His stubborn persistence seemed to have paid off when Silverman announced on June 28, 1982, that there was "insufficient credible evidence" to warrant prosecution on any criminal charge.

The details were laid out in a 708-page report, which had been partially censored for public inspection. Silverman continued at his post for another two-and-a-half months, investigating 14 additional allegations against Donovan, but in September 1982 he resigned as independent prosecutor after concluding for a second time, in an 111-page final report, that he could find no corroborating evidence against Donovan that could credibly be taken to court. Nevertheless, Silverman said he had "no reason to feel less disturbed" than he had earlier about the sheer number of allegations linking Donovan to unsavory figures.

Calling a news conference, the embattled labor secretary attempted to end the controversy by declaring himself "angry that I had to endure months of relentless press coverage of groundless charges made by shameless accusers." His parting blast marked the end of one of the most intensive investigations of a cabinet member in the history of the republic.

The results of Silverman's in-depth probe took the piercing publicity spotlight off Donovan for some months, but even then the controversy wasn't over. Almost two years after Silverman's investigation was concluded, it was revealed that yet another federal grand jury in New York City was investigating charges linking the much-maligned Schiavone company to fraud on a subway construction contract. Again the feisty Donovan came out swinging, calling the allegations a "witch hunt," but he and six other executives were indicted by the grand jury for allegedly participating in a scheme to defraud the New York City Transit Authority of $7.4 million.

The indictment announcement ultimately forced an action that two years of FBI and congressional investigations could not—the labor secretary's resignation. Several months after the indictment disclosure, on March 15, 1985, Donovan quit as labor secretary after a New York State judge ordered him to stand trial. Defense attorneys began almost two years of legal wrangling which delayed the trial until September 1986. Even then it became the longest trial in the Bronx in fifty years, lasting more than eight months. On May 25, 1987, Donovan and his co-defendants were acquitted on all charges, giving him a Pyrrhic victory in the six-and-a-half-year scandal which began with his ill-considered cabinet nomination.

Ray Donovan wasn't the only high-level Reagan appointee who became embroiled in political controversy. Richard Allen also became the focus of unflattering press attention early in the administration, but his end came much more quickly. The appointment of the bespectacled, silver-haired conservative activist as President Reagan's first national security adviser was regarded in some circles as a concession to the Republican party's right-wing hardliners.

Military officials, including a National Security Council security official named Jerry Jennings, needing space in a White House safe unexpectedly discovered a thousand dollars in cash. A well-connected, capable career bureaucrat whose later experience included serving as deputy director of the Federal Emergency Management Agency (FEMA), Jennings said that he initially wasn't sure where to turn and took the mystery to presidential counselor Ed Meese. Because finding cash in a highly classified safe was so unusual, Meese decided to refer the matter to the Justice Department for further inquiry after discussing the details of the discovery with Jennings, according to the latter's account. But when news broke concerning the Justice Department's inquiry and Allen's supposed connection to the money, another high-ranking Reagan appointee suddenly found himself on the defensive.

Steadfastly denying any wrongdoing, Allen revealed that he'd intercepted the money from a Japanese journalist who had tried to give the thousand dollars to Mrs. Reagan as an honorarium around the time of the January 1981 inaugural. The Japanese magazine sponsoring the article didn't object to offering the stipend, as such gratuities are commonplace and accepted in Japan. Realizing that as an official, he could neither accept nor sign for the money, Allen gave the envelope containing the payment to a secretary with instructions that it be passed along to appropriate authorities. Instead, it was forgotten and left in the safe.

Complicating the flap was the revelation that Allen had accepted two watches, each worth about $135, from a long-time Japanese business associate and his wife. He stated that he saw nothing wrong with taking the watches as personal gifts, since they were not connected to the interview or official business; nevertheless, FBI agents were assigned to probe the circumstances behind Allen's acceptance of the watches and the interception of the cash for the First Lady.

The ensuing investigation revealed that Allen had had a number of meetings with various Japanese business executives, and that they apparently considered Allen a valuable ally in gaining access to Reagan decision-makers. The potential appearance of influence-peddling, stoutly denied by Allen who recused himself from U.S.-Japan auto trade matters, was seized upon by some Reagan insiders as a means of forcing out the national security adviser.

Allen made a temporary comeback in the court of public opinion when the Justice Department backed his version of events and declined to take legal action against him; meanwhile, conservative friends lobbied hard on his behalf. While he had his share of political enemies, none believed that Allen, worth a salary well into six figures as a consultant in the private sector, could be compromised for a thousand dollars or a few watches he could easily afford. But the media frenzy concerning the Japanese affair caused reporters to check Allen's financial disclosure forms more closely. They found that the national security adviser had been receiving monthly payments from the sale of his lucrative consulting business to former Reagan speechwriter Peter Hannaford.

Worse yet, given the publicity circus, Allen admitted that he "had provided the wrong date" for the sale of his Potomac International Corporation. Rather than having sold his interest in the consulting firm in January 1978, as he listed in his disclosure, he had actually held on to his share until January 18, 1981, just two days prior to the inauguration. That admission didn't help Allen's cause politically.

The Justice Department declined to appoint a special prosecutor to look into the convoluted affair finding no evidence of wrongdoing by Allen. But by then, top White House officials had grown tired of blaring headlines and Allen's embarrassingly public feuds over foreign policy with the equally stubborn Alexander Haig. One of them had to go, and since hardliner Allen was considered by administration moderates as a thorn in the side of the White House's foreign policy apparatus, he resigned in January 1982 without being accused nor convicted of any crime or misbehavior.

There weren't any winners in the Allen contretemps. While few believed Allen had done anything inadvisable, the investigation and negative publicity temporarily tarnished his reputation and was an embarrassment to the Reagan White House. Moreover, the incident sparked bad feelings toward Allen by Jerry Jennings, who'd been unlucky enough to be on duty when the money was discovered. Although he claimed to have no animus toward Allen, Jennings believed that Allen's conservative friends bad-mouthed him behind his back and hurt his chances for political promotion. Jennings told Senate investigators that a friend privately confided he'd probably be fired from the White House for going to Meese with the evidence.

Many months later, however, Allen was questioned about his knowledge of whether Reagan campaign officials had illicitly gained advance copies of Jimmy Carter's briefing books prior to the pre-election presidential debate. He stated that an unnamed National Security Council employee had obtained "innocuous"Carter-related information reportedly passed along by Jennings, who said that he had been deluged with scores of phone calls from reporters asking if he'd provided Carter debate papers to Reagan campaign operatives, an allegation he later denied under oath. Allen had no specific response to Jennings' recollections, but a lengthy congressional report stated that the former national security adviser had no role in transmitting campaign documents to the Carter camp.

In any event, Allen's sudden, voluntary exodus, in what many loyal conservatives considered an unfair and untimely political purge, didn't seem to make the Reagan team any more careful about bad publicity for those chosen for key national security posts. Proof of their lack of oversight can be found in the hiring practices of Allen's replacement as national security adviser, William Clark. "Judge" Clark was a respected, long-time Reagan confidante who served as Secretary of the Interior and as a trouble-shooter at the State Department for his friend, the president. He was Reagan's "Mr. Fix-it", who could be counted upon to serve as a loyal caretaker while a particularly nettlesome problem was resolved.

Upon replacing Allen, Judge Clark saw no problem in hiring as his National Security Council assistant Thomas Reed, a former Air Force secretary who was publicly accused of making a "killing" in the stock market by backdating documents. According to documents in a civil suit filed by the Securities and Exchange Commission and obtained by the consumer group Common Cause, Reed had traded on insider information to turn a $3,000 stock option into $427,000 in profits in forty-eight hours. He wriggled out of further trouble by settling the case; he paid the amount of the questionable profits and promised not to trade on inside information again.

His own depositions to SEC attorneys prove that he considered the appropriate financial forms as "roadblocks" to the stock option bartering that he wanted to do. His greed caused him to commit a sin worse in the eyes of many than Richard Allen was accused of, but Clark apparently felt that Reed's money-grubbing manipulations were nothing to fret over. When the administration didn't get an overly adverse reaction by hiring Reed as a temporary consultant, he was kept on as a staff member of the National Security Council, the executive branch's most important and secretive foreign policy-making body.

Reagan's seemingly lax attitude about who served in sensitive national security posts would come back to haunt him even more in his second term of office, but the controversies involving Allen and Reed were a warning which went unheeded by the president and those closest to him.

President Reagan didn't know Rita Lavelle, but the mid-level bureaucrat caused him a lot of grief, and the investigation into her official granting of favors helped demonstrate how pitifully little personal input he had into the daily operation of his administration. Jimmy Carter had spent precious hours deciding, for example, which staffers would get playing time on the White House tennis courts; to his credit, Reagan didn't waste time on such trivia. But unlike the driven, detailed-oriented Carter, Reagan didn't even know the names of some of his top appointees, let alone what they did.

Lavelle certainly didn't look like a central figure in a Washington political scandal, which are usually peopled by middle-aged politicians, lawyers in drab suits, beautiful blondes who can't type, and the shapely wives and girlfriends of the fallen powerful. Plump, with a bit of a matronly appearance despite being only in her mid-thirties, Lavelle was from a close-knit Irish Catholic family in California, and like scores of other loyal young Reaganites had come East to savor the fruits of victory as a political appointee.

Her connections to Reagan confidante Ed Meese, going back to 1969, helped promote her to an enviable $67,000-a-year position at the Environmental Protection Agency. Nor was this assignment merely a high-paying, paper-pushing sinecure for past services. Her bureaucratic-sounding title of Assistant Administrator for Solid Waste and Emergency Response didn't adequately reflect the real power the stout, ambitious young woman wielded. She had been made the administration's overseer of the $1.6 billion dollar Superfund, an historic environmental project mandated by Congress to clean up hundreds of toxic waste dump sites around the country.

So ignorant of Washington's ways that she didn't even bother to read the EPA's code of ethics to guide her behavior in her new, sensitive job, Lavelle charged into the delicate task with the touch of a jackhammer. The management of the Superfund was one of the top environmental priorities on Capitol Hill, but Lavelle spurned congressional requests for cooperation and instead spent most of her working days being wined and dined by chemical industry lobbyists, who picked up dozens of pricey lunch and dinner tabs at exclusive K Street watering holes in downtown Washington. Her appointments calendar, later turned over to congressional investigators, looked more like that of a busy restaurant reviewer than the schedule of a ranking federal official.

Lavelle's elbow-rubbing with lobbyists, however reprehensible, was only indicative of her president's contempt for environmental regulations. Rather than selecting a scientist, environmental expert or top manager from industry, Reagan nominated a young, former Colorado legislator named Anne McGill Gorsuch, whose cool demeanor and hard-nosed management style earned her the sobriquet "The Ice Queen." Her main job was to reverse environmental policies deemed nettlesome to the business community, and to preside over huge personnel cutbacks totalling almost thirty percent of the agency's workforce in several critical areas.

The dedicated scientists, lawyers and researchers who populated EPA's bureaucracy were appalled at the favoritism towards corporate pollutors they observed at the agency, almost from day one of the Reagan takeover. But for the most part, their warning cries went unheeded until Lavelle's management of the Superfund program degenerated from careless to possibly criminal. Outraged over rumors that Lavelle had actively intervened to assist a former employer, Aerojet-General Corporation, with pollution problems relating to the Superfund cleanup, some disgruntled EPA employees finally decided they'd had enough. They went to congressional staffers with the details of favors being routinely performed for industry lobbyists by agency officials.

Initially, the investigators delved only into whether Lavelle had illicitly aided Aerojet-General, one of 100 companies that had dumped hazardous wastes at California's Stringfellow Acid Pits dump in Riverside, which environmental officials rated as the second worst such site in the state. Inside sources claimed that Lavelle had taken part in EPA meetings about Aerojet-General's role following instructions not to from the agency's legal counsel. Startled investigators were told that she continued participating in the sensitive negotiations even after she withdrew in writing from the case because of possible conflicts of interest.

From this relatively modest beginning in the early fall of 1982, a series of investigations dubbed "Sewergate," eventually involving six congressional subcommittees, the Justice Department and top officials from the Reagan White House, was soon to rock the agency to its foundation. Finding their access blocked to internal agency documents, two congressional subcommittees, chaired by Reps. Elliott Levitas of Georgia and the powerful, relentless John Dingell of Michigan, issued subpoenas for dozens of boxes of official papers and records. Although not unusual for an official oversight investigation, the congressional subpoenas set off a six-month power struggle between the administration and Capitol Hill which dominated the front pages for months.

Under specific instructions from the White House, admin-

istrator Gorsuch, citing the claim of executive privilege, refused to turn over the subpoenaed documents relating to her
subordinate Lavelle's actions and other alleged malfeasance.
Her unexpected defiance led to a contempt of Congress citation against her by the full House on December 16, 1982.
Meanwhile, top Reagan officials, including Meese, White
House counsel Fred Fielding, Deputy Attorney General Edward Schmults and others huddled to discuss strategy for
blocking the contempt citation. Gorsuch later claimed she
opposed the White House effort to withhold the documents
as unjustified and unwise, but she was seen as the focal point
of resistance by angry legislators.

The potential constitutional confrontation wasn't resolved
for several months, after a series of tense meetings involving
congressional staffers and administration lawyers. Meanwhile, additional revelations about "sweetheart" deals for
polluters, conflicts of interest among top EPA officials, and
the alleged existence of a secret political "hit list" aimed at the
administration's opponents trickled out and revealed Reagan's EPA as a cesspool of mismanagement and political favoritism.

The controversy escalated dramatically on February 7,
1983, when President Reagan suddenly fired Lavelle after a
memo was found in her personal computer arguing that
EPA's lawyers were too tough on industry polluters and were
"systematically alienating the primary constituents of this
administration, the business community." Apparently, that
fairly accurate reflection of administration mindset was too
much for the White House to defend publicly, and the sinking
Lavelle was left to face both congressional and criminal accusations by herself. Shocked at being abruptly cut loose and
fearing that she would quickly become a scapegoat for the
administration's critics, Lavelle literally begged long-time
benefactor Ed Meese to come to her rescue, but her desperate
entreaties fell on deaf ears. "I knew I was in the hot seat, but
I assumed the backing was there," Lavelle later told *The Washington Post*. "I was naive."

Severing Lavelle's lifeline didn't solve the White House's
problems, nor did it mollify congressional critics, who by now
were flocking in droves to the television cameras to denounce

the administration's clumsy handling of the EPA mess. The brunt of the pressure now fell upon Administrator Gorsuch's well-tailored shoulders. Right in the midst of her professional travails in February 1983, Gorsuch managed to find time to wed senior Interior Department official Robert Burford. But any new-found domestic tranquillity for the Burfords didn't lessen the turmoil at EPA's headquarters in the Southwest harbor section of the city. More heads were going to have to roll, and it soon became apparent that despite the president's initial statements supporting her, the newly-wed Anne Gorsuch-Burford was going to have to walk the plank to pay the price for the administration's environmental gaffes and attempted coverup.

The bright, tough-minded Burford wasn't exactly a victim; in many ways she was the architect of her own downfall. Her management style was brusque but woefully disorganized. She either had condoned the disastrous mismanagement over which she presided, or she was inexcusably ignorant of it. As the various "Sewergate" investigations progressed during the spring of 1983, it was revealed that Lavelle's toadying for chemical industry bigwigs wasn't the worst of the sins committed by Reagan's EPA management team—far from it. Congressional investigators unearthed evidence that Lavelle and other EPA officials had discussed how to politicize the Superfund cleanup grants by illicitly apportioning the grants to gain the most political advantage for Republicans. The handwritten notes of a former Lavelle aide, as reported by the *Washington Post*, stated that a White House aide had asked Lavelle to "bend over backwards" to help GOP candidates by orchestrating the announcements and actual release of Superfund money prior to the 1982 elections.

Evidence also came to light that Burford had surrounded herself with aides and consultants who used their influence to help private businesses gain inside access to the agency's decision-making process. One former consultant, Denver area lawyer James Sanderson, worked part-time for the EPA while continuing to represent legal clients with business before the agency, according to a Justice Department report. Nevertheless, Sanderson was pushed for the number three position at

EPA and withdrew only after details of his conflicts of interest were made public.

Disturbingly, congressional bloodhounds discovered that official agency documents had been shredded or altered to keep their true contents from prying eyes on Capitol Hill. They also learned to their shock that not only the administration's political enemies were targeted for reprisal by EPA's internal hit team. The assistants of general counsel Robert Perry kept what were referred to as "green books" which contained confidential personal information and negative references about agency employees suspected of disloyalty to the party line on environmental matters.

The sordid affair came to a head in March 1983, when it became obvious that only a springtime housecleaning at the agency would save White House officials from many more months of embarrassing revelations which they could no longer hope to contain or answer convincingly. Polls showed that the majority of Americans, while liking Reagan and giving him generally high marks, believed that he preferred protecting big business polluters to worrying about the environment. This was one fight the Reagan forces couldn't bluff their way through by invoking the president's immense public popularity.

Once a decision had been reached to cut the administration's losses, White House aides conferred over how to ease the unwilling Burford out of her job. Vilified in the media and believing she was taking the fall for the actions of others, Burford stubbornly tried to hang on. First Joseph Coors, the fabulously wealthy beer magnate from her home state of Colorado, was brought in to ask her to resign. Coors' family-funded conservative think tank, The Heritage Foundation, had provided EPA with a couple of dubious appointees. Then for the *coup de grace*, Meese later called on Burford's friend and fellow bureaucrat-basher James Watt, the fundamentalist, arch-conservative secretary of the interior, who wasn't winning any popularity contests himself in Washington. Watt privately told Burford that loyalty to the president required her to step aside. Reluctantly, Burford agreed to quit on the condition that her steep legal fees be paid. Her resignation was received with sighs of relief and allowed Reagan officials to come to terms with the cantankerous Congressman Dingell over boxes of subpoenaed EPA documents.

However, even then the battle between 1600 Pennsylvania Avenue and Capitol Hill wasn't over. Deputy Attorney General Schmults knew that the administration had withheld hundreds of pages of damaging handwritten notes concerning the EPA affair, but he didn't inform Congress about the administration's failure to fully comply with the subpoenas. Schmults maintained that he had meant to inform Congress at a later time and didn't intend to deceive investigators. His lapse and other unresolved questions prompted yet another investigation by the House Judiciary Committee, whose staff produced a detailed, 1,200-page report on the EPA tempest six months later, a review which uncovered evidence suggesting additional misconduct.

Actions against administration officials suspected of lying to Congress or withholding information in the EPA inquiry dragged on for years. In April 1986 a special, court-appointed independent counsel was named to further probe charges that a former assistant attorney general, Theodore B. Olson, gave false testimony about the withholding of the EPA documents from Congress. After almost three years of investigation, the independent counsel, Alexia Morrison, issued a report in early 1989 declaring that there was insufficient evidence to prosecute Olson and thus exonerating him.

Yet within two weeks after Burford's May 1983 resignation, the total of senior EPA officials who had left or been fired from the scandal-tainted agency reached an unlucky thirteen. Attorney William Ruckelshaus had been a victim along with his former boss, Attorney General Elliott Richardson, during Watergate's infamous "Saturday Night Massacre" when they were forced out of the Nixon Justice Department for refusing to fire Watergate special prosecutor Archibald Cox. Since the well-regarded Ruckelshaus could be counted upon to attract bipartisan support, he was asked to take charge of the EPA and neutralize the political damage. As a private lawyer, Ruckelshaus had represented several corporate clients with questionable commitments to environmentalism, but by this time no one had the energy left for a nomination fight and he was welcomed as a white knight to replace the departed Burford and her disgraced management team.

Although many figures associated with the EPA fiasco lost their jobs and professional reputations, and were saddled with sizable legal fees, perhaps the saddest figure was the forlorn and financially ruined Lavelle. She was convicted in federal court for lying to Congress concerning her EPA activities and sentenced to six months in prison and a $10,000 fine. Her attorney James Bierbower described the beleaguered Lavelle as "just another Washington casualty."

Although his aggressive pro-business, deregulation policies had helped initiate the EPA scandal by giving polluters unprecedented access to the environmental agency's decision-making process, President Reagan managed to remain personally untouched by the fallout which hit many of his high-ranking appointees. It was this uncanny ability to deftly avoid personal blame which caused his critics in Congress to begin referring to him as the "Teflon" president. Nothing stuck to him.

Even as administration officials were being blasted for gross misbehavior in the EPA affair, Reagan's own judgment in appointing the malefactors or his leadership role in misguiding environmental policy was rarely questioned. He retained such overhwelming popularity with the voters that political opponents and many reporters hesitated to criticize him personally. Jimmy Carter, whose every mistake had clung to him like flypaper, watched ruefully from the sidelines while his successor seemed to walk on water.

At just about the time that the EPA imbroglio was starting to fade from the headlines, another long-festering political controversy involving the Reagan White House was being revived in the office of an obscure House subcommittee. One morning in June 1983, John Fitzgerald, a 31-year-old counsel to the Subcommittee on Human Resources of the House Post Office and Civil Service Committee, chanced to read an opinion column by Jody Powell, Jimmy Carter's former press-secretary-turned-pundit.

Powell bemoaned the cursory treatment he said news organizations had given to allegations that an issues briefing book prepared by Carter aides somehow had found its way into the hands of top Reagan handlers prior to the critical October 28, 1980, presidential debate. Although Powell didn't know it at the time, his missive would soon generate FBI interviews of high-ranking administration officials, and would rekindle fractious infighting among feuding Reagan loyalists.

Because the subcommittee had jurisdiction over the Ethics in Government Act, which prohibits such acts of political skullduggery, Fitzgerald took the article to Micah Green, the subcommittee's staff director, according to an account in the *New York Times*. After discussing the possibility of launching a congressional investigation of the allegedly purloined campaign papers, the pair then approached their boss, Rep. Donald Albosta, a Michigan farmer in his third term of Congress. Intrigued with the information, Albosta directed that subcommittee letters of inquiry be sent to the Reagan officials named in Powell's article, asking for their written response to the charges.

Initially, reports of the Albosta panel's modest probing met with little enthusiasm, even among Washington journalists and political junkies bored with the slow pace of a hot summer. Reagan officials understandably weren't anxious to rehash three-year-old accusations which hadn't attracted much previous attention, except for a one-paragraph mention in a book by senior *Time* White House correspondent Laurence Barrett entitled *Gambling With History*. Albosta's inquiry didn't meet with much enthusiasm among House Democrats, either.

Part of the hesitance of Albosta's colleagues was probably due to the overlap of the EPA scandal, which was still in the headlines and continued to draw howls of White House-bashing from administration defenders. Another factor was that the relatively junior Albosta didn't possess much clout among his House colleagues. He wasn't regarded as a subcommittee chairman who instilled fear in the opposition. In addition, his three-person subcommittee staff was young and lacked experience in the kind of nasty confrontations which were likely to result from publicly questioning the veracity of the president's top aides.

Nevertheless, Albosta's "kiddie korps" persevered, with

the addition of a couple of investigators and lawyers, including respected former Watergate counsel James Hamilton. Less than a month after its humble beginnings, the Albosta probe was daily, front-page news in Washington's headline-starved dog days of summer, a little "midsummer madness," as described by one bemused columnist.

"Much ado about nothing," was President Reagan's succinct view of the controversy. He dismissed the allegations as partisan sour grapes. However, a steady stream of relevations in July 1983 concerning the briefing book affair caused his off-the-cuff remark to boomerang back on the White House. First, it was revealed that Central Intelligence Agency Director William Casey, Reagan's campaign manager in 1980, had set up an "intelligence operation" designed to learn whether the Carter camp would spring an "October surprise" relating to the release of the American hostages then still held in Iran. The disclosure led many to wonder what other snooping Casey's clandestine apparatus might have initiated.

A week later, documents and information from aides to President Carter were located in Reagan campaign files, which were stored at the Hoover Institute at Stanford University. The material included a memo sent by Reagan campaign volunteer Wayne Valis to White House chief of staff James Baker, which supposedly reported details of a Carter staff meeting "from a source intimately connected to a Carter debate staff member." Although administration officials described them as innocuous, the discovery of the documents shot the controversy back into the headlines and focused renewed attention on the Albosta inquiry.

In letters responding to the subcommittee's written questions, White House counselor Meese and deputy chief of staff Michael Deaver disavowed any knowledge of how the Reagan campaign obtained documents and other information from the Carter camp. Meanwhile, the Justice Department had brought the FBI into its investigation and Reagan personally ordered the cooperation of White House officials, despite his earlier public comments disparaging the allegations as unimportant.

Scores of Reagan and Carter campaign workers were interviewed separately by the FBI and the Albosta panel, including

college-aged "gofers" who had done little more than photo-
copy and deliver documents for their candidate. Hundreds of
rumors and second-hand tips were followed up by criminal
and congressional investigators.

Sex, an always-welcome element in any Washington political scandal, briefly became an issue when it was suggested
that a Reagan spy might have obtained the briefing papers by
sleeping with someone in the Carter campaign. That titillating tidbit faded almost as quickly as it blossomed after convincing denials from all sides. As the lengthy investigation
wore on, it became apparent that most of the principal suspects in what was now known as "Debategate" or "Briefing-
gate" had conveniently foggy memories.

One interviewee who claimed to have a crystal-clear recollection of events was chief of staff Baker. He sparked the
central riddle in the debate mystery when he flatly asserted
that Casey had provided the Carter briefing papers which
were used to prepare Reagan for the presidential face-off.
Irate, Casey stomped over to the *New York Times* Washington
bureau and told reporters that it would have been "totally
uncharacteristic and quite incredible" for him to have obtained or used the Carter papers. "I wouldn't touch it with a
ten-foot pole," snorted the irascible intelligence chief, whose
comments set off an embarrassing public war of words between him and the equally iron-willed Baker.

To refresh his memory, Casey had called political operative
Paul Corbin, who had received payments from the Reagan
campaign, to ask what Corbin had handed over to him. Corbin, a primary subject of the Albosta inquiry, said that he told
Casey he'd provided only speech materials on crime issues to
Reagan's team and hadn't been the source of any stolen or
secret papers.

The growing tension between Baker and Casey became, for
the White House, one of the painful by-products of the Debategate fallout. Meanwhile, Republican loyalists in the
House were wailing loudly that Albosta and his Democratic
cohorts were wasting hundreds of thousands of taxpayer dollars chasing after thin air. No crime had been committed, and
in any event the Justice Department was conducting a proper,
impartial investigation, said GOP stalwarts.

At the same time, the Albosta panel was having difficulty securing access to key documents from the Justice Department, and the bushy-haired Michigan congressman was coming under intense pressure not to hold public hearings on his subcommittee's findings. What had started out as a simple congressional letter of inquiry had turned into a protracted political controversy which, for a brief time, threatened the continued employment of top Reagan aides such as Baker, Casey and David Stockman, the boyish-looking, tousled-haired budget chief whose off-hand comments about the Reagan campaign's acquisition and use of Carter papers had helped launch the Albosta probe.

The Justice Department and Albosta investigations dragged on through the fall of 1983 and into the new year without resolution. Finally, in February 1984, Justice officials announced the end of their eight-month investigation by concluding in a pathetically brief, three-page report that it "uncovered no credible evidence that the transfer (of campaign documents) violated any criminal law." Incredibly, the diametrically conflicting views of Baker and Casey were allowed to remain unresolved. Despite months of mutual finger-pointing by the two officials and published reports that the president did not oppose the use of an FBI polygraph to check their stories, neither Baker nor Casey were subjected to lie detector tests. Weakly, the Justice investigation purported that all Reagan campaign personnel who had documents or were aware of them "denied any knowledge of how they were originally obtained and any belief the materials were stolen."

Three more months passed before Albosta's subcommittee concluded its year-long investigation and issued two volumes of findings totalling 2,314 pages and weighing over five pounds. Their version of events, including an extensive FBI search for fingerprints on the purloined documents, was considerably more detailed than the Justice Department's flimsy, three-page flier. The Albosta report concluded that it was likely that the Reagan camp received two sets of briefing papers, rather than one, prior to the debate, and that Reagan aides knew that the materials came from the Carter offices. While it could not resolve the key Casey-Baker dispute, the subcommittee sided with Baker's version of events, finding credible his assertion that Casey had provided the Carter materials used to brief Reagan. The subcommittee found no evidence that Ronald Reagan personally was involved in the pilfering of the Carter papers.

In addition, the Albosta report charged that some of the witnesses interviewed by the subcommittee "had not been entirely candid," and that while the source of the leak could not be pinpointed, investigators had deduced from the available evidence that the Carter notebooks probably came from the offices of the National Security Council, whose documents are supposed to be totally confidential. Albosta's probers also agreed with a federal judge's written opinion that the Justice Department had erred in not appointing a special, court-appointed independent counsel to pursue the Debategate inquiry, as required by the Ethics in Government Act, which the administration had ignored in this instance to its own advantage.

Ironically, Congressman Albosta may have suffered the worst outcome from the year-long Debategate drama. His management of the careless investigation was criticized as vacillating even by some Democratic colleagues, and he was blasted by angry Republicans for supposedly leading a partisan charge against the White House. Administration defenders in the House denounced the subcommittee's crusade as a waste of a half a million taxpayers' dollars even as as the results were being released. Months later, in the 1984 elections, the Michigan legislator stumbled into a fate suffered by less than three percent of congressional incumbents—he lost his seat to a young, telegenic Republican challenger, Bill Schuette. While Schuette clung tightly to Reagan's coattails, he also won at least partly because of the negative publicity resulting from Albosta's dogged pursuit of the briefing book case.

Despite all the political hoopla surrounding the scandal, the bottom line was that the Carter papers were somehow illicitly obtained by Reagan's handlers, but neither the FBI nor the meticulous, ill-fated investigation by the Albosta panel positively identified the culprits or how they pulled off the pre-election coup. What the evidence did show was that Reagan had been covertly handed an unfair, key advantage in the election race, but the Teflon President and his aides managed to turn the tables on their accusers and evade accountability.

*   *   *

Slight, bespectacled and balding, with the unassuming bearing of the loyal aide-de-camp he'd been for twenty years, Michael K. Deaver's modest appearance gave no outward sign that he was one of the most powerful and ruthless men in the Reagan White House. Viewed by his detractors as little more than Nancy Reagan's unctuous purse-carrier (fellow Reaganite Lyn Nofziger disdainfully called him the First Couple's "number one sycophant"), Deaver was an experienced public relations operative with a well-developed gift for image-shaping. Savvy about television's dominating sway over the political process and how it could be used to best advantage, he set out a carefully conceived media strategy to portray Ronald Reagan as a decisive, vital commander-in-chief and patriotic father figure for the nation.

Television network executives, anxious for Reagan video "opportunities," and to curry the good will of a hugely popular president, quickly learned that Deaver, who *Time* magazine dubbed the "vicar of visuals," could be a formidable foe when he didn't get his way. Indeed, some Reaganites who worked with the taciturn Deaver privately regarded him as an arrogant, vindictive toady who used his close personal relationship with the Reagans to grab unrivaled control of the White House image-making apparatus. For their part, both Ronald and Nancy Reagan regarded the fortyish Deaver, who they'd known for more than twenty years, almost as a son, and therefore few dared to risk the aide's icy displeasure.

At the beginning of the Reagan presidency, as White House deputy chief of staff, Deaver was part of an uneasy "troika," a power-sharing arrangement with presidential counselor Ed Meese and chief of staff James Baker. But unlike the ideological Meese or the pragmatic Baker, who each schemed to assert control over White House policy-making in his own way, Deaver was uninterested in the substance of government.

He had no agenda beyond making the Reagans look good, a job in which he had spent most of his adult life. During the first administration, with a few exceptions, he was notably successful at controlling the media's access to the amiable but distant chief executive, and in keeping an increasingly pliant press from fingering the president as the culprit for any White House policy missteps.

Deaver's only serious blunder was in advising Reagan to include a military cemetery in Bitburg as part of a state visit to Germany in the spring of 1985. Intended as an poignant, symbolic picture story for television correspondents covering the trip, the planned ceremony instead sparked an international uproar among Jewish Holocaust survivors offended by the president's plans to lay a wreath at the World War II gravesite of Nazi soldiers near Luxembourg.

Weeks of controversy over continued revisions in Reagan's planned itinerary sharpened the debate. The front-page flap over the Bitburg stopover infuriated Nancy Reagan. The intensively protective First Lady was always eager for subordinates to blame when events took a bad turn for her "Ronnie," and on this occasion she pointed her delicate but damning finger at Deaver, usually her favorite lackey. (Years later, Reagan would claim that he visited Bitburg because he believed that Nazi SS troops buried there had been killed for trying to shield Jews. Holocaust experts declared the assertion unlikely, and one opined that Reagan apparently had been given only "anecdotal" information about the cemetery.)

Even before the embarrassing Bitburg incident, which damaged his reputation as a genius of media manipulation, Deaver had begun to feel burned out. The incessant demands of the huge White House staff and its fifteen-hour workdays had taken their toll. The stress had caused him to begin drinking heavily and in secret, sometimes as much as a quart of vodka a day, although he wasn't detected as a problem drinker at the time by his administration colleagues. Most of them later expressed surprise when they learned the extent of his solitary binges, which he carefully concealed with copious rolls of breath mints.

Like several other long-time Reagan aides, Deaver had gotten a nibble of the good life as a presidential powerbroker. No one loved mixing socially with the rich and beautiful more than Deaver, who'd developed a virulent case of the illness known in Washington as "Potomac fever," whose victims developed an unslakable thirst to be recognized and fawned over. He moaned to friends that his $72,000 White House salary wasn't enough to make ends meet in Washington and that his family was living on savings. When his wife Carolyn obtained a high-paying job with a public relations firm and got the Republican National Committee as a client, the couple's political "double-dipping" helped relieve the financial pressure. But he needed more money—much more—to prosper in the rarefied social atmosphere to which he'd become accustomed while serving at Nancy Reagan's elbow.

Even before Reagan's second inaugural in January 1985, Deaver made plans to leave the palatial trappings of the White House and set up his own public relations firm. In May, he bid farewell to the Reagans, who were reluctant to see their friend and favorite door-opener depart. Within weeks, Fortune 500 corporations were lining up at Deaver's pricey Georgetown Washington Harbor complex offices to pay six-figure retainers to a man who had almost unequaled access to the president and his top aides. Proof that Deaver continued to be regarded with special affection by the First Couple was the fact that he was allowed to keep his coveted White House pass, and was provided with an invaluable copy of the president's detailed, daily personal schedule, which few outside the White House Executive Office were permitted to see.

In a city where the perception of power is prized above all else, he became such a hot commodity that within a scant ten months after leaving the White House, he was pictured on the cover of *Time* magazine, chatting on his car telephone, the Capitol in sharp focus behind him providing an unnecessary reminder of his political clout. After two decades as a glorified errand boy for the Reagans, Mike Deaver thought he'd finally arrived in the business world on his own terms. But instead, a deadly combination of hubris, alcohol, and perhaps more than a bit of repressed self-importance conspired to destroy his new-found fortune and embarrass his long-time benefactors in the White House.

Actually, the seeds of Deaver's downfall had been sown months before the *Time* story, a publicity bonanza which backfired and served rather to confirm what some observers already had suspected; the former media manipulator's connections at the White House were for sale, and he either didn't know or didn't care about the unwritten Washington rule that influence-peddlers should stay out of the capital's glaring publicity limelight and operate in the shadowy backroom corners. Deaver's enviable client list included Boeing, CBS, Phillip Morris, TWA and the government of South Korea, to name but a few of the special interests willing to pay hefty fees to a consultant whose only obvious asset was his longstanding personal relationship with the president of the United States.

By the fall of 1985, the ex-Reagan aide's wheel-greasing on behalf of his corporate clients came to the attention of Michigan congressman John Dingell, the blunt-spoken, frequently overbearing chairman of a House subcommittee with wide-ranging oversight powers. Dingell's bird-dogging staff, who earlier had clashed with the Reagan White House during the EPA scandal, heard that Deaver might have used his inside knowledge of the administration's position on the controversial acid rain problem to gain a $105,000 contract with the Canadian government to influence the issue. Irate, Dingell ordered the General Accounting Office, the congressional watchdog agency, to probe Deaver's activities on acid rain and his work on behalf of the Canadian government.

GAO's gumshoes learned from Deaver's former White House colleagues that, while still working for the administration, he'd actively sought to create a "special envoy" approach to mediate the U.S.-Canadian split on acid rain, and that he'd pushed prominent Republican operative Drew Lewis for the post at a time when Canada was pressing the U.S. to take extensive steps to curb the industrial emissions which caused the destructive precipitation. The U.S. government subsequently agreed to a five-billion-dollar cleanup plan which was more ambitious than the Reagan Administration previously had agreed to support.

GAO's findings on Deaver's lobbying activities suggested possible violations of the 1978 Ethics in Government Act, which banned contacts with former executive branch co-workers for one year after leaving office. The disclosures were enough to prompt a referral to the Justice Department for further investigation. Ultimately, under pressure from congressional Democrats, Justice officials acceded to the selection of a court-appointed, independent prosecutor, Whitney North Seymour, Jr., a New York attorney whose polite yet patrician mien matched his old-line establishment background.

Meanwhile, reporters and congressional investigators examined the details of other Deaver consulting projects, including his guidance to Boeing's Air Force One designers on the Reagans' airborne traveling requirements and decorative preferences. He'd also arranged an unusual personal meeting with President Reagan for a top South Korean trade official while simutaneously pushing to open up the Asian cigarette market for an American tobacco company. In addition, he attempted to set up a personal powwow with the chairman of the Federal Communications Commission to discuss pending business involving his client CBS.

None of the blatant favor-seeking was seen as inappropriate by either Deaver or his former employer at 1600 Pennsylvania Avenue. "I didn't use my influence with the president or the White House at any time," Deaver told the *Washington Post* in response to questions about the acid rain allegations. "Mike has never put the arm on me, or sought any influence from me since he has been out of government," snapped the president in a blunt riposte to his friend's critics.

Special prosecutor Seymour, a stickler on ethics issues, saw the evidence differently and convened a federal grand jury to hear testimony about Deaver's unique style of public relations, which included staying at the homes of U.S. ambassadors abroad while he was doing business with foreign clients. Deaver had pushed the White House's nomination of one of his ambassador/hosts, and in another instance had improperly told U.S. ambassador to South Korea Dixie Walker, who he was pressing for special favors, that the diplomat would be retained in his post by the administration.

After months of investigation, Deaver was indicted, not for violating the federal one-year ethics ban on contacting former executive branch officials, but for perjury. He was charged with lying to both Dingell's congressional committee and the grand jury, which had heard his sworn if confusing version of events.

Deaver's lawyers responded by unsuccessfully challenging the constitutional authority of the independent counsel Seymour, and then claiming that Deaver's previously unrevealed alcoholism had impaired his ability to present truthful testimony. Their gambling defense strategy unexpectedly failed, and in December 1987, he was found guilty on three of five counts and sentenced to fifteen hundred hours of community service and a $100,000 fine.

Deaver's all-too-public grab for the brass ring cost him his business, his professional reputation and, to some extent, his friendship with the Reagans. The First Lady reportedly was incensed by remarks about her and her husband made in a book which Deaver authored with a ghost writer, largely to pay legal bills which reportedly exceeded $500,000. Even former detractors at the White House shook their heads in sympathy at the total public ruination of a troubled but not evil man, who just thirty months before had been at the right hand of the president.

On a brighter note, though, the saddest chapter of Mike Deaver's saga wasn't the final one. Within months, like once-feared former Nixon aide and Watergate sinner Charles Colson, Deaver re-discovered his religion. And, in his court-ordered community service, he learned to confront the daily, gritty travails of Washington's inner-city poor and homeless, some who lived in sleeping bags and tents across the street from the cloistered White House offices, which not long before had encompassed his whole moral universe.

He also apparently mended his bridges with Nancy Reagan and, as a result, had the last word with his former rivals in the White House. In August 1991, three longtime Reagan loyalists—William Clark, Ed Meese and policy adviser Martin Anderson—were "purged" from the trustees board of the Ronald Reagan Presidential Foundation, which operated the former president's official library. Newspaper accounts reported that Nancy Reagan engineered the unexpected ouster of her husband's aides and friends. Mike

Deaver was brought in, at a reported salary of $15,000 per month, to direct the library opening.

If Michael Deaver was a coddled favorite child of the Reagan inner circle, Franklyn "Lyn" Nofziger was the black sheep of the political family. Like Deaver, Nofziger had a long history of service to the Reagans dating back to the early California days, and he regarded his unshakable fealty to Ronald Reagan as more important than even the conservative cause itself. Loyalty was what Lyn Nofziger seemed to prize above all else. It was the lifeblood of politics for him, and that conviction created a common bond with the older man he frequently referred to as "Governor," who amply rewarded those who stuck by him.

A wisecracking former newspaper reporter and conservative activist with a barroom brawler's attitude towards politics, the pot-bellied, often disheveled Nofziger never really fit in with the buttoned-down, black tie formality preferred by most of the California Reaganauts. A man whose favorite tie had a picture of Mickey Mouse wasn't likely to endear himself to Nancy Reagan and her stylish Beverly Hills friends, and in Republican political circles it was common knowledge that the president's wife regarded Nofziger's slovenly personal habits with disdain.

Not only did he not care what others thought about his deliberately rumpled persona, Nofziger reveled in his bluff, street-fighting image. His political acumen was so highly regarded that he'd survived more than one attempt to permanently exile him from the Reagan team, and he was rewarded with the title of assistant to the president for political affairs when the Reagans assumed residence in the White House. The campaign workers and hangers-on who wanted to pick political plums from the Reagan tree first had to pass the stringent Nofziger litmus test of loyalty. To the delight of his conservative soulmates, he applied it with unremitting vigor.

Out of place in the stifling, bureaucratic atmosphere of the Executive Office, however, the energetic Nofziger soon grew restless. In his late fifties and not a wealthy man, he thought about leaving the administration and cashing in on his years of sweat and toil in the political vineyards while the man he helped to put in the White House could still be of practical use to him.

In January 1982, he packed his political bag of tricks, including his bulging Rolodex, and moved out of the White House. Almost immediately he formed a consulting partnership with California businessman Mark Bragg, a handsome, well-dressed mover-and-shaker twenty years his junior. Bragg, a smooth operator who moved easily in the power offices of Washington's K Street business corridor, was in many ways the antithesis of the casual Nofziger; the one thing they had in common was their belief that access plus influence equalled money. The odd couple's fledgling firm, Nofziger and Bragg Communications, quickly gained lucrative contracts with a variety of corporations whose executives wanted favors performed quietly in high places and were willing to make wealthy men of those who could produce results.

One of many companies which appreciated Nofziger's continuing ties to top Reagan officials was Comet Rice, a subsidiary of Early California Industries of Los Angeles. Comet had gotten itself into a bind by promising to sell a rice from a specific year's crop to the South Korean government. Later, company officials realized they were short and needed to substitute rice from another year's crop. Such a switch required the support of the State Department, whose policymakers were giving Comet the bureaucratic cold shoulder. Enter Lyn Nofziger, to whom turning up the political heat a notch was second nature.

"I was hired to help get one side of the story to the governor [Reagan]," stated Nofziger in a deposition about his role with Comet, whose bosses wanted to leapfrog over the troublesome naysayers at State and get to someone in the Reagan camp who could overrule any objections to their plan. To accommodate his client, Nofziger wrote a well-placed friend in the White House, then-national security adviser William Clark, a man he'd been working with on the Reagan White House team only months before. "I would like to point out that once again the administration is on the wrong side of a political issue," stated Nofziger's personal missive to Clark. "I sure wish you would take a look at this, because it seems to me that once again we're in a position of screwing our friends and rewarding our enemies."

Nofziger wrote Clark at least twice more in the next month, complaining that State Department officials refused to see his client's representative. To his credit, the national security adviser refused to become involved in what he regarded as a domestic matter, and had an aide make a non-commital reply to Nofziger's private, impassioned pleas. Embarrassed months later when his first letter to Clark was published by a Sacramento newspaper, Nofziger admitted the note intended to influence Clark was "dumb", but insisted he was merely trying to make "others aware in this administration of what I viewed the situation to be."

But his effort to sidestep proper government policymaking channels to benefit Comet was just a minor flap compared to Nofziger's other, more profitable acts of access-peddling, several of which would eventually make him the subject of federal criminal prosecution. Fairchild Republic Corporation manufactured an aircraft, the A-10, which the Air Force and Congress wanted to stop funding. Only intervention at the highest levels could save the controversial plane, which seemed destined for the budgetary scrap heap. To the relief of harried Fairchild executives, Nofziger was hanging up his consulting shingle just as the plane's future was taking a decided nosedive. Weeks after he left the White House, Nofziger was writing urgent memos to top State and Defense Department officials urging continued A-10 production.

When letters didn't produce the desired results, Nofziger arranged to meet with National Security Council staff members to head off the A-10's demise. For these door-opening services, Fairchild funneled $25,000 to Nofziger through the office of company lobbyist Stanton Anderson the day after a dinner between Anderson, Nofziger and Thomas Guarino, then vice president of Fairchild. The aircraft manufacturer also contributed $50,000 to the the New America Foundation, an educational arm of a political action committee headed by Nofziger.

Despite warnings from his consulting firm's own legal counsel that contacting executive branch officials, such as those at the NSC, might be a violation of the ethics laws,

Nofziger blithely plowed ahead: "These are my friends and I'm going to back them if I want to," he responded, dismissing his attorney's note of caution.

The portly, suddenly-richer Nofziger was wearing the same set of ethical blinders when he accepted a $100,000 retainer from the Marine Engineers Beneficial Association (MEBA) to lobby the White House to increase the use of civilian crews on maritime ships under the control of the Navy. Although President Reagan supported the idea, the maritime bosses complained that his subordinates were foot-dragging on its implementation. Nofziger dutifully complained on their behalf to Ed Meese's top deputy, James Jenkins, and to then-chief of staff Jim Baker. Former Navy Secretary John Lehman conceded that while the Navy made progress on the civilian manning program, MEBA's pet project never would have been developed so rapidly, except for the influential shoves administered by the group's well-connected consultant.

Word got around fast that Nofziger could push the right buttons with top Reagan officeholders, many who owed their political appointments to him. The Long Island Lighting Co. (LILCO) signed up with Nofziger and Bragg for the sum of $20,000 per month. If that sounded like a lot, it was pocket change compared to the the utility's ultimate goal: getting the controversial $4.6 billion dollar Shoreham nuclear power plant opened over the objections of federal regulators unhappy with Shoreham's emergency evacuation plans and construction safety record. Nofziger approached his successor as White House political director, Ed Rollins, on behalf of LILCO, but was rebuffed after Rollins checked with the Energy Department and found that the plant had significant problems. An outraged Sen. Daniel Moynihan of New York called for an investigation of Nofziger's lobbying on behalf of LILCO.

Nofziger might have lost that round, but he was more successful in helping a private health firm loosen federal regulations protecting Medicare patients. According to a report by a congressional subcommittee headed by New York congressman Ted Weiss, Nofziger was paid $300,000 by the International Medical Centers (IMC) to assist the company in gaining a controversial waiver which would enable it to remain in the Medicare program, an exception critical to the firm's survival, as eighty percent of its clients were Medicare recipients.

"The subcommittee's investigation revealed that the key contact...was Lyn Nofziger, the former White House aide hired as IMC's lobbyist," stated the report. The importunings of Nofziger and others turned the tide, as the federal health official in charge of the rule caved in to IMC, waived the rule and after leaving his job with the Health Care Financing Administration, received $40,000 in consulting fees and salary from the insurer. As a result, concluded the report, IMC received almost $12 million in payments from the government and continued to provide poor care to Medicare patients prior to going out of business, stranding many elderly subscribers without any medical coverage.

All these feats were just a warmup for Nofziger's single most notorious feat of arm-twisting—his successful effort at helping to secure a $32 million dollar Army engines contract for the Wedtech company. A minority-owned firm in the South Bronx, Wedtech used a network of highly paid consultants and lobbyists to ride roughshod over the legitimate objections of Army and Small Business Administration officials.

Initially known as Welbilt Electronic Die Corporation, the New York manufacturing facility, located in a run-down neighborhood in the shadow of Yankee Stadium, was headed by an impulsive and somewhat emotionally unstable Hispanic businessman named John Mariotta. Prone to sudden mood swings and fond of keeping financial records scattered in shoe boxes, the erratic Mariotta nevertheless had almost boundless ambitions for his modest machine shop.

Two days before Nofziger left his White House post, Mariotta had been honored by President Reagan as a "hero of the eighties" at a reception recognizing minority business achievement. Although the poorly educated Mariotta could barely read the menu in the elegant White House dining room, he had a flash of inspiration about how he could become one of the fashionably dressed magnates who surrounded him at the ceremony. Know and use the right people—that was the secret which separated his struggling brainchild from Manhattan companies which populated the Fortune 500 list. From that cynical bit of insight was born one of the biggest scandals of the Reagan years, which tarred several of its top officials, including Nofziger.

At the time of his triumphant trip to Washington, Mariotta was attempting unsuccessfully to expand his operations by obtaining a multi-million dollar contract with the Army to mass produce a small engine commmonly used for a variety of generating purposes. Army officials didn't think Welbilt, as Wedtech was then known, could do the job, and scoffed at as ludicrous the company's initial $100 million dollar bid for the contract. Army procurement experts privately estimated that the job could be done for one-fifth Welbilt's inflated asking price.

The military's resistance to his grandiose schemes infuriated Mariotta and his equally colorful, unscrupulous business partners, who jointly decided they needed friends— powerful political friends. They already had a New York congressman and several city officials catering to them in return for money and other favors, but they needed to establish themselves in Washington and carve off a slice of the juicy federal pie.

After all, thought Mariotta, hadn't he been personally singled out for praise by the president of the United States? Why couldn't he get someone with clout to listen to how he'd built a burgeoning business, employing hundreds of productive workers, out of nothing but a dingy garage and his own sweat? Access cost money, but Mariotta wasn't about to see his dreams of glory go up in smoke over the stupidity of a few stubborn Army bureaucrats. He'd get the president's own men to intervene and make the Army listen.

Lyn Nofziger was already familiar with the mercurial Mariotta. The former political adviser had been with the "Governor" when Reagan the candidate had come to the broken glass and shattered concrete of the South Bronx in 1980 to remind its listless, unemployed denizens that, unlike Jimmy Carter, he would remember their misery when he got to the Oval Office. Now it was time to honor that pledge. Less than a month after he left the White House, Nofziger and his partner

Bragg were hired to plead Welbilt's case at the White House and the Pentagon.

Welbilt had been referred to Nofziger and Bragg by Stephen Denlinger, the director of a trade group known as LAMA, the Latin American Manufacturers Association, of which Mariotta was perhaps the most important member. Right up front, Mark Bragg told Denlinger that he and Nofziger would make the contacts necessary for Welbilt to get the engines contract, according to a 1988 Senate report on the firm's influence-peddling.

Bragg and Nofziger lost no time launching a tag team effort to loosen the Army's trenchant opposition to Welbilt. While Bragg worked on the lower-echelon civilian decision-makers, Nofziger called the secretary of the Army, John Marsh, who assembled Army officials that same day to discuss the contract. As a result of that impromptu session and a second meeting, the Army reaffirmed its decision not to award the contract to Welbilt and so informed the company in writing. That news didn't bother the confident Bragg, who told a worried Denlinger not to fret about the rejection; other chips were being moved around the table, and the Army wasn't going to have the last word.

Bragg had good reason to know why: the week before the Army had thrown out the Welbilt proposal, Nofziger wrote to presidential counselor Ed Meese to request his assistance. Giving Meese a thumbnail sketch of Welbilt's woes with recalcitrant Army purchasers, Nofziger concluded, "Ed, I really think it would be a blunder not to award that contract to Welbilt. The symbolism (of minority enterprise) "is very great here."

Meese later said he "might" have asked his deputy Jim Jenkins to look into the matter. To be certain Jenkins became aware of the combined forces backing Welbilt, Bragg and Denlinger also visited his office. Impressed, Jenkins sent a note to cabinet secretary Craig Fuller, asking for guidance. After checking with White House counsel Fred Fielding, the arbitrator of ethics matters, Fuller told Jenkins that awarding government contracts was not the business of White House officials. Stay out of it, he was warned. Jenkins, a genial former Navy officer and California state housing official, decided to ignore the directive because Fuller "wasn't my boss, so he couldn't tell me not to" help Welbilt.

Instead, Jenkins started pestering Small Business Administration officials on Welbilt's behalf while Nofziger and Bragg went to lunch with SBA's administrator, James Sanders, yet another California political appointee. When SBA continued to resist, Jenkins convened a highly unusual meeting in the "Ward Room" of the White House, ordering all the players involved in the Army engines contract to appear. Assistant Secretary of the Army Jay Sculley, obviously unhappy at being summoned to the special roundtable, "looked like he had been dragged in like a little dog on a leash," joked one of the meeting participants.

Although the mild-mannered Jenkins didn't rant or threaten anyone, all the government worker bees knew the hidden agenda of the unofficial gathering; the White House wanted Welbilt to have the engines contract, and the agencies responsible better come up with the money to make it happen. That's exactly what occurred, with Nofziger and Bragg providing behind-the-scenes pressure at key points in the months-long negotiating process. Both the Army and the SBA repeatedly violated their own regulations to come up with additional funds and revised estimates to accommodate the small but suddenly high-profile Bronx machine shop.

Just to cover their bets, the Welbilt crowd also enlisted the informal lobbying efforts of long-time Meese friend E. Robert Wallach, a San Francisco personal injury lawyer, who peppered his law school chum in the White House with a tiresome series of meandering memos. The missives touched upon subjects ranging from the engines contract to his discourses on proper dietary habits, on which the vegetarian Wallach had pronounced views. A smallish, polite, immaculately groomed man with huge, bushy eyebrows and the appearance of a graying gnome, Wallach was regarded as a bit of an eccentric in legal circles.

Like the poet e.e. cummings, he spelled his name with no capital letters, and was an inveterate name-dropper who seemed most content in the company of the well-to-do and well-connected. In fact, he was so impressed with "his good friend" Meese's proximity to the Oval Office that he moved from San Francisco to Washington to be near him, and later helped represent Meese in the contentious 1985 Senate nomination hearing which preceded his confirmation as attorney general.

A man of many faces, Wallach could come close to tears while discussing the desperate plight of poor and unemployed inhabitants of Welbilt's South Bronx deprived neighborhoods. Yet he had no hesitation in asking the company's board of directors to pay him well over a million dollars for doing little more than making a few phone calls and writing memos, some of which had nothing to do with Welbilt's problems, to Meese and others.

Although Meese would later claim to have mostly ignored his friend's endless stream of memos and letters, Wallach did persuade him to place an unusual personal call to Commerce Secretary Malcolm Baldrige. One of Baldrige's underlings, a street-smart Economic Development Administration official named Carlos Campbell, was resisting the firm's pressure for additional loan guarantees and extensions from Commerce. Campbell's private notes describing his telephone conversations showed that neither the friendly pleas of Nofziger nor repeated angry beratings from Bragg had changed his mind about the company; he knew a back-door approach when he saw one. Despite his firm stand, Campbell was later unceremoniously ousted from his job, and publicly charged that the animosity of Welbilt's consultants was the cause of his dismissal.

Welbilt's top officials didn't care about the cost; they believed in a scatter-shot approach; attack from all fronts. Frequently one of their many lobbyists didn't even know what another was doing. But the confusion sown by their hit-and-miss strategy didn't matter. Soon there would be so much government money rolling in that the huge payments and stock options handed out to influence-sellers like Nofziger and Wallach would be a bagatelle.

Mariotta's insider strategy worked. Welbilt got (or more accurately bought) the Army contract. A note from Jenkins to Meese stated that "your personal go-ahead to me saved this project." The Senate report examining the origin of the contract award stated that both Meese and Jenkins "failed to

observe the White House policy on contacts with procurement officials, which failure resulted in improper favoritism
toward a specific contractor."

Flush with success, the following year Welbilt changed its
corporate name to Wedtech. Millions of dollars in government assistance, loans and outright subsidies hadn't resulted
in the Army getting its engines; delivery was many months
and a mountain of production problems behind. Wedtech
wasn't capable of building the engines in the first place, and
by this time its officers' high-living and Atlantic City gambling had all but bankrupted the company.

Few knew it, however; the firm's high rollers conspired to
cook the books, and bought off the few outside auditors competent enough to discover their crooked shenanigans. Of
course, the company's non-performance should have meant
the end of the government gravy train and stock profits now
worth millions of dollars to the few lucky enough to catch the
manic Mariotta in a generous mood. Instead, Wedtech's embattled little gang of thieves merely stepped up the pressure
for even more federal handouts.

Having failed to deliver on the engines contract, the larcenous Wedtech crew grew bolder still. They set their sights on
a $126 million dollar Navy contract, a taxpayer-funded bo-
nanza which would keep their pyramid scheme alive and
provide enough cash influx to cover up all their past sins, if
they just could get their hooks into it.

There were two big problems standing in the path of the
Wedtech finaglers. First, the Navy construction contract in
question called for immense, ninety-ton pontoon bridges
made of fabricated metal, large enough to deploy millions of
tons worth of cargo from ship to shore. And, the Navy brass
wanted them in a hurry. Wedtech's undertrained, woefully
equipped workers couldn't adequately keep the production
schedule for relatively simple engines for the Army from a
technology forty years old. The company didn't have the
facility, tools, skills or time to perform even part of the job,
certainly not within the severely compressed delivery schedule the Navy insisted upon.

Second, because of the growing value of its stock, the company was about to be kicked out of the government's minor-

ity set-aside program, which was intended to benefit the less advantaged. With the Army contract, Wedtech couldn't any longer be considered a "mom-and-pop" operation which needed federal assistance. Small Business Administration officials, who considered Wedtech their biggest minority success story, wanted to "graduate" the contract-rich firm from the government's 8(a) program, and turn it loose to face the business world. It was time for the company to sink or swim on its own.

Losing its SBA support would have been disastrous for Wedtech, which was surviving only because more and more government money had been covering up incompetence and outright theft. Thrown into a real competitive business climate, it would no longer be eligible for any more sole source goodies like the engines contract, with Army advisers and engineers underwriting much of the actual costs and often doing much of the work on-site in order to get their product produced correctly and quickly.

No, Wedtech had to stay under the government umbrella, or its well-concealed, ruinous financial position would be revealed and the inflated value of the company's stock would come crashing down, along with the growing fortunes of its owners, lawyers, consultants and political protectors. Impossible as it seemed, Wedtech had to have that Navy construction project—all of it.

Keeping themselves in the government's minority set-aside program was the easy part. Wedtech insiders devised a phony stock scheme to make Mariotta, an Hispanic, appear to retain majority control of the company (which at this point he no longer had), and thus continue the firm's eligibility under the Small Business Administration's rules regarding minority ownership. Those at the agency who raised questions about the highly questionable arrangement were either ignored or coerced into accepting the deal, stated the Senate investigative report, which called the arrangement a "sham."

Forcing the Navy into handing over a contract four times as big as the Army engines project was a bit tougher. Initially, the Navy steadfastly refused to allow any minority contractor into the bidding process because of the time sensitivity of the pontoon construction. The pontoon bridges supported the

U.S. Rapid Deployment Force around the world, and the Navy's logistics chief, a no-nonsense admiral, wanted the gigantic floating causeways built and transported posthaste. The accelerated schedule was already slipping at the time of the bidding. With no facility and no experience in such mammoth-scale construction, Wedtech had no hope of gaining even a small portion of the hotly contested contract. But that was before Lyn Nofziger, Mark Bragg, Wallach and Wedtech's other advocates took up the cudgel on behalf of their generous friends.

Everyone except Wedtech was shocked when Assistant Navy Secretary Everett Pyatt reversed his earlier, supposedly unshakable objection to Wedtech's participation and awarded the company first a portion, then all of the $100 million-plus contract.

Captain David de Vicq, a ramrod-straight career Navy construction expert with a blond crew cut and a straight-forward attitude, had helped build military projects all over the world. Because of his expertise and excellent work record, the unlucky de Vicq had drawn the unenviable assignment of assessing Wedtech's capabilities for the important job. Wedtech officials had given him a tour of a pathetic, empty shell of a building which they proudly claimed was their production facility. It had no roof and no power, and in union-controlled New York City, Wedtech was months away from getting the site fit for anything. Shocked at what he saw, he flatly told his Navy superiors that Wedtech had no chance of completing the job *at all*, let alone on time. De Vicq's repeated objections were ignored and Wedtech got the pontoon contract.

Disturbingly, when Wedtech later fell behind and the Navy started frantically searching for a second production source for the pontoons, the Navy inexplicably awarded future "options," or contract additions to Wedtech, at a time when the company was failing to deliver unfinished pontoons for which payment had already been made. Worse yet, the first Wedtech-produced pontoons tested were so far out of alignment that workers, in a laughable fit of frustration, used a sledge hammer to try and make corners fit the exacting specifications.

Despite what was at best Wedtech's lackluster performance, a ranking Navy official, Wayne Arny, inexplicably attempted to authorize lucrative additional work on the basis of an open-ended "letter contract" with no price negotiations. An outraged Captain de Vicq termed that deal a "license to steal." Arny claimed that he didn't remember signing the order, which was rescinded, and Senate investigators subsequently interviewed thirty Navy officials in an unsuccessful attempt to learn where the document originated.

One possible explanation was contained in an affidavit from Wedtech executive Mario Moreno, who swore that the company had secretly agreed to pay Bragg and Nofziger $400,000 if the additional work for the pontoons was awarded without price negotiations. When a ranking defense audit supervisor, Colonel Don Hein, warned the Navy that Wedtech appeared to be broke, he was told to mind his own business. Hein was summarily transferred to another post after being threatened by a Wedtech official and dressed down by his boss. He and the tough-minded de Vicq, who was detested by Wedtech's flim-flam artists, were to become two more of a number of government workers who were pushed out of the way for trying to raise legitimate questions about Wedtech's shell game.

The service was throwing good money after bad, and top Navy officials were raising hell about continuing delays for a critical strategic program, but the money kept flowing to the now-infamous operation in the Bronx. By this time the Navy considered Wedtech a black hole into which its procurement money disappeared without a trace.

Senate investigators discovered why. Nofziger and Bragg's fingerprints were everywhere, along with those of the human memo machine, Bob Wallach. First, Nofziger had gone to the top and met privately with Navy Secretary John Lehman, who claimed he took no action on behalf of Wedtech as a result of the consultant's visit. Moreover, the Navy official who made the decision to give the pontoon contract to Wedtech, Ev Pyatt, testified under oath that he had not spoken to either Nofziger or Bragg prior to the award of the pontoon contract.

However, Senate probers learned from Pyatt's own scheduling calander that he had met with Nofziger at least three times during the months preceding his decision on Wedtech.

An internal memo was found in Navy files citing a call from a "Mr. Nosziger (Spelling?) President's Political Advisor, relative to the delivery date of the technical proposal from Wedtech." Pyatt testified he never saw the note, although it's unlikely a call from the president's chief political aide would have gone unheeded or unreturned.

In addition, Pyatt had accepted an invitation to an anniversary celebration of the Nofziger & Bragg firm in February 1984, the month before the Navy contract was signed. Pyatt's telephone logs also showed evidence of sixty calls between him and the lobbyists, many of them after the contract was awarded, during a period when Navy officials were sharply critical of Wedtech's non-performance. Later, Pyatt had at least a couple of lunches with Nofziger, and he attended a presidential inaugural ball in January 1985 as a guest of Nofziger and Bragg (although he claimed he had not asked them if they represented defense contractors).

Memos written to his personal file by Wallach also suggested that Bragg had spoken with and influenced Pyatt and had reported his success to both Wedtech and Wallach. (Not taking any chances, the Wedtech fixers also paid $60,000 in cash to a Navy civilian employee, Richard Ramirez, to become a "mole" for the company and provide inside information on the pontoon contract. However, it was unclear exactly how many Wedtech insiders knew about the bribing of Ramirez.)

Finally, the Senate inquiry revealed that Pyatt's nomination to become Assistant Secretary of the Navy for Shipbuilding and Logistics was held up at the White House for almost a year prior to the signing of the contract, and was released by the administration the same day the ink dried on the Wedtech agreement. This rather suspect coincidence led to the suggestion that Pyatt's nomination may have been held hostage while the consultants pressured him over Wedtech.

The affable Jenkins, still at the White House at the time that Pyatt's name came through, denied that the Navy official's nomination was used as a lever to force him to help Wedtech. But Jenkins's version of events was colored by the fact that he, too, later became a highly paid consultant to the company, after he left the White House, through his friendship with Nofziger.

The greedy Ramirez, who also admitted to taking bribes from other government contractors, and who stubbornly resisted the Justice Department's attempts to squeeze him into a plea-bargaining arrangement, ultimately pled guilty to taking illegal gratutities. Cooperatively, he disclosed to Justice Department officials that he was present at a meeting during which he was advised to tell Pyatt that his promotion depended upon Wedtech getting the Navy contract. Justice's lawyers were unable to corroborate the story despite months of interviews.

The investigating Senate subcommittee, chaired by the respected Michigan Senator Carl Levin (D), referred Pyatt's public congressional testimony to the Justice Department for further review, as his interview statements and testimony were found to be in conflict with other evidence and documents. After three years of investigation, Justice officials quietly closed the book on Pyatt, who had resigned his post in the middle of the probe, without bringing criminal charges against him. But privately, Justice attorneys admitted that "there was a lot of smoke" surrounding Pyatt's curious and unexplained flip-flop in favor of Wedtech, according to an internal Senate memo.

The Senate report concluded that the Navy improperly awarded the contract to Wedtech because of political influence, and that the Navy overpaid the company by millions of dollars for pontoons it never received, or got many months late in unusable condition.

The Wedtech facade had came tumbling down under the weight of too many lies and unfulfilled promises. The company went bankrupt, leaving its minority workforce and many helpless investors stranded, but not before Nofziger and Bragg cashed in on stock reportedly worth more than $600,000. Months later, when the company's fraud had been revealed, Wedtech's stock would be valued at pennies a share.

Nofziger's almost feverish attempts to peddle his access to the Reagan White House couldn't go unnoticed indefinitely, and a court-appointed independent counsel, James McKay, was selected to investigate the full extent of his activities.

Nofziger was subsequently indicted on several criminal counts relating to his work for Wedtech, Fairchild and the maritime union. Bragg, who hadn't been a political appointee like his partner and thus wasn't subject to the federal ethics laws, was charged with one count of aiding and abetting.

In February 1988, after a parade of witnesses detailed his enthusiastic lobbying of executive branch officials, Nofziger was found guilty on three counts of violating the Ethics in Government Act, a law he scorned as "Mickey Mouse" because it didn't apply to Congress and lower-ranking federal officials.

Sentenced to a ninety-day jail term and fined $30,000 for illegal lobbying, an unrepentant Nofziger later won a reversal when a federal appeals court overturned his convictions in a controversial split decision. Two judges ruled that independent counsel McKay had not proved that Nofziger knew what he had done was illegal, and that the White House hadn't had a "direct and substantial" interest in the projects pushed by Nofziger. The dissenting jurist on the three-judge appeals panel felt strongly the prosecution indeed had made its case convincingly against Nofziger, and that he clearly had violated the ban on lobbying executive branch officials.

Wallach, New York congressman Mario Biaggi, whose son's law firm represented Wedtech, and a handful of the company's executives and hangers-on also got close attention from criminal prosecutors. A much-decorated former New York city police officer who'd served ten terms in Congress, Biaggi was forced to resign from the House in 1988 after his conviction on charges relating to illegally pressuring Wedtech to give him $1.8 million in cash and stocks. He served 26 months in federal prison before being released for medical reasons in mid-1991.

The racketeering conviction of Wallach was reversed in May 1991 by an appeals court on the basis that one of the former Wedtech executives had testified falsely on unrelated matters. A six-term Bronx congressman, Robert Garcia, once a rising star, had his political career and reputation ruined by his Wedtech-related extortion conviction; his wife Jane was also convicted along with her husband for illicitly gaining interest-free loans from the corrupt company.

As his parting shot, Nofziger said he was sorry he ever agreed to work at the Reagan White House for a year after the election. "I never did like government," he said. "Now I know why."

Wedtech's demise also caused major headaches for Ed Meese, who always seemed to be near the epicenter of any Reagan administration storm. A separate report by independent counsel McKay on Meese's ethical behavior concluded that, while there was no direct proof that Meese benefitted financially from Wedtech, Meese "and his staff intervened" with federal officials "to facilitate Welbilt's obtaining" the Army engines contract. But for Meese's role, stated McKay's report, Wedtech "probably would not have been awarded the contract."

The independent counsel also recounted Meese's controversial involvement with two rather bizarre characters introduced into the Wedtech mix by his ever-present crony Wallach. One was W. Franklyn Chinn, a Chinese-born money mananger who ran his business from an efficiency apartment in a San Francisco residential building. The other was Dr. Rusty Kent London, a non-practicing physician from New Jersey who made his living gambling and investing. The eccentric London (whose given name was Irving Lobsenz) had written a book on card "counting," or how to beat the odds in Las Vegas casinos. An informal business partner of the mysterious Chinn, London was also Wallach's landlord.

The unlikely duo had been brought into the Wedtech mix as consultants by Wallach to improve Wedtech's scattershot management. But the real motive was a scheme for the pair to artificially inflate the price of Wedtech's stock, for which they were paid a million dollars by crooked company insiders eager to pump up their phony paper empire.

After Meese's and his wife Ursula's private financial investments were criticized at his confirmation hearings to be attorney general in 1985, Wallach suggested that the couple place their savings under Chinn's watchful eye. Wallach already had hundreds of thousands of dollars invested with Chinn. He confided to Meese that Chinn was involved with Wedtech and that Chinn was taking him as a client only as a favor to Wallach. Nevertheless, solely upon the word of his ubiquitous friend, Meese invested more than $54,000 of his family's personal savings with Chinn, despite the money manager's ties to the controversial defense contractor.

Through a complex tangle of transactions which were probed for years by patient Securities and Exchange Commission officials, Chinn earned an average of more than 34% profit for "Meese Partners" in less than two years. The independent counsel's inquiry further determined that, in violation of federal regulations, Chinn made investments for Meese for which there were not sufficient funds at the time of the transactions. In other words, the attorney general's account got a "free ride" from stock brokerage firms. McKay could find no evidence that Meese did anything improper for Wedtech or Chinn in return; but Chinn, London and Wallach all refused to provide testimony for the investigators because of other, pending criminal charges against them. The subsequent racketeering convictions of Chinn and London were reversed along with Wallach's by a New York appeals court.

As was his usual practice when confronted with evidence of conflicts-of-interest, Meese claimed to have "no recollection" of his lengthy conversations with Wallach and Chinn, or whether they might have related to Wedtech. The evidence shocked and dismayed even top Justice Department lawyers, who previously had been defensive of their amiable but hopelessly disorganized boss.

Even before the public issuance of McKay's report, two ranking Justice officials resigned their offices because of Meese's unethical conduct, according to their testimony before the Senate Judiciary Committee. One of them, William Weld, who gained considerable public stature for his principled stand in opposition to Meese's sloppy ethics, won election as governor of Massachusetts in 1990.

*　　*　　*

"He was a unique person with strong qualities, enormously committed, forceful, a born leader. But he tended to see the world in terms of black and white. When things didn't fit into his structure, he just ignored them. It clouded his vision."

Many who observed his actions during eight years as president believe the quotes would aptly describe Ronald Reagan's narrowly focused world view. However, the comments, from a former colleague, pertain to a young military officer and National Security Council employee whose impetuous, misguided actions triggered the most far-reaching scandal of the Reagan presidency, and almost caused a constitutional crisis between the executive and congressional branches of government.

The controversial figure at the center of what was to become a political maelstrom was a handsome, hard-charging Marine Corps colonel, Oliver L. North, a Vietnam veteran who loved cloak-and-dagger, but lamentably tended to exaggerate his own role in military and intelligence covert actions.

From the bowels of the Old Executive Office Building in the White House complex, North organized and coordinated an astonishing variety of secret weapons-selling, hostage-rescuing, fund-raising and intelligence-swapping activities, which collectively came to be known as the "Iran/contra" affair following their disclosure in November 1986. The true origin and legitimate presidential authorization, if any, for what North and his fellow conspirators termed "The Enterprise," confounded criminal and congressional probers for more than five years, and crippled the presidency of the chief executive whose wishes the gung-ho military aide sought to carry out.

Although generations apart in age and background, there were a number of similiarities between the determined NSC staffer and the president he so loyally served. Both men were intensely patriotic, with an overweening fear of what they regarded as the creeping threat of global communism to American security; Ronald Reagan had been preaching this message since "Ollie" North was a toddler. Specifically, each fervently believed that communism's most dangerous thrust might come from south of the U.S. borders, not far from where Cuba's Fidel Castro had established his socialist dictatorship, ninety miles from American shores, more than thirty years ago.

Reagan, North and many American policy-makers saw the 1978 overthrow of Nicaraguan strongman Anastasio Somoza Garcia and his replacement in power by leftist Sandinista revolutionaries, as a body-blow to U.S. interests in the region.

When thousands of anti-Sandinista "contras," whose Spanish name suggested their fierce opposition to the new regime's links to Moscow, took to the hills outside the capital of Managua, the Reagan White House quickly mandated financial and ideological support for the rag-tag army of resistance as one of the highest priorities of administration foreign policy.

While the contra cause eventually received considerable sympathy from a diverse cross-section of the American political spectrum, there was never a majority of members of Congress who believed that an annual check for hundreds of millions of dollars worth of non-lethal aid, in addition to tons of U.S. military weapons and hardware, were necessarily going to tip the balance of power in the rebels' favor.

Skeptical intelligence analysts concluded that there was little chance for an outright military victory over the entrenched Sandinistas by the poorly organized contra army. Other experts speculated that if the U.S. waited long enough, the repressive communist government in Managua might collapse under the crushing double-whammy of an economy devastated by civil war and punishing trade embargoes instituted in Washington.

Oliver North and the true believers in the contra cause had a dramatically different view—the guerrillas' desperate effort against the Sandinistas might be democracy's last-ditch stand against the rising threat of communism in Latin America. If the U.S. didn't help ensure the contras' overthrow of the Sandinistas, thought North, then Washington might be forced to send in American troops to rid our southern neighbor of the socialist scourge. Unlike Vietnam, this was one battlefield the determined Marine colonel didn't intend to leave without an ultimate victory for what he regarded as the heroic forces of freedom.

Significantly, North's vision of a possible political and social apocalypse in the region was enthusiastically embraced by Reagan strategists eager to draw a line in the sand and show that their president was standing tall against subversive aggression south of American borders. Nicaragua must not become another obedient client of Moscow like Cuba, and Soviet influence there must be underminded by whatever means necessary. The small, torn nation of five million people, two-thirds of mixed Indian and European mestizo blood, was to become a keystone of American foreign policy.

Out in the wooded, closely guarded confines of the Central Intelligence Agency headquarters in Langley, Virginia, there was an owlish-looking, wizened lawyer who shared the single-minded Col. North's fervent, missionary zeal. Although he had the bent frame and shuffling gait of an aging college don, with an annoying habit of mumbling almost incoherently, CIA Director William Casey was no shrinking academic violet, nor was he a man to be taken lightly, as many of his adversaries had learned the hard way.

Brilliant and unusually well-read, Casey had been an authentic World War II hero. From the Office of Strategic Services, he personally had directed some of the boldest Allied intelligence forays conducted behind enemy lines. The exhilarating role of youthful spymaster created a lifelong love for clandestine operations and an intellectual contempt for those unwilling to take risks for a greater cause.

The erudite Casey was a longtime insider in Republican political circles; he'd once written speeches for GOP presidential candidate Wendell Willkie. A former chairman of the Securities and Exchange Commission and ex-director of the Export-Import Bank, he'd managed his friend Ronald Reagan's successful 1980 presidential campaign. While he had privately longed to be named secretary of state, and was a self-made millionaire like most of the men Reagan admired, Casey wasn't a member of the California inner circle of presidential intimates. Instead, his reward was to be chosen to head the CIA, a nomination greeted with grumbles and snorts of derision by some unhappy Members of Congress.

The long knives of administration critics were waiting on Capitol Hill for Casey, whose barely-concealed contempt for the legislative branch's role in foreign policy-making was well-known; he was dubbed "the Duke of Disdain", reported his biographer, Joseph Persico. He was confirmed only after an embarrassingly public Senate confirmation battle during which both his financial dealings and personal integrity were sharply questioned by detractors anxious to keep him out of the sensitive intelligence post.

Reagan White House aides spent a fortune in political capital convincing not only Democrats, but Republican power-brokers, such as Arizona's Sen. Barry Goldwater, that Casey would behave himself and accede to Congress its traditional advice and consent role in intelligence matters. Several legislators who accepted the high-level assurances about Casey's behavior would later regret the decision as a most grievous error in judgment. Nevertheless, Casey was confirmed unanimously. Not long after he assumed control, the controversial Casey's stewardship of the CIA survived an humiliating episode involving the business dealings of his hand-picked but inexperienced deputy, Max Hugel, who came under heavy fire from the agency's old hands the moment he'd joined the Casey team as director of operations. If some of the agency's top operatives were fond of silk suits, Hugel's attire ran to lavender jumpsuits with gold chains, noted Persico in his book, *Casey*. An unexpected uproar ensued when the *Washington Post's* Bob Woodward and Patrick Tyler (who now writes for the *New York Times*) confronted the CIA's second-in-command with taped allegations suggesting that he might have provided insider information in stock transactions.

A squat, self-confident executive unschooled in the byzantine politics of Washington, Hugel vociforously denied the charges and demanded to confront his accusers, a pair of brothers named McNell who were nowhere to be found. But the reporters had more than a dozen, expletive-laced tape recordings of private conversations conducted years before between Hugel and the McNells.

Among the torrent of unprintable invectives Hugel heaped upon his former business partners on the tapes was a spasm of outrage directed at their lawyer, who supposedly had threatened a lawsuit against Hugel. "I'll put that bastard in jail...I'll kill that bastard," he ranted. Hugel's unchecked rage came back to haunt him, as the published account of his tirade and the hint of possible stock improprieties brought intense pressure for his dismissal. Following a flurry of high-level phone calls, Casey reluctantly accepted Hugel's unwilling resignation in order to avoid further investigation into his aide's affairs and to limit the front-page political fallout.

However, neither the Hugel flap nor the often bitter internal sniping which had plagued the agency since its demoralizing overhaul in the late 1970s deterred Casey from his larger mission: He was determined to revitalize what he regarded as the CIA's primary function—conducting covert operations against America's adversaries around the world.

Many Cold War veterans, including Casey, thought the agency's capability to effectively run secret intelligence operations had fallen on hard times while the White House had been occupied by Jimmy Carter. The former Georgia governor and Washington outsider didn't trust the cozy, old-boy network which had dominated the spy organization for thirty years, and he'd made no secret of his intent to roil the stagnant waters of the intelligence establishment. He was a "utopian" in the disparaging view of one former high-ranking CIA official, who felt that Carter's reluctance to utilize the agency's operations directorate made the U.S. appear weak in the eyes of its adversaries abroad.

President Carter had good reason to keep the well-entrenched intelligence bosses at arm's length. In the two years before his election, congressional investigations headed by Rep. Otis Pike (D-N.Y.) in the House and Senator Frank Church (D.-Idaho) in the Senate revealed the CIA's fingerprints on plots to assassinate foreign leaders. Astonished government investigators also unearthed the sordid details of all sorts of bizarre, off-the-books spy schemes concocted by CIA officials, who hadn't bothered to inform Congress about their clandestine machinations, as the law required. The months-long revelations and strongly worded congressional condemnations of the spy scandals painted a disturbing picture of a top-secret bureaucracy gone amok.

To rein in the spy world's dirty tricksters, Carter brought in Navy Admiral Stansfield Turner to clean house. Turner's marching orders were to ensure that no other rogue operations surfaced from Langley headquarters to damage Carter's delicate brand of personal diplomacy. The upright, articulate admiral executed the presidential directive with a ferocious energy; he cracked the adminstrative whip and forced a number top-ranking agency officials to retire or face exile in the CIA's version of bureaucratic Siberia.

The shakeup made Turner a detested figure inside the agency and a target for negative press leaks from disgruntled members of the cloak-and-dagger set, for their exclusive coterie was unused to such tight control by an outsider. *"Reagan/Bush"* campaign signs began appearing at CIA offices during the 1980 presidential campaign, according to a Senate Intelligence Committee staffer who visited the Langley headquarters often.

As soon as the hard-working Casey took control, however, he acted quickly to dispel the malaise which had descended over the intelligence community like a pall during the previous administration. He loosened the bonds which he felt had crippled the CIA's far-flung intelligence-gathering apparatus. Half a lifetime earlier, he had successfully placed spies in Berlin during the final, chaotic weeks of World War II; they became invaluable human weapons in the Cold War against the Soviet Union.

But the CIA which Casey inherited, despite a new generation of Buck Rogers electronic and satellite technology, couldn't consistently deliver reliable, real-time intelligence information from human sources in strategic areas important to U.S. interests. That fact had been made painfully obvious during Carter's pitiful, failed attempt to rescue more than fifty American hostages in Iran by means of an ill-prepared helicopter assault across the desert. The doomed mission and its sorry epilogue of recriminations helped bury his presidency.

The wily Casey was determined to revitalize the agency's reputation and morale. He knew that his friend Ronald Reagan was a chief executive who wanted results, but unlike the driven, meticulous Carter, was uninterested in the details of exactly how the job got done. "Covert action" wasn't a dirty phrase in the Casey lexicon.

In fact, Casey may have started his covert action revival as a private citizen, even before Reagan assumed residency in the White House. During the 1980 campaign, Reagan advisers had feared the Carter White House would attempt some sort of last-minute "October Surprise" to repair the damage done by the botched rescue attempt and possibly tip the balance of an otherwise fairly close election in the Democrats' favor. At least some circumstantial evidence points to the possibility that the opposite may have occurred; Reagan's campaign manager, Casey, may have struck his own secret bargain with the Iranian Islamic government on the hostage issue to assure his candidate's election victory, according to accounts which didn't surface publicly until a decade after the election.

Former National Security Council staffer Gary Sick, an expert on Iran who was in the middle of the Carter administration's attempts to free the hostages, stated that as many as fifteen witnesses have offered information about secret trips made by Casey to Paris and Madrid during the summer of 1980. Several international arms dealers and former intelligence operatives active in Europe at the time have said that Casey set up an unofficial arrangement with arms broker Cyrus Hashemi, who had close contacts within the radical Iranian government.

The alleged deal was this: The Iranian government would keep the hostages captive until after the presidential vote, which Reagan presumably would win if the Americans were still held on election day, for their imprisonment then dominated the U.S. political landscape and news coverage. Then they'd be released immediately after Reagan assumed office, in return for which the new American administration would turn a blind eye to weapons shipments to Iran by third countries such as Israel. The Iranian mullahs were desperate to gain additional weapons, and particularly precious spare parts and tires, for their escalating holy war against Saddam Hussein's Iraq.

No firm proof of any such agreement exists; and in fact, the credibility of several of the witnesses is highly suspect. But former Carter administration officials have complained publicly that backstage White House hostage negotiations suddenly went flat during the final three weeks prior to the election, with the polls almost dead even between Reagan and Carter. In addition, as it turned out, the hostages *were* held until a beaming Reagan could greet them on the White House lawn shortly after his inauguration. Moreover, former State Department and intelligence officials, as well as former President Carter himself, have asserted that weapons flowed to Iran through various circuitous routes shortly afterwards, beginning as early as January 1981.

Casey's widow, Sofia, and various Reagan insiders hotly

denied that any such transaction occurred, although one of Casey's top campaign aides, Robert Garrick, conceded that Casey was guilty of several "erratic disappearances" during the critical weeks of the campaign which were never satisfactorily explained. To date, no one has accounted for Casey's whereabouts on the days he was supposedly in Paris and Madrid's Ritz hotel for meetings with Hashemi and a representative of the Ayatollah Khomeini. In fact, a little-noticed campaign story in the *New York Times* quoted a Reagan aide as saying Casey was returning from a trip "abroad" during the time in question. Garrick, however, claimed that his "October Surprise" activities were limited to keeping a watch of several airports for military transports whose departure might signal a last-minute hostage deal by the Carter White House.

Whether or not Casey did engineer his own "October Surprise," he lost no time launching a number of covert initiatives once his friend Ronald Reagan was sitting in the Oval Office. Col. Ollie North, an action-hungry, decorated Vietnam veteran who referred to himself as "Steelhammer" and "B.G." for "Blood and Guts" in his White House computer's coded messages, was just the kind of man the cagey spy chief admired; a gung-ho, can-do Marine who unquestioningly carried out orders and whose position as a staff assistant on the National Security Council made him a valuable asset for Casey's ambitious global gameplan.

Like North, Casey was convinced that bolstering the contras' underdog struggle against the Sandinistas was a foreign policy imperative. He thought it so important, in fact, that he became an enthusiastic proponent of the so-called "Reagan Doctrine" of support for anti-communist resistance movements throughout the world.

To the Reagan administration, the Nicaraguans' nasty civil war represented a watershed struggle to keep communist influence from gaining a foothold in Latin American countries, whose shaky, inequitable economies made them inviting targets for authoritarian socialists willing to take up arms. For Bill Casey, the battle lines were clearly drawn, and he would confront the enemy just like his hero, OSS legend "Wild Bill" Donovan, had taught him forty years before— with every resource he could muster, including the underhanded where necessary. Casey was "the last great buccaneer from OSS," in the words of Clair George, his top deputy throughout much of the Iran/contra disaster.

Anxious to counter the Marxist-led revolution in Nicaragua, the Reagan administration hit the ground running. U.S. aid to the Sandinista government was cut off soon after the new president was inaugurated. Just weeks later, in March 1981, a secret presidential "finding" authorized White House support for the contras, who until then had been considered little more than a reactionary band of exiled, anti-government snipers fomenting trouble along the border. Suddenly, the largely ignored anti-Sandinista guerrillas had the biggest military presence in the hemisphere rallying to their cause.

By December, another top-level, secret document, a National Security Decision Directive, or "NSDD," was signed by Reagan and gave the U.S. intervention even more legitimacy. It authorized the CIA to conduct "political and paramilitary operations" against the despised Sandinista government in Managua. Since the contras were considered disreputable by Latin American governments friendly to the U.S., Reagan diplomats told Congress that funds would be used to interdict the flow of arms in the region—a white lie which set the stage for a grander-scale deception to follow.

Originally, the goal of State Department officials who'd pushed U.S. backing for the contras was to use the threat of their continued existence as a bargaining chip in negotiations with the Sandinistas. But that strategy was merely a coat of diplomatic veneer to the hard-liners in the Reagan White House, who nurtured a far bolder idea: if given enough arms, money and encouragement, the contras might be able to militarily overthrow the detested communists. Such a victory would send an unmistakable message to all the leftist insurgents in Latin America. Administration strategists and their friends in the press spent the next year lobbying feverishly in favor of a spiraling increase in aid and weapons for the small but increasingly well-equipped Nicaraguan army of resistance.

The real hardball began in 1983, when Congress began to second-guess the ballooning amounts of U.S. aid to the counter-revolutionaries and took action to limit arms sales.

Nervous legislators fretted that what had started out as sideline cheerleading was now escalating dangerously into direct American involvement in an escalating civil war whose ramifications could spread, with dire and unpredictable consequences, far beyond the borders of Nicaragua. To prepare for an expected cutoff of funds, Reagan intelligence officials created operation "Elephant Herd," a contingency plan to keep the aid to the contras flowing.

As a first step to slow the gathering momentum of the contra bandwagon, Congress had passed, in December 1982, the first of two versions of the "Boland Amendment," named after the then-chairman of the House Select Committee on Intelligence, Massachusetts Congressman Edward Boland. The overwhelmingly supported measure prohibited the CIA and the Department of Defense from spending funds to overthrow the Sandinista government, or to provoke hostilities between Nicaragua and neighboring Honduras, the operational base of some of the contra forces.

The growing opposition prompted Ronald Reagan to step forward as the personal champion of the beleaguered contra forces. Bringing to bear the full weight of his almost unprecedented political popularity, and the telegenic persuasiveness which was his most formidable weapon, he declared his unbridled support for Nicaragua's anti-government "freedom fighters," a rallying cry hawkish conservatives embraced with unrestained enthusiasm. The president's stirring words were backed with dirty deeds: CIA-backed operatives were secretly mining the harbors of Nicaragua, though Congress, contrary to Casey's earlier promises, would not learn of it until many months later.

When the covert, unauthorized planting of explosives in foreign harbors was fully disclosed in April 1984, its illegality and sheer audacity stunned even administration sympathizers. Such an act amounted to a declaration of war. Director Casey and his underling officials maintained that Congress had been informed about the mining, but the language was buried deep in a report submitted to the Hill, and committee chairmen were furious they had not been personally notified that the agency was directly involved in a clandestine act with far-reaching consequences. Two Casey backers let the spy boss know where he stood in no uncertain terms: Senate Intelligence committee chairman Barry Goldwater wrote to Casey that he was "pissed off," and vice chairman Daniel Patrick Moynihan temporarily resigned his post over the alleged deception. The CIA chief was summoned before an extraordinary secret session of the Senate to explain his agency's failure to inform Congress that bombs had been sown in foreign waters.

Appearing contrite, Casey apologized to the sixty senators present and pledged a "new spirit of cooperation" between Langley and Capitol Hill. His promise would be formalized into what became known as the "Casey Accords," an agreement between the CIA and the Senate Intelligence Committee on consultation guidelines for covert operations. But whatever his intentions, Casey's written assurances had no more effect than his original, verbal declarations at the time of his confirmation. Congress would remain largely in the dark about the CIA's secret wars in Nicaragua and elsewhere around the world.

Congressmen who felt hoodwinked by the contra cabal moved rapidly to introduce a new, toughened version of the Boland Amendment ban, which now directed U.S. intelligence agencies to cease furnishing *any* lethal aid to the guerrillas. Contra critics on Capitol Hill thought they'd finally put a lid on the backdoor flow of weapons and ammunition to the rebels. On the contrary, the dirty, covert war was just gathering steam; only the location of its U.S. operational headquarters would change.

The CIA and the Defense Department were now legislatively prohibited from directly providing weapons, training or other forms of deadly aid to the contras. Another avenue for channeling the administration's outpouring of support would have to be found, for it was clear that Reagan, his top aides and their fellow contra-boosters in Congress believed that the Boland amendment was an unnecessary stumbling block in the way of their unwavering determination to confront the communist menace in Nicaragua.

The solution to the congressional blockade turned out to be an amazingly simple one. The nerve center for the contra support was moved from the CIA over to the White House's

National Security Council, an executive branch staff of intelligence and foreign policy experts whose mission is to advise the president on a wide range of security issues. President Reagan contended his NSC staff was immune from the congressional restrictions, and therefore could pick up the contra ball and run with it.

Although he'd repeatedly volunteered for dangerous missions behind enemy lines in Vietnam, and had helped coordinate U.S. military movements during the successful 1983 invasion of Grenada from his NSC office, funding a civil war was a whole new ball game for Ollie North. But like everything else he did, he plunged into the task with every ounce of his considerable energy. While technically only a White House staff aide, North discovered that the entire resources of the federal government were at his beck and call.

He quickly learned that people at every level assumed his requests were backed with the authority of the White House—and therefore the president of the United States. He took advantage of that assumption at every turn, and tirelessly utilized intelligence, military and diplomatic resources to set up and manage a covert fund raising, arms selling, war planning and hostage dealing apparatus whose operations spanned several continents.

Casey, who became the young Marine's unofficial guide in the slippery world of international weapons brokering, had an office in the White House complex around the corner from North's and suggested to a hand-picked crew of former CIA and Defense Department officials that they introduce themselves to the NSC aide if they wanted to assist in the secret war he was running.

Two of the central figures recruited to what the participants called the "Enterprise," Richard Secord and Albert Hakim, were a bit of an odd couple. A grim-faced, tough-talking retired Air Force major general and former Defense Department official known to the operation's insiders by the codename "Mr. Copp," Secord knew both North and the CIA director before the weapons-selling scheme began.

A military special operations expert brought into the unofficial brotherhood by Casey, Secord had excellent connections in the intelligence community and became a prominent player in "Project Democracy," which was the euphemistic title given to the umbrella organization created to coordinate various covert programs to supply arms and supplies to the contras. Secord met privately with Casey on several occasions for advice or assistance when the operation ran into financial or logistical difficulties. And "Uncle Bill," as one of the contra leaders nicknamed Casey, also consulted with North frequently, keeping close tabs on his young protegé's activities. According to subsequent news accounts, they traveled together in Latin America after the Enterprise swung into high gear, visiting CIA station chiefs and Panama's drug-dealing dictator, General Manuel Noriega.

The more mysterious, Iranian-born Hakim, sometimes referred to as "Abe" in North's copious memos, served as money manager. The naturalized American created a complex network of overseas bank accounts and dummy companies to funnel millions of dollars coming in from a wide range of arms purchasers and private donors. Hakim and his partner Secord became "almost co-equal lieutenants" with North in the Enterprise, and were both handsomely rewarded for what they claimed were their patriotic efforts on behalf of U.S. interests.

Over a period of two years beginning in mid-1984, the Enterprise took in nearly $48 million, of which about $12 million left over from operating expenses was surplus, or profit. Much of the cash was generated by the creation of an international weapons bazaar coordinated by Secord and Hakim, with the clandestine help of ex-CIA officials, respected Swiss bankers and shadowy, often unsavory merchants from the world military arms markets.

Other pro-contra activists also drifted into North's circle of influence. Retired General John Singlaub, an outspoken anti-communist, had dared to clash with President Jimmy Carter over the wisdom of withdrawing thousands of U.S. troops from South Korea when he was American commander in Seoul. The resulting public furor created international headlines and hastened his exit from military service, but made Singlaub a hero to hard-line conservatives.

The blunt, crew-cut general headed a second, unsanctioned effort to channel weapons to the contras, and repeatedly attempted to solicit funds for them from other countries such as Taiwan and South Korea, where he had close personal contacts at the highest levels. Singlaub's prominent political and media profile had the added benefit of acting as a "lightning rod," drawing attention away from the peripatetic North and his bustling NSC command center.

North hadn't started from scratch; the hard-charging colonel controlled secret donations for the contras totaling more than thirty million dollars, contributed by Saudi Arabia's ruling princes. A number of "third party" countries, such as Saudi Arabia, were anxious to curry favor at the White House, and were only too happy to slip a few million dollars under the table, particularly when the request was being made by someone as close to President Reagan as National Security Adviser Robert "Bud" McFarlane.

During one private session with the president, Saudi diplomats related that they were prepared to double their one million dollar per month "donation" to the contras, an encouraging bit of news which the president personally passed along to McFarlane. While the Saudis publicly denied that their generous gifts were intended for the contras, North saw to it that millions of dollars from "Country Number Two", as Saudi Arabia was referred to in a congressional report, were placed directly into bank accounts controlled by contra leader Adolfo Calero. North's most trusted contact with the contras, Calero had his own complicated system of companies serving as fronts in the Caymen Islands.

But the plotters weren't satisfied with depending upon foreign governments to plug up the funding gap created by legal restrictions. Worried that Congress might not allow renewed military assistance to the contras, North hatched a backup scheme to continue the flow of ready cash by helping to organize a network of private fund-raising efforts.

The most influential was the National Endowment for the Preservation of Liberty (NEPL), whose chief fund-raiser, the dapper Carl "Spitz" Channel (Channell), and his associate Richard Miller, went to great lengths to conceal the fact that munificent donations made by rich widows and retired industrialists were being used to buy arms for the contras. Since their conservative organization was advertised as a tax-exempt foundation, the Internal Revenue Service was unlikely to look kindly upon tax deductions for anti-aircraft missiles or machine guns. Channell set up a secret account, facetiously codenamed "Toys," to handle disbursements for contra-related weapons purchases, a decision which later got him into hot water with the IRS and a court-appointed, independent prosecutor, Lawrence Walsh.

To assist Channell's group with its solicitations, North had potential big-money donors ushered into the Old Executive Office Building for private briefings on the contras' struggle to liberate Nicaragua from the repressive yoke of the Sandinistas. His personal entreaties and the impressive White House surroundings softened up wealthy sympathizers such as financier Nelson Bunker Hunt, who donated a total of $484,000. The sharply dressed Channell and North, frequently decked out in full military regalia for such occasions, were what one senator termed a "one-two punch." North dazzled the carefully selected crowd with his patriotic pitch, but as a government official was careful not to ask for money himself.

Then Spitz and his associates reconvened the meeting across the street at the fashionable Hay-Adams Hotel and passed the hat for five and six-figure donations from an audience which had been spellbound by the charismatic, earnest young Marine. North's emotional, heartfelt paeans on behalf of the contras made the habitually disorganized and often brutal guerrillas sound like the founding fathers of democracy to his attentive, admiring guests.

The smooth, well-organized efforts of Channell, Miller and North and others raised $10 million, but less than half of that went to the contras. A lot of the loot was spent on what was termed "white propaganda"—pro-contra public relations and planted press stories coordinated largely by International Business Communications (IBC), a company owned by Miller, a former Reagan bureaucrat-turned-consultant.

While Secretary of State George Schultz was kept ignorant of much of the Enterprise's shenanigans, his underlings at Foggy Bottom backed the propaganda angle to the hilt. As a result of a 1983 presidential directive, the State Department's Office of Public Diplomacy for Latin America and the Caribbean labored mightily on the contras' behalf. Its activities were managed not by the State Department, but by an "inter-agency working group" established by the NSC.

"The principal NSC staff officer was a former CIA official, with experience in covert operations, who had been detailed to the NSC staff for a year with Casey's approval," stated the congressional report on the Iran/contra affair. Given this setup, it wasn't surprising that the office blatantly used tax-payer money to funnel a series of sole source contracts, worth more than $400,000, to IBC, which was described as "a White House outside the White House." IBC helped implement the President's foreign policy in an indirect, unorthodox, but ef-fective way.

However, while the contras ultimately received as much as $20 million worth of guns, hardware, military technology and other support through air resupply operations funded by the Enterprise and its offshoots, only a fraction of the booty was flowing south. Secord and Hakim siphoned off more than $6 million worth of commissions for themselves from the Enter-prise's bulging coffers.

"Secord and Hakim...never negotiated with Calero or any-one else for these commissions; they simply took what they wanted out of the general pool of money in the Enterprise accounts," according to congressional investigators who traced the labyrinthian tentacles of the operation's financial network around the world. Lavish parties and padded ex-pense accounts for contra leaders headquartered in Miami also consumed much of the money raised by the well-groomed NEPL middlemen who worked with "Mr. Goode," as North was sometimes known to his compatriots.

The Enterprise schemers seemed immune by their connec-tion to the White House from any outside oversight; they were actually running a secret government within the NSC. While its members were busy hustling exotic weapons, such as British-made Blowpipe missiles, and hiding millions of dollars in numbered Swiss bank accounts, their unofficial leader, Colonel "Blood and Guts," acted as a one-man State Department and intelligence agency. Although it wasn't part of his White House job description, North supervised aid to the insurgents through a U.S. military officer in El Salvador named Steele, and initiated the construction of a hidden airstrip in northern Costa Rica which was to have a special purpose.

Oblivious to whether the host government actually wanted to be dragged into the Nicaraguan conflict, North ordered the CIA station chief in Costa Rica, "Tomas Castillo" (whose real name was Joe Fernandez), to tell U.S. Ambassador Lewis Tambs that the Reagan administration wanted to open a "Southern Front" for the contras to fight the Sandinistas in southern Nicaragua.

A history professor who'd became a diplomat through his political connections, the inexperienced Tambs thought he was in no position to refuse such an audacious command. Prior to reporting to his post he'd received instructions from the "RIG" (Restricted Interagecy Group) about aiding the Nicaraguan resistance. The only members of the RIG group were North, CIA Central America Task Force director Alan Fiers, and Tambs's superior, Assistant Secretary of State Elliott Abrams, a staunch contra backer. The group reported directly to Casey and his deputy, Clair George.

The acerbic Abrams, an admirer of North's, later denied that he'd given Ambassador Tambs permission to operate outside normal diplomatic channels. But many in Congress disbelieved his self-serving comments, and accused Abrams of lying about the details of his own backstage role in aiding and abetting the contras, for his version of events was pointedly contradicted by other administration officials. Abrams would later plea bargain with lawyers in order to avoid a possible felony charge for withholding information from Congress.

After months of logistical problems, North got his airstrip, and the Enterprise organized resupply operations through the efforts of former Air Force lieutenant Richard Gadd, who had past experience providing air support to the Pentagon. But things weren't moving fast enough for the impatient North. Without the knowledge of his superiors, he drew the Nicaraguan Humanitarian Assistance Office (NHAO), created to channel non-lethal food and other aid to the contras, into the Enterprise's web.

His tool was a tall, cherubic-looking former Senate staffer and public relations aide named Robert Owen, known as

"T.C.," or "The Courier" to the pro-contra plotters. The earnest Owen looked like an overgrown choirboy, but had the single-minded tenacity of an ideological fanatic. His moral universe was painted starkly in black and white, with no shades of gray tinting his robust determination to prevent communism from gaining more converts in the western hemipshere. Traveling extensively in Latin America, he became North's loyal "eyes and ears."

After insistent prodding aimed at recalcitrant State Department bureaucrats, North was able to get Owen's company, the Institute for Democracy, Education and Assistance (IDEA) a contract with the United Nicaraguan Opposition (UNO), to assist in disbursing humanitarian aid. But the arrangement was a convenient front; Owen used the UNO contract as a cover to spy for North and keep tabs on the contra resupply operation, despite State Department regulations forbidding such activities (North's favorite code name for the State Department was "Wimp"). No problem or setback deterred the determined North for long. On one occasion, he and a CIA official failed to stop an ill-advised contra air attack, which resulted in the loss of the rebels' only operating helicopter. Undaunted, North asked his boss McFarlane for permission to replace the lone chopper with a private donation. After some hesitation, the national security adviser responded, "I don't think this is legal," for once putting the brakes on his energetic aide.

The rebuke didn't stop the imaginative North from fantasizing about a glorious victory for the overmatched contra forces, who besides their relatively weak military position were split into quarreling camps by their own internal, petty bickering. One of his hundreds of memos on the White House "PROF" (professional office system) IBM computer suggested that the contras were poised to capture a piece of Nicaraguan territory, and that the U.S. should rush to their assistance, rather than suffer another humiliating Bay of Pigs episode. North repeated this grandiose claim to other potential donors, but even the most rabid contra supporters in the administration regarded such a scenario as totally implausible, and merely another example of his lamentable tendency to confuse hard reality with his own frequent flights of fanciful bravado.

Eventually, the expanding circle of people in the know about the Nicaraguan supply scheme prompted congressional inquiries to the White House demanding an explanation of North's activities, which had become the subject of scattered news reports triggering alarm bells on Capitol Hill. McFarlane, the taciturn, poker-faced Texan then running the National Security Council, knew that revealing secrets detailing the contra support operation to Capitol Hill would finish the operation, so he decided instead to stonewall the interrogators.

For example, the national security adviser's written response to a letter from Indiana Democrat Rep. Lee Hamilton, the respected, brush-cut chairman of the House Permanent Select Committee on Intelligence, was a flat-out lie. "I can state with deep personal conviction that at no time did I or any member of the National Security Council staff violate the letter or spirit of the law," McFarlane's letter pompously and falsely asserted.

Worse yet, he brazenly repeated the denial to Hamilton's face in a subsequent closed-door session with the powerful committee chairman. To his later chagrin, the low-key Indiana representative told McFarlane that "I for one am willing to take you at your word", and didn't probe any further.

Apparently not content with a broad-brush assertion of White House innocence, McFarlane dug himself a deeper hole with a second, even stronger reply to questions raised by Maryland Congressman Michael Barnes three weeks later. "There have not been, or will there be, any expenditures of NSC funds which would have the effect of supporting directly or indirectly military or paramilitary operations in Nicaragua by by any nation, group, organization, movement or individual."

When the persistent Barnes asked to examine documentation of this claim during a visit to McFarlane's office, the national security adviser imperiously dumped a pile of carefully selected papers in front of the bespectacled congressman and told Barnes he could read them, but not make notes or take copies out of the room. The congressman declined the condescending, take-it-or-leave-it offer, and didn't learn until later that as a direct result of his stubborn inquiries, he'd been put on the contra sympathizers' "hit list" for election defeat. Meanwhile, other congressional questioners got a similar line of malarkey from McFarlane and North when they asked about the NSC's activities on behalf of the contras.

The White House made a feeble attempt to justify its actions by conducting a brief, internal "investigation" of the covert activities by the President's Intelligence Oversight Board. While McFarlane and North were successfully deceiving the curious congressmen, the Board's counsel, a young lawyer named Bretton Sciarioni, concluded after a five-minute interview with North that he "had not provided military or fund-raising assistance to the Nicaraguan Resistance." In fairness, NSC officials improperly withheld documents from the Board, but Sciarioni didn't press his inquiry beyond North's blanket denial, despite the possibly catastrophic consequences for the president if trust in the White House staff turned out to be misplaced.

To top it off, an undated, classified legal opinion from the Board asserted that the National Security Council was not subject to the legislative prohibitions specified in the congressional restrictions and aimed at U.S. intelligence-related agencies. The secret memorandum, authored by Sciarioni and tucked away in North's White House safe, went so far as to bluntly declare that "None of Lt. Col North's activities during the past year constitutes a violation of the Boland Amendment." Of course, this controversial document was probably not intended to see the light of day unless the NSC's barricade of obfuscation failed to stymie the flurry of congressional inquiries.

Nevertheless, neither the pressure generated by the congressional skeptics nor the published reports of possible violations of law by White House officials deterred the tight little band of top-level Reagan appointees who knew all or part of what was really happening behind-the-scenes. Their hubris might be attributed, at least in part, to the persistent personal and political popularity of their leader. Following his astoundingly one-sided, forty-nine-state re-election victory over Walter Mondale in the fall of 1984, Ronald Reagan became, at least temporarily, the proverbial 800-pound gorilla of Washington politics.

Reagan critics in Congress and the press, sensing a massive outpouring of affection for the second-term president, which was reflected in opinion polls and translated into bruising political clout, shied away from confronting the White House juggernaut head-on. If many woke up in Reagan's "morning in America" with a hangover, few were anxious to take on the thankless and potentially painful mission of publicly assaulting a chief executive beloved and trusted by an overwhelming majority of Americans. The former actor had succeeded where his predecessor Jimmy Carter had failed—he had convinced the public he would not tell a lie.

Emboldened by the ease with which they had deflected outside scrutiny, North and his cohorts escalated their risk-taking and raised the foreign policy and constitutional stakes they were playing for to an even higher level. As badly as Ronald Reagan wanted the contras to remain a well-armed thorn in the side of the Sandinistas, he wanted something else more—the return of the remaining American hostages from the Middle East.

Never a stickler for detail, Reagan preferred to delegate responsiblity to subordinates. Usually, his White House staff presented him with option papers, which boiled down complex issues into simpler, condensed summaries; the president would then check his preference of actions from a brief menu of choices. Several of Reagan's top aides who'd had no personal contact with him prior to their service in the White House, such as McFarlane, were shocked by the president's apparent inability to retain the main points of substantive briefings for more than a day or two. Others realized that Reagan seemed genuinely to dislike disappointing anyone, and frequently would agree with the staffer who had seen him last on a particular issue.

Such was not the case when it came to discussing the hostages, however. Reagan had forced Jimmy Carter from the White House by harshly attacking, even ridiculing, his handling of the hostage tragedy. It grieved him that well into his second term of office, there were American citizens still being kidnapped and held for long periods of time by Middle East-

ern terrorists, including Shiite Muslim radicals allied with the
Iranian revolution. His friend Bill Casey was especially obsessed with the abduction of CIA operative William Buckley,
who had been reported by intelligence sources to have been
excrutiatingly tortured and murdered by his captors.

Photos of the hostages' gaunt, drawn faces were frequently
on the nightly network news broadcasts. Their families' desperate pleas for assistance underscored repeated media reports about the administration's failure to come to terms with
the Ayatollah Khomeini's revolutionary Islamic government,
whose ruling mullahs regarded Washington with contempt
and issued daily denounciations of the "Great Satan" America.

The plight of the Iranian hostages was a wretching human
story, with more emotional immediacy for Reagan than the
arcane terminology employed by his arms control negotia-
tors, or the endless flow charts favored by numbers crunchers
at the Office of Management and Budget. He wanted action,
and uncharacteristically, he pestered his briefers almost on a
daily basis for updated information on what was being done
to gain the release of the Middle East hostages.

During the late spring of 1985, a CIA Middle East expert
named Graham Fuller wrote an issue paper restricted to the
eyes of a handful of administration decision-makers. His
analysis suggested that the U.S. government consider easing
its worldwide arms embargo against Iran and perhaps seek
some sort of diplomatic and political accommodation with
the more moderate elements of the Islamic regime. The secret
proposal wasn't exactly a hit with key Reagan advisers: Defense Secretary Caspar Weinberger read it with dismay and
scribbled "This is too absurd to comment on" in the margin.

It didn't seem to have much impact at the White House,
either. Weeks after it circulated, in a speech to the American
Bar Association, Reagan blasted Iran's government as part of
a "confederation of terrorist states...a new, international version of Murder, Incorporated." Despite a continuing fusillade
of equally tough public rhetoric, however, White House officials privately conceded that placating Iran might be necessary in order to secure the hostages' release.

In fact, at a time when the U.S. relations with Iran were

seemingly at the lowest point in years, the Enterprise conspirators secretly initiated a backdoor approach to Iran through Israel. David Kimche, an Israeli foreign ministry official and former intelligence officer, served as the unofficial intermediary. In the midst of some of Reagan's harshest public diatribes against Iran, Kimche met privately with Bud McFarlane and proposed that U.S. political discussions be conducted with Teheran's revolutionary government through an Iranian middleman, Manucher Ghorbanifar. As a show of good faith, Kimche suggested, the Iranians would expect something for their efforts, namely weapons.

The mere hint that the president's national security adviser would entertain the thought of providing U.S. arms to Iran was startling, but Kimche held out a carrot the Reagan White House found difficult to resist. In exchange for 100 or so "TOW" anti-tank missiles from the Israeli arsenal, the Iranians were said to be willing to release all seven American hostages then being held prisoner.

Getting the Ayatollah Khomeini to send the hostages home, while squeezing his hostile regime for millions of dollars to add to the Enterprise's growing coffers, was just too delicious a thought to resist. Despite the incredible political risks, McFarlane was authorized by Reagan to assure Kimche that Washington would replace from U.S. arsenals whatever Israeli missiles were sold to the Iranians.

Ghorbanifar, a portly, bearded Iranian businessman and self-proclaimed "wheeler dealer," was brought in as a go-between even though he reportedly had flunked an earlier lie detector test administered by CIA officials, who regarded him as an inveterate liar and schemer. Distaste for him was so intense that the agency circulated a rarely issued "Fabricator Notice," warning U.S. law enforcement personnel that Ghorbanifar "should be regarded as an intelligence fabricator and a nuisance." (A disgusted McFarlane later called him a "borderline moron.")

Having failed to convince officials from the CIA, State Department and the Army that he could help ransom the hostages, the persistent Ghorbanifar finally weaseled his way into the top levels of the U.S. government through a New York businessman, Roy Furmark, a friend and former law client of

Bill Casey's. The slippery Iranian was then accepted into the unofficial ring of conspiracy in spite of repeated warnings that he couldn't be trusted.

The Enterprise had opened up yet another new front. After several weeks of fitful negotiations, the first two planeloads of arms arrived in Iran through the brokering of Israeli arms merchants. In mid-September one of the hostages, Reverend Benjamin Weir, was released, although only the Enterprise insiders and their supporters knew the real reason why. The steep price for his freedom had been more than 500 missiles— and perhaps the administration's credibility.

Encouraged by Weir's release, the White House acceded to the delivery of even more weapons—this time HAWK (Homing All-the-Way Killers) anti-aircraft missiles—from Israel to Iran in the hope additional hostages would be freed. The president was told that a phony cover story would be circulated asserting that the transporting airplane contained "oil drilling equipment" if the transfer was disclosed. But the Iranians angrily rejected the HAWK models, some of which to their displeasure still had Israeli markings on them. The suddenly greedy brokers also apparently had exaggerated the missiles' shootdown potential. No other hostages were returned as a result of the HAWK shipment.

Meanwhile, the cast of characters involved in the transcontinental arms bazaar had grown so large that State Department diplomats got wind of the "men-for-missiles" bartering. As a result, White House officials were pressed to hold a top-level discussion about the wisdom of selling weapons of mass destruction to an enemy government whose agents were holding U.S. citizens in chains. Secretary of State George Schultz and Defense Secretary Weinberger, who rarely agreed on anything, both expressed strenuous opposition to the controversial arms deals in White House meetings which the president attended.

Reagan turned a deaf ear to the objections of his two old friends, however, and soon after signed a secret presidential "finding" which authorized a slightly revised continuation of the weapons sales in which the U.S., not Israel, would play the lead role. At the same time, the president ordered CIA Director Casey in writing not to inform the congressional committees with oversight responsibility, contrary to an earlier written agreement between Capitol Hill and the intelligence chief.

Since the Israeli middlemen couldn't be trusted to deliver weapons acceptable to the Iranians, they were told their services were no longer required. From that time on, the lethal bargaining chips came from the Pentagon's overflowing stocks. The U.S. was now involved in a direct attempt to trade arms for hostages. A memorandum accompanying the Presidential Finding provided that the "initiative" would be shut down if the hostages were not released after the delivery of 1,000 TOW missiles to Iran.

Ollie North, who'd long been burning the midnight oil at the NSC, added several new jobs to his bulging resume. Not only was he supervising a secret air resupply operation for the contras in Central America, he was moonlighting as a travel agent, air traffic controller, banker and accountant, making certain that the Pentagon and CIA were transferring hundreds of U.S. anti-tank missiles to Israel. From there the tons of armaments were flown to Teheran.

Proceeds from the sales, less generous commissions and other expenses, were deposited in the Enterprise's "Lake Resources" Swiss account and other well-concealed escrows in order to fund the secret government's global adventures. Secord, it was agreed, would be employed as a "commercial cut-out." He and his private company would serve as a conduit for the money to be paid by the Iranians to the U.S. for the missiles. This indirect arrangement supposedly legitamized the transaction in the view of Casey and other administration officials, as Secord would be acting as an "agent" of the CIA.

It was at about this time that the Enterprise schemers realized there was $800,000 in excess of expenses left over from the initial HAWK missile sales to the Iranians. Although it was unclear who originated the proposal, North then put into motion what he termed a "neat idea." He directed Secord to spend the extra money, which he referred to as the "residuals", on the contras. He later told CIA contact Alan Fiers that the weapons sales were "kicking dollars into the contras' pot."

The Enterprise's irate Iranian customers eventually figured out they were being grossly overcharged for missiles and spare parts (North was billing them at almost four times cost). There were no refunds at this marketplace, though. A portion of the high-percentage profits were being used to underwrite a guerrilla war half a world away. The Nicaraguan rebels would eventually receive a total of about $3.8 million dollars in diverted arms sales profits (or about a quarter of the Enterprise's total capital gains), according to the calculations of congressional auditors.

In the midst of the internal administration power struggle over the weapons deals, McFarlane had resigned as national security adviser and had been replaced by his deputy, John Poindexter. An intellectual, pipe-puffing navy admiral, Poindexter had an almost obsessive penchant for secrecy and disdain for the press even more pronounced than his predecessor's. There was no letup or delay in the Enterprise's business during Poindexter's watch; the new national security adviser kept tabs on the activities of his eager aide North through a steady stream of confidential messages on the White House's PROF computer.

While he had escaped the pressure cooker at the White House, the dutiful McFarlane hadn't washed his hands of the Enterprise. On the contrary, he continued be a principal player as a private citizen. With the president's express approval, he traveled to Teheran in May 1986, six months after his resignation from government, in an attempt to secure further hostage releases. His covert mission had been preceded by months of secret talks and preparations. He was so hopeful that his visit would be triumphant that he ordered a chocolate cake from an Israeli baker as a gift for the Iranians.

His hosts didn't have much of a sweet tooth, however. Although he arrived with a planeload of spare parts for HAWK missiles, the dejected McFarlane departed empty-handed after several days of unproductive, frustrating negotiations at the top floor of the Hilton hotel, which the revolutionary Islamic government ironically had renamed the "Independence."

At the Teheran meeting with McFarlane, the Iranians escalated their demands to include the release of Shiite Muslim terrorists being held in Kuwaiti prisons. While North thought it possible the American side might quietly pressure Kuwait to free at least some of the Islamic "Da'Wa" inmates, McFarlane realized such a proposal would outrage Secretary Schultz and other administration officials who'd put the terrorism issue on the front-burner.

The impasse didn't stop further deliveries of U.S. arms to Iran via Israel—the shipments continued unabated for another five months after McFarlane's secret, failed mission. Ultimately, two more hostages, the Reverend Lawrence Jenco and David Jacobsen, were released before the 1986 election. But by then the Americans had delivered an incredible total of more than 2,000 missiles and 200 spare parts for HAWK missile batteries in exchange for only three hostages. During this period other Americans were kidnapped by extremist groups with ties to radical factions in Iran, nullifying the hard-won purchase of prisoners. "Our guys...got taken to the cleaners", as Shultz disdainfully described the bottom line.

Suddenly, in October 1986, the facade covering the Enterprise's "off-the-shelf" activities began to crumble. North and his boss Poindexter had kept inquiring reporters at bay by repeatedly lying about the extent of White House efforts to aid the contras. The few piecemeal stories which leaked out were ridiculed by North as inaccurate distortions and fantasies.

But on October 5, a C123 cargo plane ferrying ammunition, uniforms and medicine was shot down over Nicaragua. Three crew members died in the crash, but Sandinista soldiers captured the lone survivor, Eugene Hasenfus, who was held captive and eventually tried on terrorist charges. Documents aboard the seized plane connected it to Southern Air Transport (SAT), a CIA front based in Miami.

Feverishly, North and his cohorts tried to establish damage control. Acting far beyond his authority as usual, North quickly attempted to slow FBI and Customs Service investigations into SAT, as an extensive probe undoubtedly would have revealed the Enterprise's connection to both the contra resuppply effort and the Iran arms shipments undertaken by the intelligence-controlled airline. Meanwhile, Fiers and his superior George decided to misled congressional committees which had requested information on the secret resupply flight and the CIA's knowledge of it; being truthful would "put the spotlight" on the administration and blow North's cover. So once again, they lied. Reporters who'd stumbled across bits and pieces of the Enterprise puzzle suddenly smelled paydirt, even while administration officials swore there was no connection between the Hasenfus incident and the White House.

At about the same time, Casey's friend Furmark called the CIA director and told him that Middle East investors, including the well-known international moneyman Adnan Khashoggi, were owed as much as $10 milllion dollars by the elusive Ghorbanifar. Hoping for handsome commissions when the deals were finalized, Ghorbanifar had borrowed a fortune to fund the weapons purchases. Their influential lenders were being stiffed and were going to take their grievances to Congress unless they got repaid soon, Furmark warned the intelligence chief.

Discussing the problem with Israeli contacts, North wrote in his notebooks that the best thing to do might be to "overcharge (the Iranians) on subsequent deliveries" to "pay off Furmark *et al.*" Casey tried to placate his former client Furmark by offering to review the finances of the Iranian arms transactions. When the figures showed that the deals had resulted in excess funds, Casey claimed he didn't know what had happened to the extra money.

Before the delicate dispute could be resolved, the Lebanese magazine *Al Shiraa* disclosed that McFarlane had been on a secret mission in Teheran. The following day, Ali Akbar Hashemi Rafsanjani, the speaker of the Iranian parliament, confirmed the published account. The White House circled the wagons.

The bombshell disclosures set off a bitter backstage battle in the administration. Secretary Schultz, who'd fought against the arms sales to the Iranians and was appalled by the extent to which he and other top officials had been kept in the dark, lobbied the president to "give the key facts to the public." Not wanting his arms-for-hostages deal to be seen for what it was, Reagan stubbornly resisted. The result was a cacophony of conflicting lies and half-truths.

In an televised address to the nation on the Iran arms sales,

the president delivered a half-baked account of what his subordinates and their hirelings had been doing. While he had
signed multiple presidential findings authorizing the sale of
more than 2,000 missiles and other weapons parts to Iran,
Reagan falsely asserted that "These modest deliveries, taken
together, could easily fit into a single cargo plane." A week
later, at a news conference, he claimed that no "third" country
was involved in the arms dealings, a statement embarrassed
administration spokesmen had to admit was untrue a scant
twenty minutes after it was uttered.

Reagan's shaky explanations weren't helped by North,
Poindexter and McFarlane, who all conspired to falsify National Security Council chronologies, which were supposed to
give an accurate account of key facts and documents concerning the Iranian weapons transfers. The trio committed "the
President of the United States to a false story," as North's later
testimony confirmed. Casey did his part by deliberately mis-
leading congressional committees about the CIA's active role
in the sordid affair.

The worst was yet to come. Attorney General Meese, sensing catastrophic political damage to his friend the president,
convened top administration advisers in an attempt to make
a coherent story out of the jumble of rumor and innuendo
flowing from the White House. North and other NSC officials
responded by having "shredding parties" to destroy documents which conflicted with the administration's untrue public assertion that the U.S. had nothing to do with the November 1985 shipment of HAWK missiles to Iran. North also
instructed his willowy, loyal blonde secretary, Fawn Hall, to
alter or remove other NSC memoranda as part of the attempted coverup.

On November 22, 1986, Justice Department officials found
a "smoking gun" in the NSC files—a memorandum which
stated that as much as $12 million worth of funds from the
arms sales would be used to buy supplies for the "Nicaraguan
Democratic Resistance Forces," to "bridge" the gap between
current shortages and "when Congressional approved lethal
assistance...can be delivered." Not long afterward, the officials went to the fashionable Old Ebbitt Grill near the White
House, where Meese was having lunch, and related the bad

news that millions of dollars from the Iran weapons sales might have been diverted to the contras.

Confronted with possible criminal activity at the highest level of government, Meese's curious reaction was not to call in the FBI, but rather to begin a series of one-on-one interviews with knowledgeable participants, during which he took no notes. After telling FBI Director William Webster that his help would not yet be necessary, the attorney general spoke privately with North, Poindexter, Casey and Vice-President George Bush, among others. Meanwhile, given a temporary reprieve from federal subpoenas, North and his cohorts continued to lacerate documents at a rate which finally jammed his shredding machine.

Three days later, the president announced at a news conference that North had been fired from the NSC staff, and that Poindexter had requested a transfer from the White House. In a ham-handed effort at handling questions after Reagan's brief statement, Meese dug his boss in deeper when he told reporters that the CIA didn't know of the diversion, and that money had gone to the contras straight from the Israelis into bank accounts controlled by the Nicaraguan guerrillas. The latter assertion outraged Israeli government officials, who began burning up the phone lines between Jerusalem and Washington, demanding to know what the hell Meese thought he was doing. Finally, on November 26, the embattled attorney general belatedly requested that a criminal probe be initiated, but by then much of the documented evidence had been vaporized.

Under intense congressional and public pressure to clean up the mess at the White House, Reagan announced the appointment of a three-person, special presidential review board to analyze the Iran/contra fiasco and make constructive recommendations about how to reform the renegade NSC. The board was referred to as the "Tower Commission," after its chairman, the late, diminutive former Senator John Tower, a Texan who favored expensive Saville Row English-cut suits and European cigarettes.

Following three months of incomplete and somewhat inconclusive interviews, the board issued a somber, highly detailed, 300-page report which concluded that "the President

appeared to be unaware of key elements of the operation."
Reagan initially told the board that the White House had
given prior approval to an August 1985 Israeli shipment of
antitank missiles to Iran. Later, reading from a script prepared
by aides, Reagan did a one hundred and eighty degree about-
face and denied he'd ever assented to the arms transfer.

The Tower panel, which included former Secretary of State
Edmund Muskie and national security adviser Brent Scow-
croft, was especially critical of the president's chief of staff,
Donald Regan. Before his death in a Georgia plane crash in
April 1991, Tower charged that President Reagan's shifting
stories to the presidential review board about his knowledge
of the HAWK shipment "bore all the earmarks of a deliberate
effort to conceal White House chief of Staff Donald Regan's
involvement in the Iran/contra affair."

Former Merrill Lynch chief executive Regan had served as
Treasury Secretary during the first Reagan administration. In
a move many observers considered one of the worst decisions
of the entire Reagan presidency, Regan traded jobs with chief
of staff James Baker at the outset of the second term and
became the president's story-swapping, bosom pal. While
probably no more ruthless than the steely Baker, Regan lacked
the political sense to remain out of the limelight; he made
many enemies with his imperious attitude and a lamentable
tendency to view himself as power in his own right.

Angrily, he denied orchestrating the president's confusing
turnaround concerning whether or not he'd authorized the
Iran arms shipments. But the Tower report, which essentially
concluded that the White House was being poorly administered, damaged Regan's special relationship with his presidential friend. Soon his many detractors, including First Lady
Nancy Reagan, called their favorite journalists to suggest in
no uncertain terms that the president needed a new chief of
staff unsullied by the fallout from the Iran/contra scandal. To
the relief of all concerned, former Senator Howard Baker
agreed to come in and supervise a reordering of the shaken
Reagan White House.

The Tower commission's harsh portrait of a White House
careening out of control reinforced the conventional wisdom
that Ronald Reagan was a leader out of touch with his subor-

dinates and the policy direction of his own administration. However, as Haynes Johnson of the *Washington Post* and others have convincingly argued, that ninety-day judgment may have been premature, at least as it related to the Iran/contra affair. The culmulative evidence uncovered by House and Senate congressional probers and Independent Counsel Lawrence Walsh painted a different picture; one of an activist, risk-taking chief executive who was a bold initiator, rather than a doddering, ignorant figurehead whose military-trained aides seized control of the White House from under his nose.

For example, while the president was not accused of breaking any laws by the Iran/contra congressional committee, its final majority report portrayed Reagan as actively and repeatedly attempting to conceal key aspects of the scandal. He also failed to "leave the members of his administration in doubt that the rule of law governs." Significantly, concluded the report, "The ultimate responsibility for the events in the Iran-contra affair must rest with the president. If the president did not know what his national security adviser was doing, he should have."

Admiral Poindexter told the Iran/contra special congressional committee more than 180 times that his memory failed him regarding the details of the most important events of his life. Yet the supposedly fuzzy-brained navy admiral graduated first in his class of nine hundred at Annapolis, and had earned a doctorate in nuclear physics from the California Institute of Technology.

Neither he, Oliver North nor Bud McFarlane had ever done anything in their careers which even remotely suggested a rebellious streak of independence of action from the proper lines of authority. On the contrary, each was regarded as an totally reliable "team player", who followed rather than led. Yet even while found guilty of lying under oath, Poindexter continued to profess that he had kept the details of the Iran funds diversion from the president in order to protect him from knowledge that might have resulted in impeachment.

There was considerable speculation, but no proof, that Casey had engineered a contingency "fall guy" backup plan which called for North or Poindexter to accept full responsiblity and take the political and legal heat off the president if their activities were uncovered. No one would ever know for certain, however, as two weeks following the White House's embarrassed admissions, Casey suffered a massive stroke and died after months of incapacitation, possibly taking many of the Iran/contra's darkest secrets to the grave with him. In his book *Veil*, detailing Casey's use of the CIA in a worldwide covert action campaign, *Washington Post* editor Bob Woodward wrote that the dying intelligence boss admitted from his hospital bed that he had known of the diversion of arms funds to the contras. Administration defenders and Casey's wife hotly disputed Woodward's version of events, though, and no firm conclusion regarding Casey's full role was documented.

Bud McFarlane, despondent over the humilating discovery of the secret underground government's illegal activities, and feeling the pressure of congressional and criminal investigations, tried to end his life with an overdose of pills. Fortunately, he survived the impetuous suicide attempt. After a brief recovery, he decided to recant many of his earlier lies concerning the Enterprise's far-flung operations.

Many unanswered questions remain about what Ronald Reagan knew or ordered others to do, either directly or implictly. Certainly much of what has been made public since the fateful, initial disclosures of November 1986 has been tainted with deception. Unraveling the mosaic of falsehoods was the primary reason why the frustratingly complex, $32 million-dollar investigation of special prosecutor Walsh continued through more than five-and-a-half years, numerous criminal convictions, appeals and several grand juries.

The patrician-looking Walsh, energetic in his mid-seventies, persevered through endless, often petty attempts by the Justice Department to block his office's access to documents on supposed grounds of national security. He and his staff of more than thirty lawyers and support personnel also weathered perhaps the worst mistake of the Iran/contra probes: the decision by the select congressional committee to grant limited immunity in exchange for the testimony of North and Poindexter, a move Walsh termed "the most damaging single factor hampering the prosecution of Iran/contra activity."

Ollie North was convicted by Walsh's team for obstructing

Congress, destroying government documents and accepting an illegal gratuity (a security fence at his home which was paid for from Enterprise funds; North later asked the builder to produce a phony receipt). While an appeals court reversed the convictions and the Supreme Court refused to reinstate them, North was transforming himself into what the *Los Angeles Times* called a "one-man conglomerate."

Paid up to $25,000 for speeches to conservative audiences, he also sold bullet-proof vests manufactured by Guardian Technologies, a firm he founded with Joe Fernandez, a former CIA agent who was implicated with him for illegally defying the congressional ban on contra resupply. None of the Iran/contra principals convicted except the tight-lipped, forgetful Poindexter and former CIA official Thomas Clines were sentenced to prison terms. Poindexter's conviction and six-month jail term for lying to Congress was appealed, as was Clines' sixteen-month sentence and $40,000 fine for federal tax violations relating to his Iran/contra activities. In July 1991, the CIA's Alan Fiers pleaded guilty to two misdemeanor counts of unlawfully withholding information from Congress and promised to assist the prosecution as part of a plea bargaining agreement.

The indefatigable Walsh, under fire from the administration and other critics of his prolonged, expensive prosecution, doggedly pursued the mountainous trail of paper evidence. When the discovery of unexamined private notes of Caspar Weinberger suggested that he might have known more about the controversial arms sales than he'd admitted to Walsh's lawyers or congressional probers, a crack of light shone through what the independent counsel seemed to believe was a well-planned, concerted effort by top administration officials to cover the president's tracks. The much-maligned investigation continued right through four years of the presidency of Reagan's successor, George Bush, whose own role in the foreign policy fiasco remained murky.

*   *   *

Like the Iran/contra affair, several of the administration's other notable blunders didn't come to light until well into Reagan's second term of office. "Deregulation" is the single word which best describes the root cause of the fiscal and political woes unearthed during the final three years of the Reagan revolution.

Acting on Reagan's fervently held belief that less government is better government, administration loyalists enthusiastically stripped the oversight and regulatory bark from as many federal agencies as possible. "Privatization," or the contracting out of federal services to private hands, was embraced as the holy grail of government management. While a determined effort to emasculate the Environmental Protection Agency backfired on the White House during the first term, the full, devastating effect of this misguided philosophy wouldn't be felt until years later.

During the Reagan years, "we tried as a Government not to get on anyone's back," said Frederick D. Wolf, a former financial management official at the General Accounting Office, an investigative arm of Congress. But when resources are reduced in the critical "oversight area, you're going to have a problem," he conceded.

In terms of sheer burden to the taxpayers, certainly the most disastrous single result of weakened federal regulation was the savings and loan debacle, which was the worst financial catastrophe since the Depression. By some estimates it will cost the unimaginable sum of a half a trillion dollars to clean up. In more easily understandable terms, that amounts to approximately five thousand dollars per American household.

When Reagan took office, the savings and loan industry had been a mainstay of American finance for more than a century. S&Ls, as they were commonly called, had an important role in the Norman Rockwell vision of America favored by the president. They were local institutions where middle-class Americans obtained mortgages for their homes and businesses. Many savings and loans were the financial bedrocks of their communities.

By early in the acquisitive Eighties, however, the combination of increasing inflation, relaxed regulatory rules and cutbacks at enforcement agencies created a world of riskier high finance which overwhelmed the S&Ls. To compete, they had to offer higher interest rates to attract depositors. Many solid

S&Ls were taken over by inexperienced incompetents or crooks, who used the new freedoms to turn them into casinos, investing in speculative real estate deals, questionable construction projects, unsecured bonds, and even the roller-coaster futures market.

The S&L free-booters often squandered their depositors' funds on lavish lifestyles for themselves and other insiders. And, why not? There was no risk for them. Beginning in 1980, the federal government insured all individual account deposits up to $100,000. For the unscrupulous, the looser operating rules of the savings and loans gave them a license to steal; up to forty percent of the savings and loan failures discovered to date have been connected to criminal misconduct.

In fairness, not all the blame for the S&L debacle can be laid at the door of the Reagan White House. Congress passed the short-sighted legislation which opened the financial floodgates, and congressional powerbrokers, such as former House Speaker Jim Wright of Texas, were only too eager to help wealthy S&L owners evade fiscal discipline by intimidating the few federal regulators bold enough to question their high-flying antics. The sad spectacle of the Senate's "Keating Five" ethics hearings demonstrated the embarrassing lengths to which influential and respected legislators were willing to go to help a fabulously rich campaign contributor, whose misdeeds wiped out the life savings of thousands of innocent S&L investors.

But there's no question that the Reagan team was ultimately responsible for the floodtide of greed which dominated the decade of the Eighties and may yet finish the S&L industry. The administration's timid enforcers repeatedly blocked or slowed attempts by regulators in the field to clamp down on the high rollers.

Edwin Gray, an amiable public relations executive with no banking experience, was appointed as chairman of the Federal Home Loan Bank Board, which was supposed to help oversee the S&L industry. He benefitted from thousands of dollars worth of expensive perks paid for by the banks his agency regulated. Later, in the unaccustomed role of S&L whistleblower, Gray claimed that he was ignored when he warned White House budget officers that his office was de-

sparately short of qualified examiners. The purse watchers at
the Office of Management and Budget, said Gray, were
"blindly infatuated with deregulation." Several Bank Board
examiners told congressional investigators that they were
pressured into signing audits which misrepresented or over-
estimated the assets of troubled S&Ls. Nothing was done
until years too late.

Even after the depth of the S&L scandal surfaced, federal
regulators mishandled the disposal of failed savings institiu-
tions and added hundreds of millions of dollars to the cost of
the bailout. According to a report prepared for the Treasury
Department's Resolution Trust Corporation (RTC), wealthy
investors took advantage of the S&L debacle to gain sweetheart deals from the federal government on real estate and
commercial buildings at the expense of the taxpayers. Although the RTC was trying hard to turn around a desperate
situation, the administration tried to cut its legal staff in 1992,
and experienced financial analysts believe the savings and
loan bailout has become a "black hole" which could indefinitely swallow public capital.

While there was plenty of blame to spread around in the
S&L debacle, the scandal at the federal Department of Housing and Urban Development (HUD) more clearly revealed the
cynical depths to which Reagan's deregulators were willing
to stoop. The administration's activist ideologues saw federal
housing programs as little more than welfare handouts, and
would have preferred eliminating HUD from the government
landscape altogether. Since that political pipe dream was a
practical impossibility, the budget-cutters slashed the HUD
staff from 16,000 to 11,000, while reducing federal housing
subsidies over a period of years from $26 billion to less than
$8 billion.

To ensure its demise as an effective government program,
the White House then turned the agency into a dumping
ground for political hacks, a "turkey farm" in the words of
one former top HUD veteran. In one of Reagan's most disastrous appointments, Samuel Pierce was chosen as Secretary of
HUD to administer what amounted to a dismantling of the
agency.

A brilliant, able black attorney with a glittering resume and a stiff personality, Pierce reportedly harbored a secret desire to be named to the Supreme Court and supposedly thought the HUD job would elevate his profile for a lifetime appointment to the high tribunal. Bored by his management duties and uninterested in the details of complex housing programs, he spent most of his time watching soap operas in his office and indulging a passion for travel, most often to the Soviet Union, whose officials were, of course, breathlessly waiting to hear about America's housing problems. He said so little at Cabinet meetings that he was derisively nicknamed "Silent Sam" by his Reagan colleagues, who wondered among themselves why enigmatic Pierce had bothered to accept the job in the first place.

The budget and staffing cuts, together with Pierce's lackluster leadership, resulted in administrative chaos at the already troubled agency, which continued dispensing billions of dollars worth of housing grants, loans and guarantees. If HUD couldn't be deregulated out of existence, then its critics intended to milk it for all it was worth. An army of consultants, influence-peddlers and political hangers-on descended on the vulnerable agency like a horde of hungry locusts.

"During much of the Eighties," according to a report by a House Government Operations Subcommittee, "HUD was enveloped by influence peddling, favoritism, abuse, greed, fraud, embezzlement and theft. In many housing programs, objective criteria gave way to political preference and cronyism, and favoritism supplanted fairness. 'Discretionary' became a buzzword for '"giveaway."'" The favorite Reagan management tool, "privatization" became "piratization" at HUD, in the words of congressional investigators.

Internal investigations by the agency's Inspector General and other audits had revealed a decade-long pattern of mismanagement, theft and waste, but the warnings had gone completely unheeded by Pierce and his favor-dispensing subordinates. Not until the spring of 1989, months after Reagan left office, did investigators for Rep. Thomas Lantos (D-CA) notice an agency report which charged that developers had paid consultants to "influence awards" of rehabilitation funds for public housing projects.

The distinguished-looking, silver-haired Lantos had a dif-

ferent background than most of his colleagues in the House.
He and his lovely, petite wife Annette had barely escaped the
Nazis as teenagers, and were among thousands of Eastern
Europeans saved through the heroic efforts of a Swedish diplomat named Raoul Wallenberg. With not much more than his
diplomatic credentials, the thirtyish Wallenberg boldly faced
down German Gestapo officials while supervising the departure of a huge number of ethnic refugees, many of whom
otherwise were destined for Nazi concentration camps and
almost certain death.

When advancing Soviet troops later drove out the retreating Germans, Wallenberg was taken into custody and never
heard from again. The articulate Lantos conducted a personal
crusade to publicize Wallenberg's selfless deeds and to pressure the Soviets for a documented accounting of the fate of the
young diplomat, who some witnesses claimed had been swal-
lowed up by the infamous Soviet gulag prison system.

The searing, unforgettable memories of wartime Europe
made Washington influence-peddling seem tame, and Lantos
unhesitatingly ordered his subcommittee staff to pry open the
Pandora's box at HUD. They found that the agency had been
turned into a grabbag for those with the right connections.
The corruption was so pervasive that the Justice Department
had initiated more than 600 separate investigations relating to
the agency's programs.

It wasn't hard to understand why. Pierce's executive assistant was an inexperienced, blonde socialite named Deborah
Gore Dean, whose previous jobs had included bartending and
running a local social magazine. Dean and her friends, who
came to be called "the brat pack" for their arrogance and rude,
demanding behavior, presided over the handing out of millions of dollars in federal housing contracts to influential
Republicans, who sent her scores of request letters addressed
"Dear Debbie."

One of the beneficiaries was former Interior Secretary
James Watt, who'd previously portrayed himself as a dedicated disciple of reduced government spending. "While in
government," noted the Lantos report, "Secretary Watt often
belittled federal programs to assist the poor and less fortunate. He spoke of the dangers of being 'lured by the crumbs

of subsidies, entitlements and giveaways.'" The ex-Cabinet official was paid a total of $420,000 for making a few phone calls on behalf of developer Joseph Strauss, who candidly admitted that he'd hired Watt "because of his access and influence."

Carla Hills, a former HUD secretary who also later served as the U.S. Trade Representative, personally lobbied the pliant Pierce to lift restrictions on the DRG Funding Corp., which defaulted on loans that may eventually cost HUD as much as $300 million dollars. GOP campaign consultant Paul Manafort unabashedly confessed to the Lantos committee that his firm engaged in "influence-peddling."

Several top-ranking HUD bureaucrats, anxious to cash in on the gravy train, left government service and set up consulting firms to tap into the lucrative buddy system. Millions of dollars intended to be spent on the rehabilitation of housing for poor and moderate income people instead "became the trough from which former HUD officials and the politically well-connected fed." All the while, deserving housing programs without political patrons went unaided or remained underfunded.

Checks and balances were non-existent. In what may have been one of the largest thefts of government funds by a single individual in American history, real estate closing agent Marilyn Harrell was accused of embezzling a total of $5.6 million dollars from property sales, simply by not remitting the proceeds to HUD. When she claimed to have stolen the money for charitable purposes, she was dubbed "Robin HUD" by the press. It was later revealed that Harrell had kept much of the diverted money for herself.

"Silent Sam" didn't exactly cover himself with glory when he was asked about his role in directing HUD grants to friends and political contacts. Pierce stubbornly insisted he'd had nothing to do with his aides' blatant favoritism. But the committee concluded that he was "less than honest about his involvement in abuses...in HUD funding decisions." An independent counsel, retired Philadelphia appeals court judge Arlin Adams, was appointed to determine the veracity of Pierce's confusing version of events, a probe which resulted in criminal indictments for the former cabinet secretary and his assistant, Deborah Gore Dean.

Even staunch conservative Jack Kemp, the former football star quarterback and Buffalo congressman who inherited the unenviable task of straightening out the disaster caused by ten years of neglect, admitted that HUD had been "rotten to the core" when it was dumped in his lap.

The treacherous "swamp" at HUD symbolized the mismanagement of the Reagan years; the rich and well-connected got richer, and the victims—the homeless, disenfranchised and voiceless—got poorer. It's a sad legacy which Americans will be paying for well beyond the year 2000.

LIST OF SOURCES

Colonial Capers

Abernathy, Thomas P. *Burr Conspiracy*. New York: Oxford University Press, 1954.

Adams, Charles F. *The Life of John Adams*. Philadelphia: J. P. Lippincott, 1968.

Barzman, Sol. *Madmen and Geniuses: The Vice Presidents of the United States*. Chicago: Follett Publishing, 1974.

Brant, Irving. *James Madison*. Indianapolis, New York: Bobbs-Merrill, 1941.

Brodie, Fawn. *Thomas Jefferson: An Intimate History*. New York: W. W. Norton, 1974.

Brown, Ralph Adams. *The Presidency of John Adams*. Lawrence: University of Kansas, 1975.

Chinard, Gilbert. *Thomas Jefferson: Apostle of Americanism*. Ann Arbor: University of Michigan, 1957.

Cresson, William P. *James Monroe*. Hamden, Connecticut: Archon Books, 1971.

Dabney, Virginius. *The Jefferson Scandals*. New York: Dodd, Mead, 1981.

East, Robert A. *John Adams*. Boston: Twayne Publishers, 1979.

Emery, Noemie. *Washington: A Biography*. New York: G. P. Putnams Sons, 1976.

Hecht, Marie B. *John Quincy Adams: A Personal History of an Independent Man*. New York: Macmillan, 1972.

Hunt, Gaillard. *Life of James Madison*. New York: Doubleday and Page, 1968.

Jones, Conover Hunt. *Dolley and the Great Little Madison*. Washington D.C.: American Institute of Archivists Foundation, 1977.

Kitman, Marvin. *George Washington's Expense Account*. New York: Simon and Schuster, 1970.

Koch, Adrienne. *Adams to Jefferson: Prosterity Must Judge*. Chicago: Berkeley Series in American History, McNally, 1963.

Lipsky, George A. *John Quincy Adams: His Theories and Ideas*. New York: Thomas Crowell, 1950, 1965.

Marble, Harriet C. *James Monroe: Patriot and President*. New York: Putnams Sons, 1970.

McDonald, Forrest. *The Presidency of George Washington*. Lawrence: University of Kansas, 1974.

Shepherd, Jack. *The Adams Chronicles*. Boston: Little, Brown, 1975.

Shepherd, Jack. *Cannibals of the Heart: A Personal Biography of Catherine and John Q. Adams*. New York: McGraw Hill, 1980.

Steinberg, Alfred. *The First Ten: The Founding Fathers and Their Administrations*. Garden City, New York: Doubleday, 1967.

Stephenson, Nathaniel W., and Dunn, Waldo H. *George Washington, 1778-1799*. London and New York: Oxford University Press, 1940.

van der Linden, Frank. *The Turning Point*. Washington, D.C.: Robert B. Luce, 1962.

Woodward, W. E. *George Washington: The Image and the Man*. New York: Blue Ribbon Books, 1926.

Cooper, Joseph. "The Press Did a Hatchet Job on George." *New York Times*, (21 February, 1984).

Wallace, Irving and Amy, and Wallechinsky, David. "Significa." *Parade*. (29 November, 1981): pg. 17.

An Old Hero for a Troubled Age

Chidsey, Donald B. *And Tyler, Too*. Nashville, New York: Thomas Nelson, 1978.

Cleaves, Freeman. *Old Tippecanoe*. New York: Charles Scribners Sons, 1939.

Curtis, James C. *The Fox at Bay*. Lexington: University of Kentucky Press, 1970.

Farrell, John J. *James K. Polk*. Dobbs Ferry, New York: Oceana, 1970.

Frank, Sid, and Melnick, Arden Davis. *The Presidents: Tidbits & Trivia*. Maplewood, New Jersey: Hammond, Inc., 1975, 1977.

Gerson, Noel Bertram. *That Eaton Woman: In Defense of Peggy O'Neale Eaton*. New York: Crown, 1974.

Goebel, Dorothy G. *William Henry Harrison*. Philadlephia,: Porcupine Press, 1974.

Koenig, Louis. *Invisible Presidency*. New York: Rinehart, 1960.

Lynch, Denis T. *An Epoch and a Man*. Port Washington, New York: Kennikat Press, 1928.

Merk, Fredrick. *Fruits of Propaganda in the Tyler Administration*. Cambridge: Harvard University, 1971.

Niven, John. *Martin Van Buren: The Romantic Age of American Politics*. Princeton,: Oxford University Press, 1984.

Remini, Robert. *The Election of Andrew Jackson*. Philadelphia, New York: J. P. Lippincott, 1963.

Sellers, Charles G. *James K. Polk*. Princeton: Princeton University Press, 1957.

Steinberg, Alfred. *The First Ten: The Founding Fathers and Their Administrations*. Garden City, New York: Doubleday, 1967.

Van Deusen, Glyndon. *Martin Van Buren and the American Political System*. Phildelphia: University of Pennsylvania, 1953.

The Spoils of a Divided Nation

Auchampaugh, Philip G. *James Buchanan and His Cabinet (On the Eve of Succession)*. Lanchester Press, 1926.

Bailey, Thomas A. *Presidential Saints and Sinners*. New York and London: The Free Press, 1975.

Benson, George. *Political Corruption in America*. Toronto: Lexington Books, 1978.

Cotrell, John. *Anatomy of an Assassination*. New York: Funk and Wagnalls, 1966.

Dyer, Brainard. *Zachary Taylor*. New York: Barnes and Noble, 1946.

Griffis, William E. *Millard Fillmore*. Ithaca: Church and Andrus, 1915.

Hamilton, Holman. *Zachary Taylor: Soldier in the White House*. Hamden, Connecticut: Archon, 1966.

Nichols, Roy F. *Franklin Pierce*. Philadelphia: University of Pennsylvania, 1931.

Oates, Stephen B. *With Malice Toward None—The Life of Abraham Lincoln*. New York: New American Library, Mentor Books, 1977.

O'Toole, George. *The Cosgrove Report*. New York: Rawson, Wade, 1979.

Randall, J. G. *Lincoln the President: From Springfield to Bull Run*. New York: Dodd, Mead, 1956.

Rayback, Robert J. *Millard Fillmore*. Buffalo: Henry Stewart, 1959.

Ross, Ishbel. *The President's Wife: Mary Todd Lincoln*. New York: G. P. Putnams Sons, 1973.

Sefton, James E. *Andrew Johnson and the Use of Constitutional Power*. Boston, Toronto: Little, Brown, 1980.

Smith, Gene. *High Crimes and Misdemeanors: The Impeachment and Trial of Andrew Johnson*. New York: William Morrow, 1977.

Wallace, Irving and Amy, and Wallechinsky, David. "Significa." *Parade*. (27 September, 4 October, 1 November, 1981.

Grant's Grabbag, Rutherfraud and Big Steve's Baby

Bailey, Thomas A. *Presidential Saints and Sinners*. New York, London: The Free Press, 1981.

Bates, Richard O. *The Gentleman from Ohio: An Introduction to Garfield*. Durham: Moore, 1973.

Davison, Kenneth E. *The Presidency of Rutherford B. Hayes*. Westport, Connecticut: Greenwood Press, 1972.

Collidge, Louis A. *Ulysses S. Grant*. Boston, New York: Houghton, Mifflin, 1924.

Doenecke, Justus D. *The Presidencies of James Garfield and Chester A. Arthur*. Lawrence: Regents, 1981.

Faulkner, Harold U. *Politics, Reform and Expansion*. Boston, New York: Houghton Mifflin, 1959.

Gould, Lewis. *The Presidency of William McKinley*. Lawrence: Regents Press of Kansas, 1980.

Hesseltine, William. *Ulysses S. Grant, Politician*. New York, London: Fredrick Ungar, 1957.

Haworth, Paul Leland. *The Hayes-Tilden Disputed Presidential Election of 1876* (1906). New York: Russell and Russell (Antheneum House), 1966.

George F. Howe. *Chester A. Arthur: A Quarter Century of Machine Politics*. New York: Fredrick Ungar, 1935, 1957.

Jones, Henry Ford. *The Cleveland Era: A Chronicle of the New Order*. New York: U. S. Publishers Association, 1972.

Josephson, Matthew. *The Politicos, 1865-1896*. New York: Harcourt, Brace, 1938.

Leach, Margaret, and Brown, Henry J.. *The Garfield Orbit*. New York: Harper and Row, 1978.

McFeeley, William S. *Grant*. New York, W. W. Norton, 1981.

Nevins, Allan. *Grover Cleveland*. New York: Dodd, Mead, 1962.

Peskin, Allan. *Garfield*. Norwalk, Connecticut: Easton Press, 1987.

Reeves, Thomas. *Gentleman Boss: The Life of Chester Alan Arthur*. New York: Alfred Knopf, 1975.

Sievers, Harry J. *Benjamin Harrison, 1833-1901*. New York: Oceana, 1969.

Dickinson, James, "How the scandals of history left...mud on the White House steps." *National Observer* (June 9, 1973).

Congressional Quarterly. (April 25, 1987): 756-757. (March 11, 1989): 533.

The Era of the Muckrakers

Busch, Noel. *T. R.: The Story of Theodore Roosvelt and his Influence on Our Times*. New York: Reynal, 1963.

Butt, Archie. *Taft and Roosevelt: The Intimate Letters of Archie Butt*. Garden City, New York: Doran, 1930.

Coletta, Paulo E. *The Presidency of William Howard Taft*. Lawrence: University of Kansas, 1973.

Chalmers, David M. *Social and Political Ideas of the Muckrakers*. Freeport, New York: Books for Libraries Press, 1970.

Frank, Sid, and Melnick, Arden Davis. *Presidential Tidbits and Trivia*. Maplewood, New Jersey: Hammond, 1975, 1977.

Gatewood, Willard B. *Theodore Roosevelt and the Art of Contro-*

versy: Episodes of the White House Years. Baton Rouge: University of Louisiana, 1970.

Miller, Nathan. *The Roosevelt Chronicles.* Garden City, New York: Doubleday, 1979.

Pringle, Henry J. *Theodore Roosevelt.* London: Jonathon Cape, 1931.

Archer, William, in *Fortnightly Review* (May, 1910).

Pearson, Drew. "The Washington Merry-Go-Round." *Washington Post* (24 January, 1964).

Presidential Amorists and a Teapot Tempest

Baker, Ray Stannard. *Woodrow Wilson—Life and Letters.* New York: Doran, 1931.

Blum, John M. *Woodrow Wilson and the Politics of Morality.* New York: Brown, Little, Brown, 1956.

Britton, Nan. *The President's Daughter.* New York: Elizabeth Ann Guild, 1927.

Burner, David. *Herbert Hoover: A Public Life.* New York: Alfred Knopf, 1979.

Caufield, Leon. *The Presidency of Woodrow Wilson.* Rutherford, New Jersey: Fairleigh Dickinson, 1966.

Feuss, Claude. *Calvin Coolidge—The Man from Vermont.* Boston: Little, Brown, 1940.

Feuss, Claude. *The Reminisences of Claude Moore Fuess.* New York: Oral History Collection of Columbia University, 1962.

Green, Carol Wilson. *Herbert Hoover: A Challenge for Today.* New York: Evans, 1968.

Hoover, Irwin Hood. *Forty-Two Years in the White House.* Boston: Riverside, 1934.

Lisio, Donald J. *The President and Protest.* Columbia: University of Missouri, 1974.

Means, Gaston. *The Strange Death of President Harding.* New York: Guild, 1930.

Mee, Charles Jr. *The Ohio Gang.* New York: Evans, 1981.

Meyers, William S. *The Hoover Administration.* St. Clair Shores, Michigan: Scholarly, 1971.

Murray, Robert K. *Harding Era.* Minneapolis: University of Minnesota, 1969.

Seward, Keith. *The Legend of Henry Ford*. New York: Antheneum, 1972.

Smith, Gene. *When the Cheering Stopped*. New York: William Morrow, 1964.

Shachtman, Tom. *Edith and Woodrow: A Presidential Romance*. Thorndike, Maine: Thorndike, 1981.

Trani, Eugene P., and Wilson, David L. *The Presidency of Warren G. Harding*. Lawrence: University of Kansas, 1977.

Tribble, Edwin (ed.). *A President in Love: The Courtship Letters*. Boston: Houghton Mifflin, 1981.

White, William Allen. *A Puritan in Babylon—The Story of Calvin Coolidge*. New York: Capricorn, 1938.

Editorial page. *Houston Chronicle* (1 April, 1982).

O'Toole, Thomas, in the *Washington Post* (3 September 3, 1982).

Sidey, Hugh. "Old Cal Makes a Comeback". *Time* (15 August, 1983).

Lippman, Thomas, in the *Washington Post* (6 July, 1989).

Martello, Thomas, in the *Washington Post* (26 November, 1990).

The Presidential Plotter

Asbell, Bernard. *Mother and Daughter: The Letters of Eleanor and Anna Roosevelt*. New York: Fromm International, 1988.

Baker, Leonard. *Roosevelt and Pearl Harbor*. New York: Macmillan, 1970.

Barlett, Bruce. *Cover-Up: The Politics of Pearl Harbor*. New Rochelle, New York: Arlington House, 1978.

Burns, James MacGregor. *Roosevelt: The Lion and the Fox*. New York: Harcourt, Brace, 1956.

Fehrenbach, T. R. *FDR's Undeclared War*. New York: David McKay, 1967.

Hickok, Lorena. *Eleanor Roosevelt: Reluctant First Lady*. New York: Dodd, Mead, 1961.

Ickes, Harold. *Secret Diary of Harold Ickes: Volume II, the Inside Struggle*. New York: Simon and Schuster, 1954.

Lash, Joseph P. *Eleanor and Franklin*. New York: New American Library, 1971.

Prange, Gordon. *At Dawn We Slept*. New York: McGraw Hill, 1981.

Roosevelt, Elliott, and Brough, James. *The Roosevelts of Hyde Park: An Untold Story*. New York: G. P. Putnams Sons, 1973.

Roosevelt, Elliott, and Brough, James. *The Roosevelts of the White House: A Rendezvous with Destiny*. New York: G. P. Putnams Sons, 1975.

Schlesinger, Arthur, Jr. *Age of Roosevelt*. Cambridge: Riverside, 1957.

Theobald, Robert A. *The Final Secret of Pearl Harbor*. New York: Devon Adair, 1954.

Winslow, Susan. *Brother, Can You Spare a Dime?* New York, Paddington, 1976.

Wolfskill, George, and Hudson, John A. *All But the People: FDR and His Critics*. New York: MacMillan, 1969.

Pearson, Drew. "The Washington Merry-Go-Round" files (1932-45).

Bode, Carl. "Quest for the Day of Infamy." *Washington Post*: (6 December, 1981).

O'Toole, Thomas. "Did Hoover Know of Pearl Harbor?" *Washington Post*: (2 December, 1982).

"The New Deal: FDR's Disputed Legacy." *Time*: (1 February, 1982).

Butow, R. T. C. in *American Heritage*: (February/March, 1982).

Omang, Joanne. "Secret Hoover Files Show Misuse of FBI." *Washington Post*: (12 December, 1983).

Anderson, Jack, and Spear, Joseph, "Memo May Hold Clue to FDR's Death." *Washington Post*: (28 December, 1985).

Taking Hell Harry

Allen, Robert S., and Shannon, William V. *Truman Merry-Go-Round*. New York: Vanguard, 1950.

Anderson, Jack and Boyd, James. *Confession of a Muckraker*. New York: Random House, 1979.

Bailey, Thomas A. *Presidential Saints and Sinners*. New York: Macmillan, 1981.

Cochran, Bert. *Harry Truman and the Crisis Presidency*. New York: Funk and Wagnalls, 1973.

Donovan, Robert J. *Conflict and Crisis: The Presidency of*

Harry S. Truman, 1945-1948. New York: W. W. Norton, 1977.

Ferrell, Robert (ed.). *Off the Record: The Private Papers of Harry S. Truman*. New York: Harper and Row, 1977.

Harper, Alan D. *The Politics of Loyalty: The White House and the Communist Issue, 1946-53*. Westport, Connecticut: Greenwood, 1969.

McCullough, David. *Truman*. New York: Simon & Schuster, 1992.

Miller, Merle. *Plain Speaking: An Oral Biography of Harry S. Truman*. New York: Berkeley, 1973, 1974.

Mollenhoff, Clark. *Washington Cover-Up*. Garden City, New York: Doubleday, 1962.

Robbins, Charles. *Last of His Kind: An Informal Portrait of Harry S. Truman*. New York: William Morrow, 1979.

Robbins, J. *Bess and Harry: An American Love Story*. New York: G. P. Putnams Sons, 1980.

Watzman, Sanford. *Conflict of Interest: Politics and the Money Game*. New York: Cowles (Henry Regnery), 1971.

Weinstein, Allen. *Perjury: The Hiss-Chambers Case*. New York: Alfred Knopf, 1978.

Daniel, Margaret Truman. "Bess: Margaret Truman Daniel's Story of Her Mother." *Parade*: (30 March, 1986).

Maxa, Rudy. "Did Harry Truman Bequeth Us Joe McCarthy?" *Washington Post Magazine*: (31 January, 1982).

McDowell, Edwin. "1,300 Letters of Truman's Made Public." *New York Times*: (24 March, 1983).

Strout, Richard L. "Harry Truman: A Not-So-Great Haberdasher, A 'Near Great' President." *Christian Science Monitor*: (23 April, 1983).

"Truman Made Slurs in Early Letters." *Philadelphia Inquirer*: (11 April, 1983).

Gifts for the General

Childs, Marquis. *Eisenhower: Captive Hero*. New York: Harcourt, Brace and World, 1956.

David, Lester and Irene. *Ike and Mamie: The Story of the General and His Lady*. New York: G. P. Putnams Sons, 1981.

Donovan, Robert J. *Eisenhower: The Inside Story*. New York: Harper and Brothers, 1956.

Ewald, William Bragg, Jr. *Eisenhower the President: Critical Days 1951-1960.* Englewood Cliffs, New Jersey. Prentice Hall, 1981.

Frier, David. *Conflict of Interest in the Eisenhower Administration.* Ames: The University of Iowa Press, 1969.

Larson, Arthur. *Eisenhower: The President Nobody Knew.* New York: Charles Scribners Sons, 1968.

Miller, Merle. *Plain Speaking: An Oral Biography of Harry S. Truman.* New York: G. P. Putnams Sons, 1973.

Mollenhoff, Clark. *Washington Cover-Up.* Garden City, New York: Doubleday, 1962.

Mollenhoff, Clark. *The Pentagon.* New York: G. P. Putnams Sons, 1967.

Morgan, Kay Summbersby. *Past Forgetting: My Love Affair with Dwight D. Eisenhower.* New York: Simon and Schuster, 1976.

Pusey, Merlo J. *Eisenhower, the President.* New York: Macmillan, 1956.

Steel, Ronald. *Walter Lippman and the Twentieth Century.* Boston: Little, Brown, 1980.

Waltzman, Sanford. *Conflict of Interest: Politics and the Money Game.* New York: Cowles, 1971.

Brennan, Christy, Lee, David, and Clayton, Bill. "Eisenhower had own secret tapes." *Houston Chronicle* (21 October, 1979).

Loewenheim, Francis L. "Eisenhower's Secret Diaries." *Houston Chronicle* (16-17 September, 1979).

Pearson, Drew, and Anderson, Jack. "Washington Merry-Go-Round" news column, 1952-61.

The Playboy President

Blakey, G. Robert, and Billings, Richard N. *The Plot to Kill the President.* New York: New York Times Books, 1981.

Burns, James MacGregor. *John F. Kennedy.* New York: Harcourt, Brace, 1960.

Eddowes, Michael. *The Oswald File.* New York: Clarkson N. Potter, 1977.

Epstein, Edward J. *Counterplot.* New York: Viking, 1969.

Exner, Judith, with Demaris, Ovid. *Judith Exner: My Story.* New York: Grover, 1977.

Johnson, Haynes B. *Bay of Pigs*. New York: W. W. Norton, 1974.

Kantor, Seth. *Who Was Jack Ruby?* New York: Everest House, 1978.

Lane, Mark. *Rush to Judgment*. New York, Chicago, San Francisco: Holt, Rinehart and Winston, 1966.

Lasky, Victor. *J. F. K.: The Man and the Myth*. New York: Macmillan, 1963.

Lifton, David S. *Best Evidence*. New York: Macmillan, 1980.

Meagher, Sylvia. *Accessories After the Fact*. New York: Vintage Books (Random House), 1967.

Miroff, Bruce. *Pragmatic Illusions: The Presidential Politics of John F. Kennedy*. New York: David McKay, 1976.

Nixon, Richard M. *Six Crises*. Garden City, New York: Doubleday, 1962, 1969.

Reeves, Thomas C. *A Question of Character: A Life of John F. Kennedy*. New York: Free Press, 1991.

Rensselaer, Mary Van. *Jacqueline Kennedy: The White House Years*. Boston: Little, Brown, 1971.

Smith, Malcolm E. *Kennedy's Thirteen Greatest Mistakes in the White House*. New York: National Forum of America, 1968.

Summer, Anthony. *Conspiracy*. New York: McGraw Hill, 1980.

Wallechinsky, David, and Wallace, Irving. *The People's Almanac, Volume #3*. New York: William Morrow, 1981.

Wicker, Tom. *JFK and LBJ*. New York: William Morrow, 1968.

Wofford, Harris. *Of Kennedy and Kings*. New York: Farrar, Straus, Giroux, 1980.

Lindsey, Robert. "Reopening of Inquiry into Marilyn Monroe's Death Raises Imbroligo in Los Angeles." *New York Times*: (29 October, 1985).

Shearer, Lloyd. "Two Little-Known Women in JFK's Life." *Parade*: 24 April, 1983).

Summers, Anthony. Three-part series on Judith Exner. *Washington Times*: (6-9 October, 1991).

"Nightline." ABC-TV: (4 February, 1982).

"Entertainment Tonight" broadcast. (16 September, 1982).

Pearson, Drew, and Anderson, Jack. The "Washington Merry-Go-Round news column files, 1958-70.

Tall Tales from Texas

Baker, Bobby, with King, Larry L. *Wheeling and Dealing: Confessions of a Capitol Hill Operator.* New York: W. W. Norton, 1968.

Bell, Jack. *The Johnson Treatment.* New York: Harper and Row, 1965.

Caro, Robert A. *The Years of Lyndon Johnson (Vol. 1): The Path to Power.* New York: Alfred Knopf, 1982.

Caro, Robert A. *The Years of Lyndon Johnson (Vol. 2): Means of Ascent.* New York: Alfred Knopf, 1990.

Christian, George. *The President Steps Down.* New York: Macmillan, 1970.

Comier, Frank. *LBJ the Way He Was—A Personal Memoir of the Man and His Presidency.* Garden City, New York: Doubleday, 1967.

Deakin, James. *Lyndon Johnson's Credibility Gap.* Washington, D.C.: Public Affairs Press, 1968.

Dugger, Ronnie. *The Politician: The Life and Times of Lyndon Johnson.* New York: W. W. Norton, 1962.

Evans, Rowland. *Lyndon Johnson and the Exercise of Power.* New York: The New American Library, 1966.

Goldman, Eric F. *The Tragedy of Lyndon Johnson.* New York: Alfred Knopf, 1969.

Harwood, Richard, and Johnson, Haynes B. *Lyndon.* New York: Praeger, 1973.

Kearns, Doris. *Lyndon Johnson and the American Dream.* New York: Harper and Row, 1976.

Miller, Merle. *Lyndon: An Oral Biography.* Toronto: Academic Press, 1980.

Mollenhoff, Clark. *Despoilers of Democracy.* New York: Doubleday, 1965.

Mooney, Booth. *LBJ: An Irreverent Chronicle.* New York: Thomas Y. Crowell, 1976.

Murphy, Bruce Allen. *The Rise and Ruin of a Supreme Court Justice.* New York: William Morrow, 1988.

Roberts, Chalmers. *LBJ's Inner Circle.* New York: Delacorte, 1965.

Steinberg, Alfred. *Sam Johnson's Boy.* New York: MacMillan, 1968.

Winter-Berger, Robert. *The Washington Payoff.* Secaucus, New Jersey: Lyle Stuart, 1972.

"The Uncounted Eenemy—A Vietnam Deception." CBS Reports: (23 January, 1982).

Atlantic. (October, 1981): 35-75.

The Washington Journalism Review. (April, 1982): 46-48.

Pearson, Drew, and Anderson, Jack. The "Washington Merry-Go-Round" files, 1963-73.

High Crimes and Misdemeanors

Ambrose, Stephen E. *Nixon: The Education of a Politician 1913-1962.* New York: Simon and Schuster, 1988.

Ambrose, Stephen E. *Nixon: The Triumph of a Politician 1962-72.* New York: Simon and Schuster, 1989.

Anderson, Jack, with Clifford, George. *The Anderson Papers.* New York: Random House, 1973.

Bernstein, Carl, and Woodward, Bob. *The Final Days.* New York: Simon and Schuster, 1976.

Brodie, Fawn M. *Richard M. Nixon: The Shaping of His Character.* New York: W. W. Norton, 1981.

Colodny, Len, and Gettlin, Robert. *Silent Coup: The Removal of a President.* New York: St. Martin's Press, 1991.

Colson, Charles. *Born Again.* Old Tappan, New Jersey: Chosen Books, Fleming H. Revell, 1976.

Dean, John. *Blind Ambition.* New York: Simon and Schuster, 1976.

Ehrlichman, John. *Witness to Power.* New York: Simon and Schuster, 1982.

Evans, Rowland, Jr., and Novak, Robert D. *Nixon in the White House: The Frustration of Power.* New York: Random House, 1971.

Klein, Herbert. *Making It Perfectly Clear.* Garden City, New York: Doubleday, 1980.

Knappman, Edward (ed.). *Watergate and the White House, Volume 1.* New York: Facts on File, 1973.

Kutler, Stanley I. *The Wars of Watergate: The Last Crisis of Richard Nixon.* New York: Alfred Knopf, 1990.

Magruder, Jeb Stuart. *An American Life: One Man's Road to Watergate.* New York: Antheneum, 1974.

Mankiewicz, Frank. *Perfectly Clear: From Whittier to Water-*

gate. New York: Quadrangle, New York Times Books, 1973.

Mollenhoff, Clark. *Game Plan for Disaster*. New York: W. W. Norton, 1976.

Orman, John M. *Presidential Secrecy and Deception*. Westport, Connecticut: Greenwood, 1980.

Powers, Thomas. *The Man Who Kept the Secrets: Richard Helms and the CIA*. New York: Pocket Books, Simon and Schuster, 1979.

Rangell, Leon. *The Mind of Watergate*. New York: W. W. Norton, 1980.

Sanford, Robinson Rojas. *The Murder of Allende*. New York: Harper and Row, 1975.

Sirica, John. *To Set the Record Straight*. New York: W. W. Norton, 1979.

White, Theodore H. *Breach of Faith: The Fall of Richard Nixon*. New York: Antheneum, 1975.

Wicker, Tom. *One of Us: Richard Nixon and the American Dream*. New York: Random House, 1991.

Witcover, Jules. *White Knight: The Rise of Spiro Agnew*. New York: Random House, 1972.

Woodward, Bob and Bernstein, Carl. *All the President's Men*. New York: Simon and Schuster, 1974.

Washington Post staff. *The Fall of a President*. New York: Delacorte, 1974.

The Nixon Presidential Archives: Alexandria, Virginia.

Hersh, Seymour. "Kissinger and Nixon in the White House." *Atlantic*: (May, 1982); 35-68.

David Frost Interview with Richard Nixon. (13-17 June, 1977).

Ford's Follies

Barber, James David. *The Presidential Character: Predicting Performance in the White House*. Englewood Cliffs, New Jersey: Prentice Hall, 1977.

Casserly, John. *The Ford White House: The Diary of a Speechwriter*. Boulder: Colorado Associated University Press, 1977.

Ford, Betty, with Chase, Chris. *Betty Ford: The Times of My Life*. New York: Ballentine, 1978.

Ford, Gerald. *A Time to Heal: The Autobiography of Gerald R. Ford*. New York: Harper and Row, 1979.

Hartmann, Robert T. *Palace Politics*. New York: McGraw Hill, 1980.

Hersey, John. *The President*. New York: Alfred A. Knopf, 1975.

Nessen, Ron. *It Sure Looks Different from the Inside*. Chicago: Playboy Press, 1978.

Mollenhoff, Clark. *The Man Who Pardoned Nixon*. New York: St. Martin's Press, 1976.

Osborne, John. *White House Watch: The Ford Years*. Washington, D. C.: New Republic Books, 1977.

Reeves, Richard. *A Ford, Not a Lincoln*. New York: Harcourt, Brace, Jovanovich, 1975.

Sidey, Hugh and Ward, Fred. *Portrait of a President*. New York: Harper and Row, 1975.

Terhorst, J. F. *Gerald Ford and the Future of the Presidency*. New York: The Third Press, Joseph Okpaku Publishing, 1974.

Vestal, Bud. *Jerry Ford: Up Close*. New York: Coward, McCann and Geoghegan, 1974.

Hersh, Seymour. "The Pardon—Nixon, Ford, Haig and the Transfer of Power." *Atlantic*: (August, 1983).

Hersh, Seymour, articles on the Central Intelligence Agency, in the *New York Times*: 1975-76.

Rushford, Gregory G. "Making Enemies: The Pike Committee's Struggle to Get the Facts." *The Washington Monthly*: (July-August, 1976).

U. S. House of Representatives, 94th Congress. *Proceedings Against Henry A. Kissinger, Report No. 94-693*. Pike Select Committee on Intelligence, (10 December, 1975).

Congressional Record. Documents relating to investigations of the Central Intelligence Agency by the U. S. Senate Committee on Foreign Relations, House Intelligence Committee, and the Rockefeller Committee, (1975-77).

The Peanut Preacher

Anderson, Patrick. *High in America*. New York: Viking, 1981.

Carter, Jimmy. *Why Not the Best?* New York: Bantam, 1975.

Collins, Tom. *The Search for Jimmy Carter*. Waco, Texas: Word, Incorporated.

Germond, Jack and Witcover, Jules. *Blue Smoke and Mirrors*. New York: Viking, 1980.

Jordan, Hamilton. *Crisis: The Last year of the Carter Presidency*. G. P. Putnams, 1982.

Meyer, Peter. *James Earl Carter: The Man and the Myth*. Kansas City: International Press Syndicate, 1978.

Mollenhoff, Clark. *The President Who Failed: Carter Out of Control*. New York: MacMillan, 1980.

Norton, Howard. *Rosalynn: A Portrait*. Plainfield, New Jersey, 1977.

Wheeler, Leslie. *Jimmy Who?* New York: Barron's Woodbury, 1976.

Wooten, James. *Dasher: The Roots and Rising of Jimmy Carter*. New York: Summit, 1978.

Kaiser, Robert G. "Wasn't Carter the President Who Said He'd Never Lie to Us?" *Washington Post*: (7 November, 1982).

Maitland, Leslie. "At the Heart of Abscam." *New York Times Magazine*: (25 July, 1982).

Maxa, Rudy, "Ruth." *Washington Post Magazine*: (8 October, 1978).

Safire, William. "Cover-Up Scorecard." *New York Times*: (10 September, 1979).

Steele, Richard, Camp Holly, and Smith, Vern E. "Bert Lance—His Life and Good Times." *Newsweek* (29 August, 1977).

"The Burden of Billy." *Time* :(4 August, 1980).

"The Iran Rescue Mission: The Untold Story." *Newsweek*: (12 July 12, 1982).

Status Report of the Office of Professional Responsibility on the Investigation Conducted Concerning Various Matters Pertaining to Billy Carter. U. S. Department of Justice, 1980.

The Undercover Investigation of Robert L. Vesco's Alleged Attempts to Reverse a State Department Ban Preventing the Export of Planes to Libya. Staff report of the Committee on the Judiciary of the United States Senate, September, 1982.

Anderson, Jack. The "Washington Merry-Go-Round" news column files, 1975-1981.

The Teflon President

Boyarksy, Bill. *Ronald Reagan: His Life and Rise to the Presidency*. New York: Random House, 1968.

Brownstein, Ronald, and Easton, Nina. *Reagan's Ruling Class*. Washington, D.C.: The Presidential Accountability Group, 1982.

Cannon, Lou. *Reagan*. New York: Putnams and Sons, 1982.

Cannon, Lou. *Ronald Reagan: The Role of a Lifetime*. New York: Simon and Schuster, 1991.

Edwards, Lee. *Ronald Reagan: A Political Biography*. Houston: Norland Publishing, 1980.

Germond, Jack and Witcover, Jules. *Blue Smoke and Mirrors*. New York: Viking, 1981.

Johnson, Haynes B. *Sleepwalking Through History*. New York: W. W. Norton, 1991.

Persico, Joseph. *Casey—The Lives and Secrets of William J. Casey: From the OSS to the CIA*. New York: Viking, 1990.

Reagan, Ronald, and Hubler, Richard. *Where's the Rest of Me?* New York: Dell, 1965.

Steinberg, William, and Harrison, Matthew C. *Feeding Frenzy*. New York: Henry Holt, 1989.

Traub, James. *Too Good to Be True: The Outlandish Story of Wedtech*. New York: Doubleday, 1990.

Woodward, Bob. *Veil: The Secret Wars of the CIA, 1981-1987*. New York: Simon and Schuster, 1987.

van der Linden, Frank. *The Real Ronald Reagan*. New York: Wiliam Morrow, 1981.

Hearing record: *Raymond Donovan of New Jersey to Be Secretary of Labor, January 12-27, 1981*. U. S. Senate Labor and Human Resources Committee.

Hearing Before the Select Committee on Intelligence of the United States Senate, 97th Congress, First Session: Nomination of William J. Casey to be Director of the Central Intelligence Agency, Tuesday, June 13, 1981.

Unauthorized Transfers of Nonpublic Information During the 1980 Election: A Report of the Subcommittee on Human Resources, Committee on Post Office and Civil Service: May 17, 1984.

Statement of James. F. Hinchman, Deputy General Counsel,

General Accounting Office, before the Subcommittee on Oversight and Invesitgations, House Energy and Commerce Committee, on Michael Deaver's Compliance with the Ethics in Government Act: May 12, 1986.

Documents from the Office of Independent Counsel Whitney North Seymour, Jr., U. S. Courthouse, One Marshall Place, Washington, D.C., 1987.

Documents from the Office of Independent Counsel Alexia, Morrison, Washington, D. C., Documents from the Office of Independent Counsel James McKay, Washington, D. C.

Documents from the Office of Independent Counsel Lawrence Walsh, Washington, D. C.

Chronology of events, Environmental Protection Agency, U. S. Senate Subcommittee on Oversight of Government Management, U. S. Senate, Washington, D. C., 1987.

Report of the President's Special Review Board. New Executive Office Building, Washington, D. C.: (26 February, 1987).

Report of the Congressional Committees Investigating the Iran/Contra Affair with the Minority View). New York: Random House, 1988.

Wedtech: A Review of Federal Procurement Decisions: A report Preapred by the Subcommittee on Oversight of Government Management of the Committee on Governmtnal Affairs, United States Senate: May, 1988.

Abuse and Mismanagement at HUD: Twenty-Fourth Report by the Committee on Government Operations, together with Additional Views: November 1, 1990.

Starobin, Paul. "Going Overboard." *National Journal* (21 April, 1990).

Wells, F. Jean. "Banks and Thrifts, Restructuring and Solvency 1990. *Congressional Research Service*: (14 March, 1990).

Failed Thrifts: FDIC Oversight of 1988 Deals Needs Improvement: U. S. General Accounting Office report to the Chairman, Committee on Banking, Housing and Urban Affairs, U. S. Senate, and the Chairman, Committee on Banking, Finance and Urban Affairs, House of Representatives.

The Election Held Hostage. "Frontline" broadcast: (16 April, 1991).

General

Anderson, Jack. *Washington Expose.* Washington, D.C.: Public Affairs Press, 1967.

Bollens, John C. and Schmandt, Henry J. *Political Corruption: Power, Money and Sex.* Palisades, CA: Palisades Publishers, 1978.

Chambliss, William J. *On the Take: From Petty Crooks to Presidents.* Bloomington: Indiana University Press, 1978.

Heidenheimer, Arnold J., Johnston, Michael, and Levine, Victor T. *Political Corruption.* New Brunswick: Transaction Books, 1978.

Loth, David. *Public Plunder.* Westport, Connecticut: Greenwood Press, 1970.

Miller, Hope Ridings. *Scandals in the Highest Office: Facts and Fictions in the Private Lives of Our Presidents.* New York: Random House, 1973.

Miller, Nathan. *The Founding Finaglers.* New York: David McKay, 1976.

Punke, Harold H. *Education, Lawlessness and Political Corruption.* North Quincy: Christopher Publishers, 1978.

Salter, J. T. *Public Men In and Out of Office.* Chapel Hill: University of North Carolina Press, 1946.

Ross, Shelley. *Fall From Grace: Sex Scandal and Corruption in American Politics From 1702 to the Present.* New York: Ballatine Books, 1988.

Woodward, C. Vann. *Responses of the Presidents to Charges of Misconduct.* New York: Dell, 1974.

Index

A.B. Plot, 41
Abrams, Elliott, 374
ACTION agency, 291
Adams administration, 23, 24-28; foreign policy, 23-26
Adams (J.Q.) administration, 44-45
Adams, Arlin, 397
Adams, John, 22, 23, 24, 25, 31, 38, 43, 44; family of, 26-27; and Hamilton, 26, 29; and Jefferson, 23; nepotism of, 27-28; as president, 22, 23, 24, 25, 26; slander against, 28-29
Adams, Charles, 27
Adams, John Quincy, 27, 42, 55, 66; family of, 45; as president, 43, 44-45, 46
Adams, Louisa, 45
Adams, Sherman, 211-215
Aerojet General Corporation, 323
Agnew, Spiro, 256-259, 270; family of, 257; as governor, 257, 258; resignation of, 259; as vice president, 256-257, 258
Agricultural Adjustment Act (AAA), 168
Akins, James, 256
Albosta, Donald, 329-330, 333, 334; probe of "Debategate," 329-334
Albright, Jack, 249
Alcorn, Meade, 214, 215
Alger, Russell, 128
Alien Property Office, 148, 151
Allende, Salvador, 251
Allen, Richard, 318-321
Alto, Vincent, 297
Ambrose, Stephen E., 254
American hostages, arms for, in Middle East deal, 379-386; CIA and, in Middle East, 379; in Iran, 256, 305, 306, 330, 363-367; see also Iran/contra affair; Iran hostage crisis
Ames, Oakes, 102, 112
Anderson, Jack, 253, 279, 280, 293, 302
Anderson, Martin, 339
Anderson, Stanton, 342
Anderson, Vernice, 195
Annenberg, Moe, 172
Archbold, John, 133
Army Corps of Engineers, 208
Arny, Wayne, 352
Arthur administration, 115
Arthur, Chester A., 109, 112, 131; as president, 114-118
Atomic Energy Commission (AEC), 205-206, 207

Babcock, Orville, 98, 104, 105
Bache, Benjamin Franklin, 21, 22, 27
Baker, Bobby, 233-236, 237-238, 242; relationship with LBJ, 234, 235, 236-238
Baker, James, 330, 331, 333, 335, 343, 388; and William Casey, 331, 332, 333
Baldrige, Malcolm, 348
Ballinger-Pinochet controversy, 139-142, 148
Ballinger, Richard, 140, 141-142
Barnburners, 72
Barnes, Edward, 314
Barnes, Michael, 376-377
Barry, William, 56, 58, 60
Baruch, Bernard, 211
Bay of Pigs invasion, 223-224, 264
Becker, Benton, 274
Beecher, William, 253
Belknap, William, 103-104
Bell, Griffin, 299, 302
Benedict, Elias, 126
Bennett, David, 186
Bernstein, Carl, 247, 264, 274
Berrien, John, 56, 57
Biaggi, Mario, 355
Biddle, Nicholas, 59, 60-61, 62
Bierbower, James, 328
Billygate, 303-306
Bissell, Richard, 224
"Black Friday," 99, 101
Black, Hugo, 175
Black, Jeremiah, 85, 87
Blaine, Harriet, 115, 119
Blaine, James, 102, 111, 113, 117, 117, 122
Blakely, G. Robert, 231
Bliss, Betty, 76
Bliss, Cornelius, 133-134
Boeing, 227, 228, 229
Boland Amendment, 367, 368, 377
Boland, Edward, 367
Bolich, Daniel, 192
Boone, Pat, 281, 282
Booth, John Wilkes, 92
Borah, William, 157
Botts, John, 69
Bourne, Peter, 291-293, 295
Bowman, George, 87
Boyle, William, 190
Bradlee, Benjamin, 287
Bradley, Omar, 195
Brady, Thomas, 110, 112-113, 117
Bragg, Mark, 241; and Wedtech scandal, 346, 347, 348, 351, 352, 354, 355

418

Helms, Richard, 251
Hemings, Sally, 8, 31-32
Heritage Foundation, 327
Hermann, Binger, 140
Herring, R.L., 301, 302
Hersh, Seymour, 251, 277, 278, 280
Hickok, Lenora, 173-174
Hills, Carla, 396-397
Hiss, Alger, 201
Hoover administration, 160-163
Hoover, Herbert, 149, 168; as presi-
dent, 160-161, 162-163; rout of war
veterans, 161-162; wiretapping by,
162-163
Hoover, J. Edgar, 197, 221, 230-231,
240-241, 242, 249, 250
House Judiciary Committee, 266
House of Representatives, 29, 95, 138,
324, 329, 333
House Select Committee on Assassi-
nations, 231
House Select Committee on Intelli-
gence, 278
Houston, Sam, 62
Howe, Louis, 169
Howrey, Edward, 213
Hoyt, Jesse, 64
Hugel, Max, 361
Hughes, Charles Evans, 147, 149
Hughes, Howard, 188, 260, 263, 279
Hulbert, Mary, 146
Hull, Cordell, 179
Humphrey, Hubert, 248, 261
Hungate, William, 275
Hunt, E. Howard, 247, 263, 264, 266
Hunt, J.V., 185
Hunt, Nelson Bunker, 372
Hurley, Patrick, 162
Hussein (King), 286-287
Huston Plan, 250
Huston, Thomas Charles, 250
Huygens (Chevalier), 55
Huygens (Madame), 54

Ickes, Harold, 170, 171-172, 187
India, 251-252
Indianapolis News, 136
Indian Service, 134
Ingham, Samuel, 56, 57
Institute for Democracy, Education
and Assistance (IDEA), 375
Internal Revenue Service (IRS), 170,
171-172, 190-193, 262, 266, 289, 371-
372
International Business Communica-
tions (IBC), 372, 373
International Medical Centers (IMC),
344
International Telephone and Tele-
graph (ITT), 251

Interstate Commerce Commission,
212
Iran, 254-255, 379-380, 381, 382-384,
385, 386, 388
Iran/contra affair, 7, 358-360, 365-391;
Casey and 367-368, 369, 370, 373;
Congress and, 366-367, 371, 374, 376-
377, 389, 390-391; Oliver North and,
358, 359, 369, 370, 371, 372, 373-374,
375-376, 377-378, 382-287; Reagan
and, 368, 369, 371, 380, 381, 385-386,
387-389, 390; *see also* American hostages; Iran hostage crisis
Iran hostage crisis, 256, 305, 306, 330;
Carter administration and, 363, 364;
and Congress, 366-367; and 1980
presidential election, 363-365; William Casey and, 363-365; *see also*
American hostages; Iran/contra affair
Iran/Iraq War, 364
Iraq, 364
Israel, 380, 381, 382, 384, 387

Jackson administration, 49-62, 63
Jackson, Andrew, 8, 43-44, 45-46, 47-
49, 63, 64, 72; duels of, 48-49; as
president, 51, 52, 53, 54, 55, 56, 57-
58, 60-62, 70; and Second Bank, 59,
60-62
Jackson, Henry, 228, 261
Jackson, Rachel, 8, 46, 47-48, 53; slan-
der against, 47-48, 49
Jacobsen, David, 384
Japan, 179
Jaworski, Leon, 264, 273
Jay, John, 109
Jay Treaty, 24, 38
Jefferson administration, 30-33, 35
Jefferson, Martha, 29
Jefferson, Thomas, 8, 16, 19, 21, 22-23,
24-25, 29-33, 37, 38, 39-40, 43, 44; ille-
gitimate children of, 8, 31-32; and
John Adams, 23; as president, 30-33;
romantic affairs of, 29-33; in Wash-
ington administration, 18-19
Jenco, Lawrence, 384
Jenkins, James, 343, 346-347, 348, 349,
353-354
Jenkins, Walter, 235, 237, 241-243
Jennings, Jerry, 318, 320
Jingoism, 128, 135
Johnson (Andrew) administration, 94-
95
Johnson (Lyndon) administration,
234-246
Johnson, Andrew, 92-93, 266; attempted impeachment of, 95-96; as
president, 94-96; as vice president,
92-93, 239